THE MONTAGUE TWINS

THE DEVIL'S MUSIC

NATHAN PAGE & DREW SHANNON

ALFRED A. KNOPF
NEW YORK

To my friends and family, who are always there
waiting for me when I return from Narnia

—N.P.

For Sammy, whose love and support
is imbued into every single panel

—D.S.

THIS IS A BORZOI BOOK PUBLISHED BY ALFRED A. KNOPF

Text copyright © 2021 by Nathan Page
Jacket art and interior illustrations copyright © 2021 by Drew Shannon
Jacket design by Ray Shappell

Visit us on the Web! rhcbooks.com

Educators and librarians, for a variety of teaching tools, visit us at RHTeachersLibrarians.com

Library of Congress Cataloging-in-Publication Data is available upon request.
ISBN 978-0-525-64680-8 (trade) — ISBN 978-0-525-64683-9 (ebook) —
ISBN 978-0-525-64681-5 (trade pbk.)

MANUFACTURED IN CHINA
December 2021
10 9 8 7 6 5 4 3 2 1

First Edition

CHAPTER 1

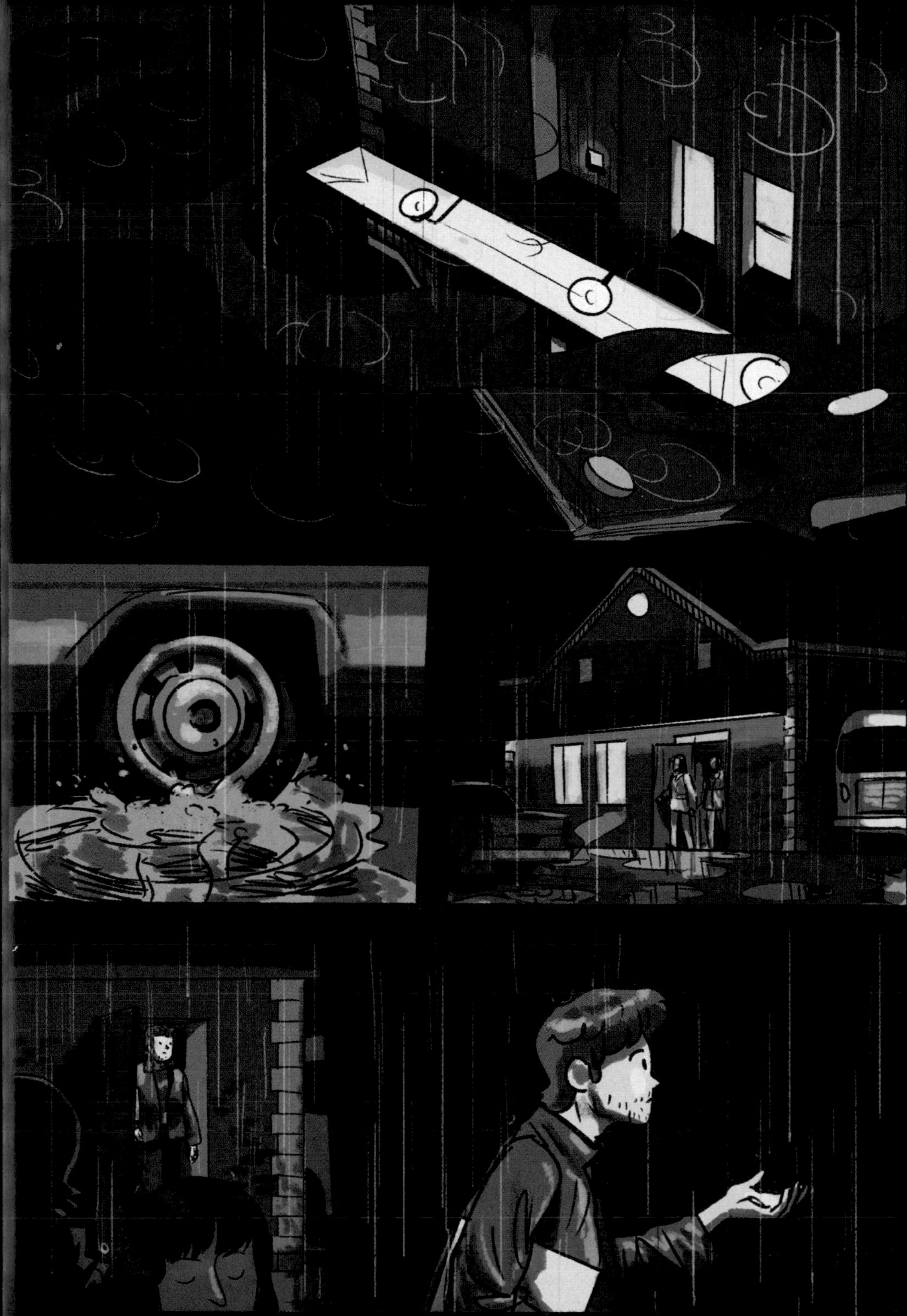

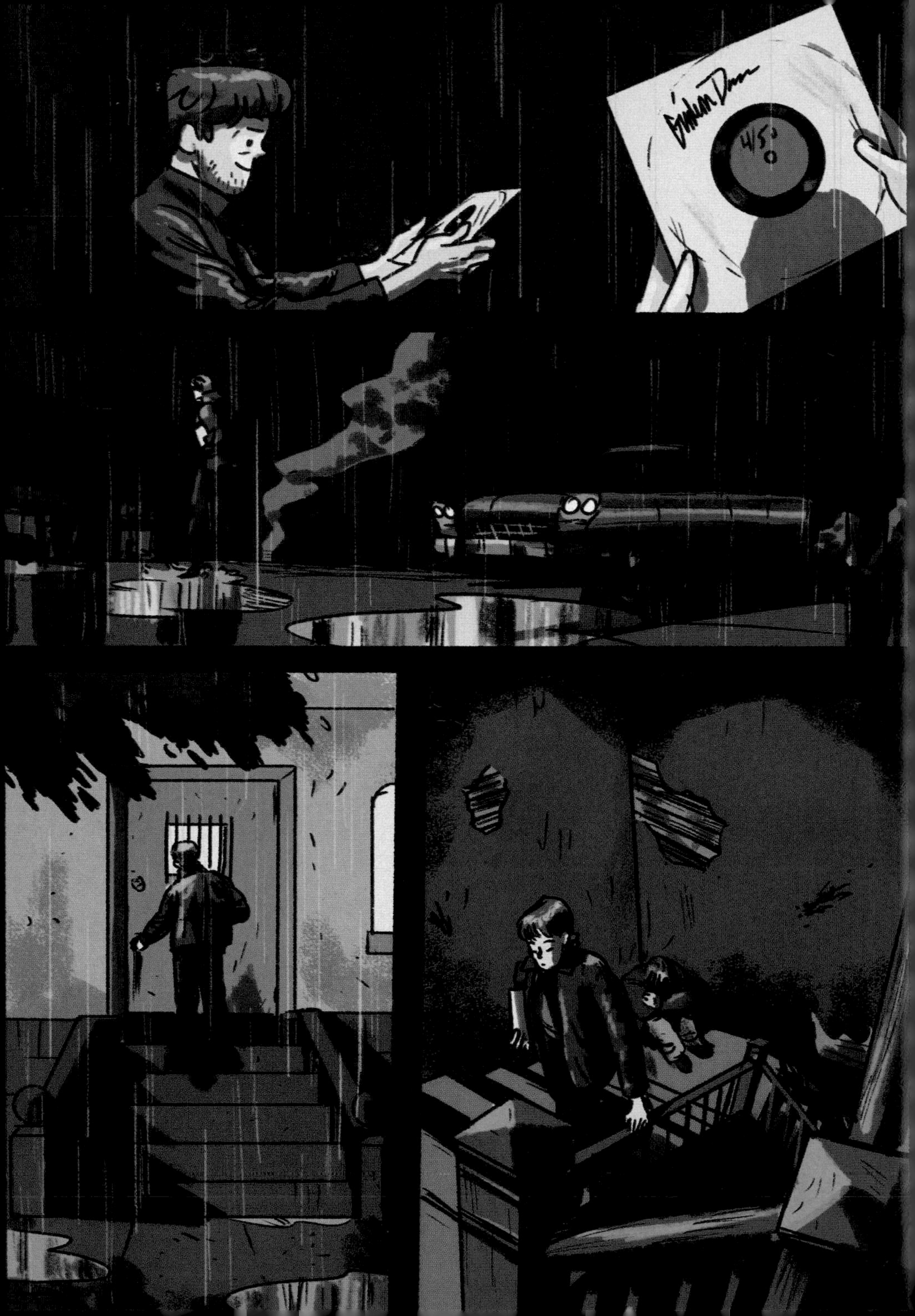

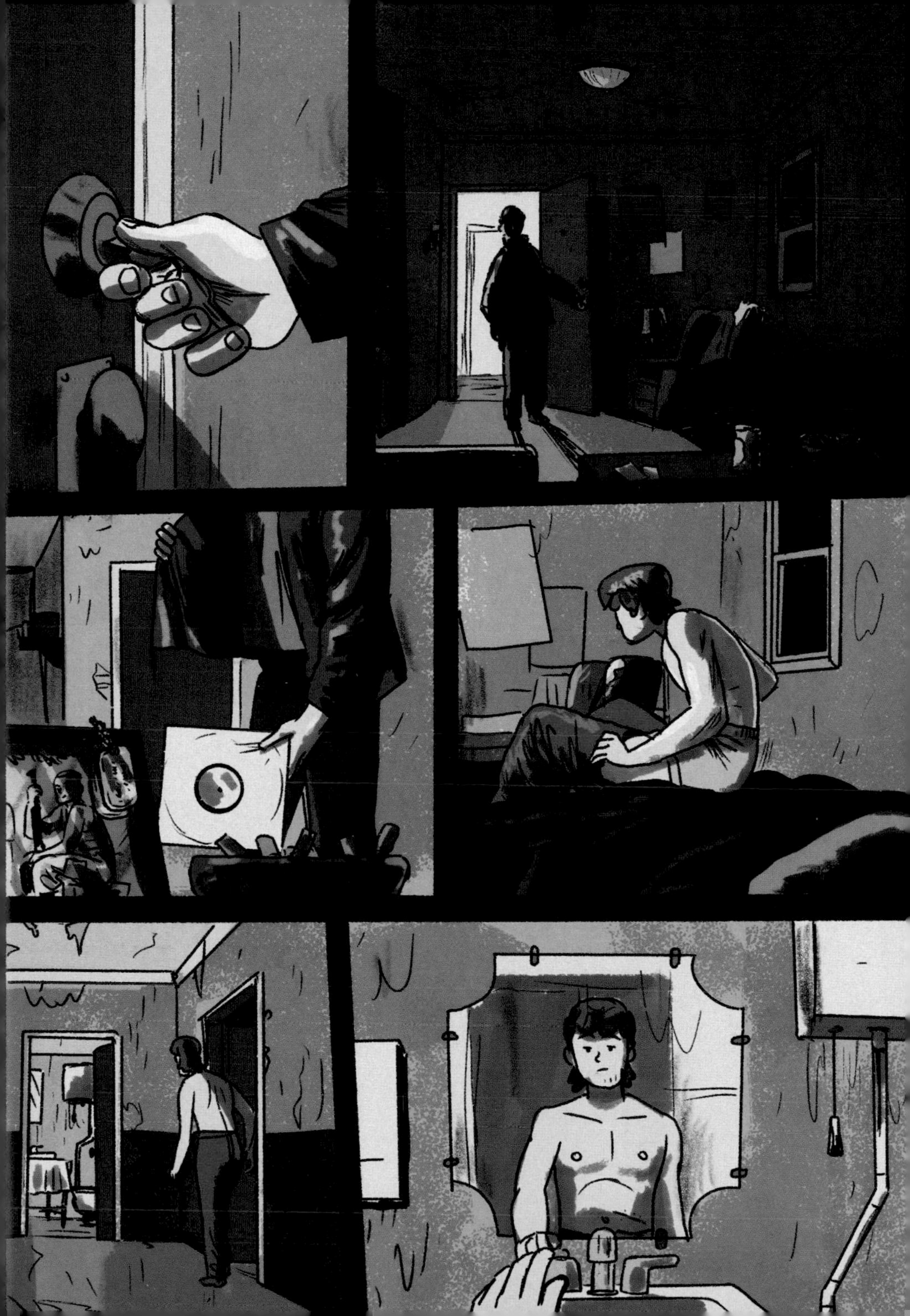

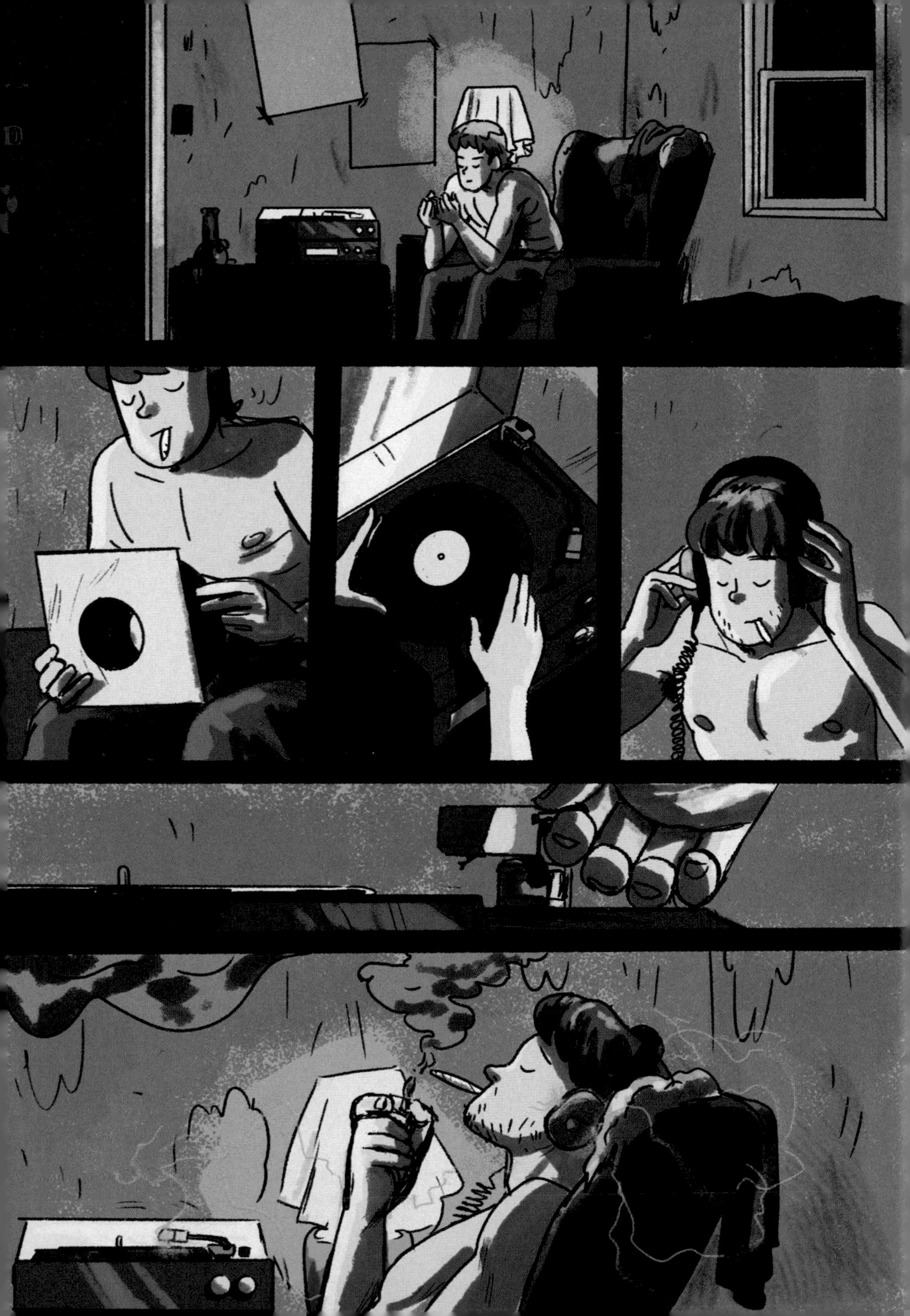

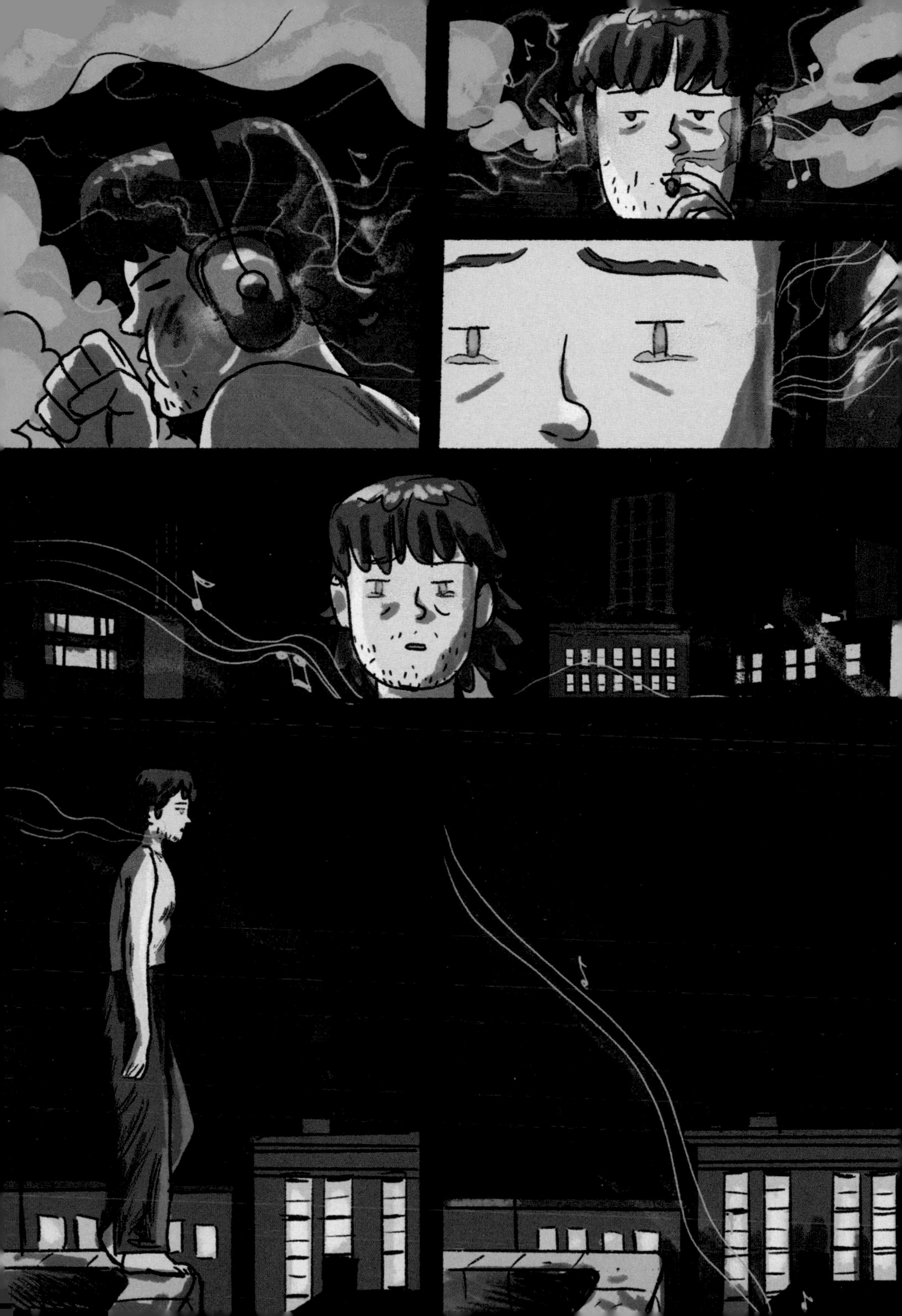

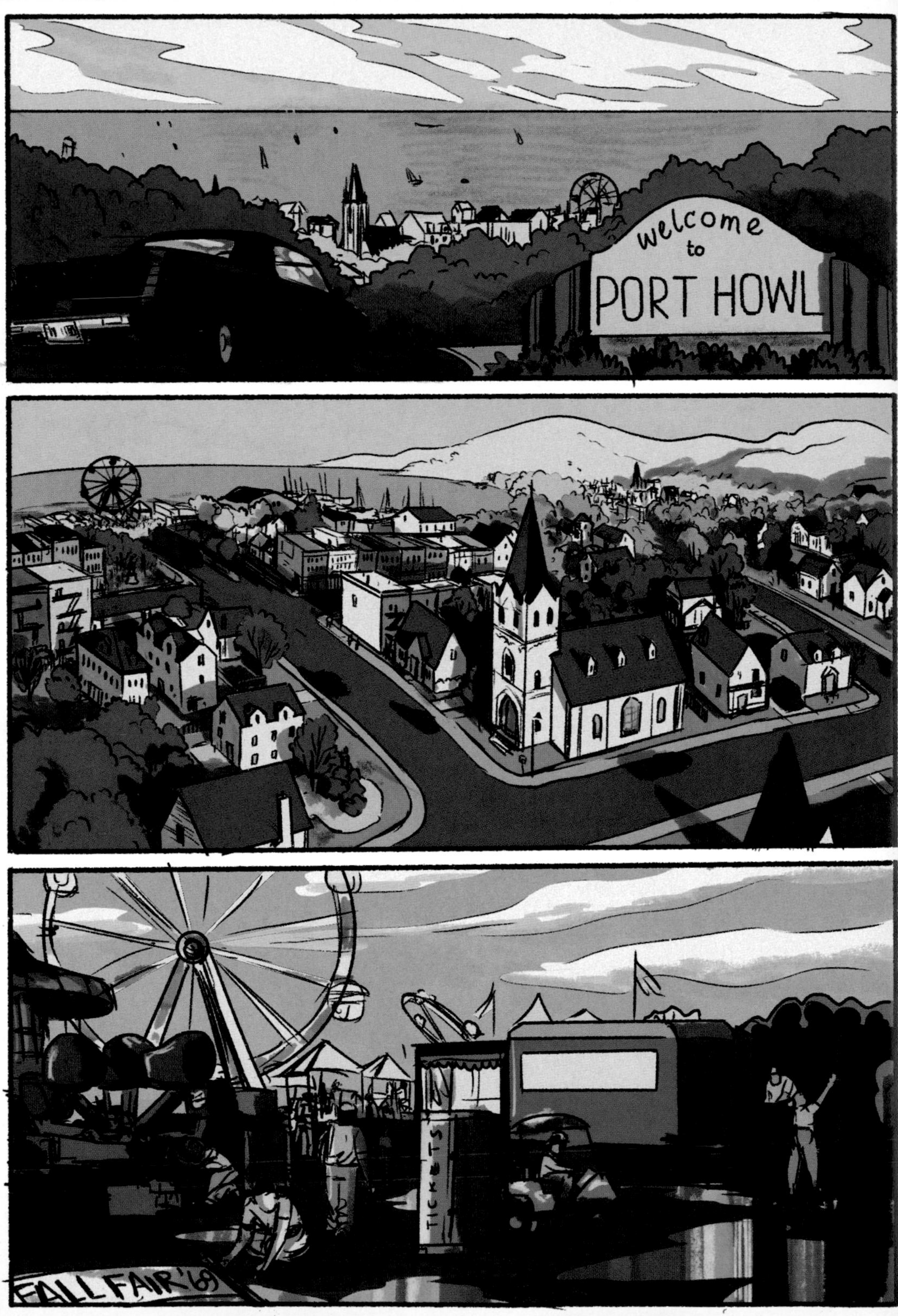
welcome
to
PORT HOWL
TICKETS
FALL FAIR '69

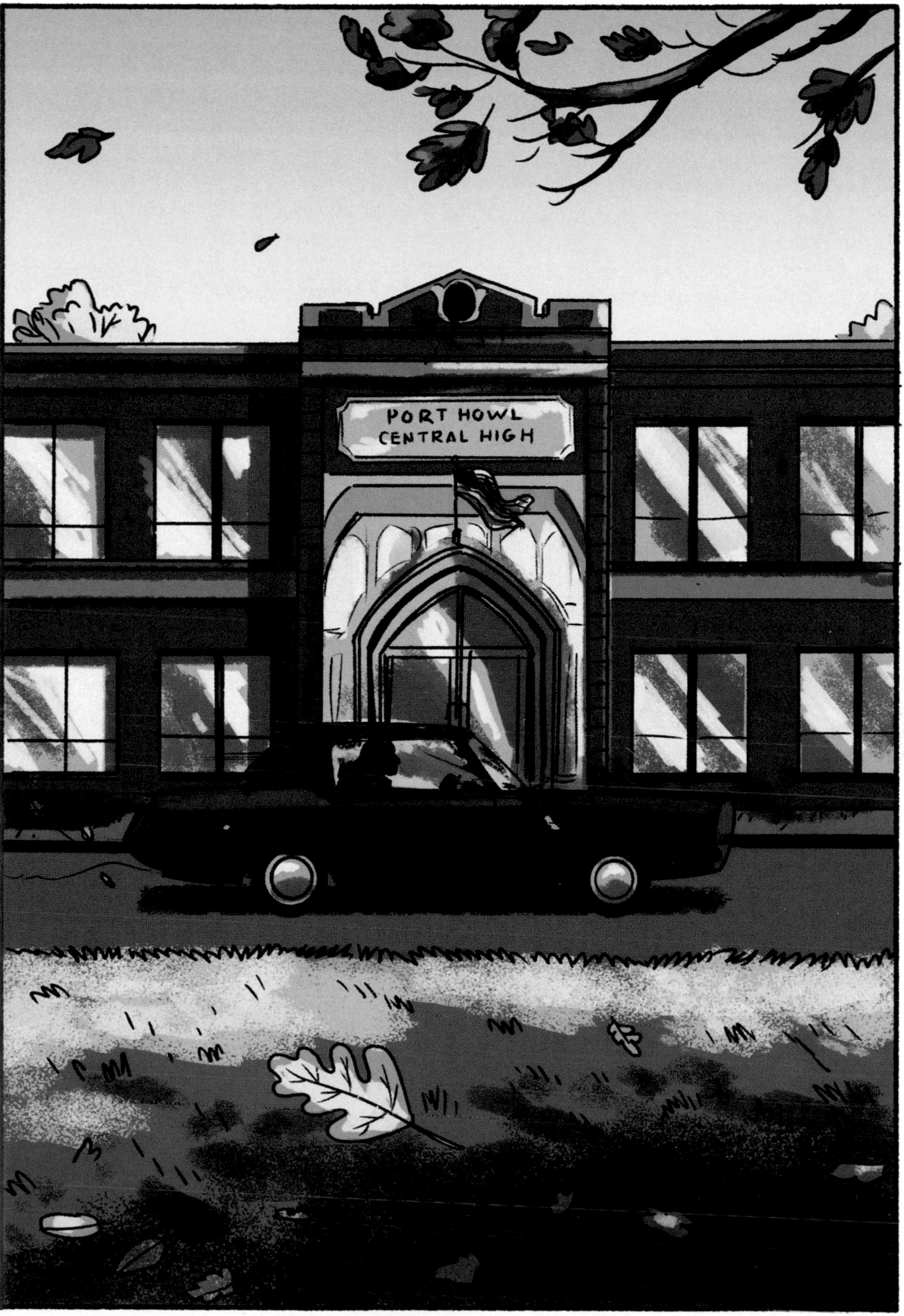
PORT HOWL
CENTRAL HIGH

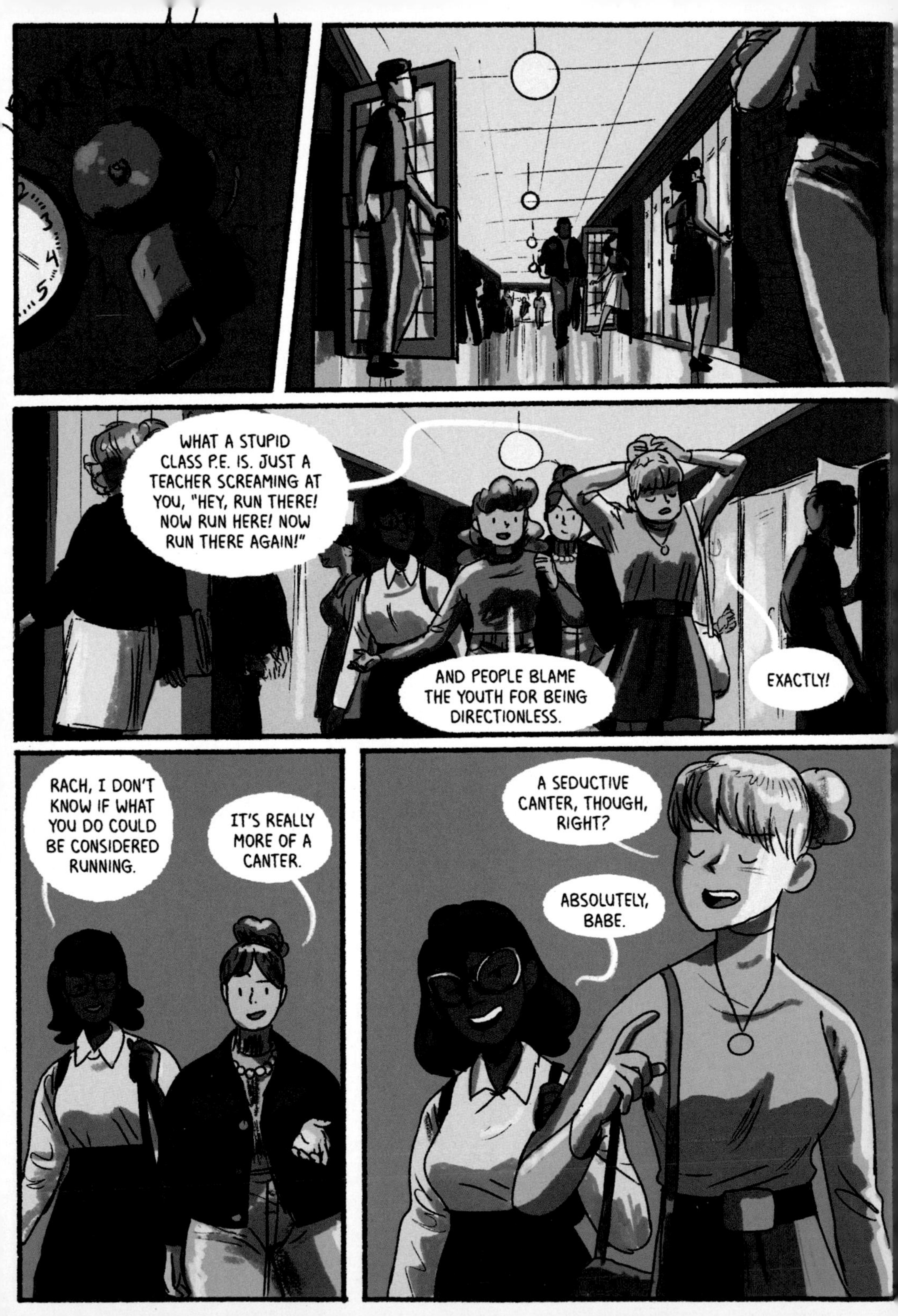
WHAT A STUPID CLASS P.E. IS. JUST A TEACHER SCREAMING AT YOU, "HEY, RUN THERE! NOW RUN HERE! NOW RUN THERE AGAIN!"
AND PEOPLE BLAME THE YOUTH FOR BEING DIRECTIONLESS.
EXACTLY!
RACH, I DON'T KNOW IF WHAT YOU DO COULD BE CONSIDERED RUNNING.
IT'S REALLY MORE OF A CANTER.
A SEDUCTIVE CANTER, THOUGH, RIGHT?
ABSOLUTELY, BABE.

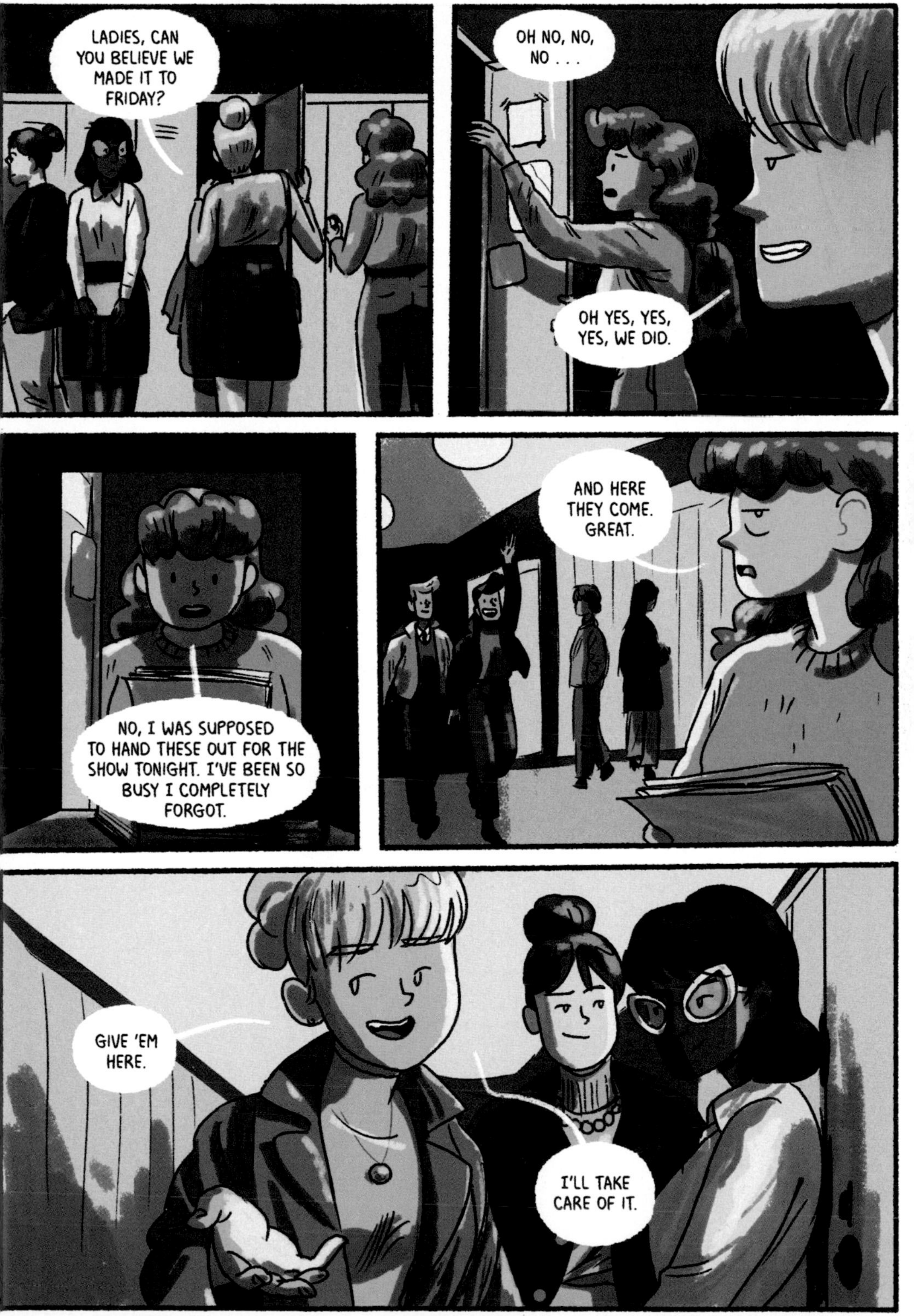
LADIES, CAN YOU BELIEVE WE MADE IT TO FRIDAY?
OH NO, NO, NO . . .
OH YES, YES, YES, WE DID.
NO, I WAS SUPPOSED TO HAND THESE OUT FOR THE SHOW TONIGHT. I'VE BEEN SO BUSY I COMPLETELY FORGOT.
AND HERE THEY COME. GREAT.
GIVE 'EM HERE.
I'LL TAKE CARE OF IT.

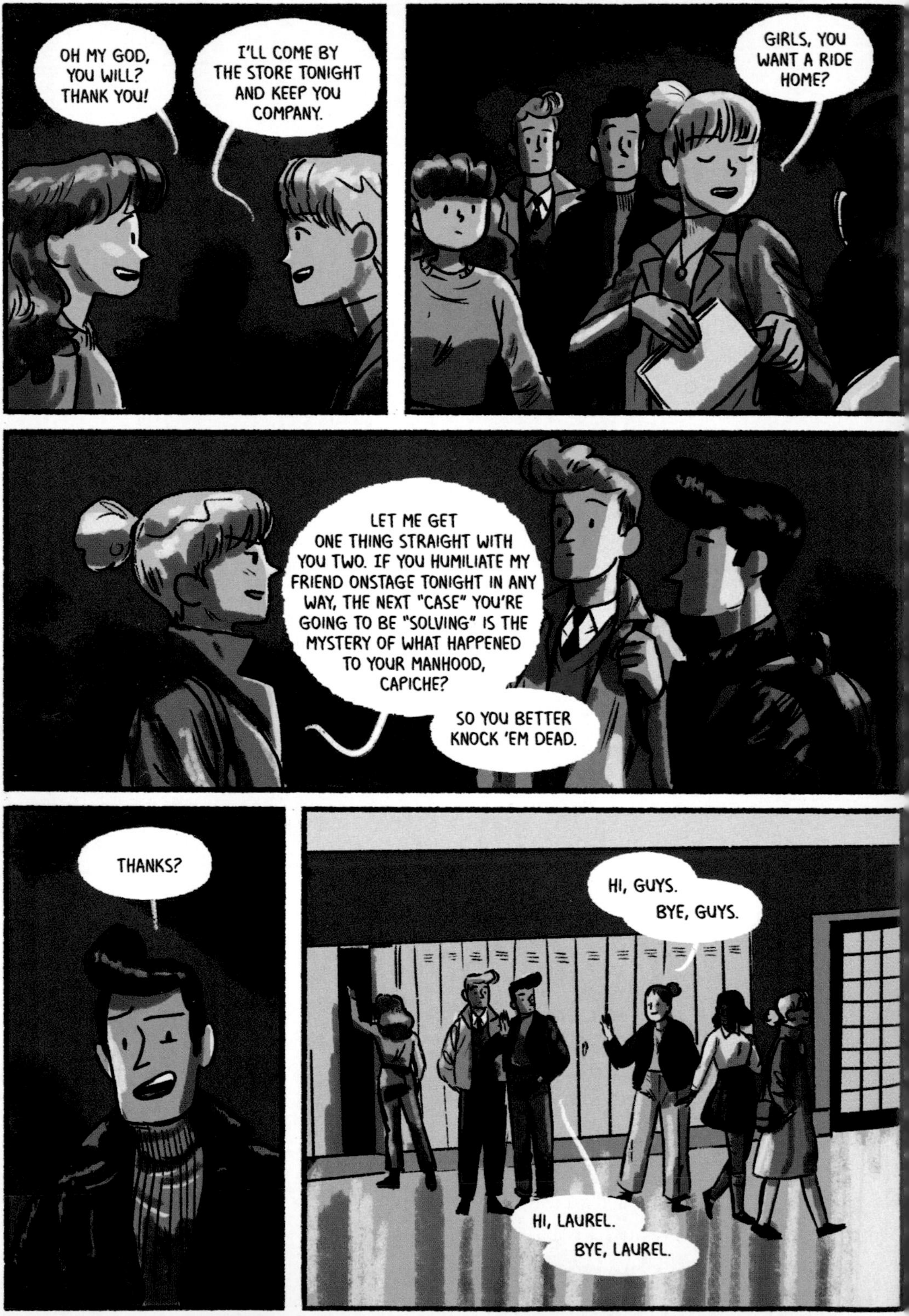
OH MY GOD, YOU WILL? THANK YOU!
I'LL COME BY THE STORE TONIGHT AND KEEP YOU COMPANY.
GIRLS, YOU WANT A RIDE HOME?
LET ME GET ONE THING STRAIGHT WITH YOU TWO. IF YOU HUMILIATE MY FRIEND ONSTAGE TONIGHT IN ANY WAY, THE NEXT "CASE" YOU'RE GOING TO BE "SOLVING" IS THE MYSTERY OF WHAT HAPPENED TO YOUR MANHOOD, CAPICHE?
SO YOU BETTER KNOCK 'EM DEAD.
THANKS?
HI, GUYS.
BYE, GUYS.
HI, LAUREL.
BYE, LAUREL.

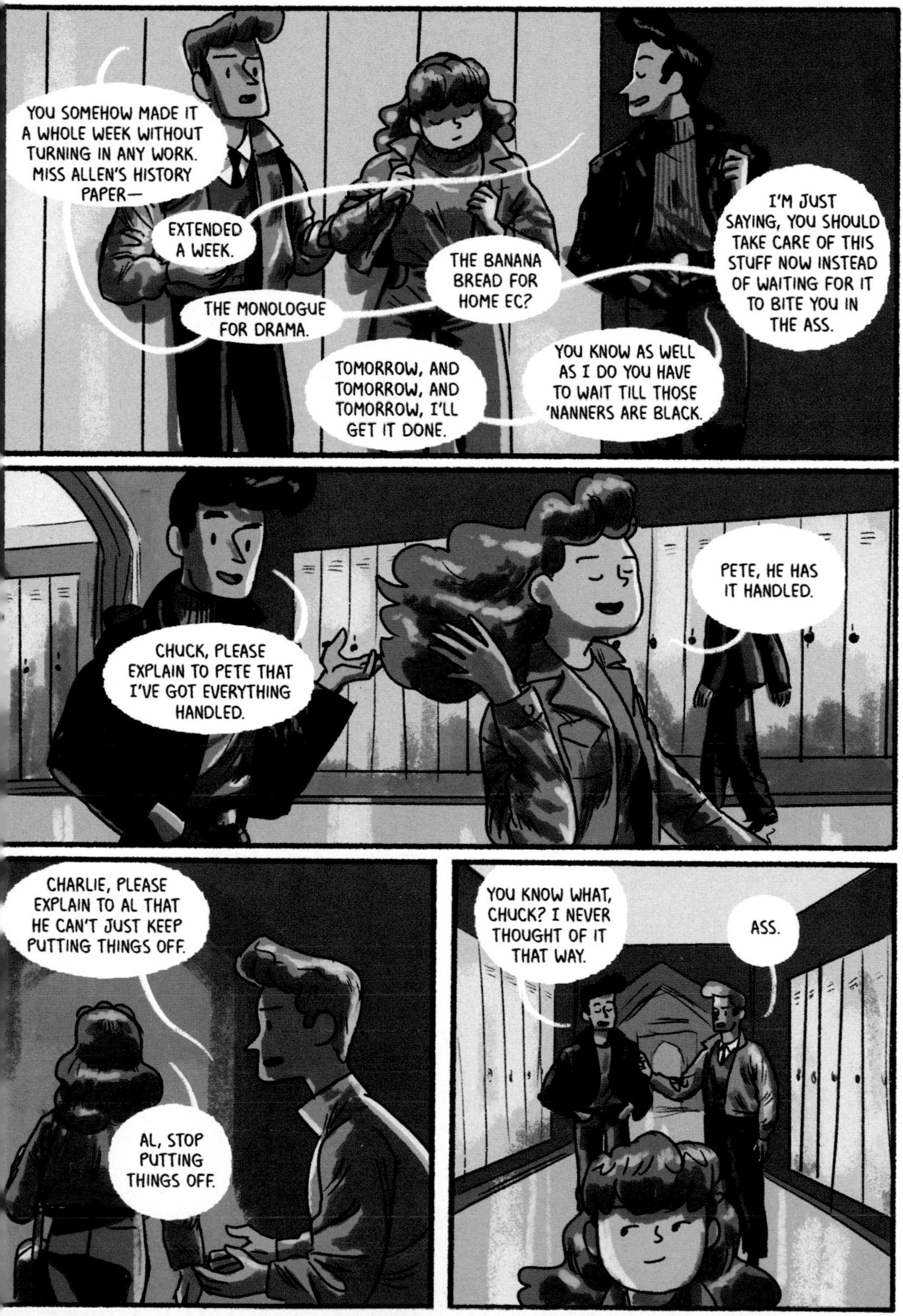
YOU SOMEHOW MADE IT A WHOLE WEEK WITHOUT TURNING IN ANY WORK. MISS ALLEN'S HISTORY PAPER—
EXTENDED A WEEK.
THE MONOLOGUE FOR DRAMA.
THE BANANA BREAD FOR HOME EC?
I'M JUST SAYING, YOU SHOULD TAKE CARE OF THIS STUFF NOW INSTEAD OF WAITING FOR IT TO BITE YOU IN THE ASS.
TOMORROW, AND TOMORROW, AND TOMORROW, I'LL GET IT DONE.
YOU KNOW AS WELL AS I DO YOU HAVE TO WAIT TILL THOSE 'NANNERS ARE BLACK.
CHUCK, PLEASE EXPLAIN TO PETE THAT I'VE GOT EVERYTHING HANDLED.
PETE, HE HAS IT HANDLED.
CHARLIE, PLEASE EXPLAIN TO AL THAT HE CAN'T JUST KEEP PUTTING THINGS OFF.
AL, STOP PUTTING THINGS OFF.
YOU KNOW WHAT, CHUCK? I NEVER THOUGHT OF IT THAT WAY.
ASS.

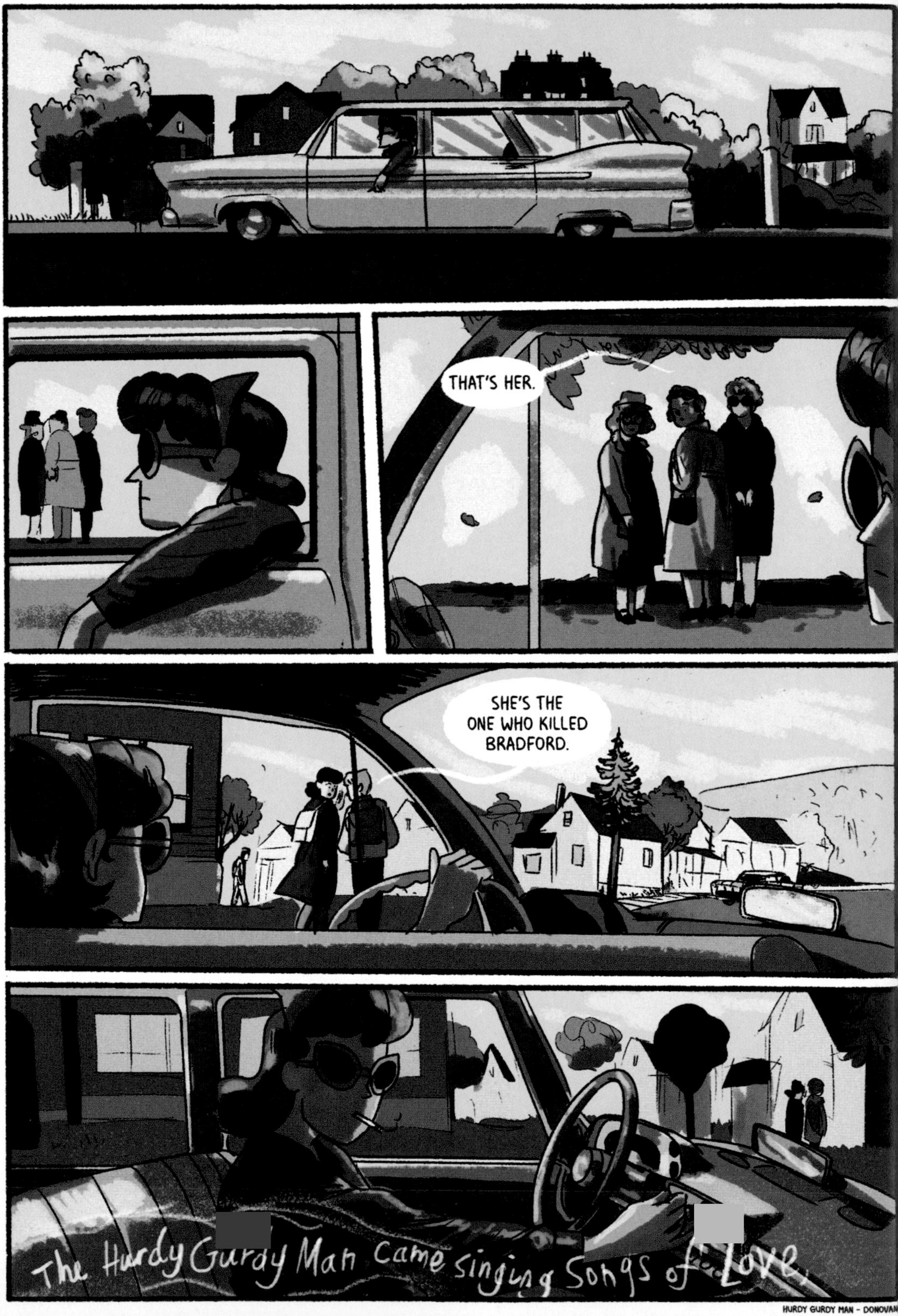
THAT'S HER.
SHE'S THE ONE WHO KILLED BRADFORD.
The Hurdy Gurdy Man came singing Songs of Love,

HURDY GURDY MAN - DONOVAN

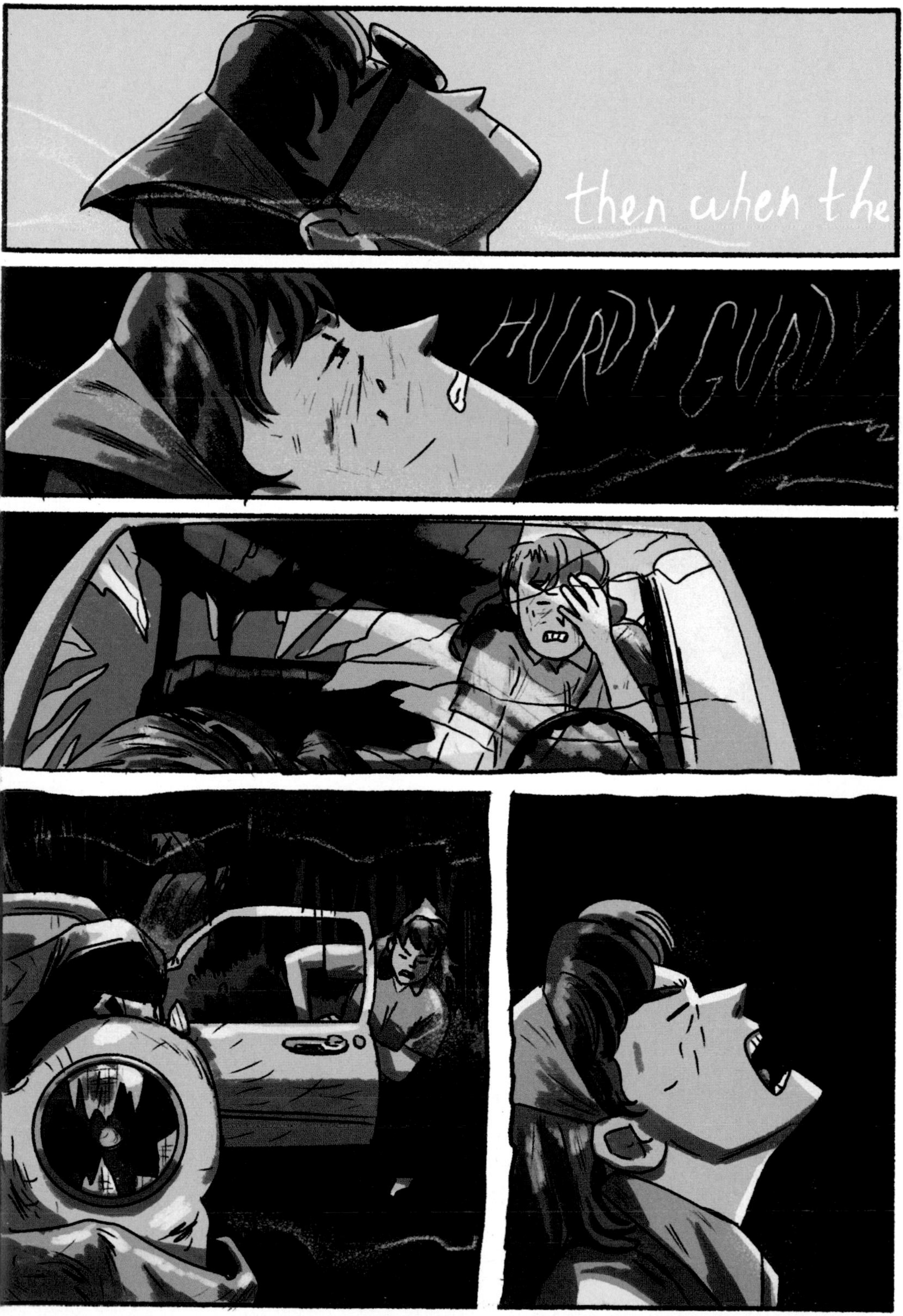
then when the
HURDY GURDY

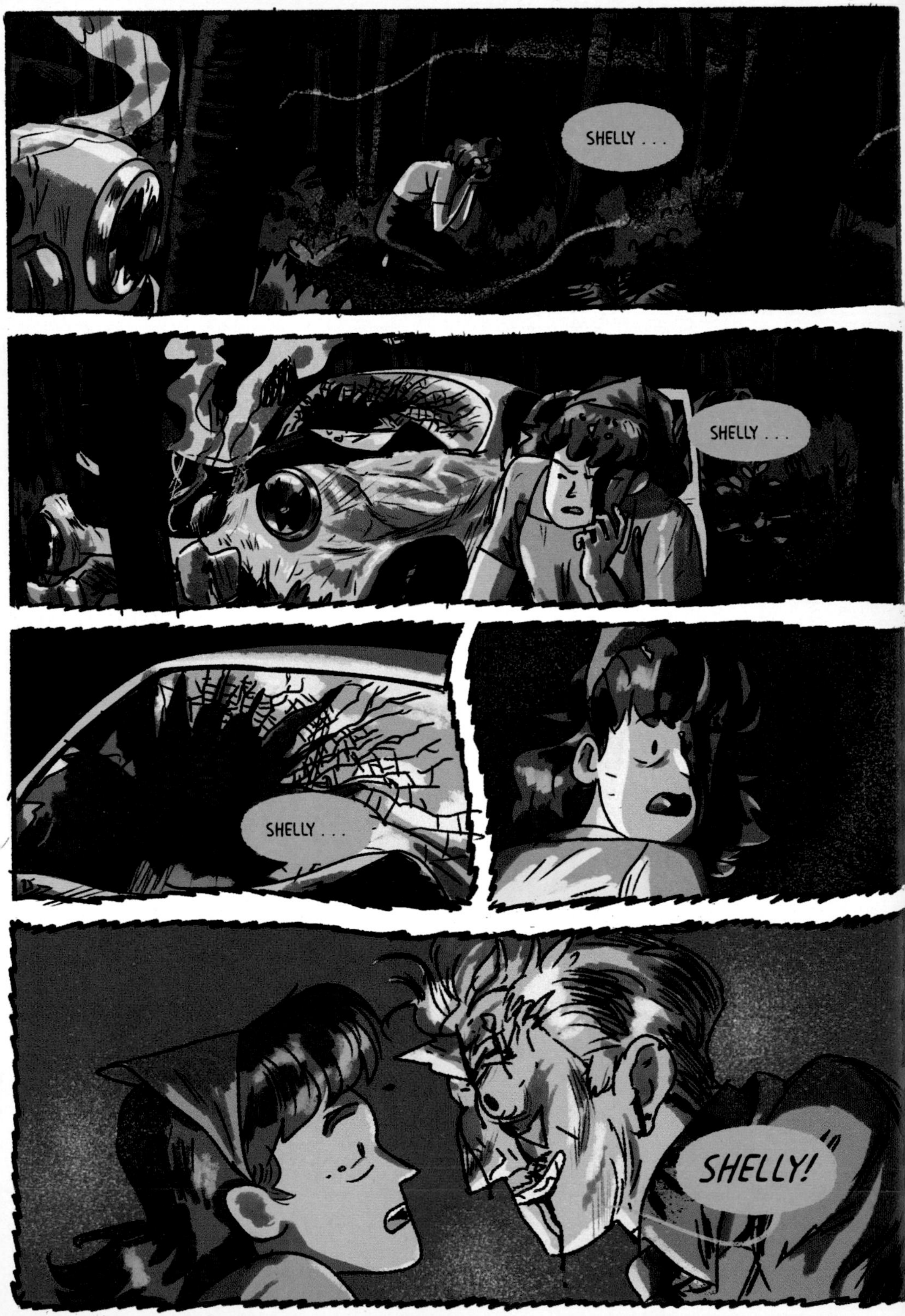
SHELLY . . .
SHELLY . . .
SHELLY . . .
SHELLY!

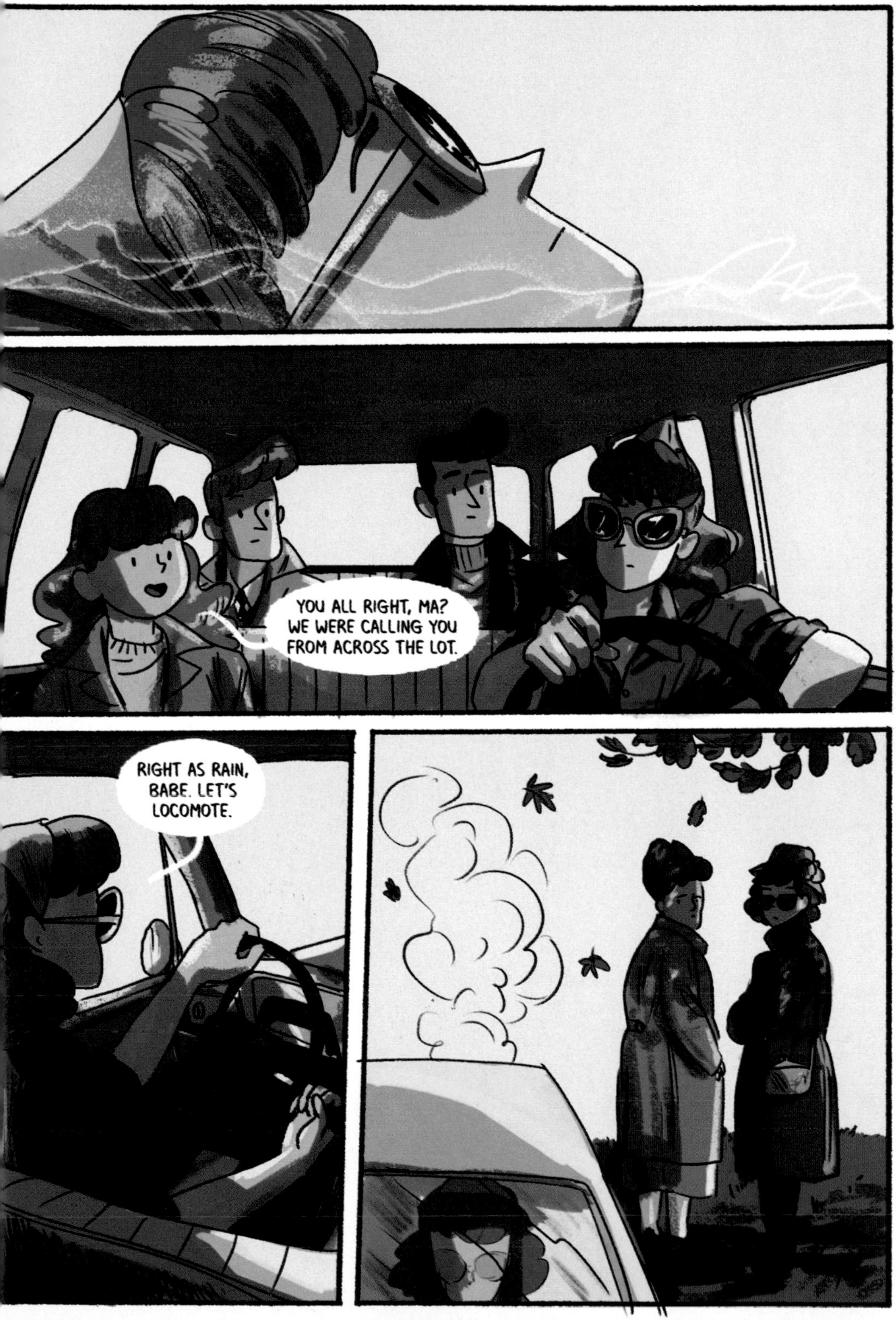
YOU ALL RIGHT, MA? WE WERE CALLING YOU FROM ACROSS THE LOT.
RIGHT AS RAIN, BABE. LET'S LOCOMOTE.

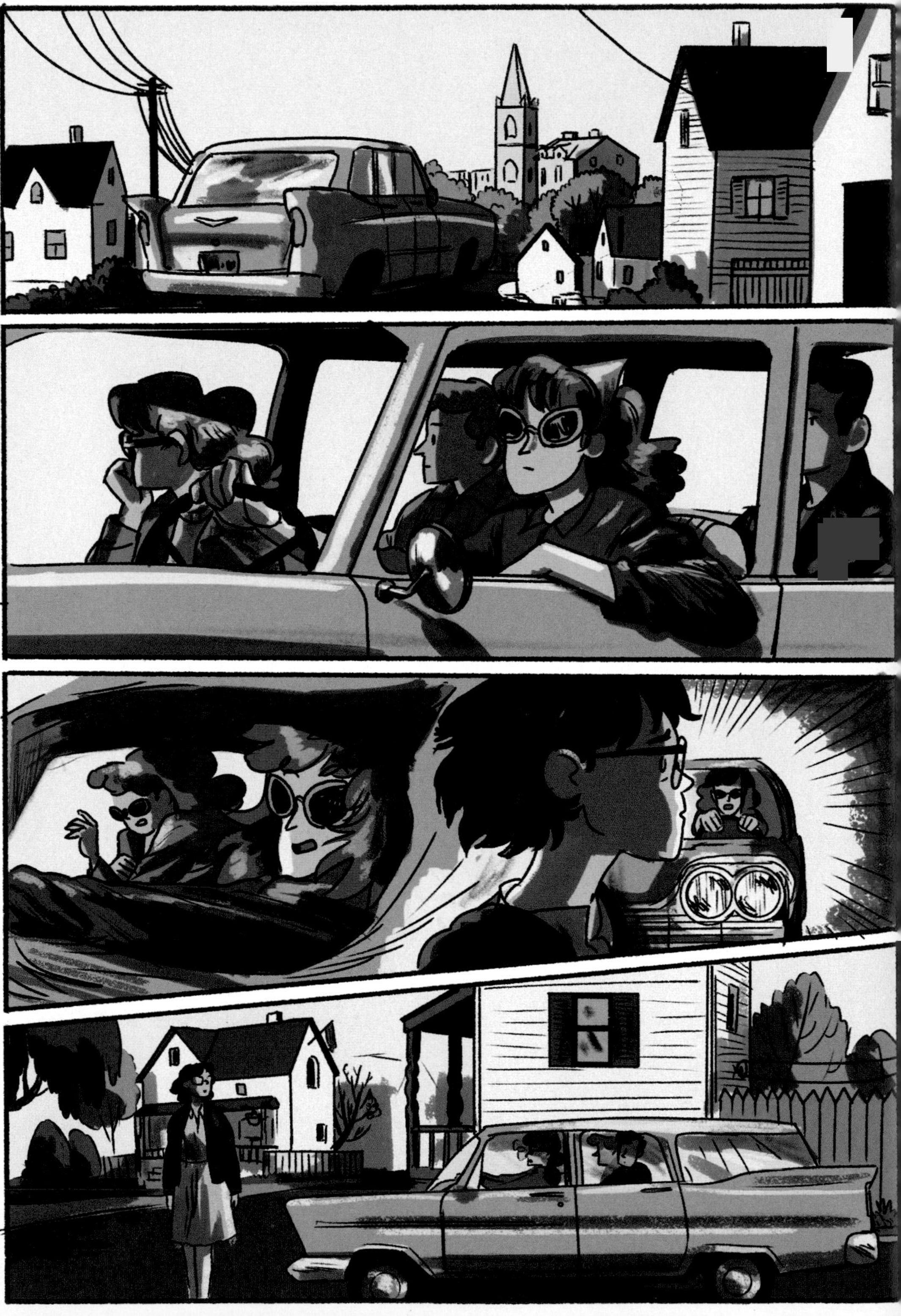

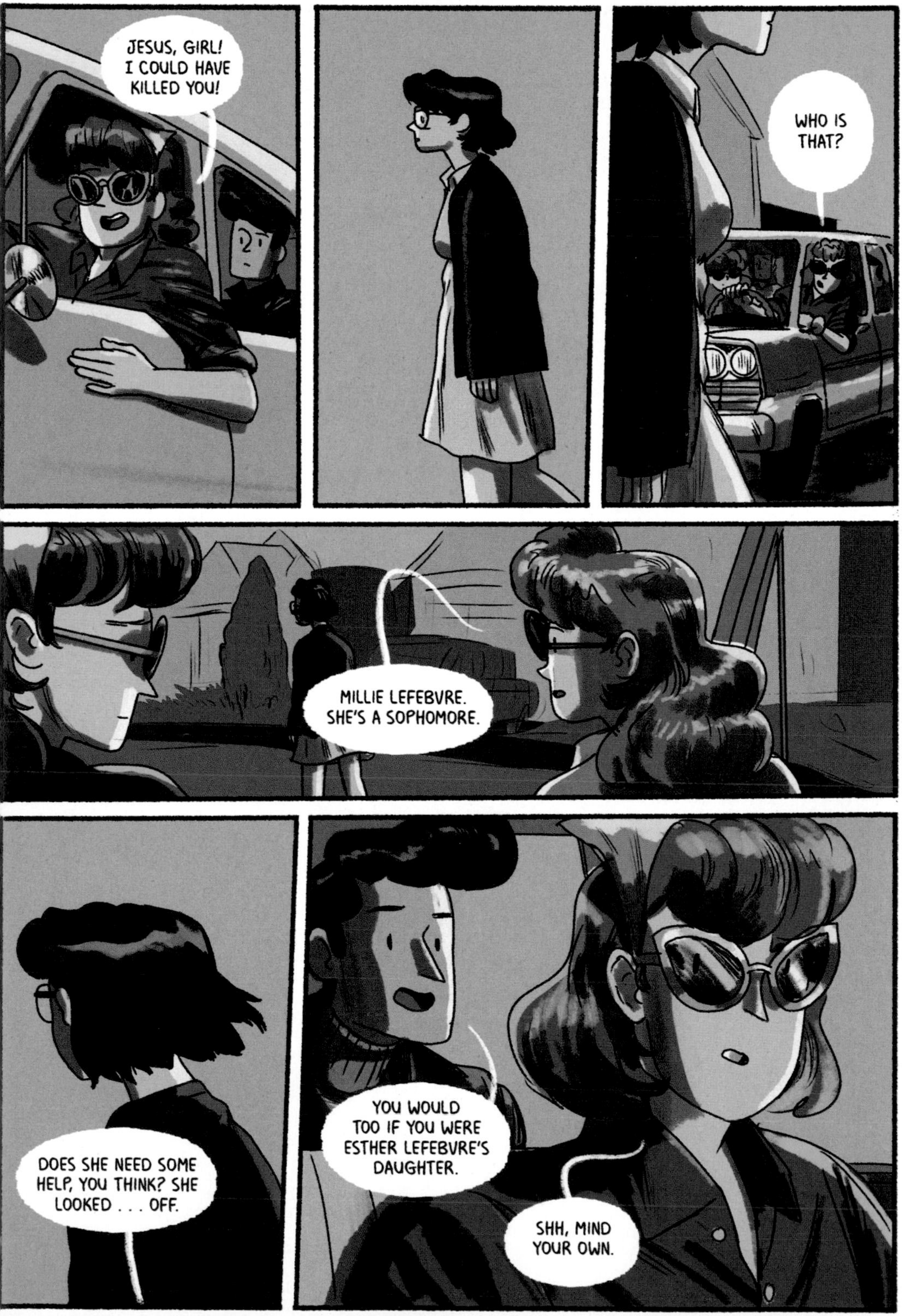
JESUS, GIRL! I COULD HAVE KILLED YOU!
WHO IS THAT?
MILLIE LEFEBVRE. SHE'S A SOPHOMORE.
DOES SHE NEED SOME HELP, YOU THINK? SHE LOOKED . . . OFF.
YOU WOULD TOO IF YOU WERE ESTHER LEFEBVRE'S DAUGHTER.
SHH, MIND YOUR OWN.

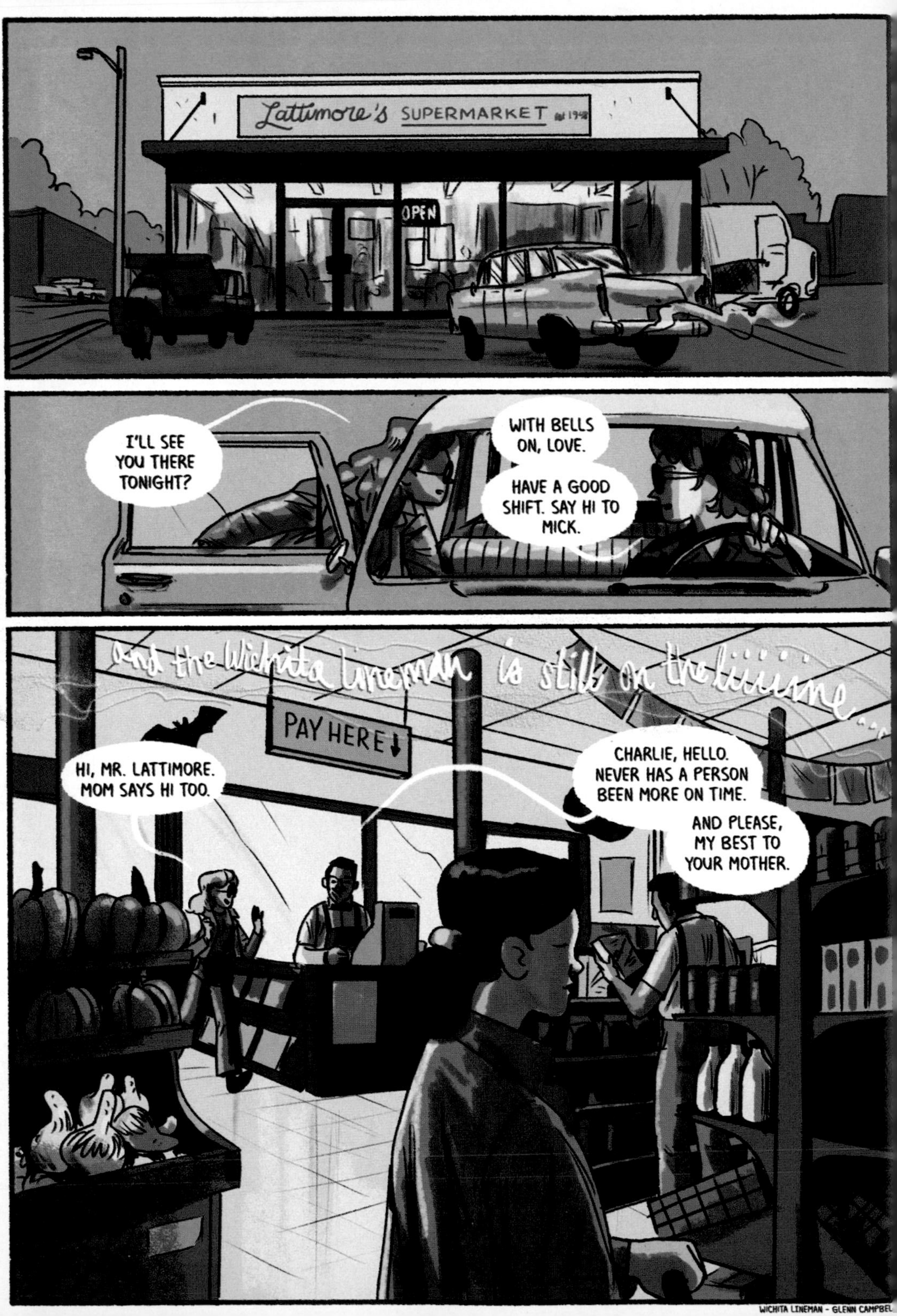
Lattimore's SUPERMARKET
OPEN
I'LL SEE YOU THERE TONIGHT?
WITH BELLS ON, LOVE.
HAVE A GOOD SHIFT. SAY HI TO MICK.
and the Wichita Lineman is still on the liiiiine...
PAY HERE
HI, MR. LATTIMORE. MOM SAYS HI TOO.
CHARLIE, HELLO. NEVER HAS A PERSON BEEN MORE ON TIME.
AND PLEASE, MY BEST TO YOUR MOTHER.

WICHITA LINEMAN - GLENN CAMPBEL

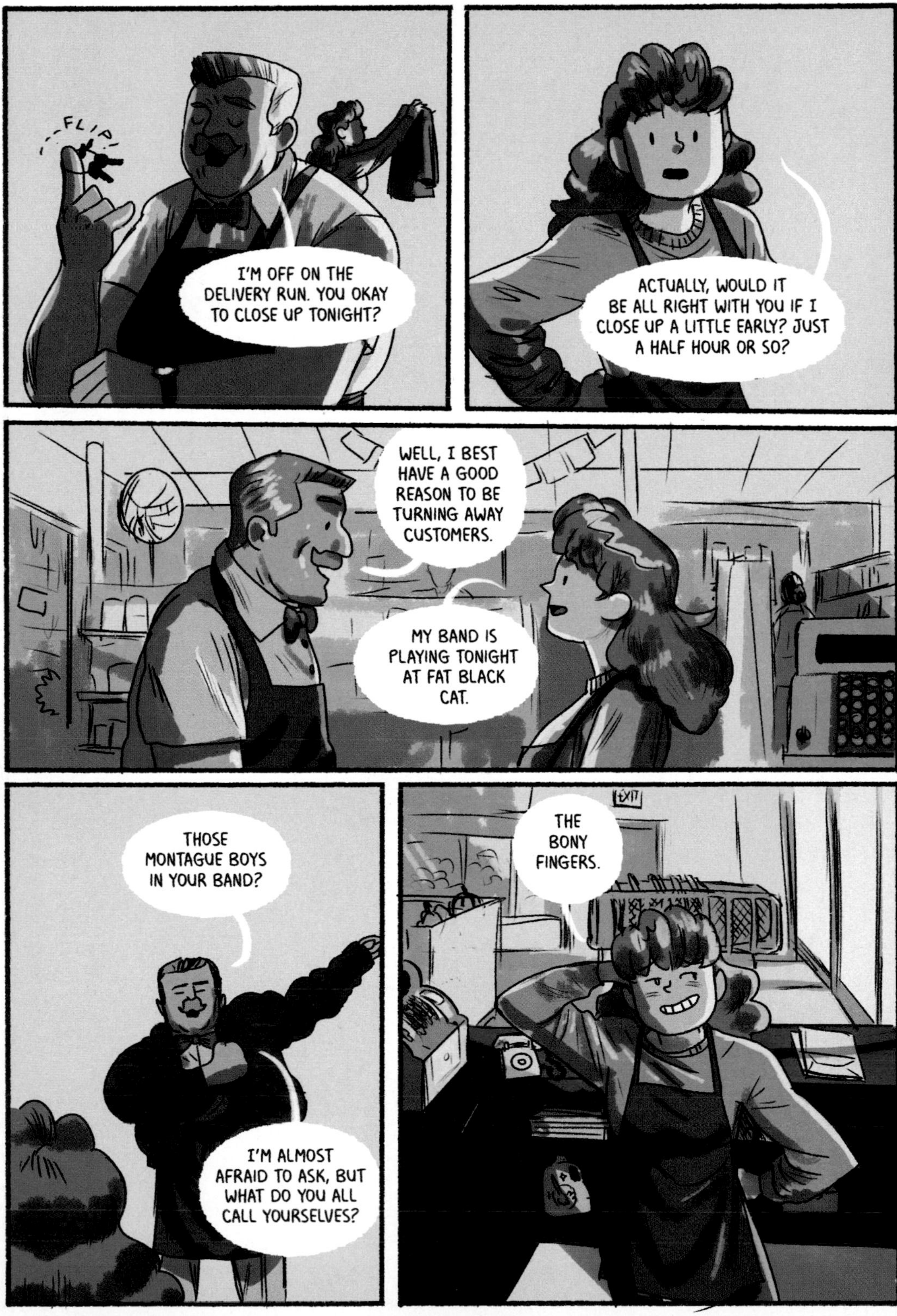
FLIP!
I'M OFF ON THE DELIVERY RUN. YOU OKAY TO CLOSE UP TONIGHT?
ACTUALLY, WOULD IT BE ALL RIGHT WITH YOU IF I CLOSE UP A LITTLE EARLY? JUST A HALF HOUR OR SO?
WELL, I BEST HAVE A GOOD REASON TO BE TURNING AWAY CUSTOMERS.
MY BAND IS PLAYING TONIGHT AT FAT BLACK CAT.
THOSE MONTAGUE BOYS IN YOUR BAND?
I'M ALMOST AFRAID TO ASK, BUT WHAT DO YOU ALL CALL YOURSELVES?
EXIT
THE BONY FINGERS.

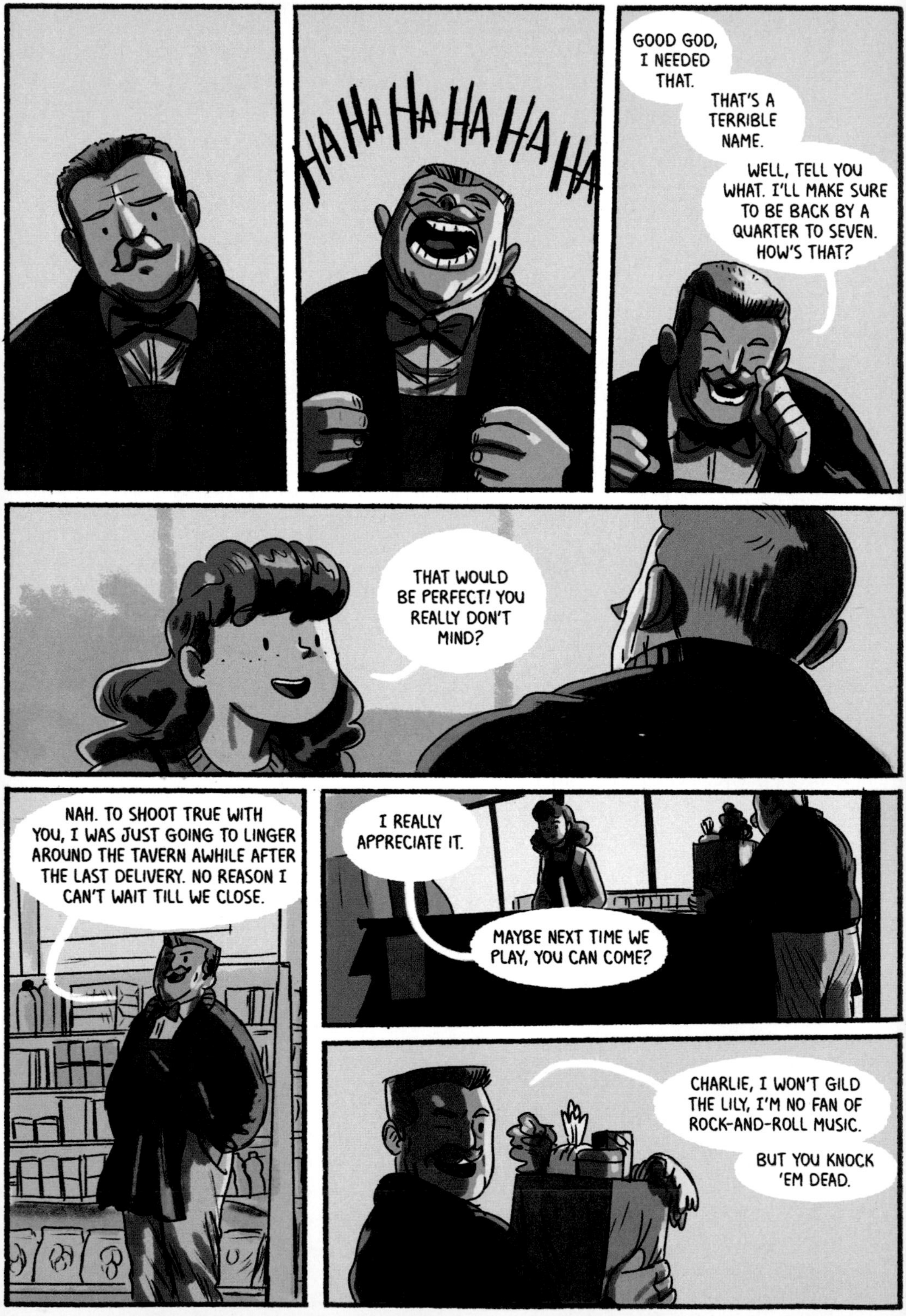

HA HA HA HA HA HA HA HA HA
GOOD GOD, I NEEDED THAT.
THAT'S A TERRIBLE NAME.
WELL, TELL YOU WHAT. I'LL MAKE SURE TO BE BACK BY A QUARTER TO SEVEN. HOW'S THAT?
THAT WOULD BE PERFECT! YOU REALLY DON'T MIND?
NAH. TO SHOOT TRUE WITH YOU, I WAS JUST GOING TO LINGER AROUND THE TAVERN AWHILE AFTER THE LAST DELIVERY. NO REASON I CAN'T WAIT TILL WE CLOSE.
I REALLY APPRECIATE IT.
MAYBE NEXT TIME WE PLAY, YOU CAN COME?
CHARLIE, I WON'T GILD THE LILY, I'M NO FAN OF ROCK-AND-ROLL MUSIC.
BUT YOU KNOCK 'EM DEAD.

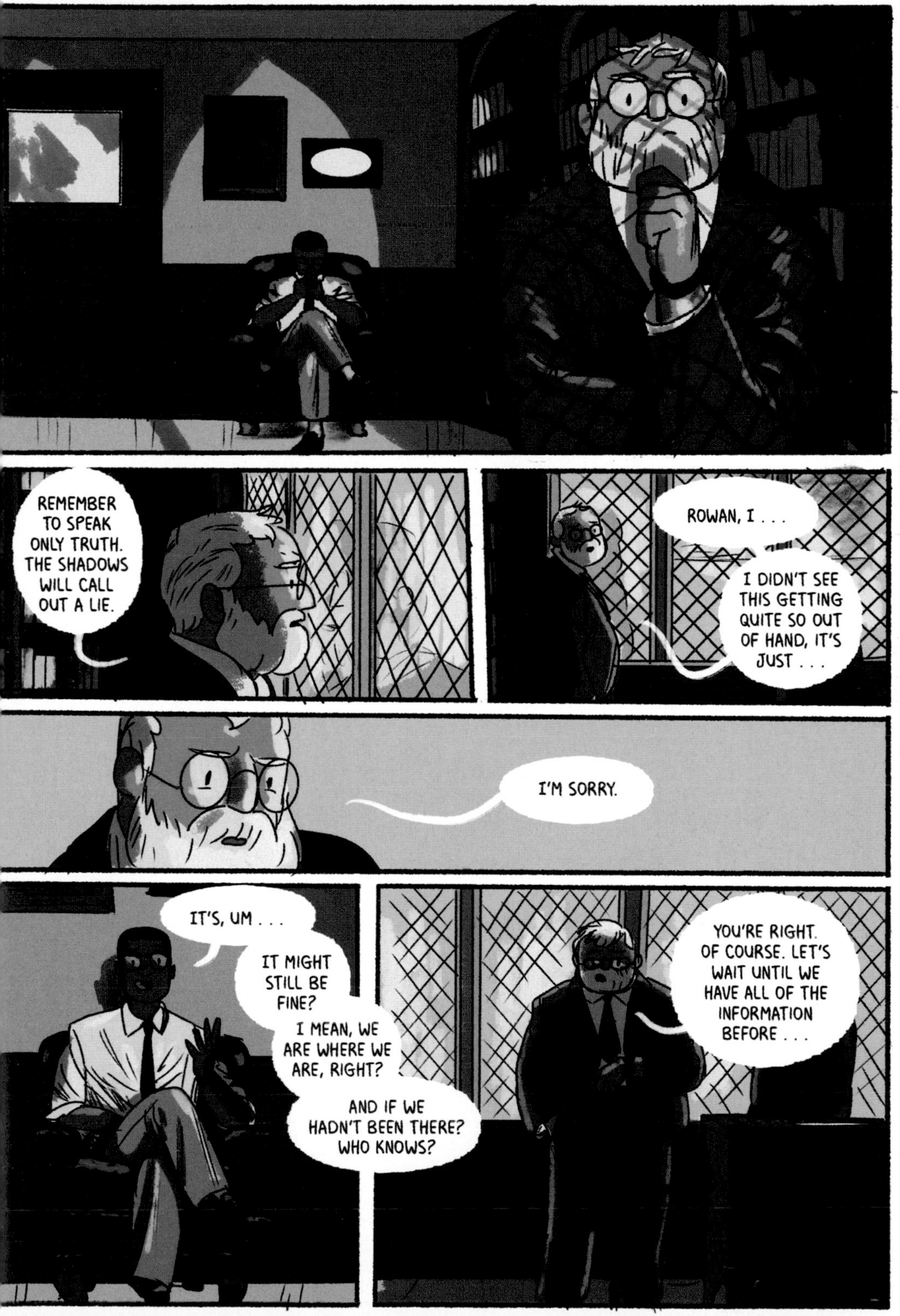
REMEMBER TO SPEAK ONLY TRUTH. THE SHADOWS WILL CALL OUT A LIE.
ROWAN, I . . .
I DIDN'T SEE THIS GETTING QUITE SO OUT OF HAND, IT'S JUST . . .
I'M SORRY.
IT'S, UM . . .
IT MIGHT STILL BE FINE?
I MEAN, WE ARE WHERE WE ARE, RIGHT?
AND IF WE HADN'T BEEN THERE? WHO KNOWS?
YOU'RE RIGHT. OF COURSE. LET'S WAIT UNTIL WE HAVE ALL OF THE INFORMATION BEFORE . . .

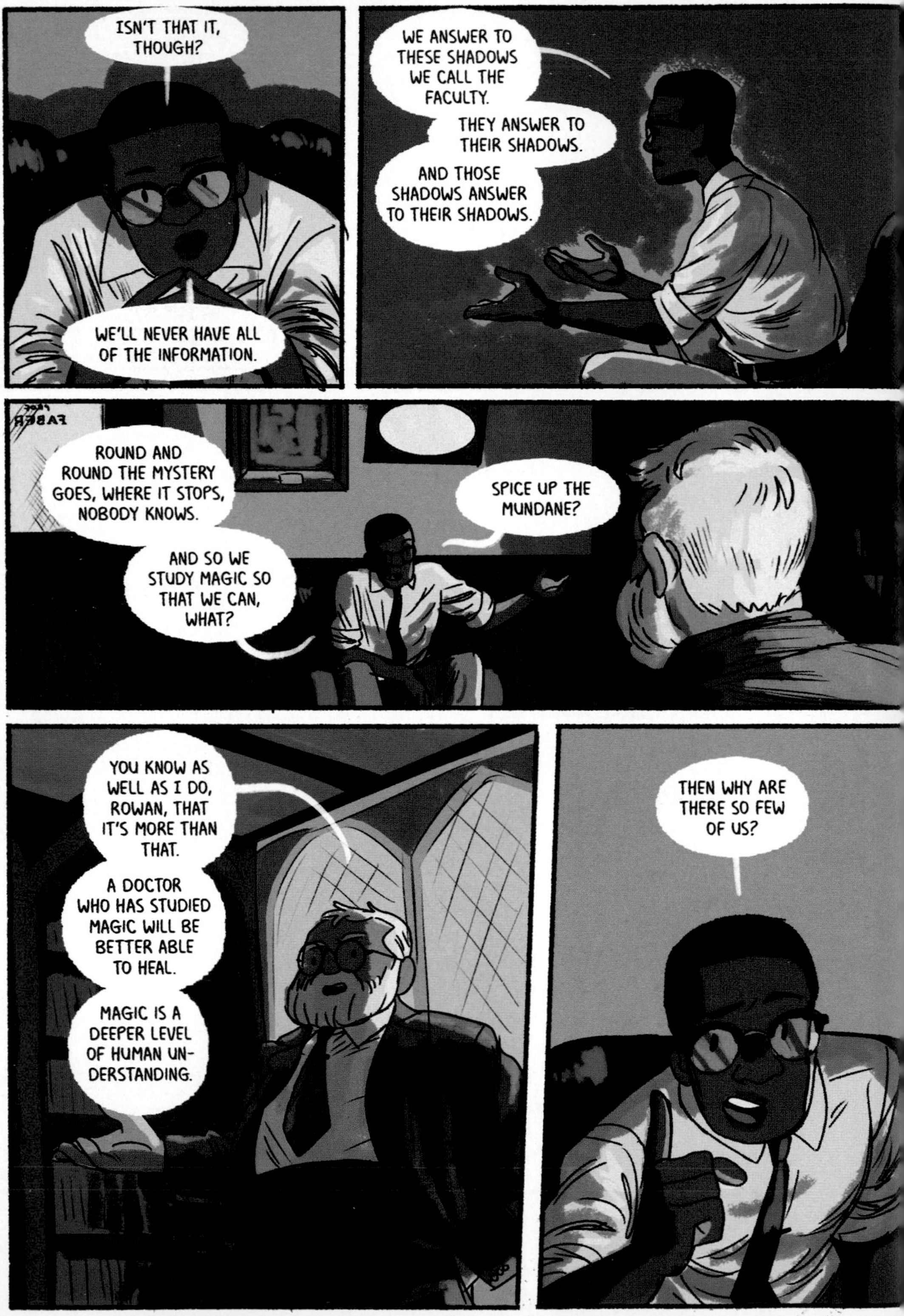
ISN'T THAT IT, THOUGH?
WE'LL NEVER HAVE ALL OF THE INFORMATION.
WE ANSWER TO THESE SHADOWS WE CALL THE FACULTY.
THEY ANSWER TO THEIR SHADOWS.
AND THOSE SHADOWS ANSWER TO THEIR SHADOWS.
ROUND AND ROUND THE MYSTERY GOES, WHERE IT STOPS, NOBODY KNOWS.
AND SO WE STUDY MAGIC SO THAT WE CAN, WHAT?
SPICE UP THE MUNDANE?
YOU KNOW AS WELL AS I DO, ROWAN, THAT IT'S MORE THAN THAT.
A DOCTOR WHO HAS STUDIED MAGIC WILL BE BETTER ABLE TO HEAL.
MAGIC IS A DEEPER LEVEL OF HUMAN UN-DERSTANDING.
THEN WHY ARE THERE SO FEW OF US?

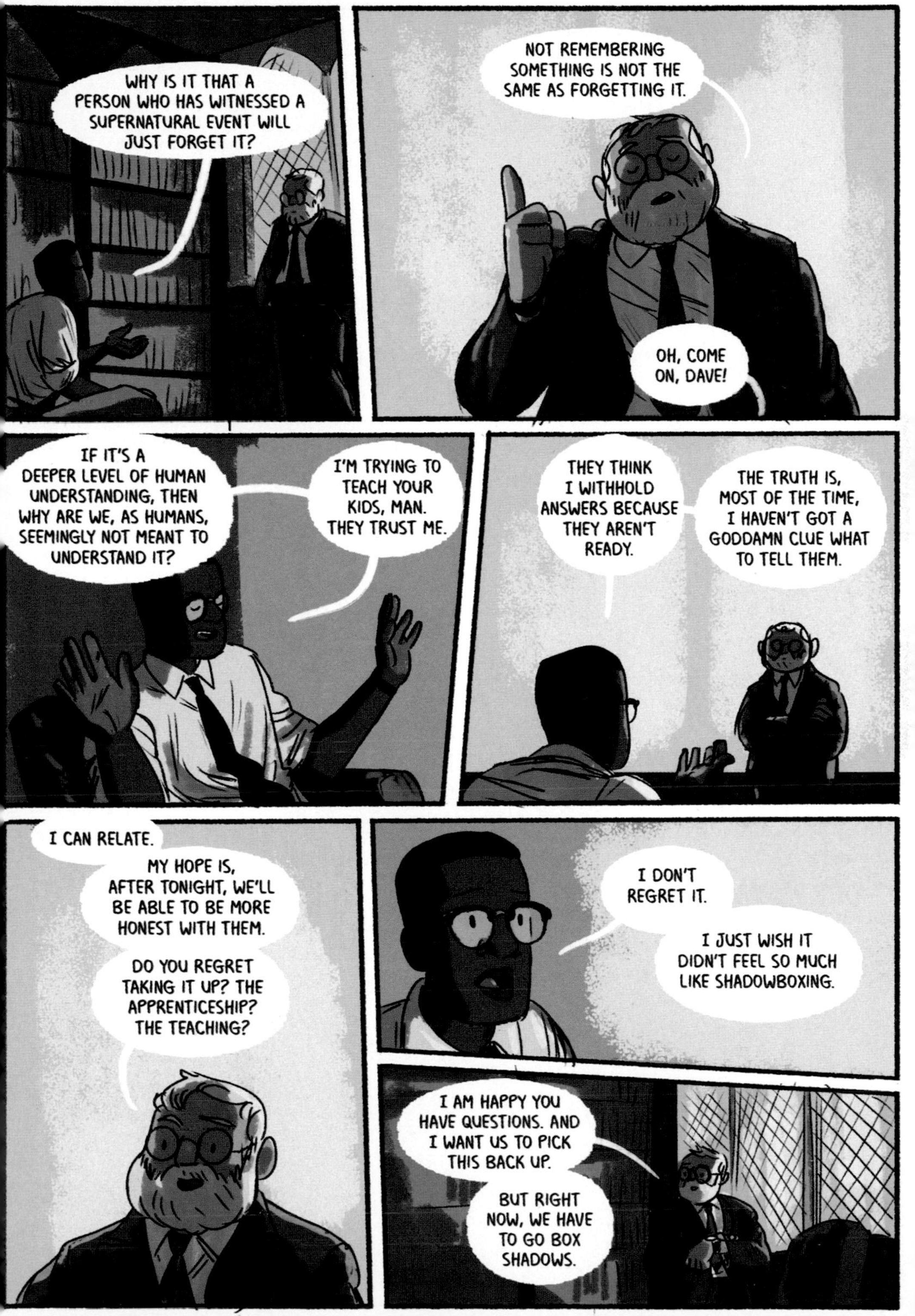
WHY IS IT THAT A PERSON WHO HAS WITNESSED A SUPERNATURAL EVENT WILL JUST FORGET IT?
NOT REMEMBERING SOMETHING IS NOT THE SAME AS FORGETTING IT.
OH, COME ON, DAVE!
IF IT'S A DEEPER LEVEL OF HUMAN UNDERSTANDING, THEN WHY ARE WE, AS HUMANS, SEEMINGLY NOT MEANT TO UNDERSTAND IT?
I'M TRYING TO TEACH YOUR KIDS, MAN. THEY TRUST ME.
THEY THINK I WITHHOLD ANSWERS BECAUSE THEY AREN'T READY.
THE TRUTH IS, MOST OF THE TIME, I HAVEN'T GOT A GODDAMN CLUE WHAT TO TELL THEM.
I CAN RELATE.
MY HOPE IS, AFTER TONIGHT, WE'LL BE ABLE TO BE MORE HONEST WITH THEM.
DO YOU REGRET TAKING IT UP? THE APPRENTICESHIP? THE TEACHING?
I DON'T REGRET IT.
I JUST WISH IT DIDN'T FEEL SO MUCH LIKE SHADOWBOXING.
I AM HAPPY YOU HAVE QUESTIONS. AND I WANT US TO PICK THIS BACK UP.
BUT RIGHT NOW, WE HAVE TO GO BOX SHADOWS.

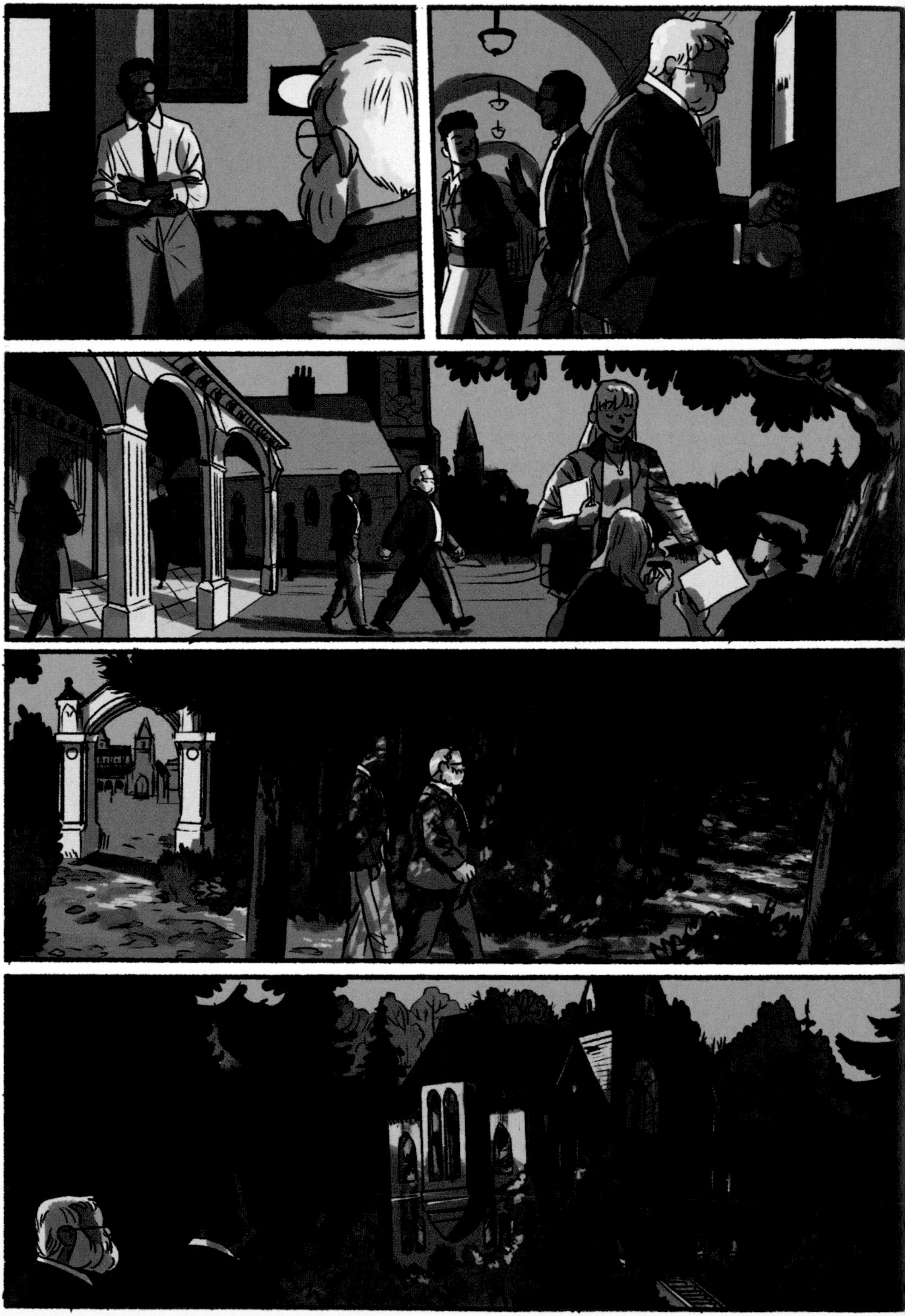

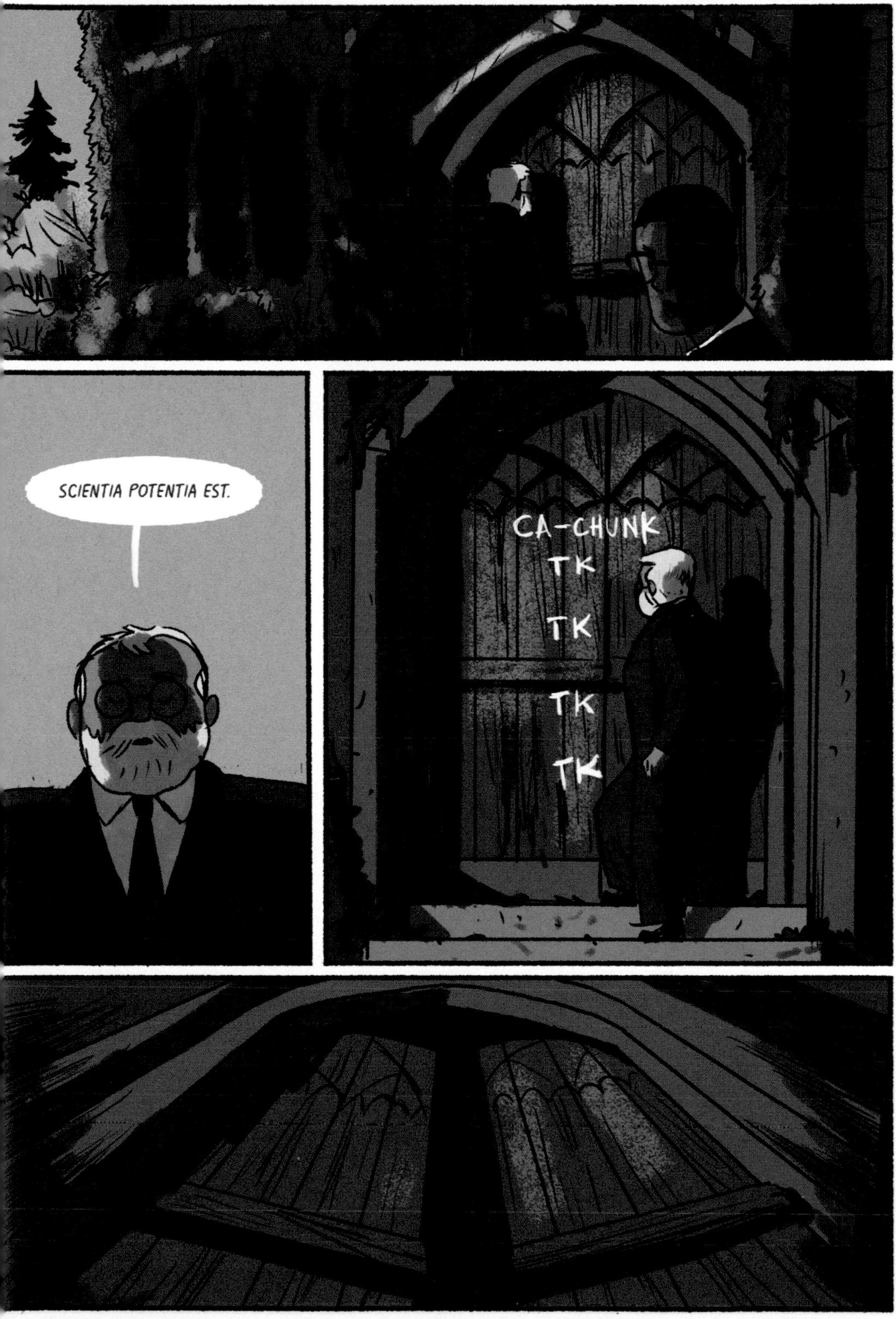
SCIENTIA POTENTIA EST.
CA-CHUNK
TK
TK
TK
TK

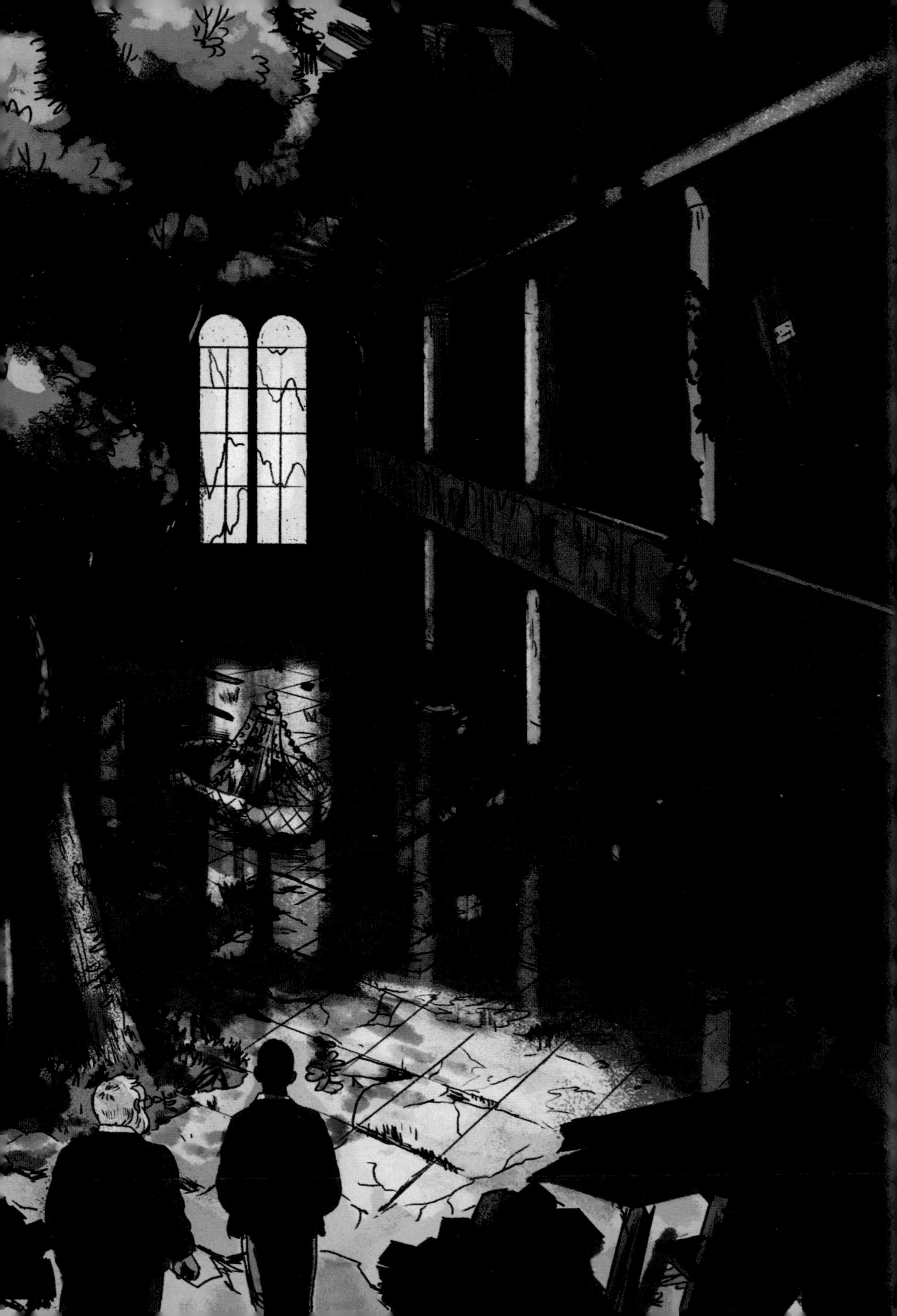

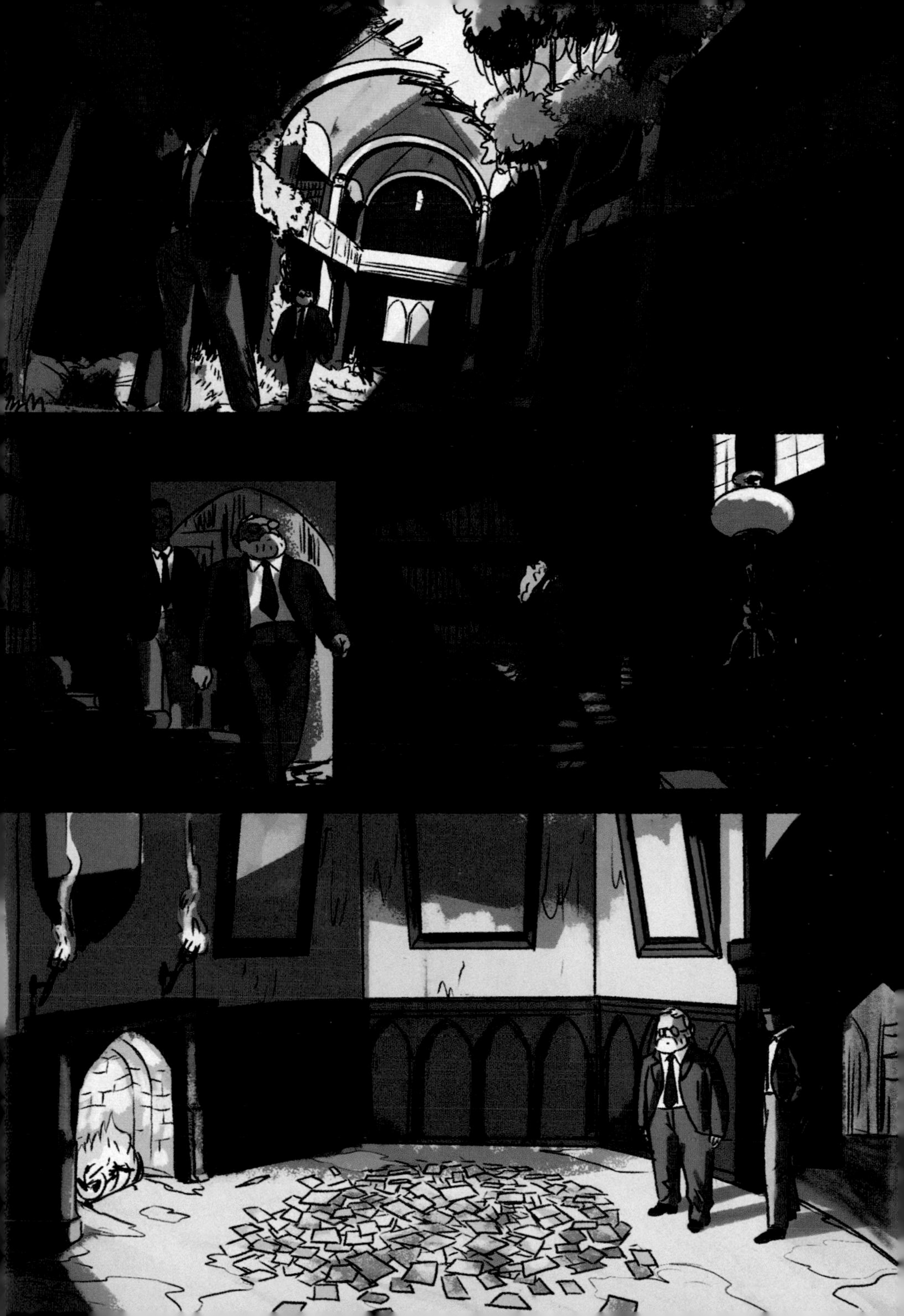

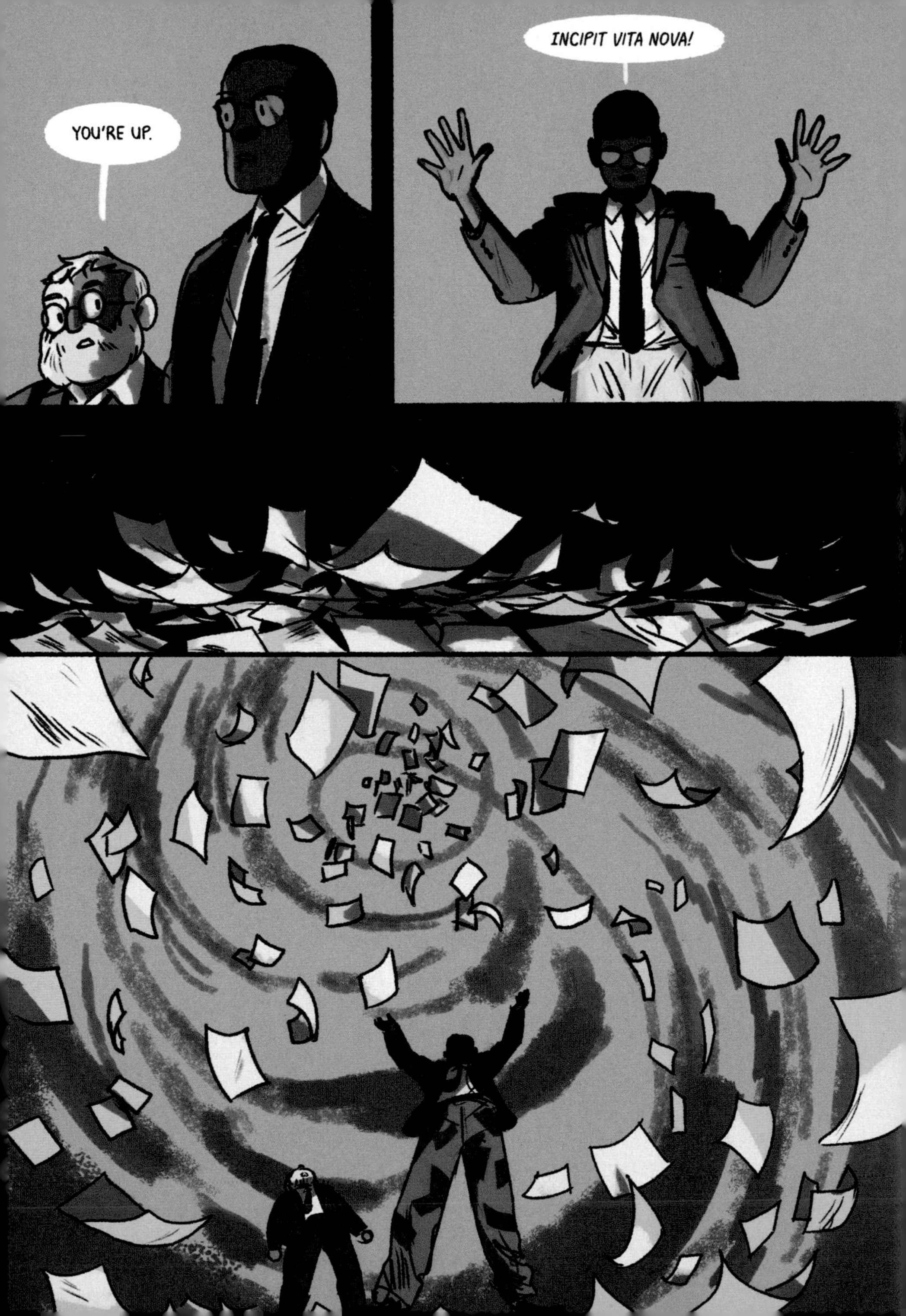
YOU'RE UP.
INCIPIT VITA NOVA!

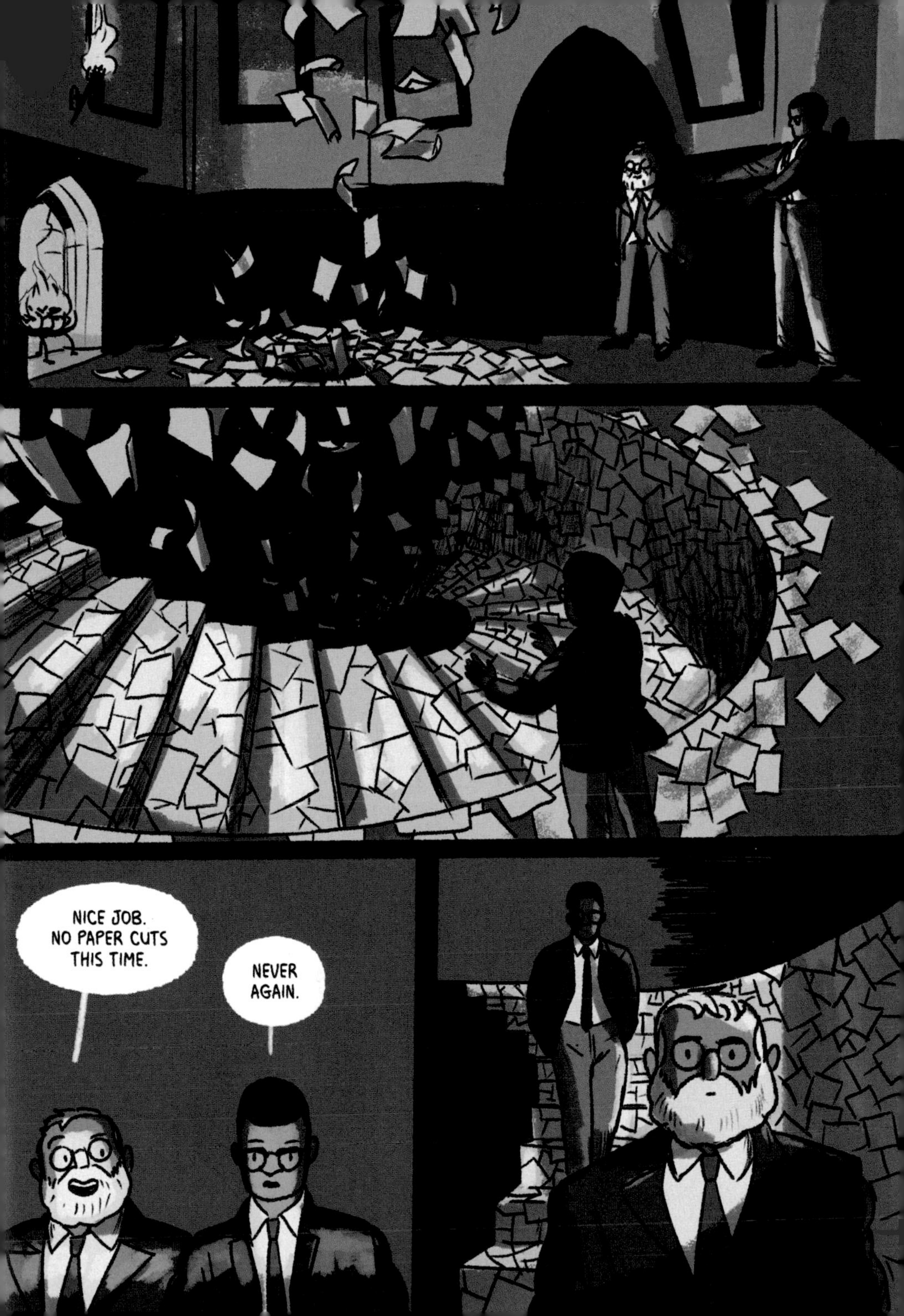
NICE JOB.
NO PAPER CUTS
THIS TIME.
NEVER
AGAIN.

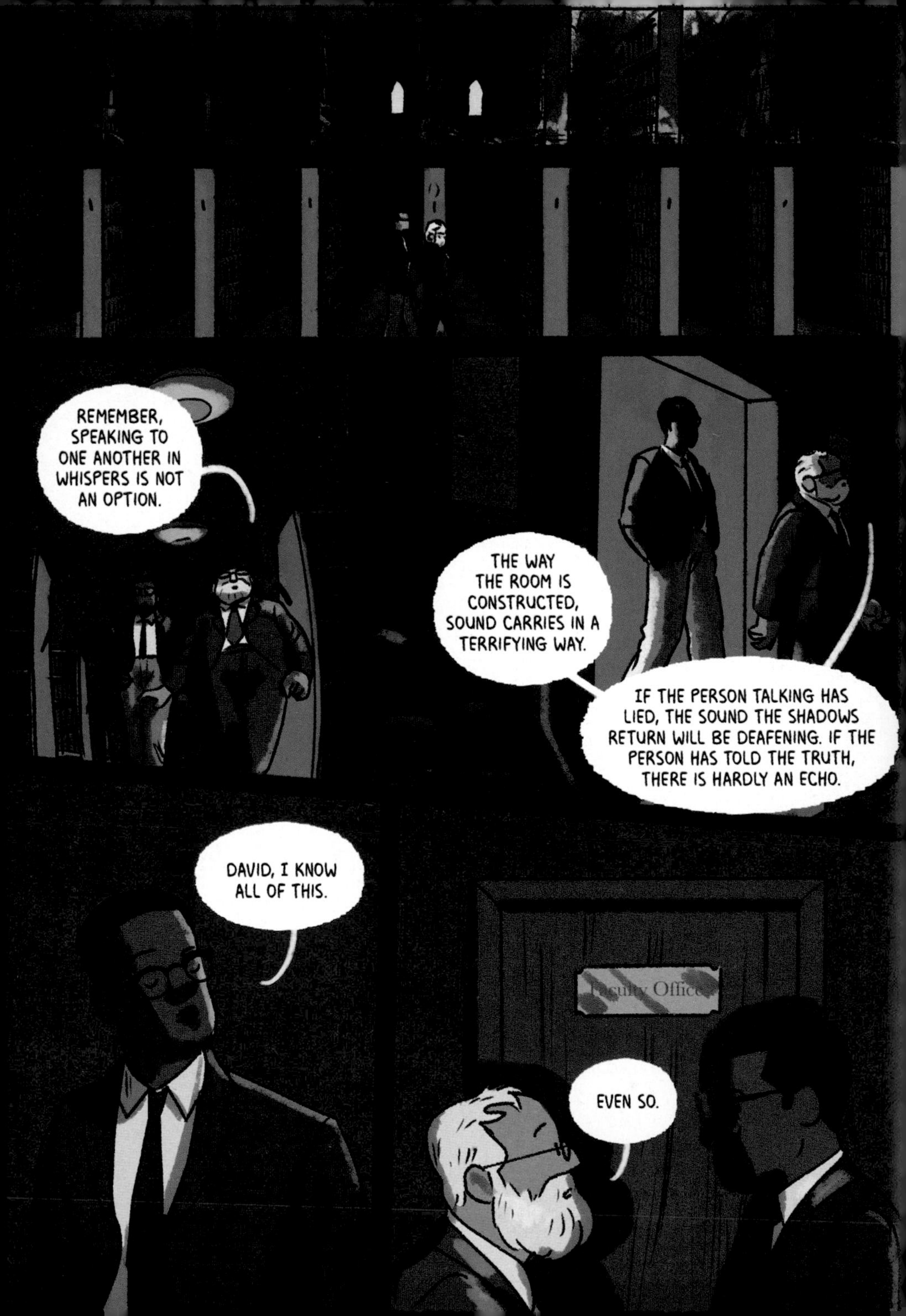
REMEMBER, SPEAKING TO ONE ANOTHER IN WHISPERS IS NOT AN OPTION.
THE WAY THE ROOM IS CONSTRUCTED, SOUND CARRIES IN A TERRIFYING WAY.
IF THE PERSON TALKING HAS LIED, THE SOUND THE SHADOWS RETURN WILL BE DEAFENING. IF THE PERSON HAS TOLD THE TRUTH, THERE IS HARDLY AN ECHO.
DAVID, I KNOW ALL OF THIS.
Faculty Office
EVEN SO.

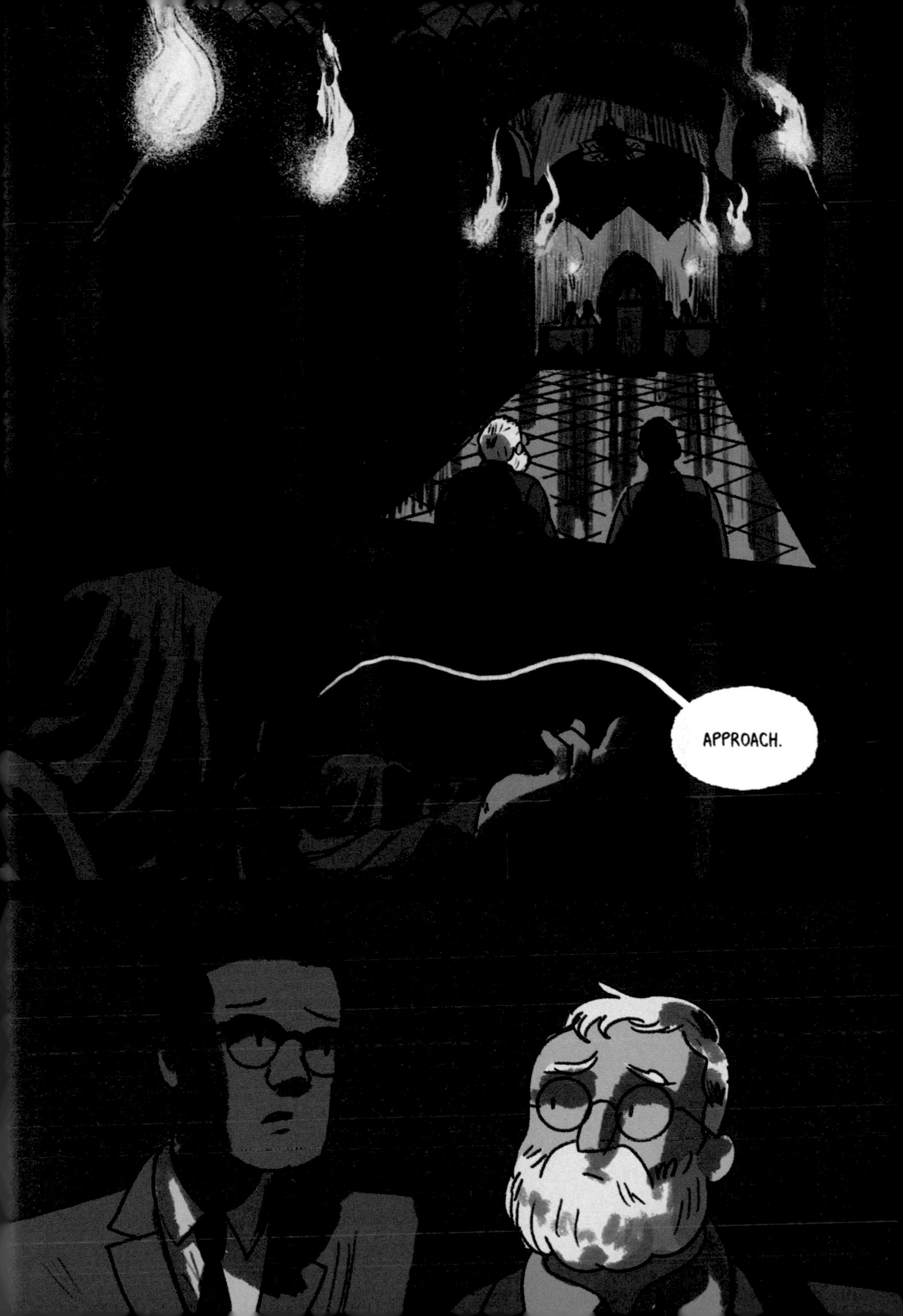
APPROACH.

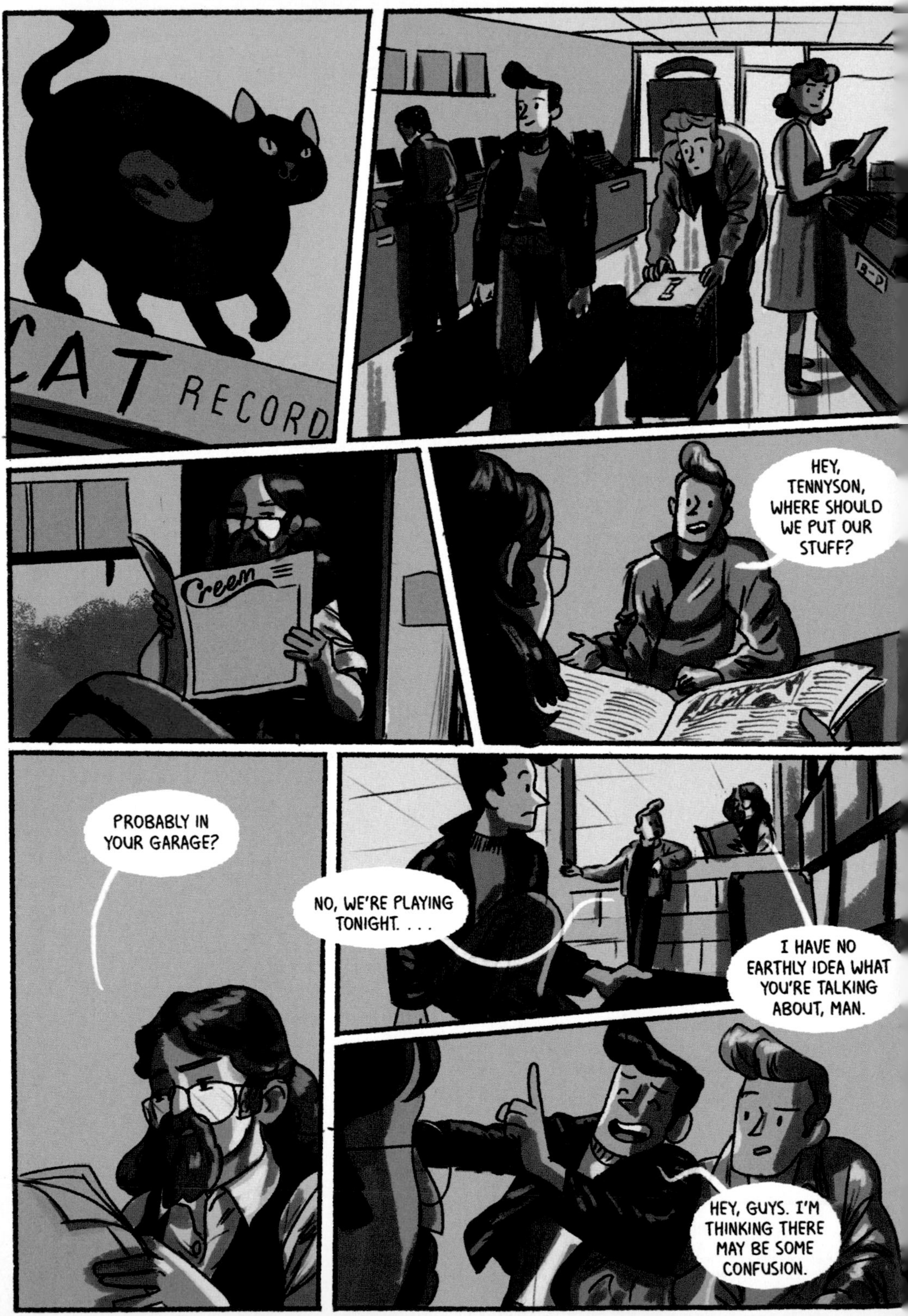
CAT RECORD
Creem
HEY, TENNYSON, WHERE SHOULD WE PUT OUR STUFF?
PROBABLY IN YOUR GARAGE?
NO, WE'RE PLAYING TONIGHT. . . .
I HAVE NO EARTHLY IDEA WHAT YOU'RE TALKING ABOUT, MAN.
HEY, GUYS. I'M THINKING THERE MAY BE SOME CONFUSION.

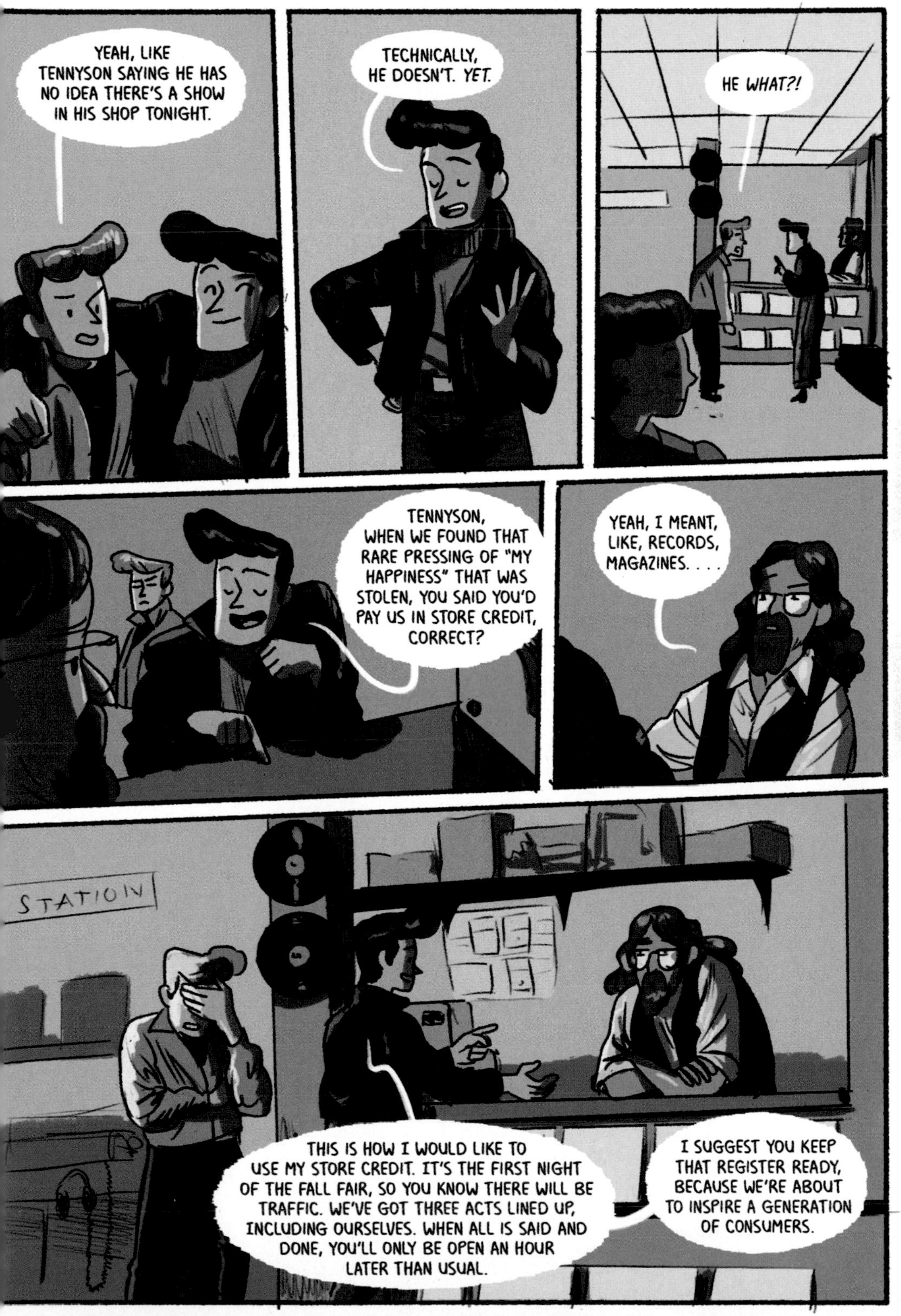
YEAH, LIKE TENNYSON SAYING HE HAS NO IDEA THERE'S A SHOW IN HIS SHOP TONIGHT.
TECHNICALLY, HE DOESN'T. *YET.*
HE *WHAT?!*
TENNYSON, WHEN WE FOUND THAT RARE PRESSING OF "MY HAPPINESS" THAT WAS STOLEN, YOU SAID YOU'D PAY US IN STORE CREDIT, CORRECT?
YEAH, I MEANT, LIKE, RECORDS, MAGAZINES. . . .
STATION
THIS IS HOW I WOULD LIKE TO USE MY STORE CREDIT. IT'S THE FIRST NIGHT OF THE FALL FAIR, SO YOU KNOW THERE WILL BE TRAFFIC. WE'VE GOT THREE ACTS LINED UP, INCLUDING OURSELVES. WHEN ALL IS SAID AND DONE, YOU'LL ONLY BE OPEN AN HOUR LATER THAN USUAL.
I SUGGEST YOU KEEP THAT REGISTER READY, BECAUSE WE'RE ABOUT TO INSPIRE A GENERATION OF CONSUMERS.

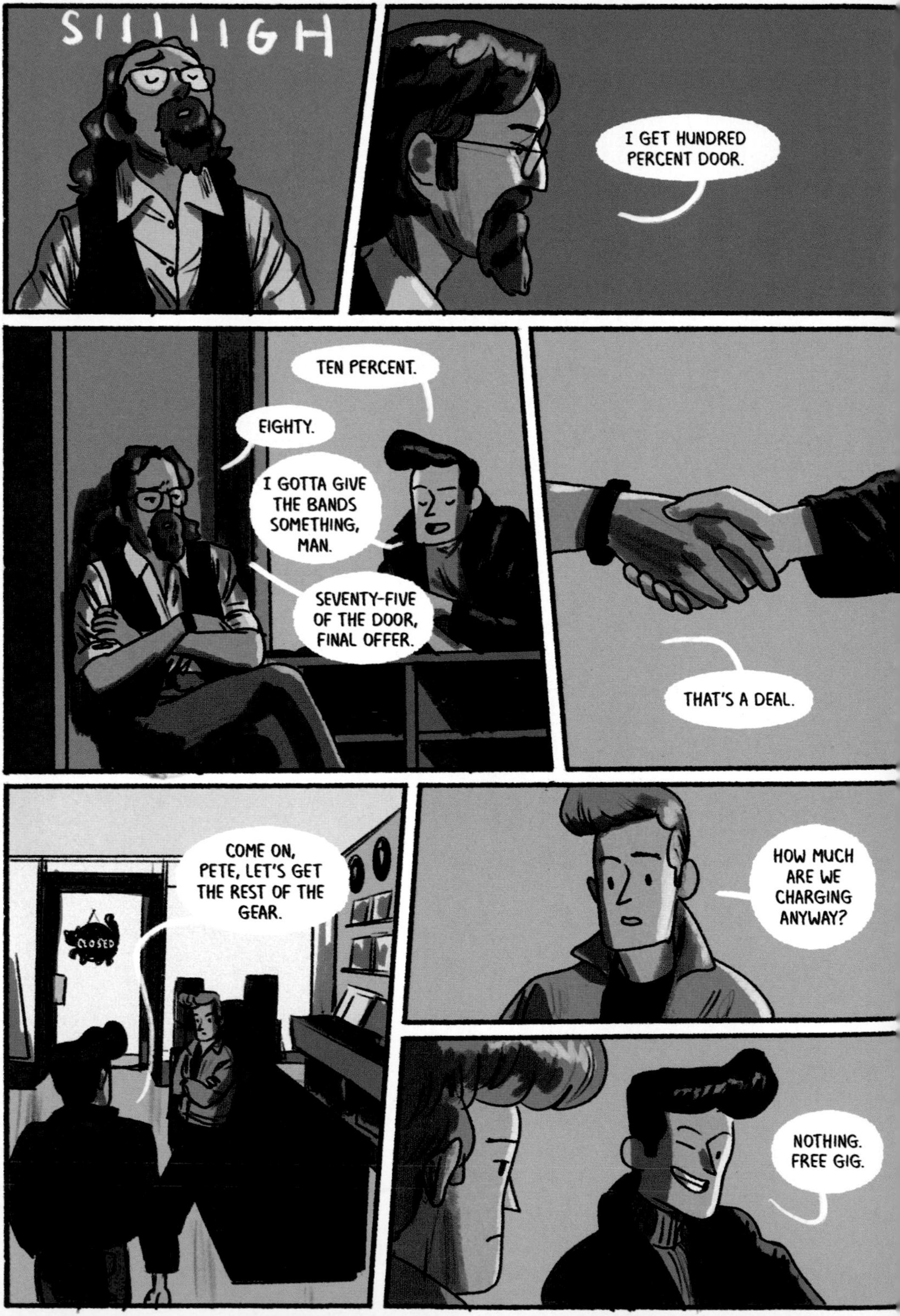
SIIIIIGH
I GET HUNDRED PERCENT DOOR.
TEN PERCENT.
EIGHTY.
I GOTTA GIVE THE BANDS SOMETHING, MAN.
SEVENTY-FIVE OF THE DOOR, FINAL OFFER.
THAT'S A DEAL.
COME ON, PETE, LET'S GET THE REST OF THE GEAR.
CLOSED
HOW MUCH ARE WE CHARGING ANYWAY?
NOTHING. FREE GIG.

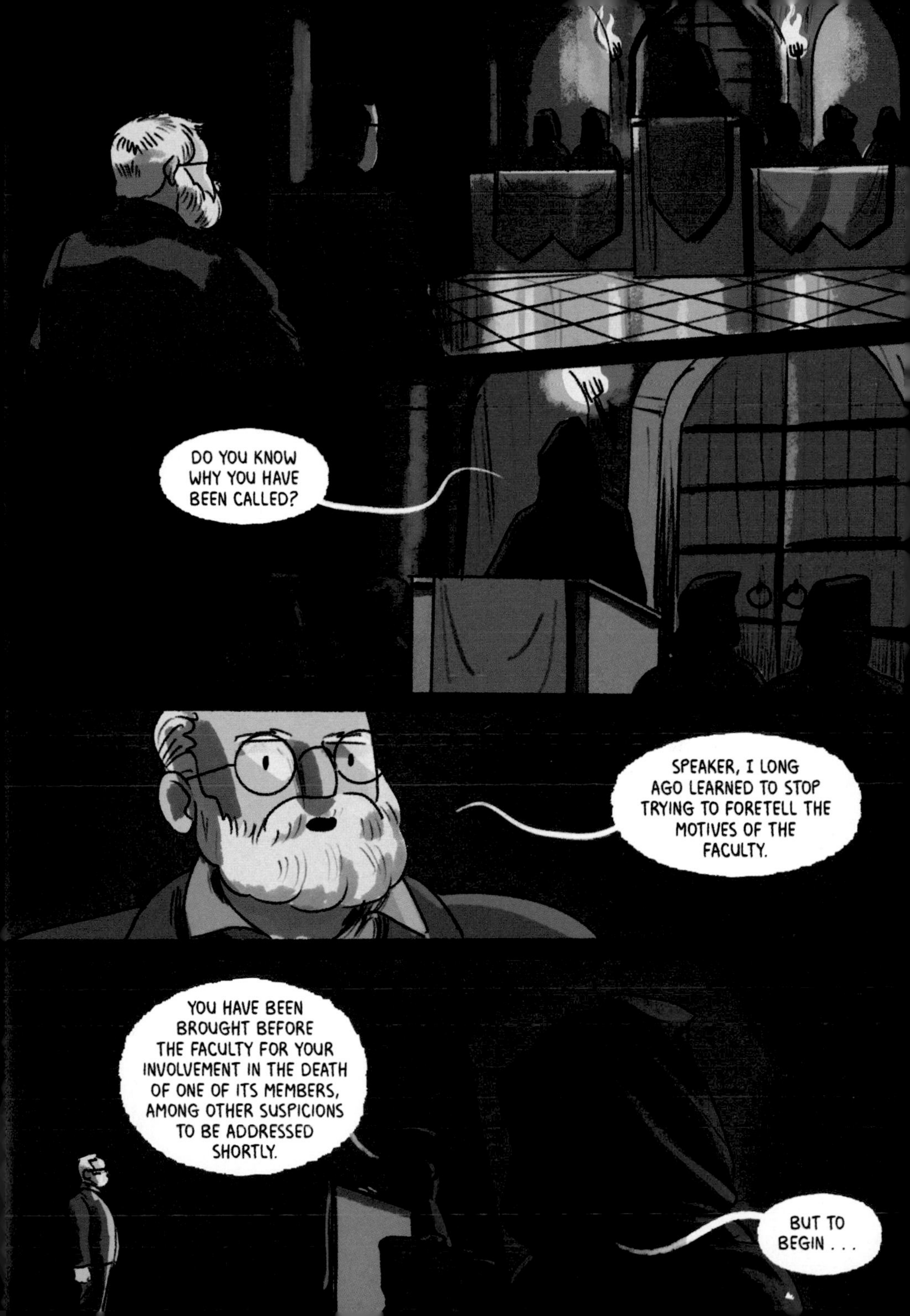
DO YOU KNOW WHY YOU HAVE BEEN CALLED?
SPEAKER, I LONG AGO LEARNED TO STOP TRYING TO FORETELL THE MOTIVES OF THE FACULTY.
YOU HAVE BEEN BROUGHT BEFORE THE FACULTY FOR YOUR INVOLVEMENT IN THE DEATH OF ONE OF ITS MEMBERS, AMONG OTHER SUSPICIONS TO BE ADDRESSED SHORTLY.
BUT TO BEGIN . . .

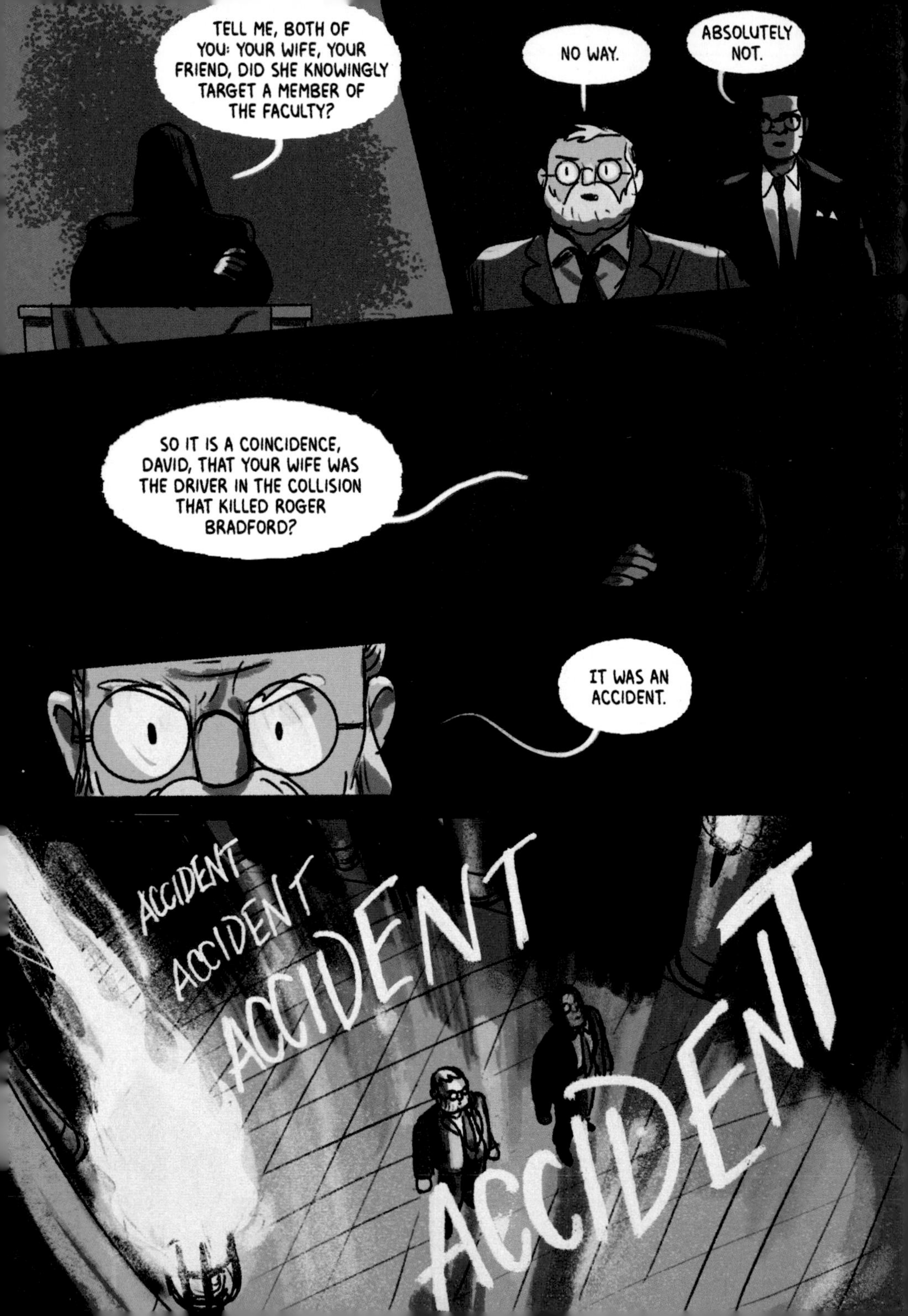
TELL ME, BOTH OF YOU: YOUR WIFE, YOUR FRIEND, DID SHE KNOWINGLY TARGET A MEMBER OF THE FACULTY?
NO WAY.
ABSOLUTELY NOT.
SO IT IS A COINCIDENCE, DAVID, THAT YOUR WIFE WAS THE DRIVER IN THE COLLISION THAT KILLED ROGER BRADFORD?
IT WAS AN ACCIDENT.
ACCIDENT
ACCIDENT
ACCIDENT
ACCIDENT

NO, THAT'S NOT . . .

SHE HAD TO DO IT. IT WAS SELF-DEFENSE. A FULL INVESTIGATION BY THE AUTHORITIES CORROBORATED THAT.

ROGER BRADFORD THREATENED THE LIVES OF MY CHILDREN AND WOULD HAVE KILLED MY WIFE. ASIDE FROM THAT, HAD WE NOT BEEN THERE, HE WOULD HAVE MURDERED HIS OWN DAUGHTER.

COULD THE QUESTION NOT BE ASKED: WAS THE FACULTY TARGETING MY FAMILY?

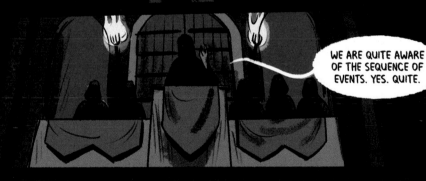

WE ARE QUITE AWARE OF THE SEQUENCE OF EVENTS. YES. QUITE.

WE NEED TO SPEAK TO THE CHILDREN.

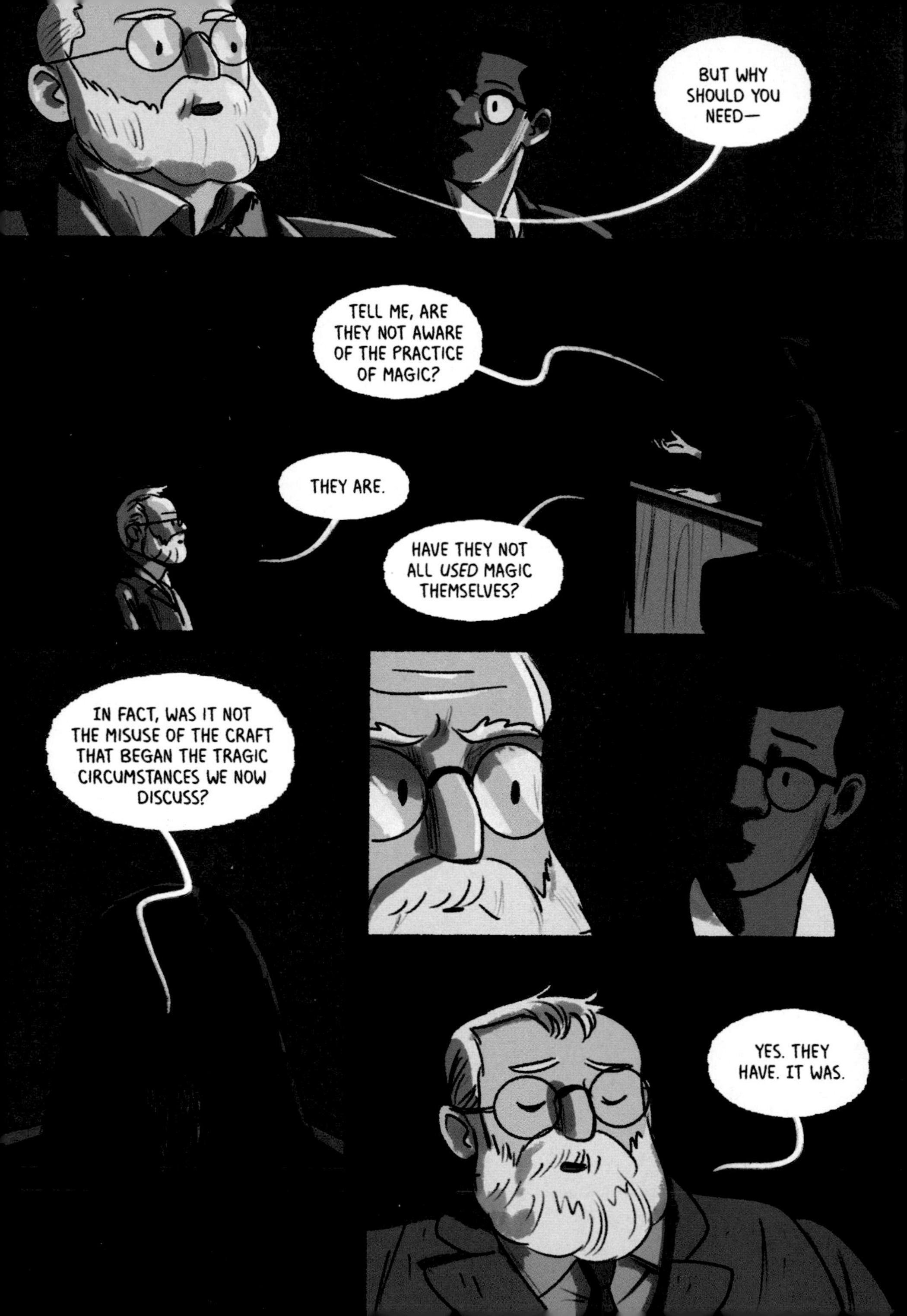
BUT WHY SHOULD YOU NEED—
TELL ME, ARE THEY NOT AWARE OF THE PRACTICE OF MAGIC?
THEY ARE.
HAVE THEY NOT ALL *USED* MAGIC THEMSELVES?
IN FACT, WAS IT NOT THE MISUSE OF THE CRAFT THAT BEGAN THE TRAGIC CIRCUMSTANCES WE NOW DISCUSS?
YES. THEY HAVE. IT WAS.

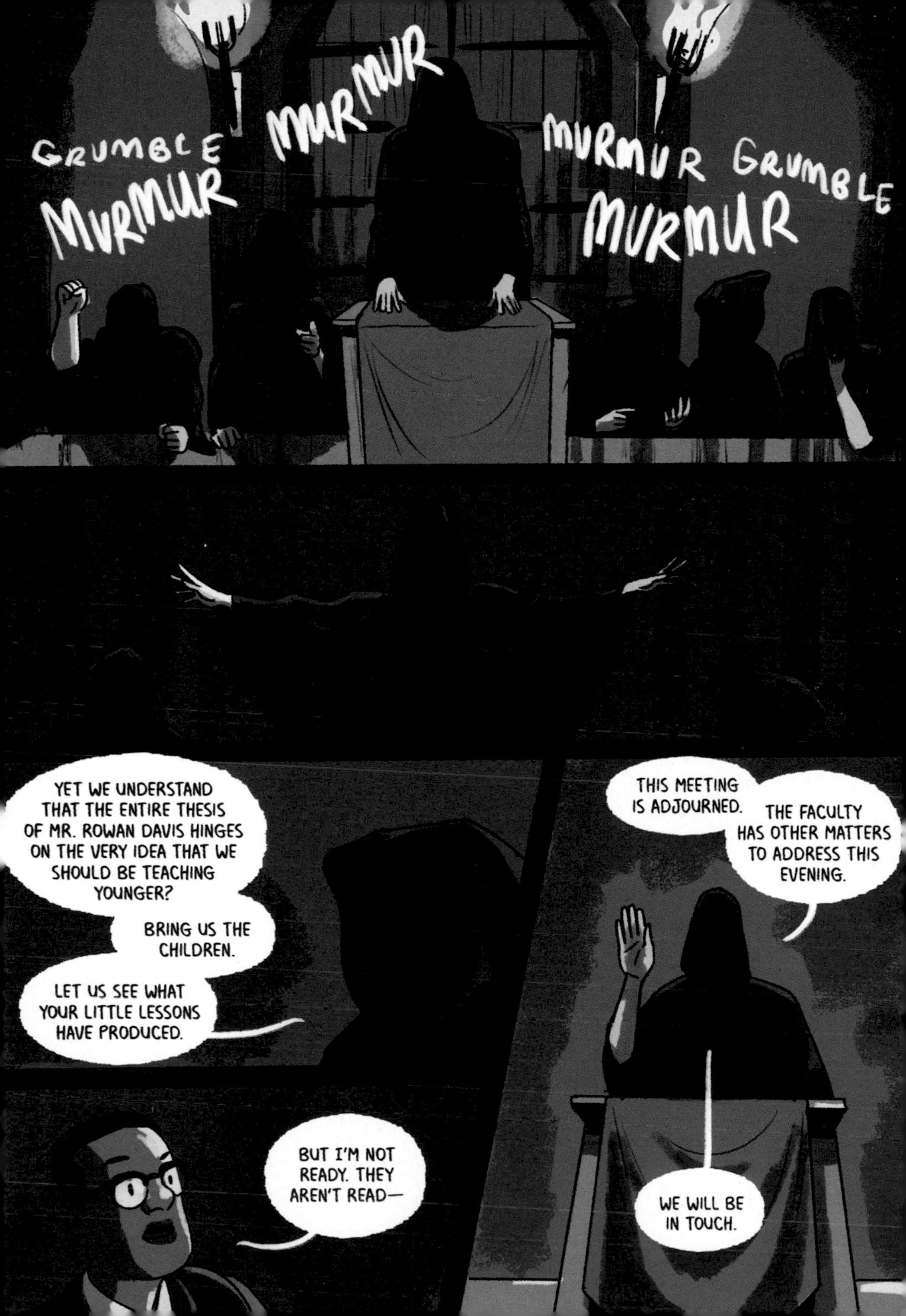
GRUMBLE
MURMUR
MURMUR
MURMUR GRUMBLE
MURMUR
YET WE UNDERSTAND THAT THE ENTIRE THESIS OF MR. ROWAN DAVIS HINGES ON THE VERY IDEA THAT WE SHOULD BE TEACHING YOUNGER?
BRING US THE CHILDREN.
LET US SEE WHAT YOUR LITTLE LESSONS HAVE PRODUCED.
BUT I'M NOT READY. THEY AREN'T READ—
THIS MEETING IS ADJOURNED.
THE FACULTY HAS OTHER MATTERS TO ADDRESS THIS EVENING.
WE WILL BE IN TOUCH.

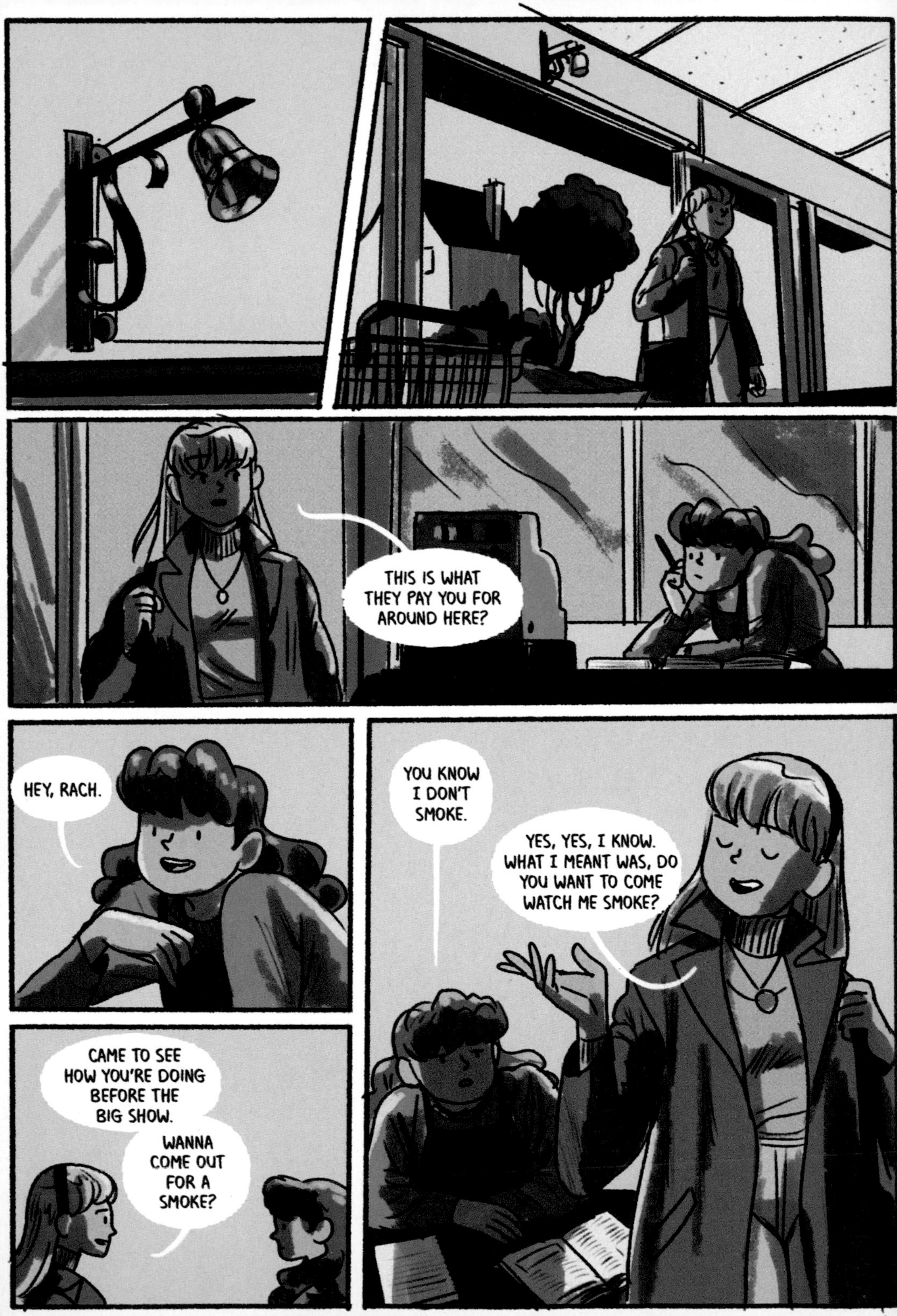
THIS IS WHAT THEY PAY YOU FOR AROUND HERE?
HEY, RACH.
CAME TO SEE HOW YOU'RE DOING BEFORE THE BIG SHOW.
WANNA COME OUT FOR A SMOKE?
YOU KNOW I DON'T SMOKE.
YES, YES, I KNOW. WHAT I MEANT WAS, DO YOU WANT TO COME WATCH ME SMOKE?

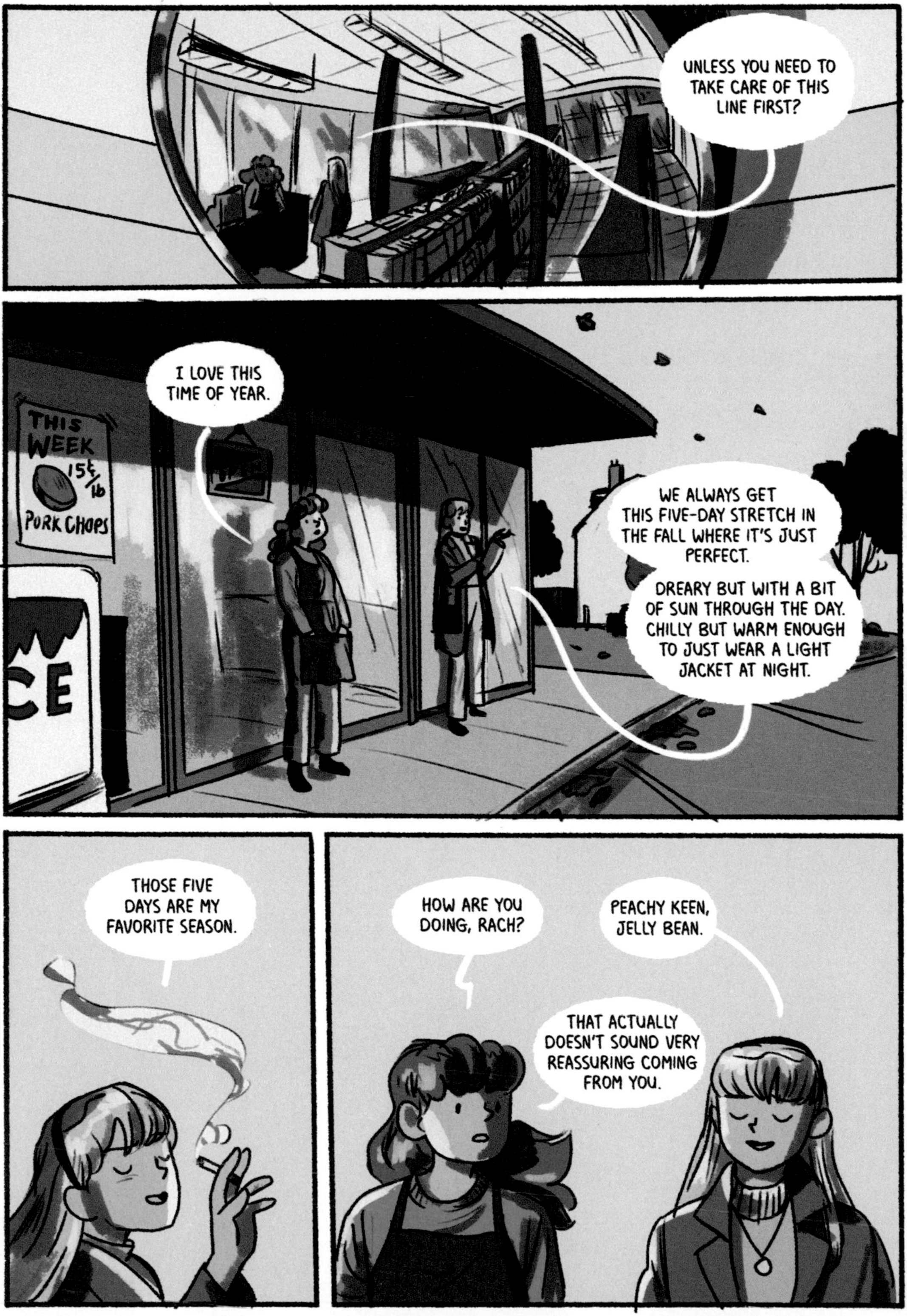
UNLESS YOU NEED TO TAKE CARE OF THIS LINE FIRST?
THIS WEEK 15¢/lb PORK CHOPS
I LOVE THIS TIME OF YEAR.
WE ALWAYS GET THIS FIVE-DAY STRETCH IN THE FALL WHERE IT'S JUST PERFECT.
DREARY BUT WITH A BIT OF SUN THROUGH THE DAY. CHILLY BUT WARM ENOUGH TO JUST WEAR A LIGHT JACKET AT NIGHT.
THOSE FIVE DAYS ARE MY FAVORITE SEASON.
HOW ARE YOU DOING, RACH?
PEACHY KEEN, JELLY BEAN.
THAT ACTUALLY DOESN'T SOUND VERY REASSURING COMING FROM YOU.

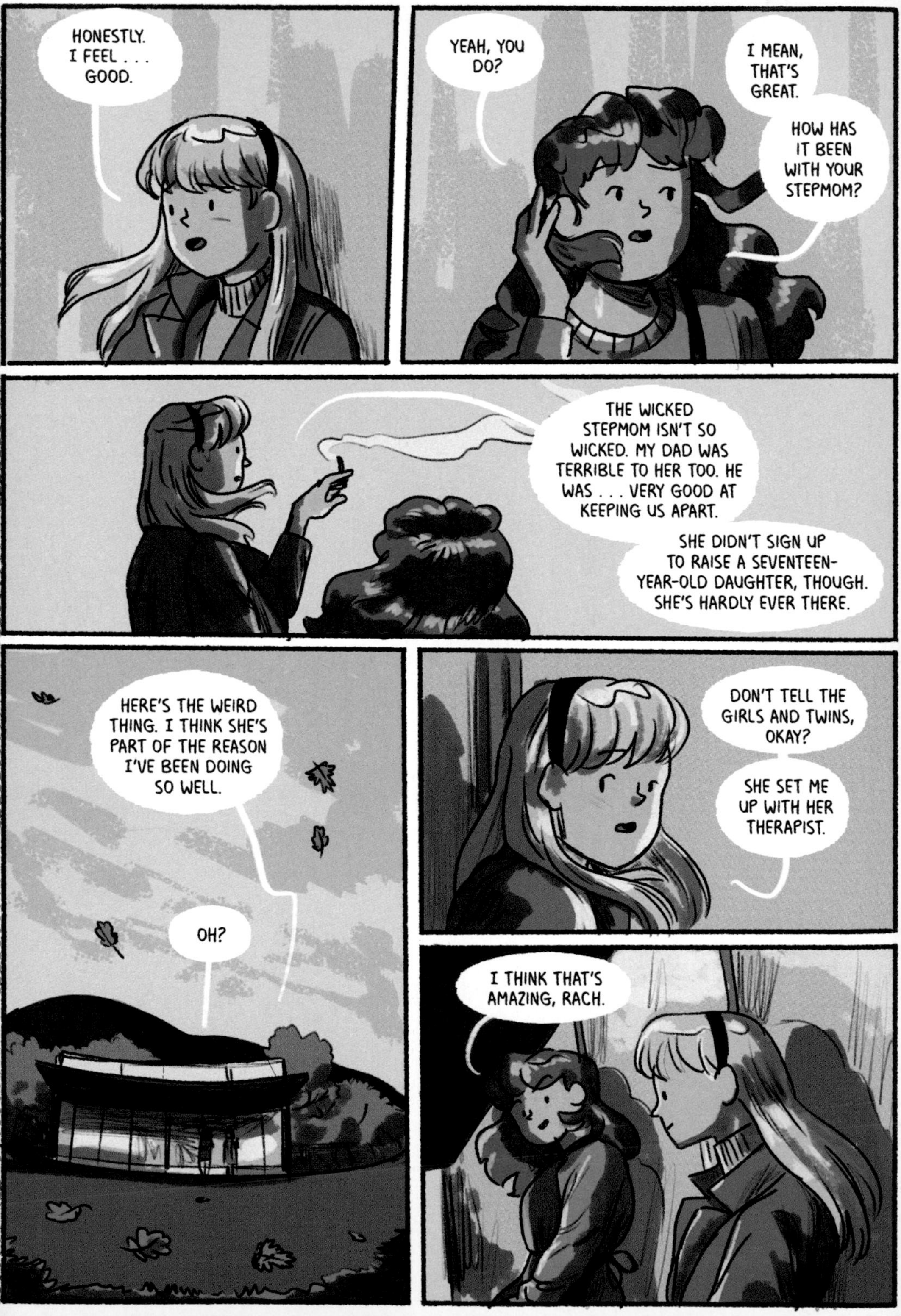
HONESTLY. I FEEL . . . GOOD.
YEAH, YOU DO?
I MEAN, THAT'S GREAT.
HOW HAS IT BEEN WITH YOUR STEPMOM?
THE WICKED STEPMOM ISN'T SO WICKED. MY DAD WAS TERRIBLE TO HER TOO. HE WAS . . . VERY GOOD AT KEEPING US APART.
SHE DIDN'T SIGN UP TO RAISE A SEVENTEEN-YEAR-OLD DAUGHTER, THOUGH. SHE'S HARDLY EVER THERE.
HERE'S THE WEIRD THING. I THINK SHE'S PART OF THE REASON I'VE BEEN DOING SO WELL.
OH?
DON'T TELL THE GIRLS AND TWINS, OKAY?
SHE SET ME UP WITH HER THERAPIST.
I THINK THAT'S AMAZING, RACH.

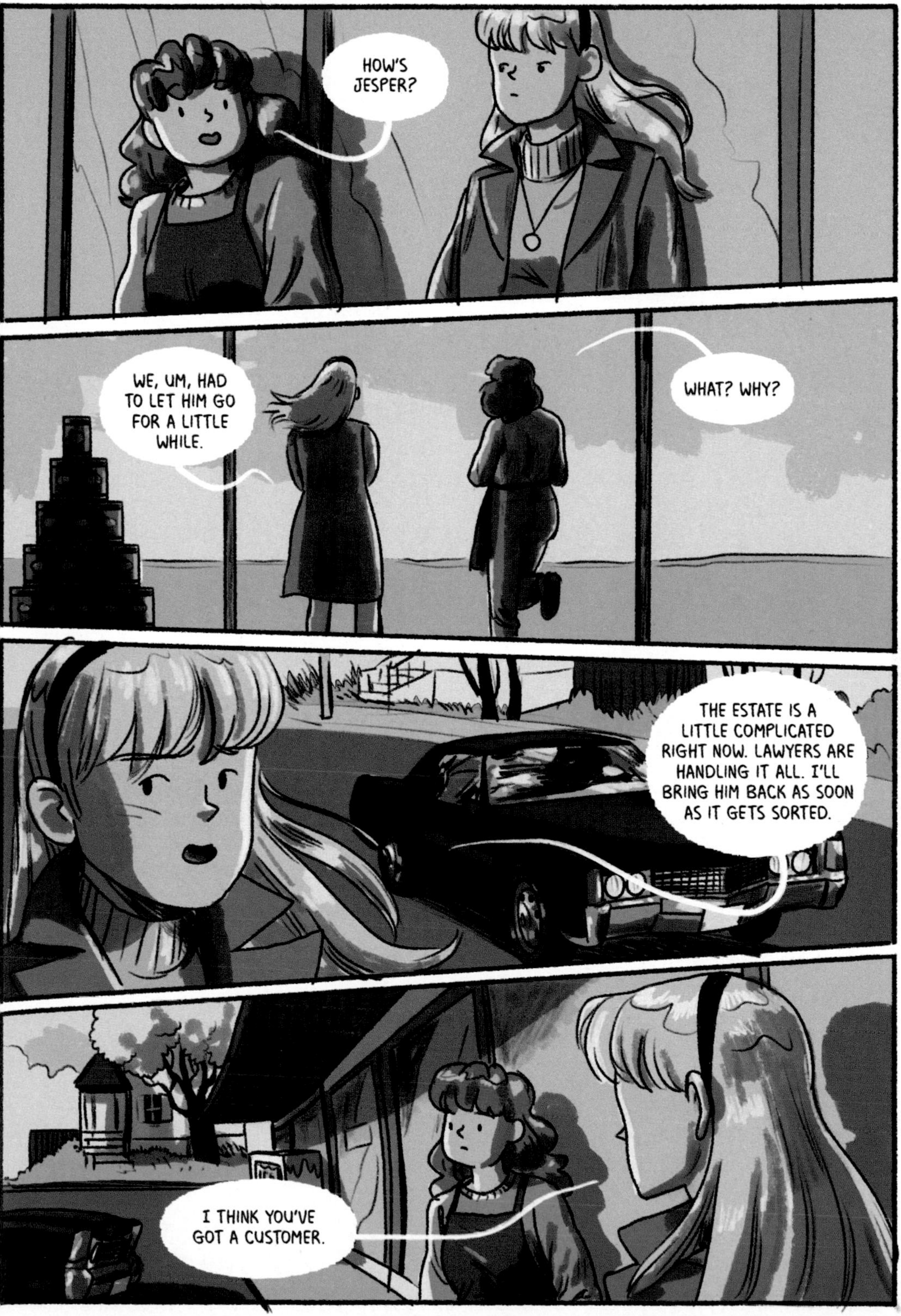
HOW'S JESPER?
WE, UM, HAD TO LET HIM GO FOR A LITTLE WHILE.
WHAT? WHY?
THE ESTATE IS A LITTLE COMPLICATED RIGHT NOW. LAWYERS ARE HANDLING IT ALL. I'LL BRING HIM BACK AS SOON AS IT GETS SORTED.
I THINK YOU'VE GOT A CUSTOMER.

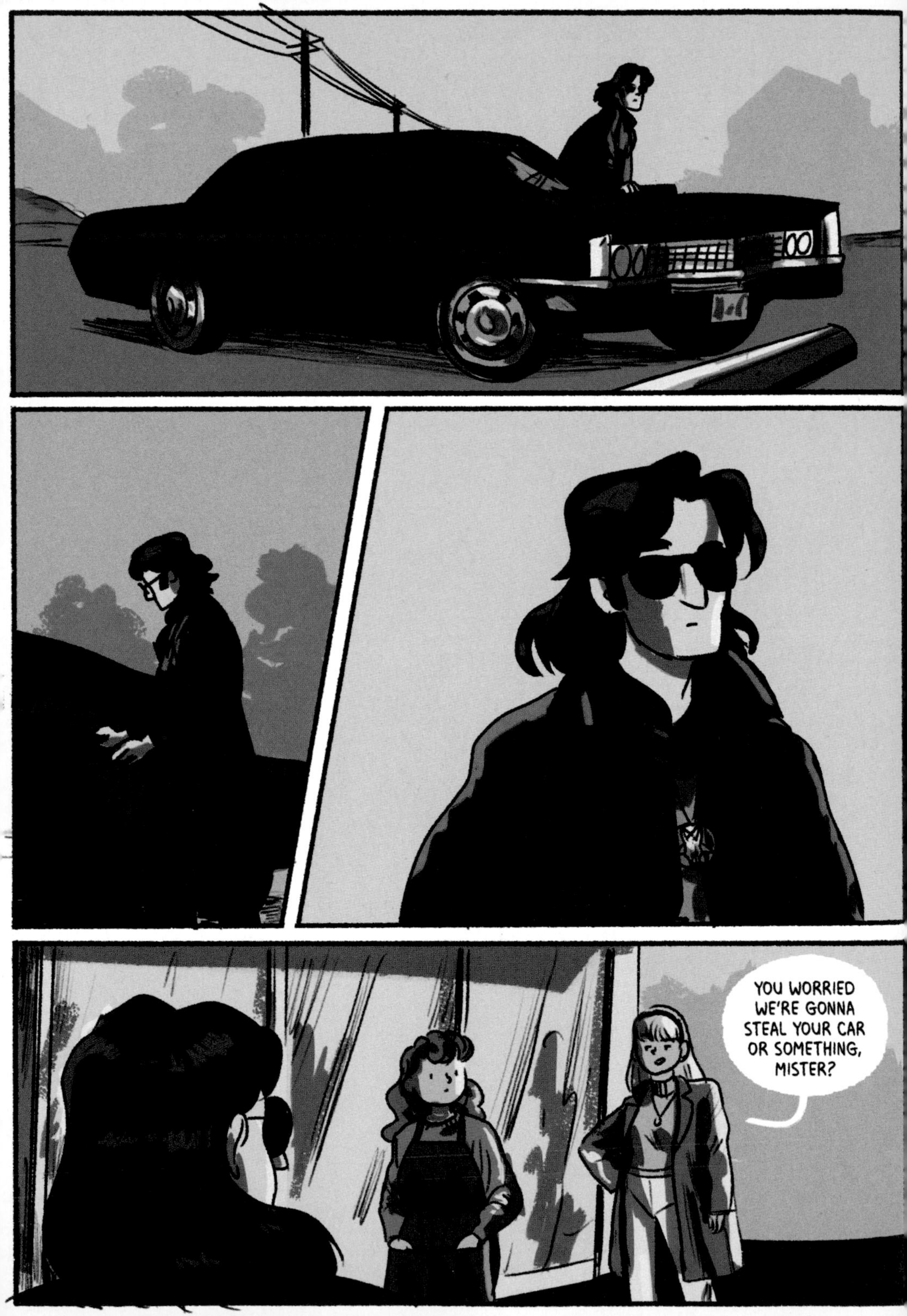
YOU WORRIED WE'RE GONNA STEAL YOUR CAR OR SOMETHING, MISTER?

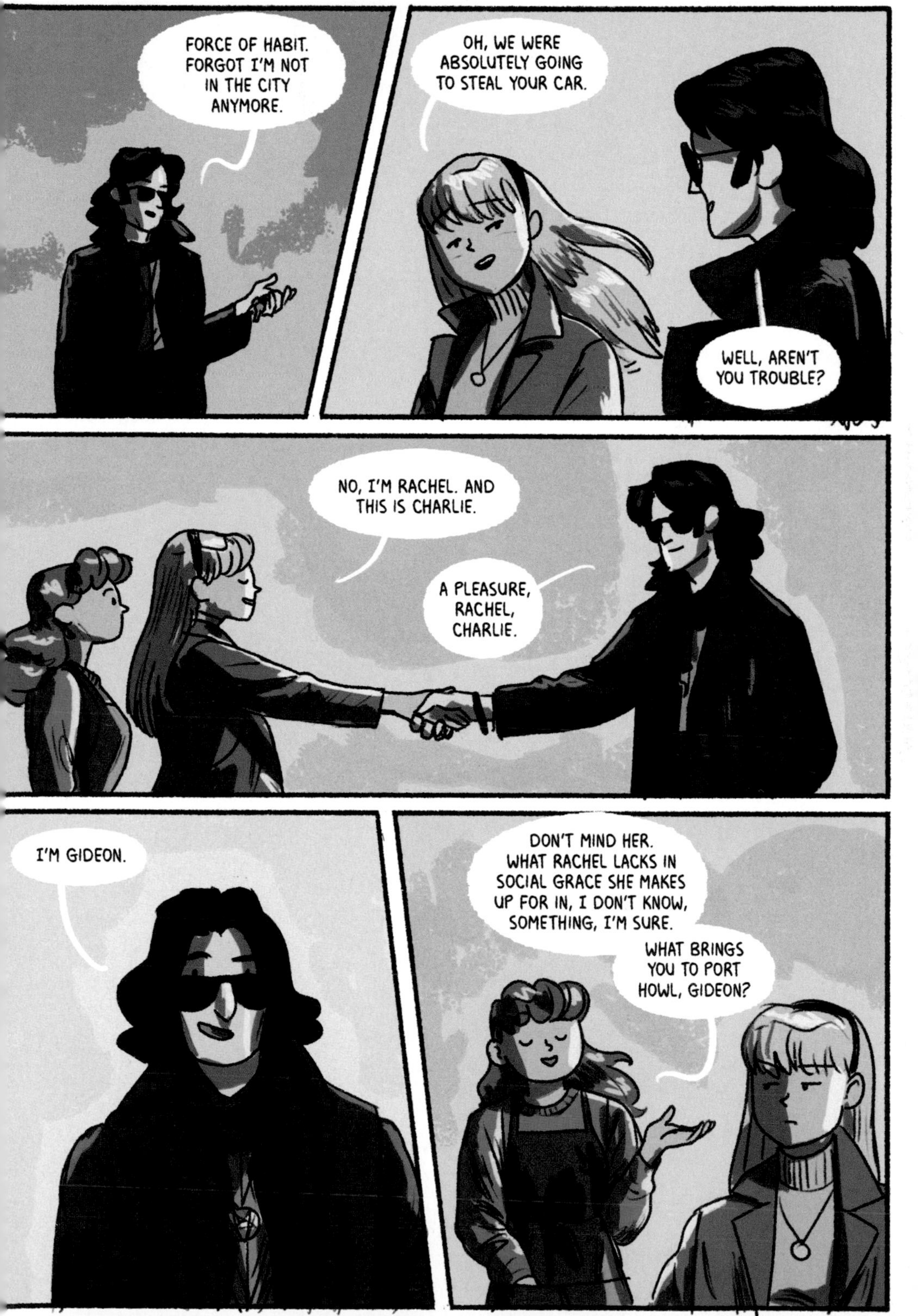
FORCE OF HABIT. FORGOT I'M NOT IN THE CITY ANYMORE.
OH, WE WERE ABSOLUTELY GOING TO STEAL YOUR CAR.
WELL, AREN'T YOU TROUBLE?
NO, I'M RACHEL. AND THIS IS CHARLIE.
A PLEASURE, RACHEL, CHARLIE.
I'M GIDEON.
DON'T MIND HER. WHAT RACHEL LACKS IN SOCIAL GRACE SHE MAKES UP FOR IN, I DON'T KNOW, SOMETHING, I'M SURE.
WHAT BRINGS YOU TO PORT HOWL, GIDEON?

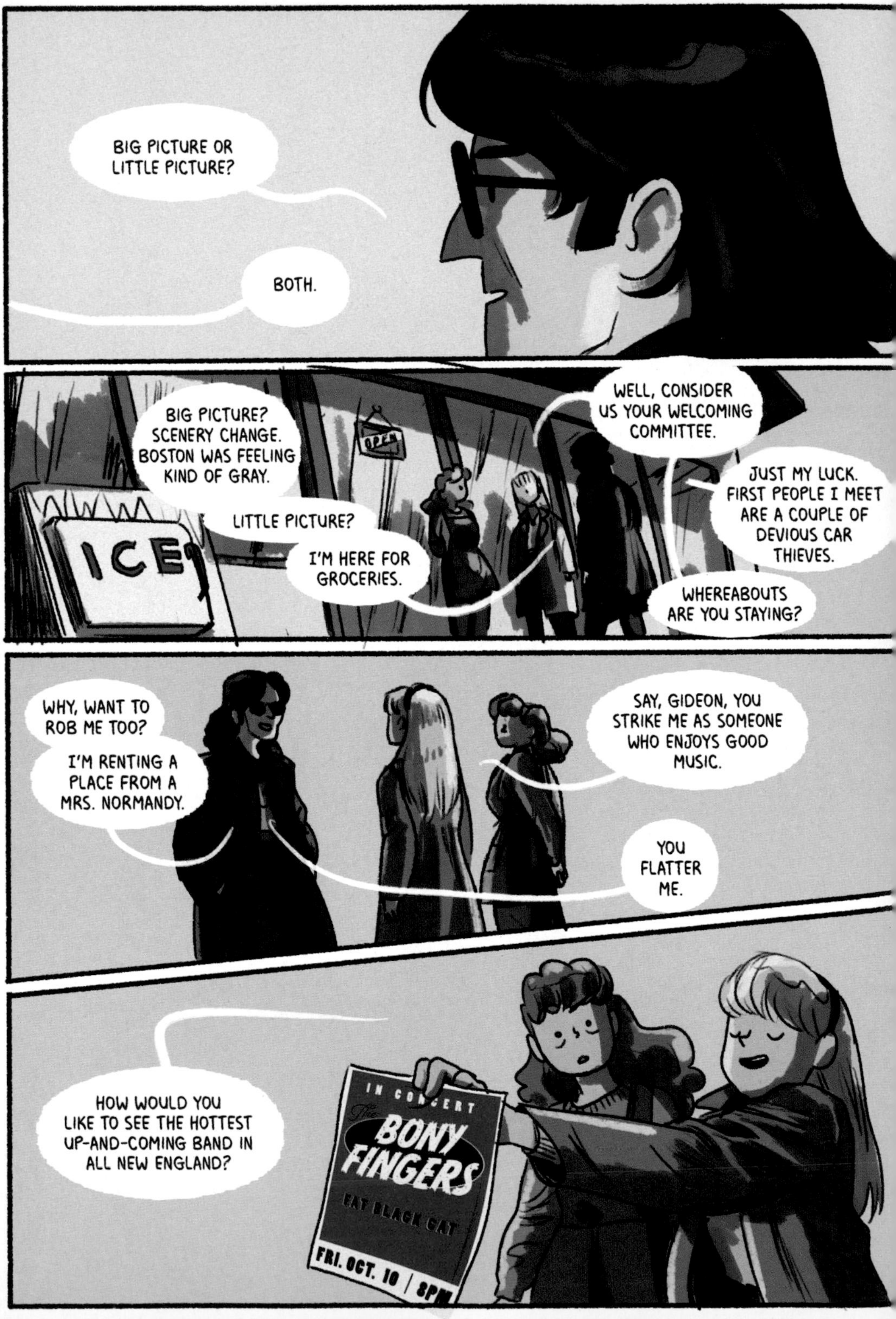
BIG PICTURE OR LITTLE PICTURE?
BOTH.
BIG PICTURE? SCENERY CHANGE. BOSTON WAS FEELING KIND OF GRAY.
LITTLE PICTURE?
I'M HERE FOR GROCERIES.
WELL, CONSIDER US YOUR WELCOMING COMMITTEE.
JUST MY LUCK. FIRST PEOPLE I MEET ARE A COUPLE OF DEVIOUS CAR THIEVES.
WHEREABOUTS ARE YOU STAYING?
ICE
OPEN
WHY, WANT TO ROB ME TOO?
I'M RENTING A PLACE FROM A MRS. NORMANDY.
SAY, GIDEON, YOU STRIKE ME AS SOMEONE WHO ENJOYS GOOD MUSIC.
YOU FLATTER ME.
HOW WOULD YOU LIKE TO SEE THE HOTTEST UP-AND-COMING BAND IN ALL NEW ENGLAND?
IN CONCERT
The BONY FINGERS
EAT BLACK CAT
FRI. OCT. 10 / 8PM

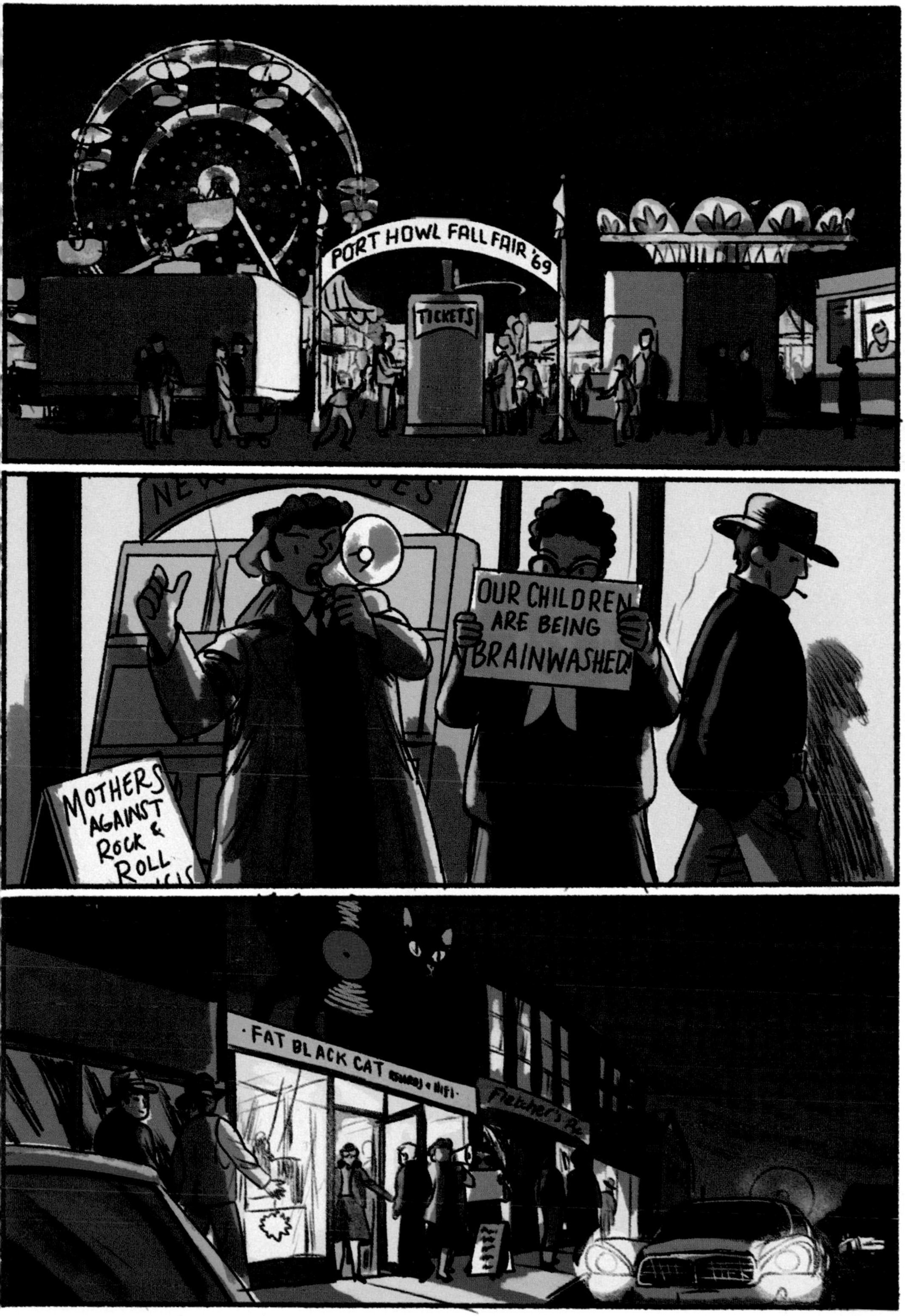
PORT HOWL FALL FAIR '69
TICKETS
OUR CHILDREN ARE BEING BRAINWASHED!
MOTHERS AGAINST ROCK & ROLL
FAT BLACK CAT

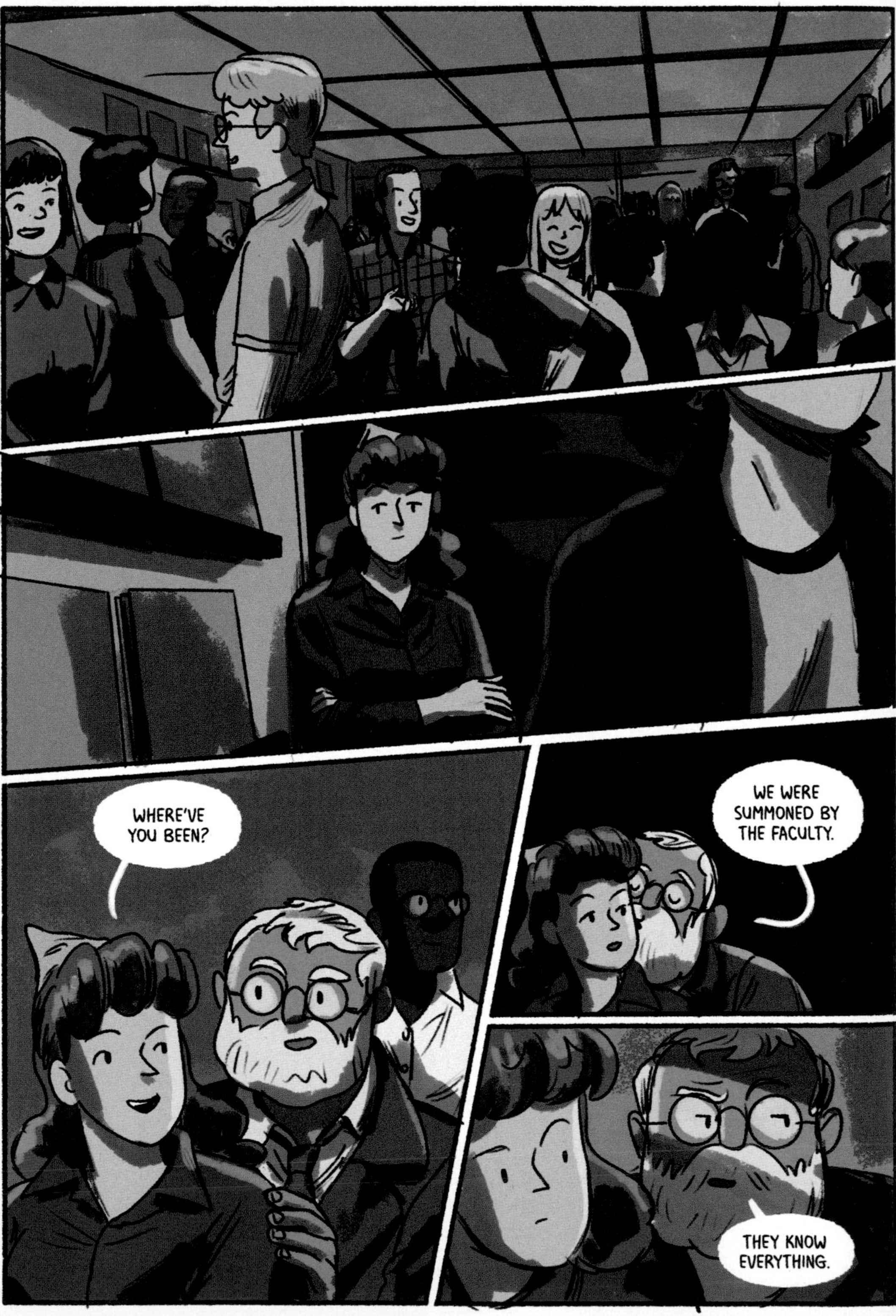
WHERE'VE YOU BEEN?
WE WERE SUMMONED BY THE FACULTY.
THEY KNOW EVERYTHING.

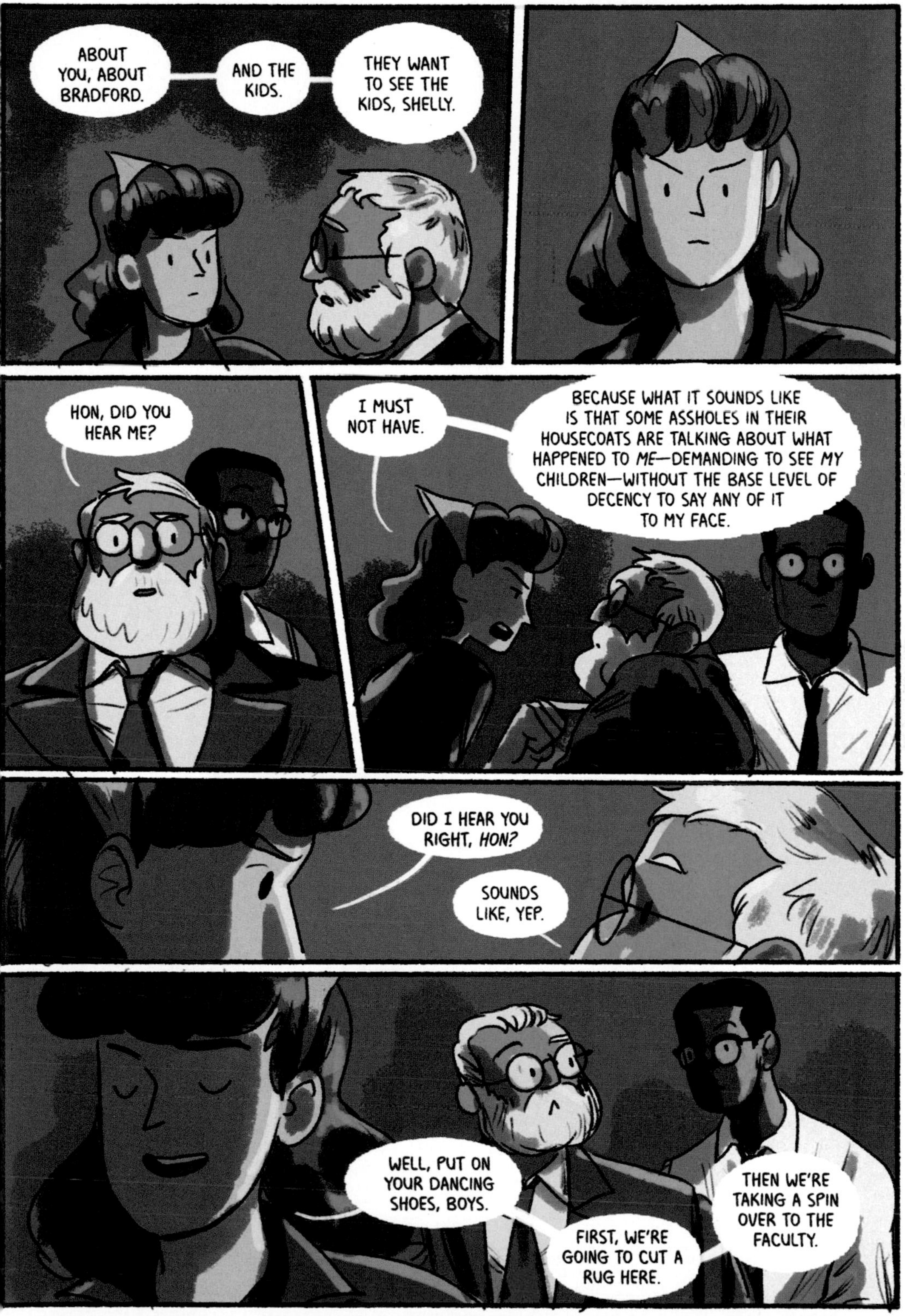
ABOUT YOU, ABOUT BRADFORD.
AND THE KIDS.
THEY WANT TO SEE THE KIDS, SHELLY.
HON, DID YOU HEAR ME?
I MUST NOT HAVE.
BECAUSE WHAT IT SOUNDS LIKE IS THAT SOME ASSHOLES IN THEIR HOUSECOATS ARE TALKING ABOUT WHAT HAPPENED TO *ME*—DEMANDING TO SEE *MY* CHILDREN—WITHOUT THE BASE LEVEL OF DECENCY TO SAY ANY OF IT TO MY FACE.
DID I HEAR YOU RIGHT, *HON?*
SOUNDS LIKE, YEP.
WELL, PUT ON YOUR DANCING SHOES, BOYS.
FIRST, WE'RE GOING TO CUT A RUG HERE.
THEN WE'RE TAKING A SPIN OVER TO THE FACULTY.

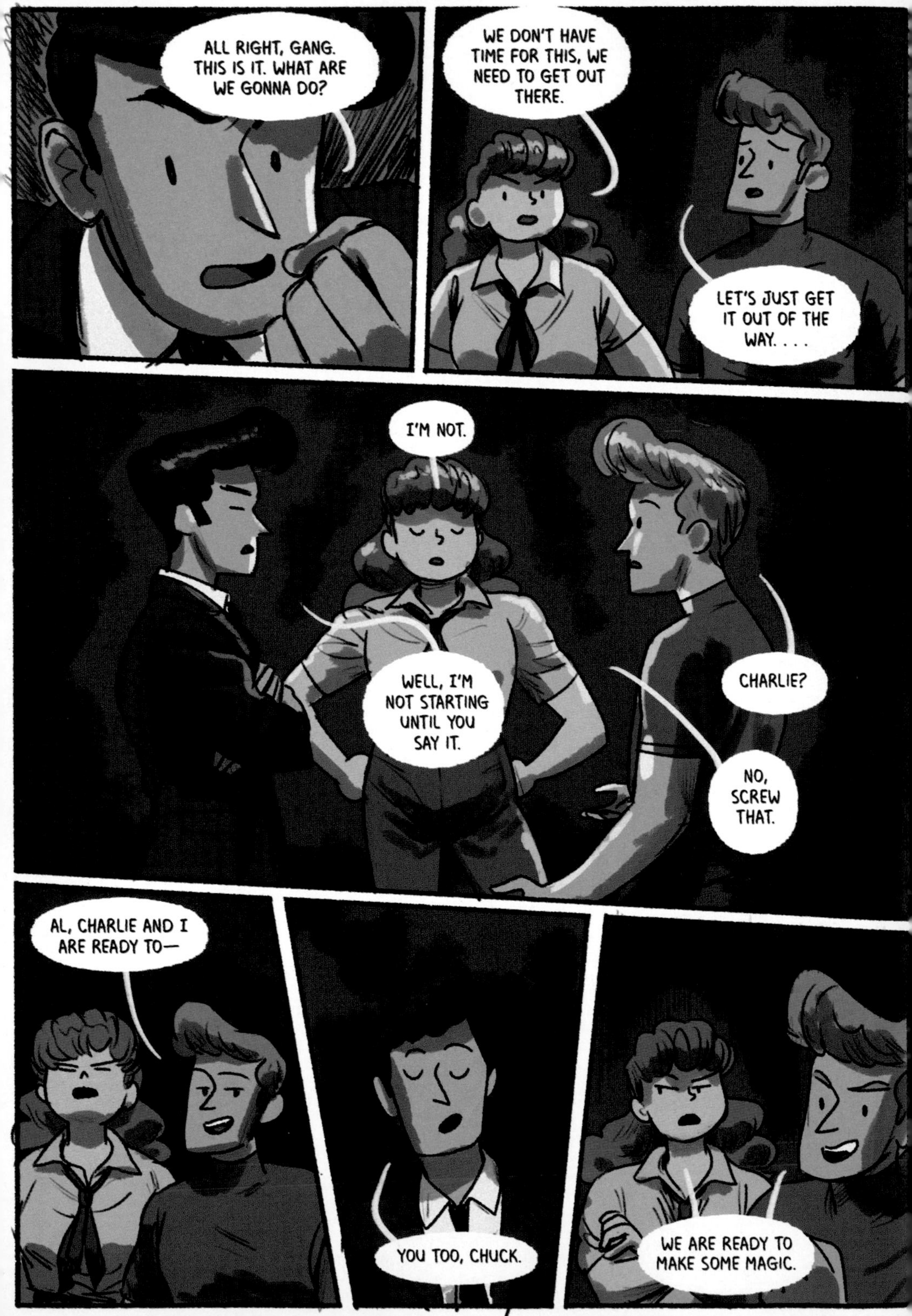
ALL RIGHT, GANG. THIS IS IT. WHAT ARE WE GONNA DO?
WE DON'T HAVE TIME FOR THIS, WE NEED TO GET OUT THERE.
LET'S JUST GET IT OUT OF THE WAY. . . .
I'M NOT.
CHARLIE?
WELL, I'M NOT STARTING UNTIL YOU SAY IT.
NO, SCREW THAT.
AL, CHARLIE AND I ARE READY TO—
YOU TOO, CHUCK.
WE ARE READY TO MAKE SOME MAGIC.

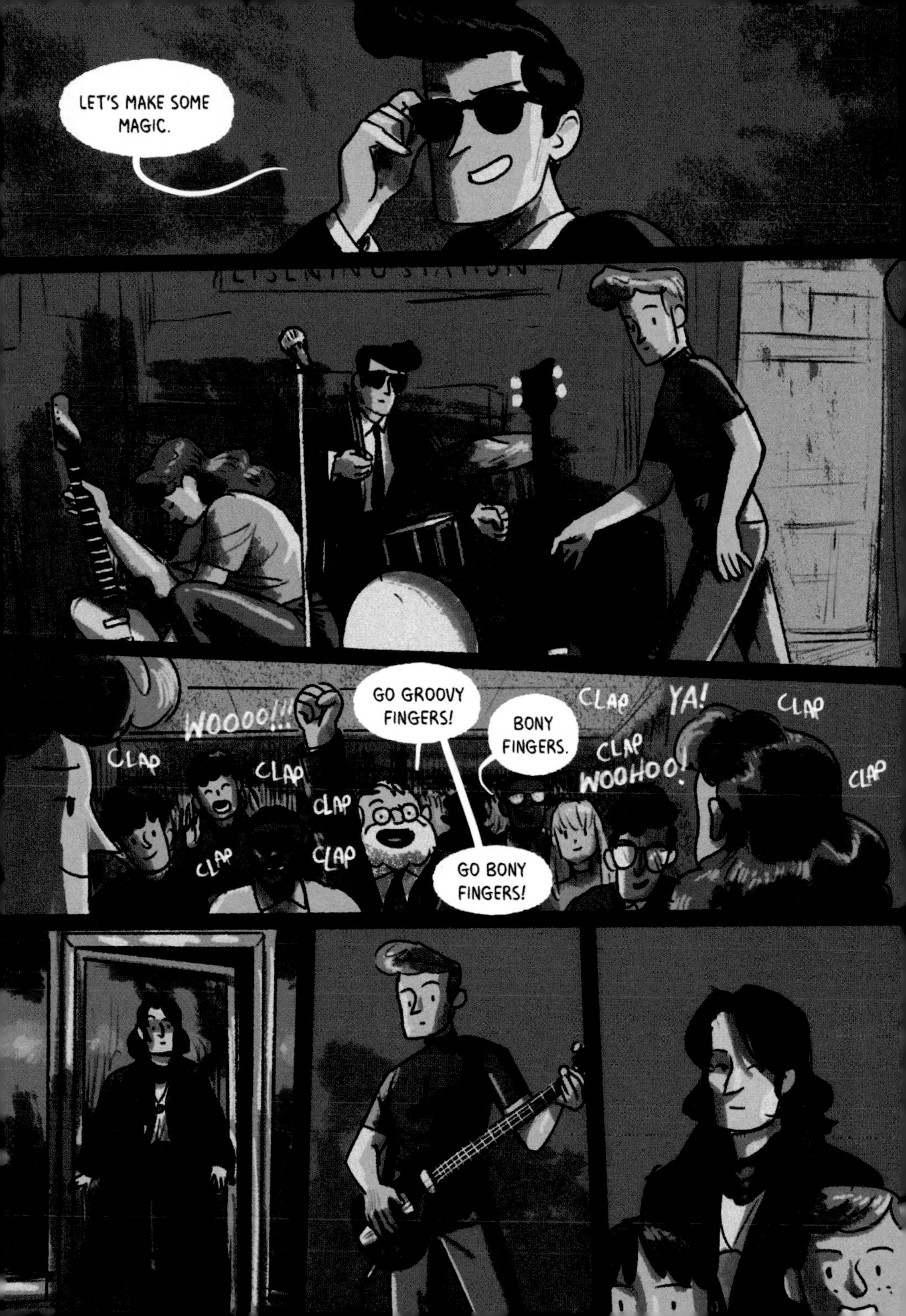
LET'S MAKE SOME MAGIC.
WOOOO!!!
CLAP
CLAP
CLAP
CLAP
CLAP
GO GROOVY FINGERS!
GO BONY FINGERS!
BONY FINGERS.
CLAP
YA!
CLAP
CLAP
WOOHOO!
CLAP

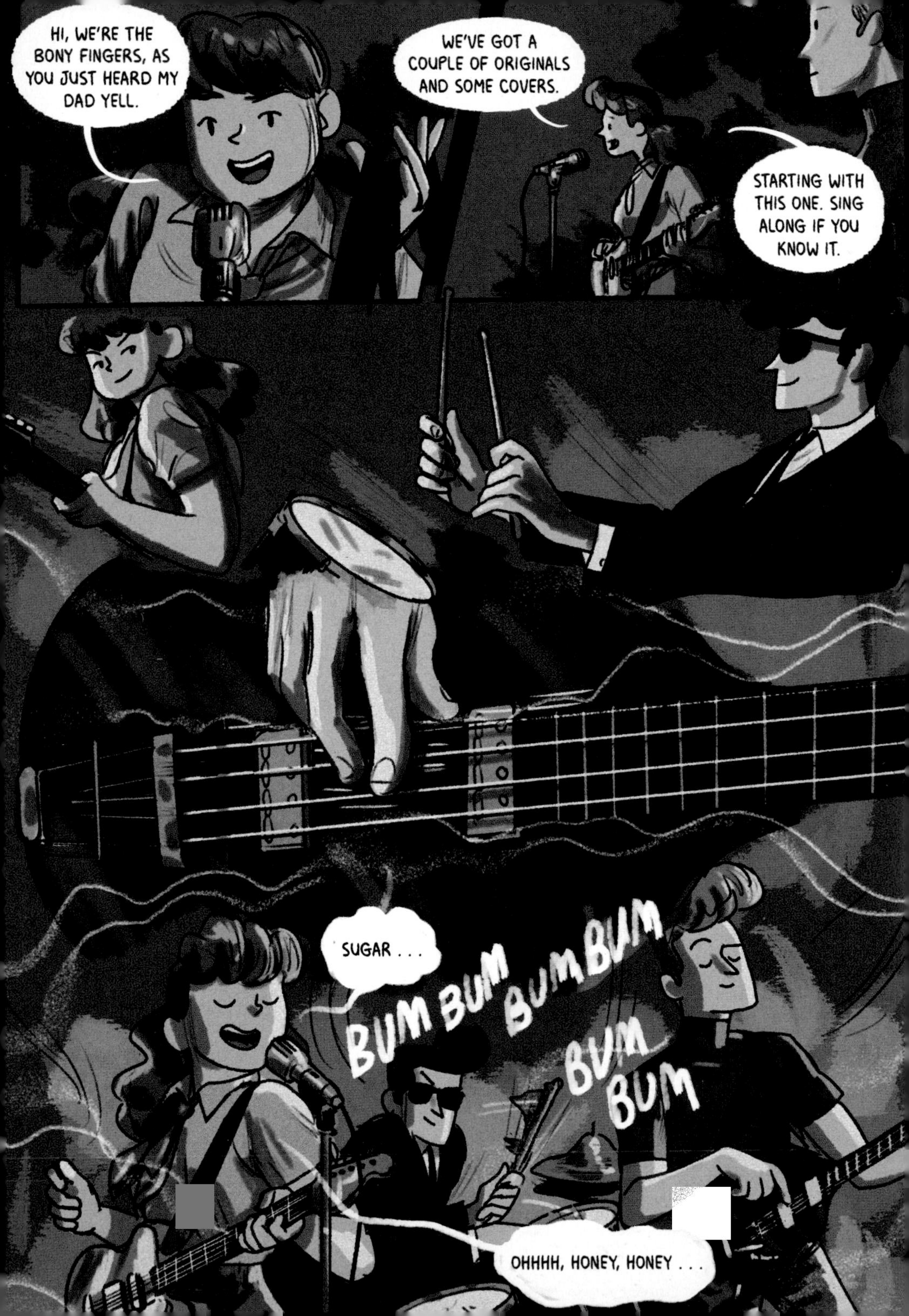
HI, WE'RE THE BONY FINGERS, AS YOU JUST HEARD MY DAD YELL.
WE'VE GOT A COUPLE OF ORIGINALS AND SOME COVERS.
STARTING WITH THIS ONE. SING ALONG IF YOU KNOW IT.
SUGAR . . .
BUM BUM BUM BUM
BUM BUM
OHHHH, HONEY, HONEY . . .

CHAPTER 2

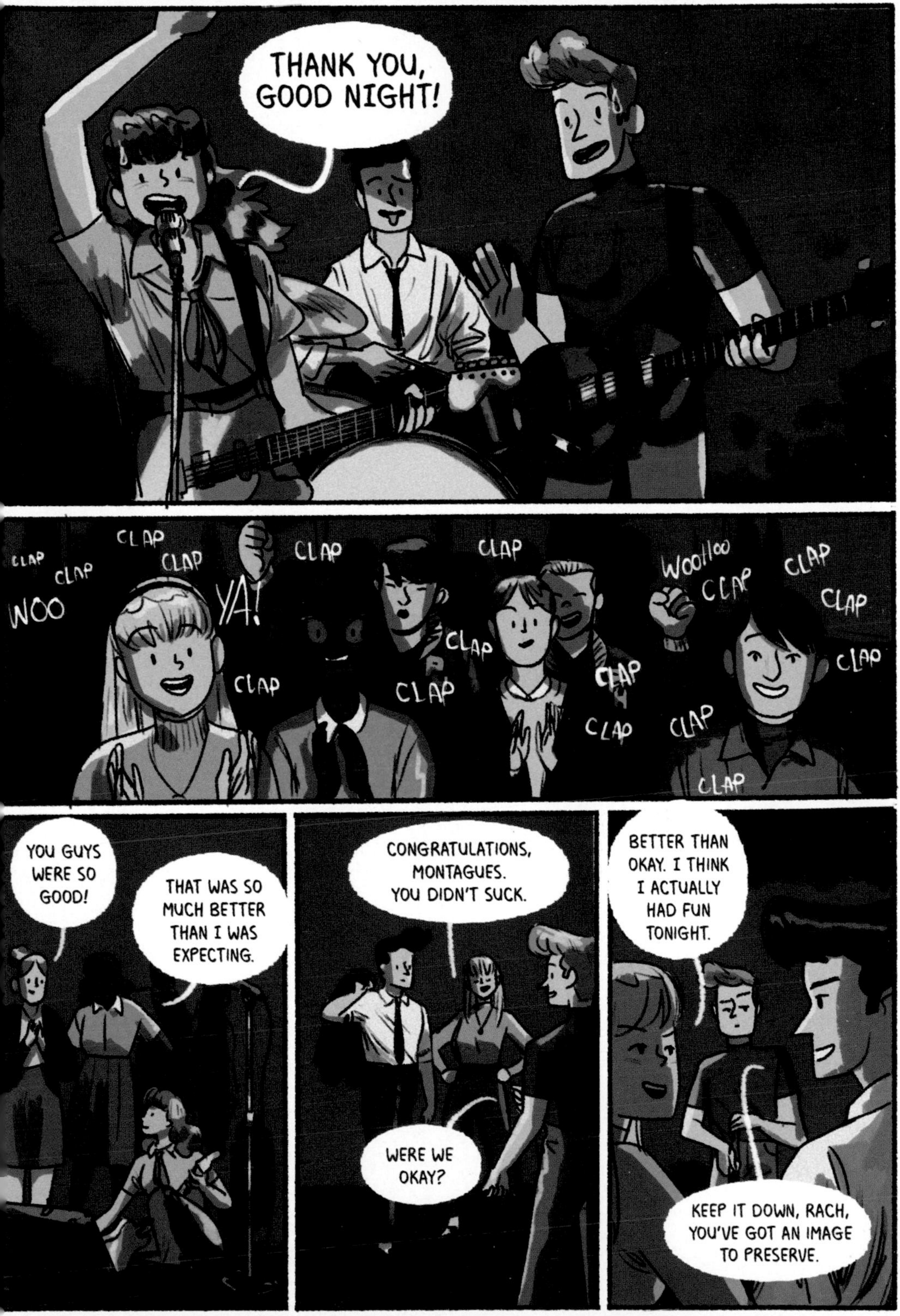
THANK YOU, GOOD NIGHT!
CLAP CLAP CLAP CLAP WOO YA! CLAP CLAP CLAP CLAP CLAP CLAP CLAP CLAP WOOHOO CLAP CLAP CLAP CLAP CLAP
YOU GUYS WERE SO GOOD!
THAT WAS SO MUCH BETTER THAN I WAS EXPECTING.
CONGRATULATIONS, MONTAGUES. YOU DIDN'T SUCK.
WERE WE OKAY?
BETTER THAN OKAY. I THINK I ACTUALLY HAD FUN TONIGHT.
KEEP IT DOWN, RACH, YOU'VE GOT AN IMAGE TO PRESERVE.

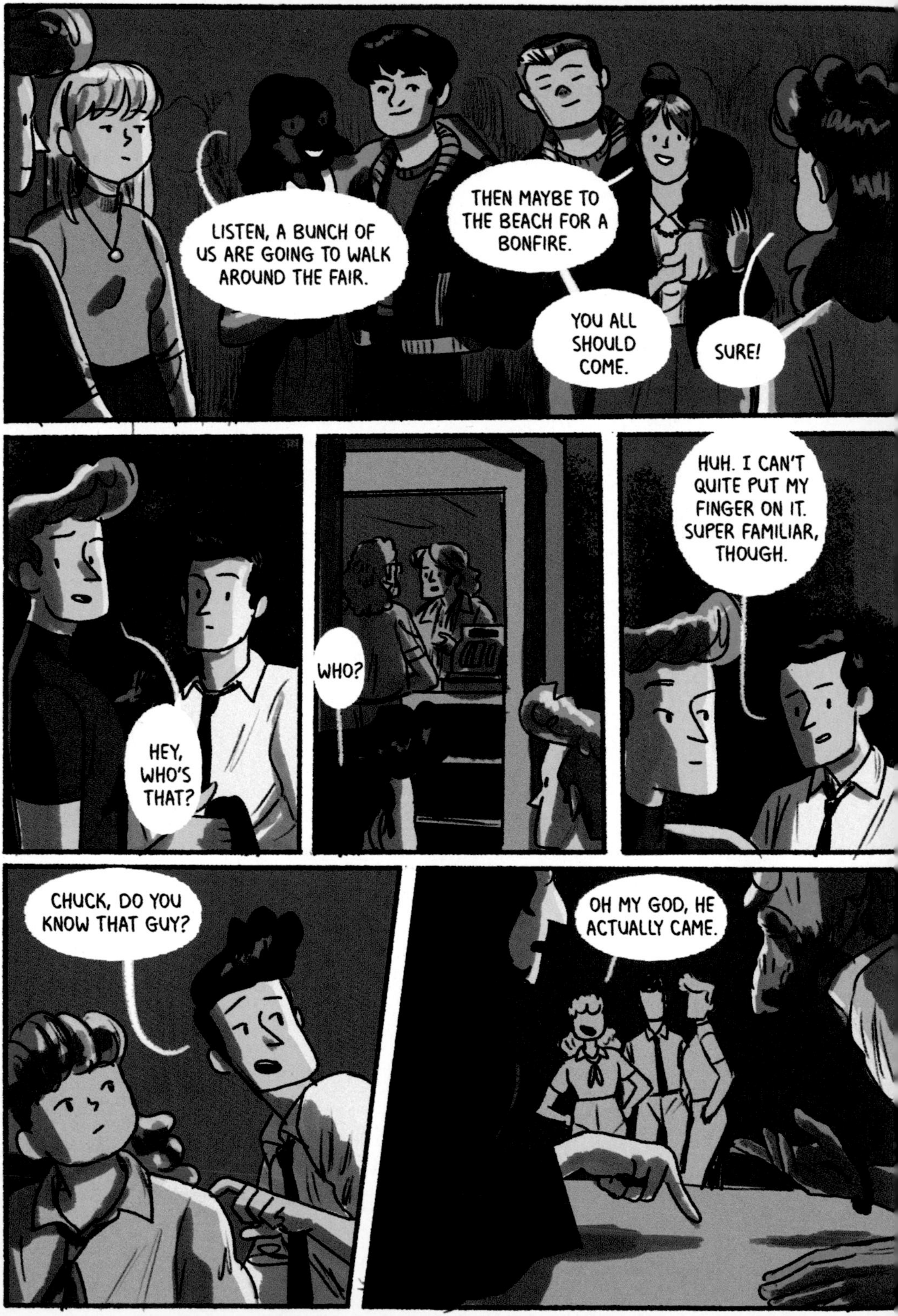
LISTEN, A BUNCH OF US ARE GOING TO WALK AROUND THE FAIR.
THEN MAYBE TO THE BEACH FOR A BONFIRE.
YOU ALL SHOULD COME.
SURE!
HEY, WHO'S THAT?
WHO?
HUH. I CAN'T QUITE PUT MY FINGER ON IT. SUPER FAMILIAR, THOUGH.
CHUCK, DO YOU KNOW THAT GUY?
OH MY GOD, HE ACTUALLY CAME.

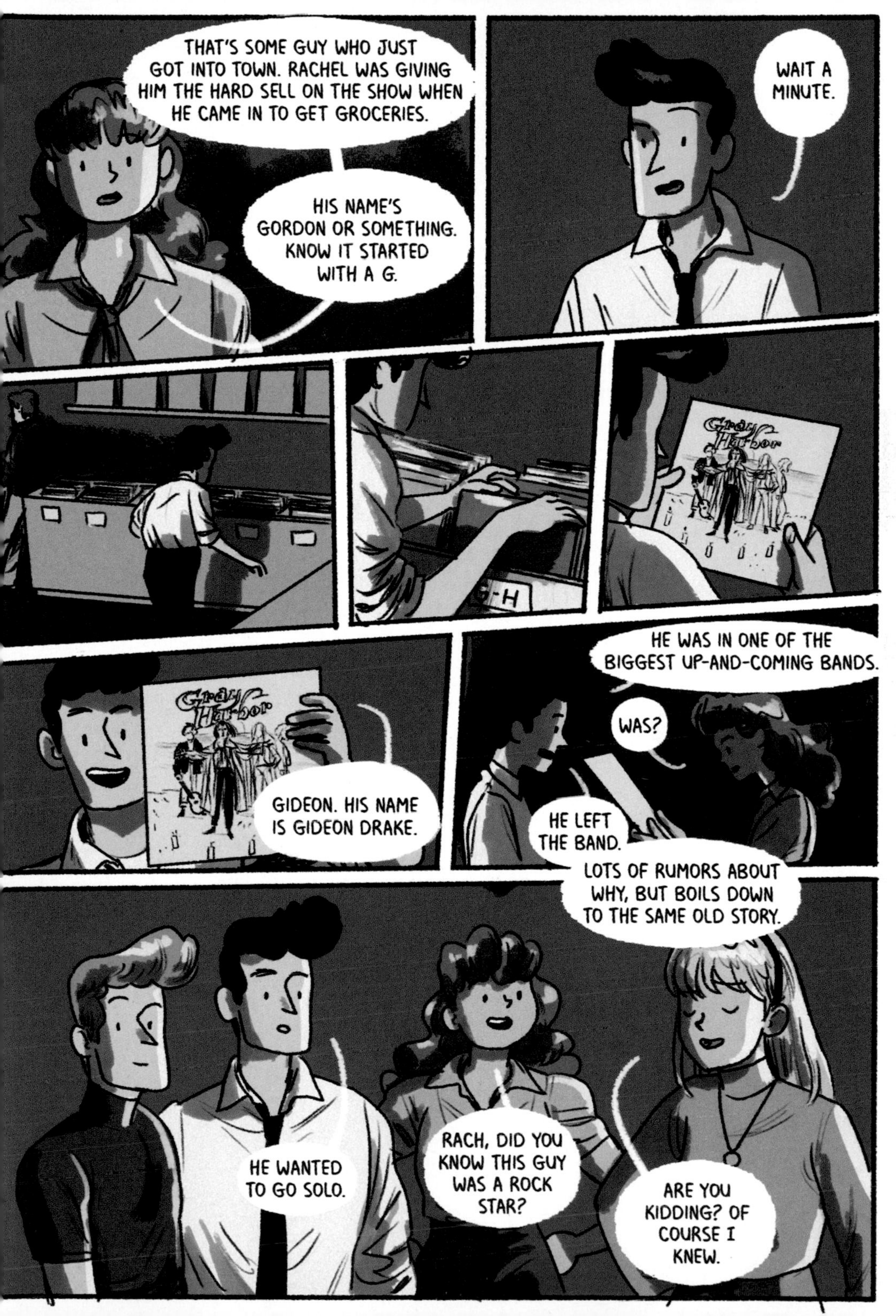
THAT'S SOME GUY WHO JUST GOT INTO TOWN. RACHEL WAS GIVING HIM THE HARD SELL ON THE SHOW WHEN HE CAME IN TO GET GROCERIES.
HIS NAME'S GORDON OR SOMETHING. KNOW IT STARTED WITH A G.
WAIT A MINUTE.
G-H
Gray Harbor
Gray Harbor
GIDEON. HIS NAME IS GIDEON DRAKE.
HE WAS IN ONE OF THE BIGGEST UP-AND-COMING BANDS.
WAS?
HE LEFT THE BAND.
LOTS OF RUMORS ABOUT WHY, BUT BOILS DOWN TO THE SAME OLD STORY.
HE WANTED TO GO SOLO.
RACH, DID YOU KNOW THIS GUY WAS A ROCK STAR?
ARE YOU KIDDING? OF COURSE I KNEW.

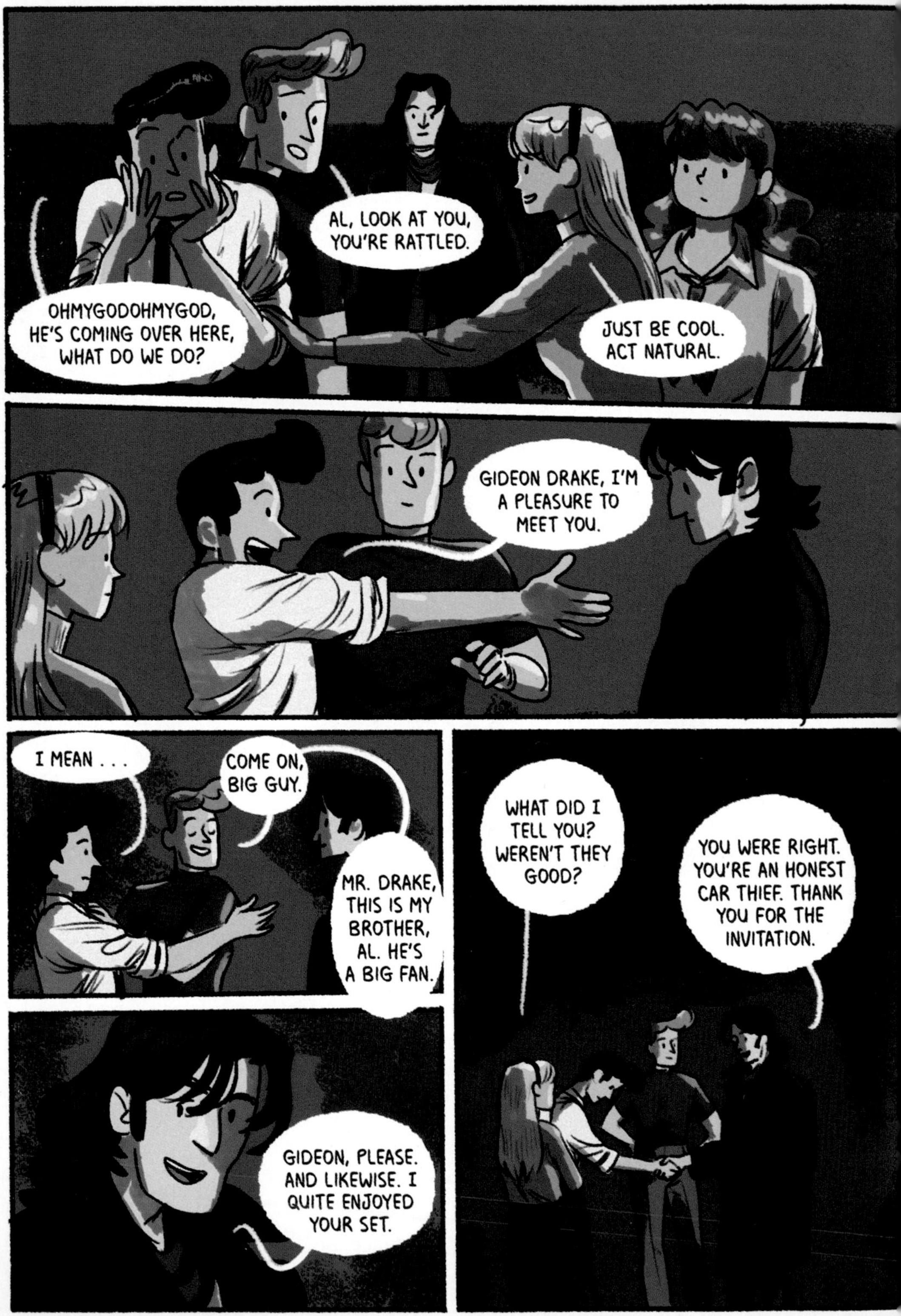
AL, LOOK AT YOU, YOU'RE RATTLED.
OHMYGODOHMYGOD, HE'S COMING OVER HERE, WHAT DO WE DO?
JUST BE COOL. ACT NATURAL.
GIDEON DRAKE, I'M A PLEASURE TO MEET YOU.
I MEAN . . .
COME ON, BIG GUY.
MR. DRAKE, THIS IS MY BROTHER, AL. HE'S A BIG FAN.
GIDEON, PLEASE. AND LIKEWISE. I QUITE ENJOYED YOUR SET.
WHAT DID I TELL YOU? WEREN'T THEY GOOD?
YOU WERE RIGHT. YOU'RE AN HONEST CAR THIEF. THANK YOU FOR THE INVITATION.

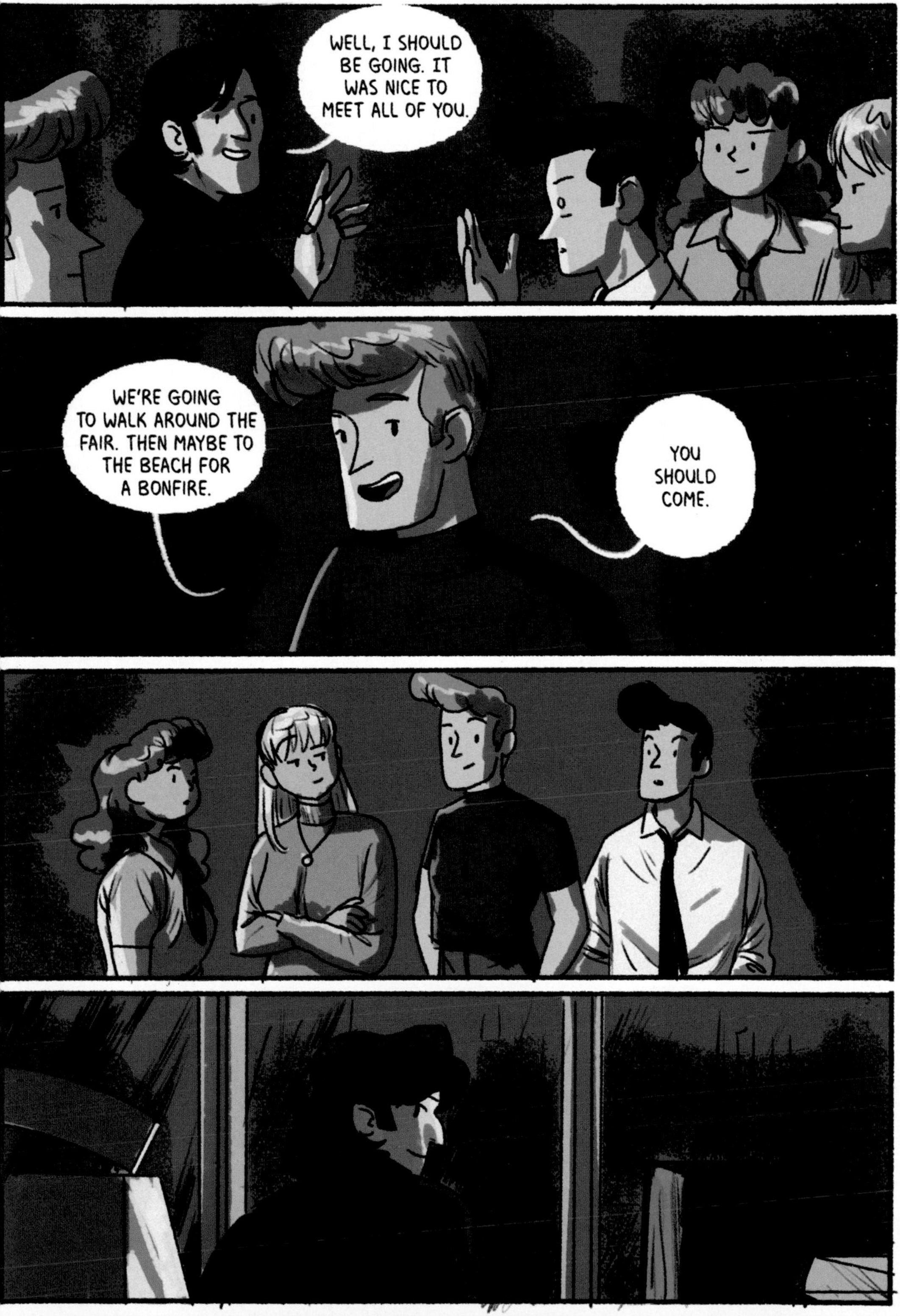
WELL, I SHOULD BE GOING. IT WAS NICE TO MEET ALL OF YOU.
WE'RE GOING TO WALK AROUND THE FAIR. THEN MAYBE TO THE BEACH FOR A BONFIRE.
YOU SHOULD COME.

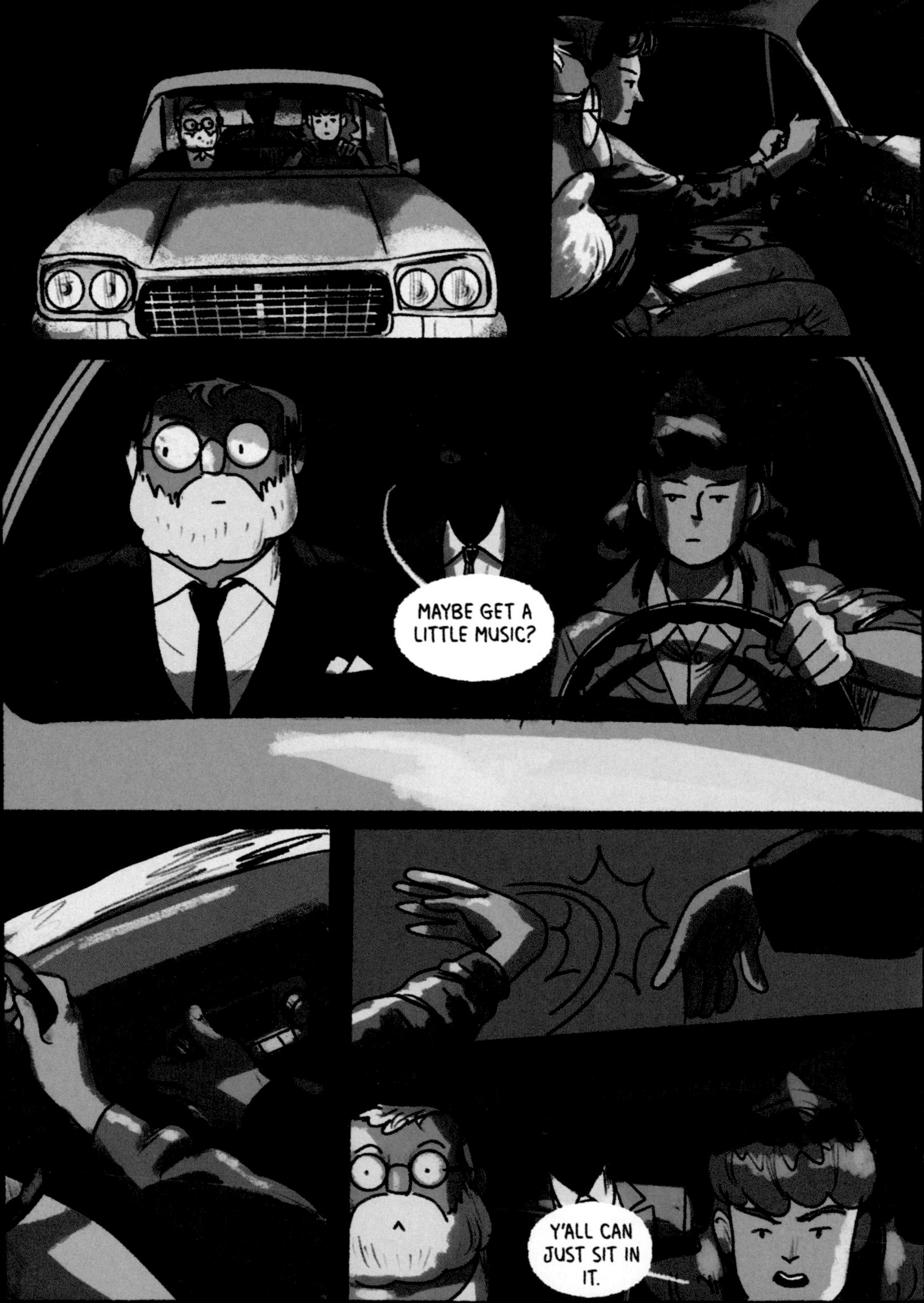
MAYBE GET A LITTLE MUSIC?
Y'ALL CAN JUST SIT IN IT.

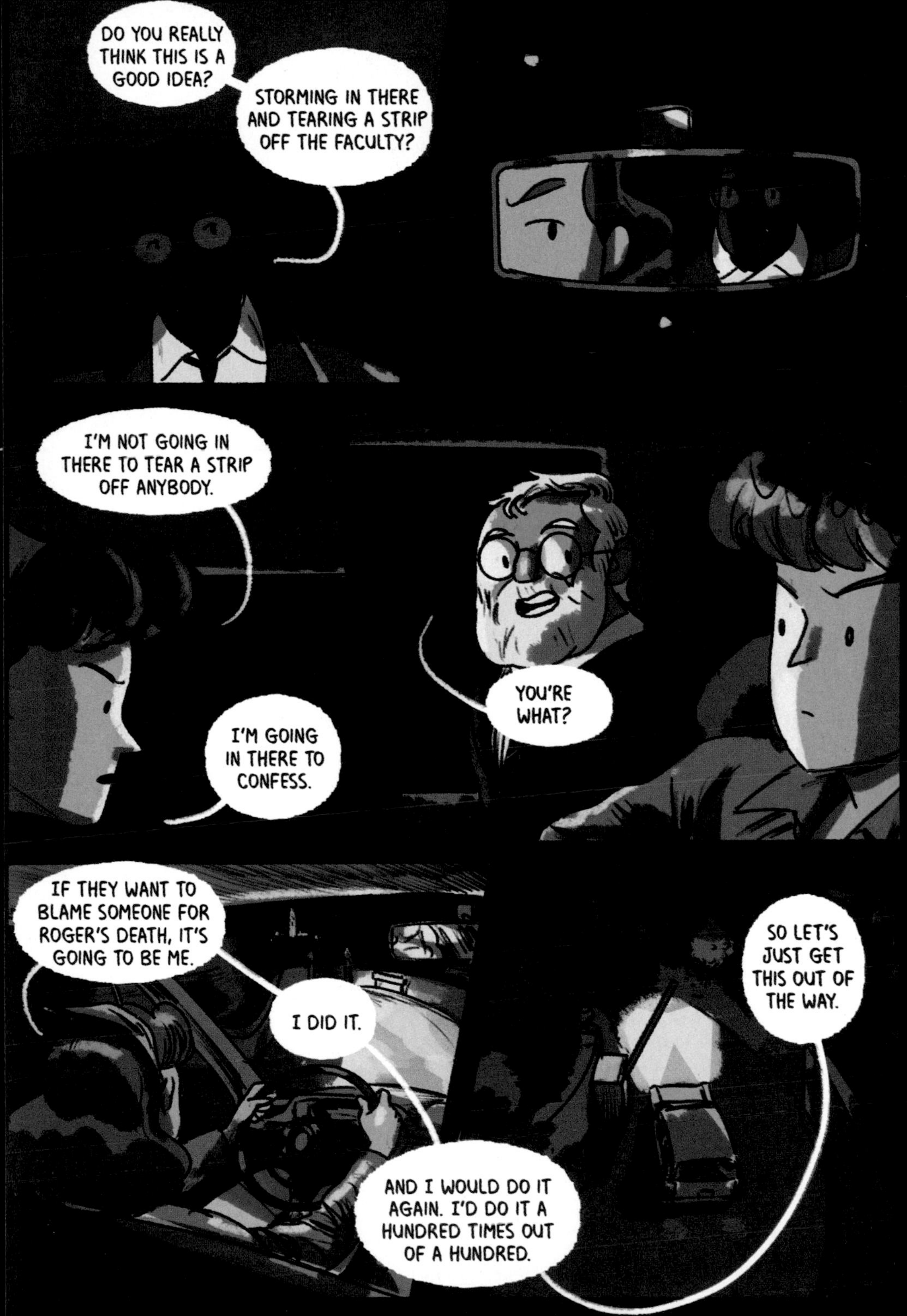
DO YOU REALLY THINK THIS IS A GOOD IDEA?
STORMING IN THERE AND TEARING A STRIP OFF THE FACULTY?
I'M NOT GOING IN THERE TO TEAR A STRIP OFF ANYBODY.
I'M GOING IN THERE TO CONFESS.
YOU'RE WHAT?
IF THEY WANT TO BLAME SOMEONE FOR ROGER'S DEATH, IT'S GOING TO BE ME.
I DID IT.
AND I WOULD DO IT AGAIN. I'D DO IT A HUNDRED TIMES OUT OF A HUNDRED.
SO LET'S JUST GET THIS OUT OF THE WAY.

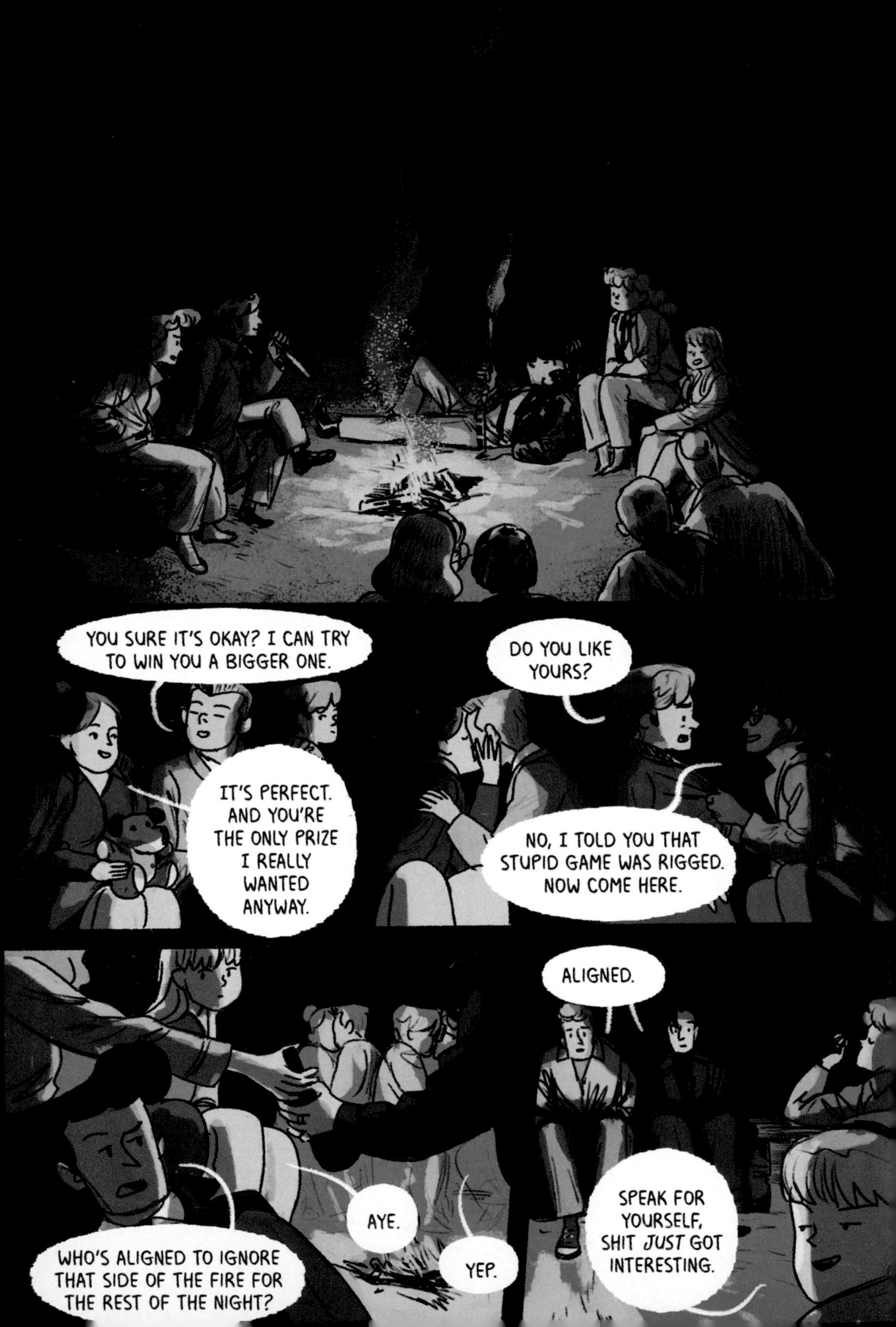
YOU SURE IT'S OKAY? I CAN TRY TO WIN YOU A BIGGER ONE.
IT'S PERFECT. AND YOU'RE THE ONLY PRIZE I REALLY WANTED ANYWAY.
DO YOU LIKE YOURS?
NO, I TOLD YOU THAT STUPID GAME WAS RIGGED. NOW COME HERE.
WHO'S ALIGNED TO IGNORE THAT SIDE OF THE FIRE FOR THE REST OF THE NIGHT?
AYE.
YEP.
ALIGNED.
SPEAK FOR YOURSELF, SHIT *JUST* GOT INTERESTING.

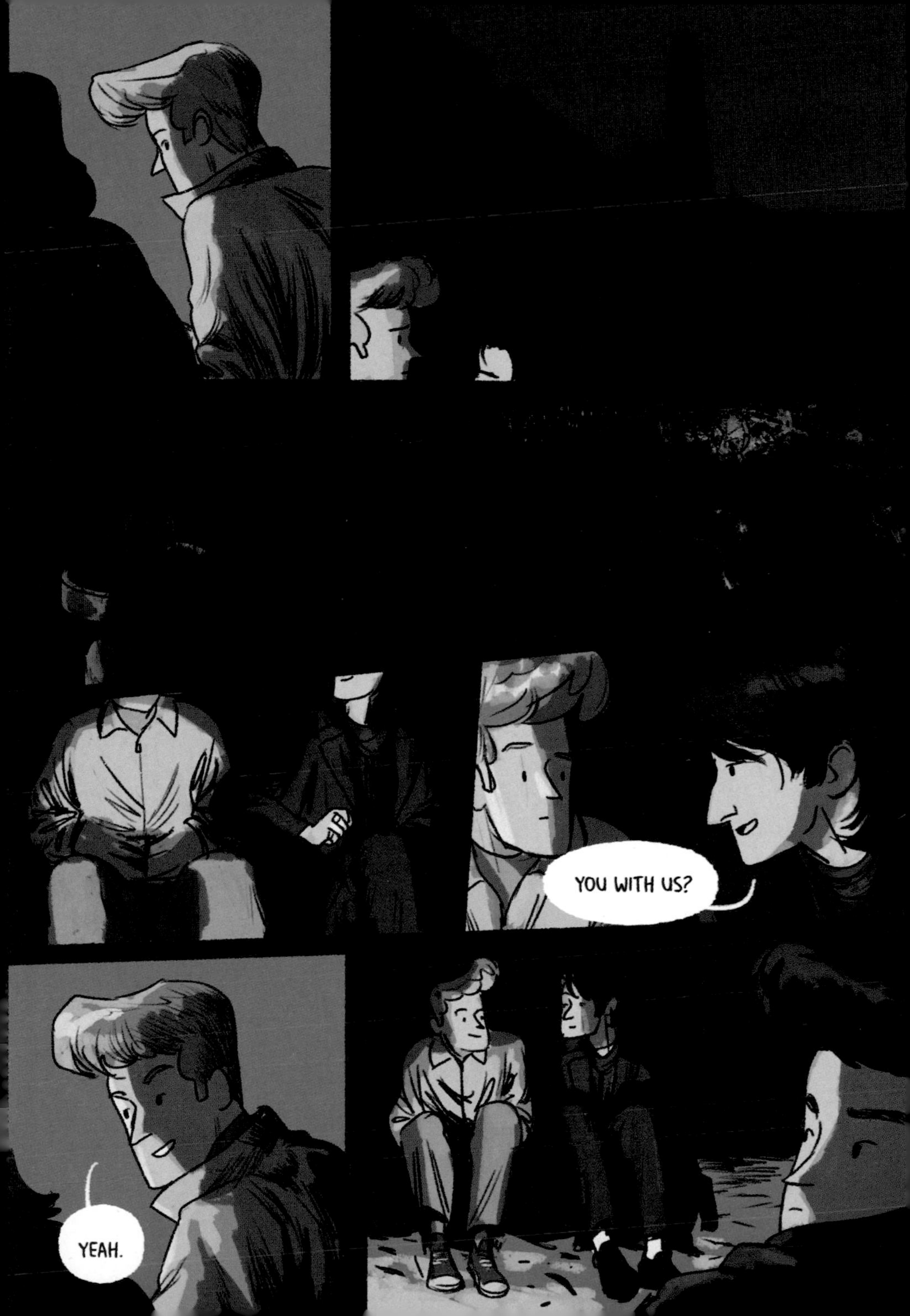
YOU WITH US?
YEAH.

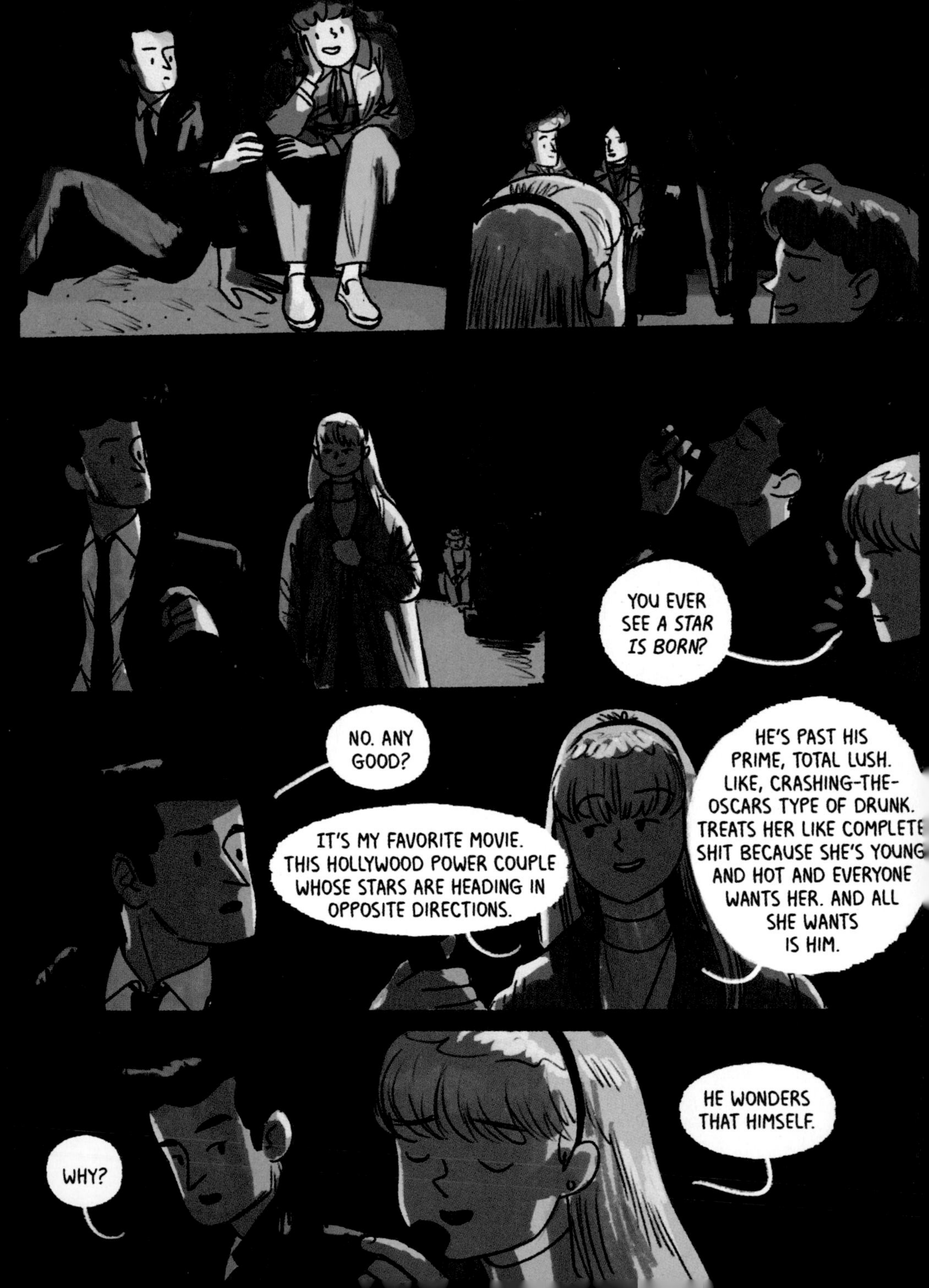
YOU EVER SEE A *STAR IS BORN*?
NO. ANY GOOD?
IT'S MY FAVORITE MOVIE. THIS HOLLYWOOD POWER COUPLE WHOSE STARS ARE HEADING IN OPPOSITE DIRECTIONS.
HE'S PAST HIS PRIME, TOTAL LUSH. LIKE, CRASHING-THE-OSCARS TYPE OF DRUNK. TREATS HER LIKE COMPLETE SHIT BECAUSE SHE'S YOUNG AND HOT AND EVERYONE WANTS HER. AND ALL SHE WANTS IS HIM.
WHY?
HE WONDERS THAT HIMSELF.

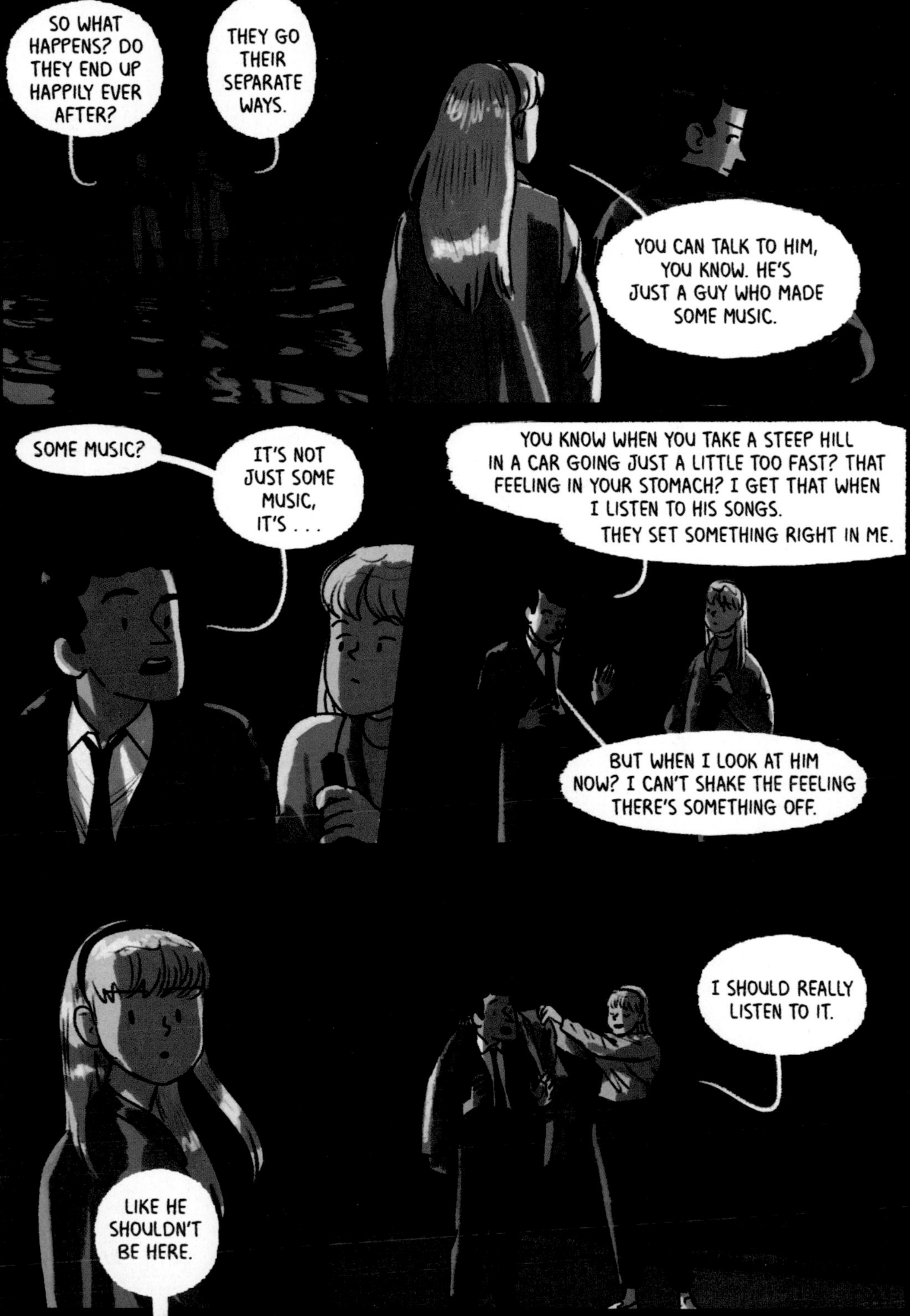
SO WHAT HAPPENS? DO THEY END UP HAPPILY EVER AFTER?
THEY GO THEIR SEPARATE WAYS.
YOU CAN TALK TO HIM, YOU KNOW. HE'S JUST A GUY WHO MADE SOME MUSIC.
SOME MUSIC?
IT'S NOT JUST SOME MUSIC, IT'S . . .
YOU KNOW WHEN YOU TAKE A STEEP HILL IN A CAR GOING JUST A LITTLE TOO FAST? THAT FEELING IN YOUR STOMACH? I GET THAT WHEN I LISTEN TO HIS SONGS. THEY SET SOMETHING RIGHT IN ME.
BUT WHEN I LOOK AT HIM NOW? I CAN'T SHAKE THE FEELING THERE'S SOMETHING OFF.
LIKE HE SHOULDN'T BE HERE.
I SHOULD REALLY LISTEN TO IT.

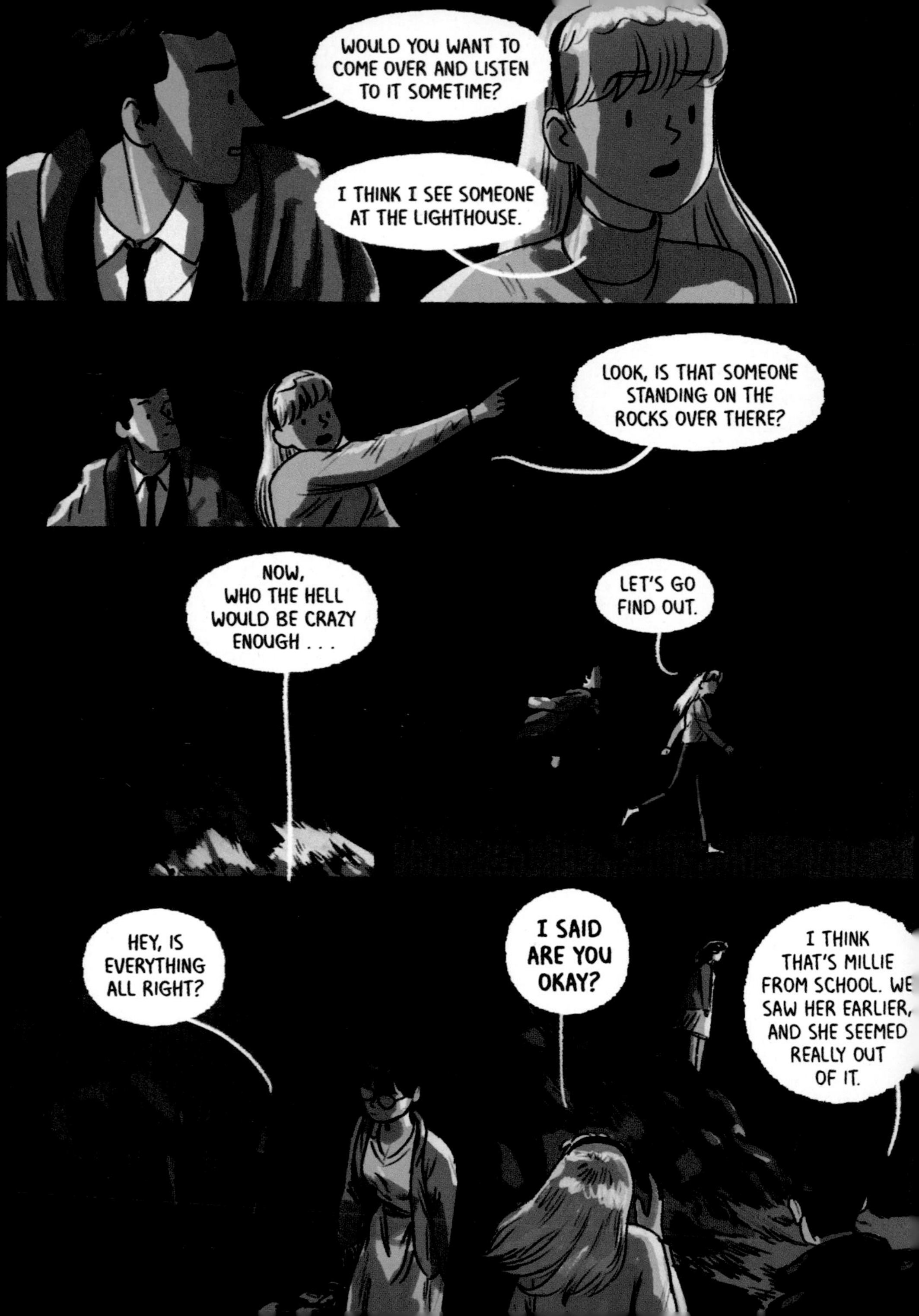
WOULD YOU WANT TO COME OVER AND LISTEN TO IT SOMETIME?
I THINK I SEE SOMEONE AT THE LIGHTHOUSE.
LOOK, IS THAT SOMEONE STANDING ON THE ROCKS OVER THERE?
NOW, WHO THE HELL WOULD BE CRAZY ENOUGH . . .
LET'S GO FIND OUT.
HEY, IS EVERYTHING ALL RIGHT?
I SAID ARE YOU OKAY?
I THINK THAT'S MILLIE FROM SCHOOL. WE SAW HER EARLIER, AND SHE SEEMED REALLY OUT OF IT.

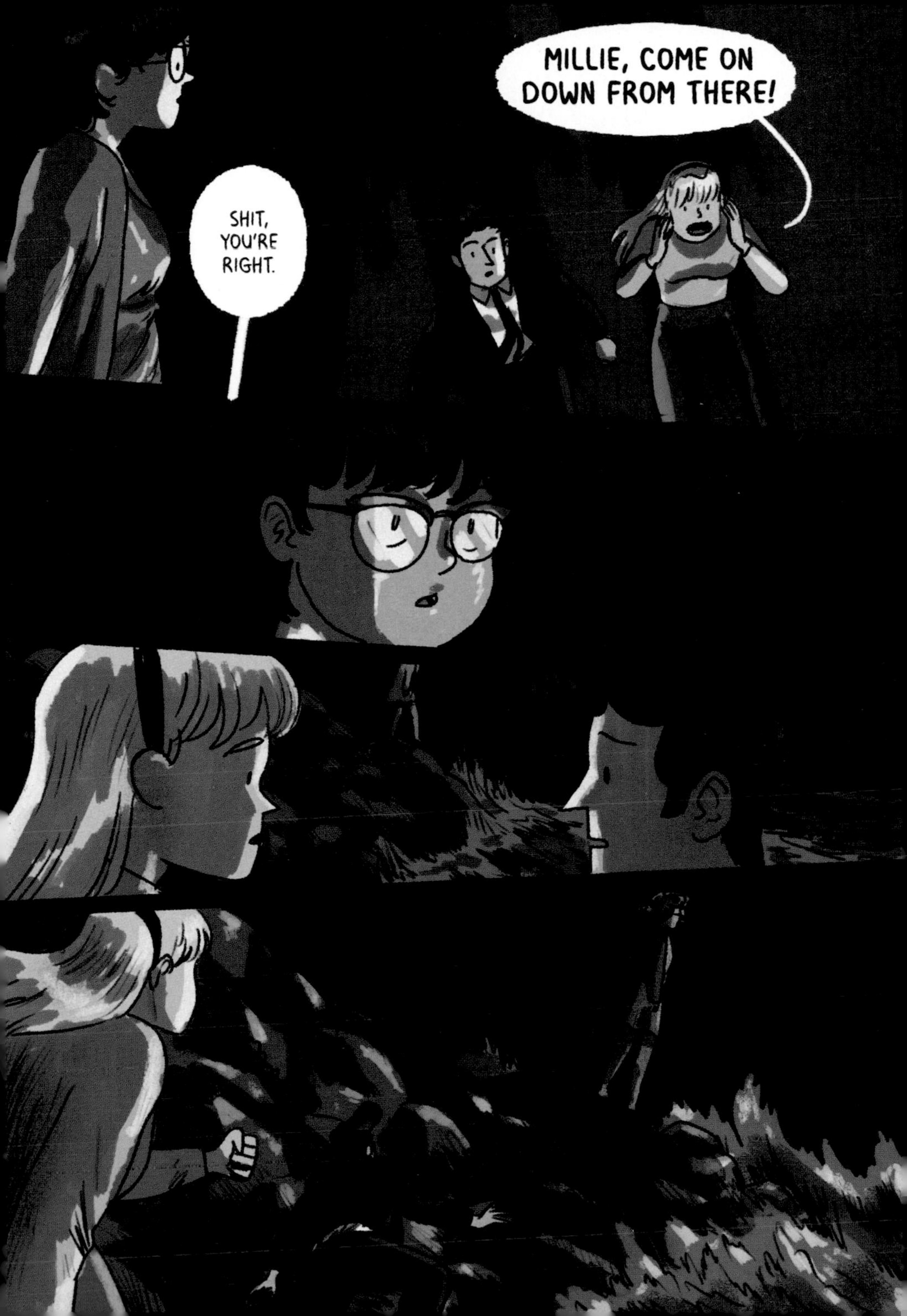
SHIT, YOU'RE RIGHT.
MILLIE, COME ON DOWN FROM THERE!

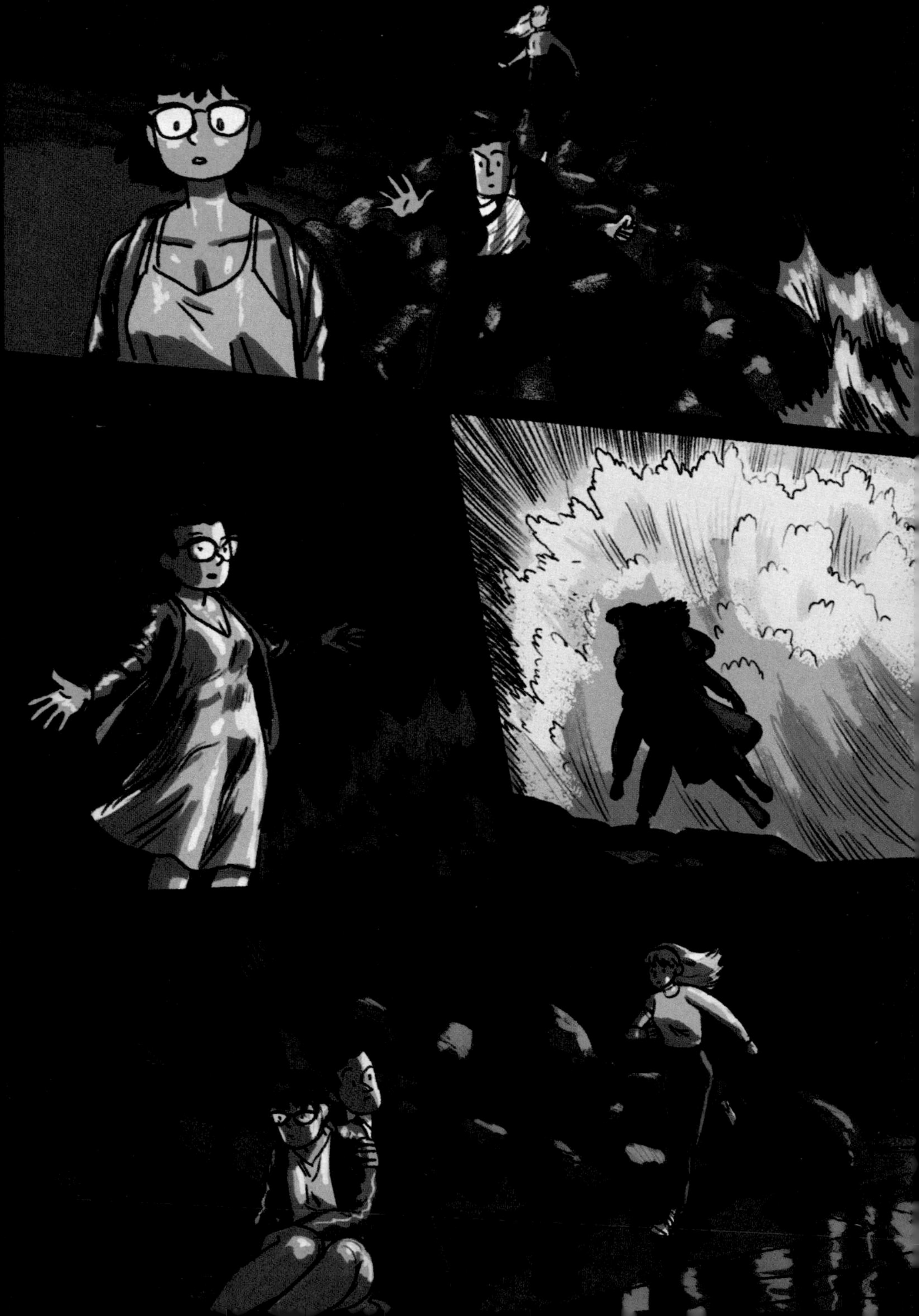

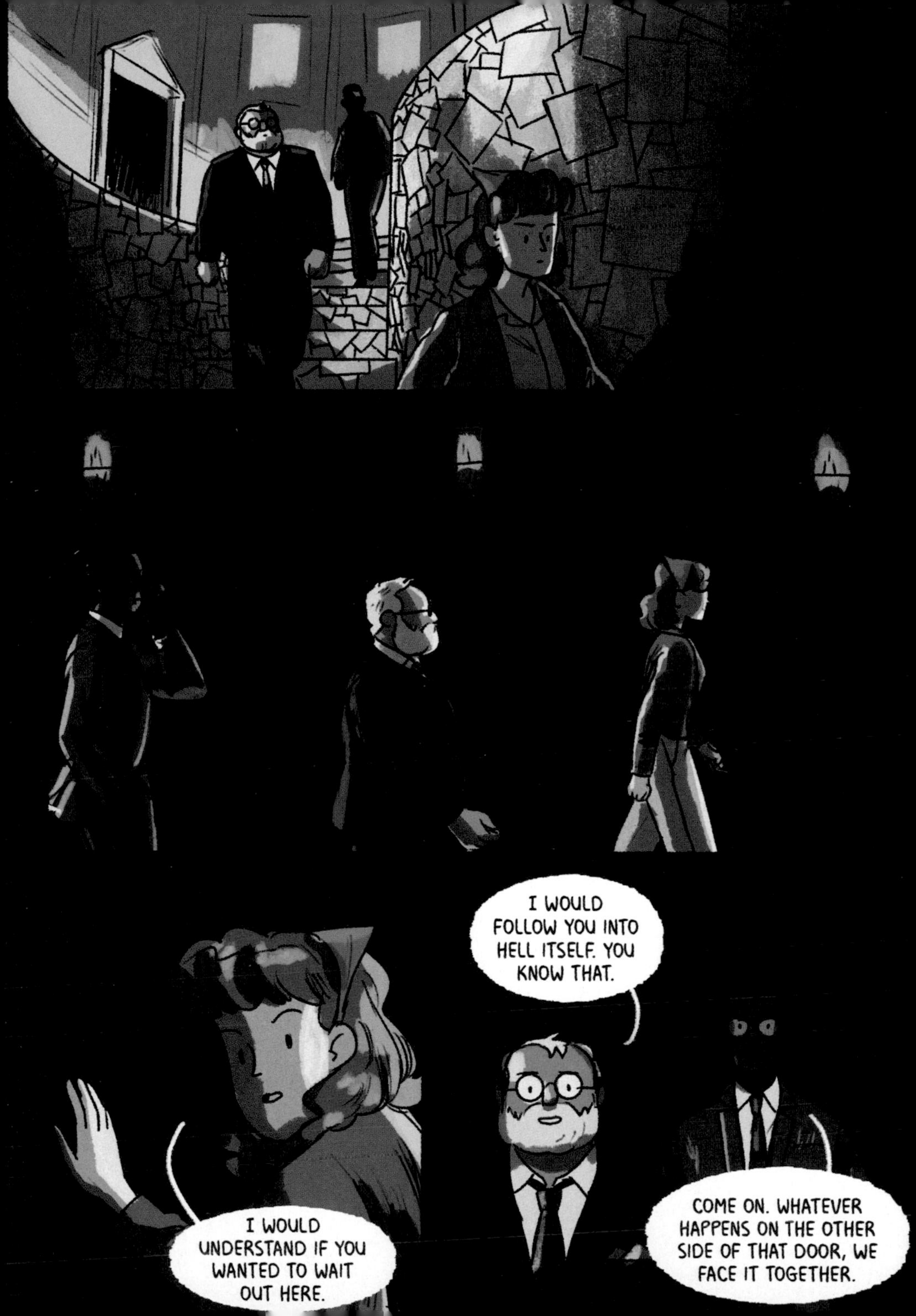
I WOULD UNDERSTAND IF YOU WANTED TO WAIT OUT HERE.
I WOULD FOLLOW YOU INTO HELL ITSELF. YOU KNOW THAT.
COME ON. WHATEVER HAPPENS ON THE OTHER SIDE OF THAT DOOR, WE FACE IT TOGETHER.

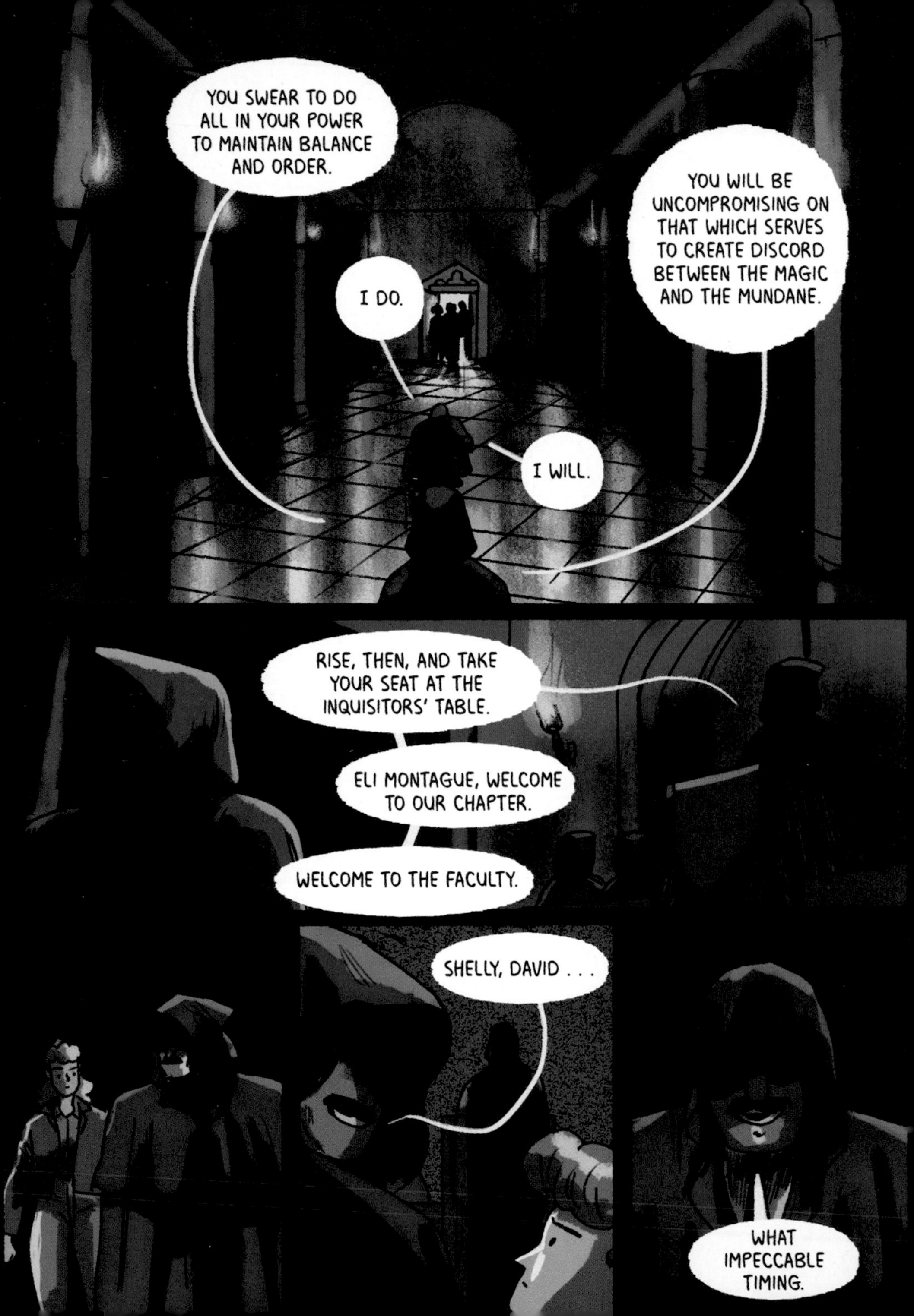
YOU SWEAR TO DO ALL IN YOUR POWER TO MAINTAIN BALANCE AND ORDER.
I DO.
YOU WILL BE UNCOMPROMISING ON THAT WHICH SERVES TO CREATE DISCORD BETWEEN THE MAGIC AND THE MUNDANE.
I WILL.
RISE, THEN, AND TAKE YOUR SEAT AT THE INQUISITORS' TABLE.
ELI MONTAGUE, WELCOME TO OUR CHAPTER.
WELCOME TO THE FACULTY.
SHELLY, DAVID . . .
WHAT IMPECCABLE TIMING.

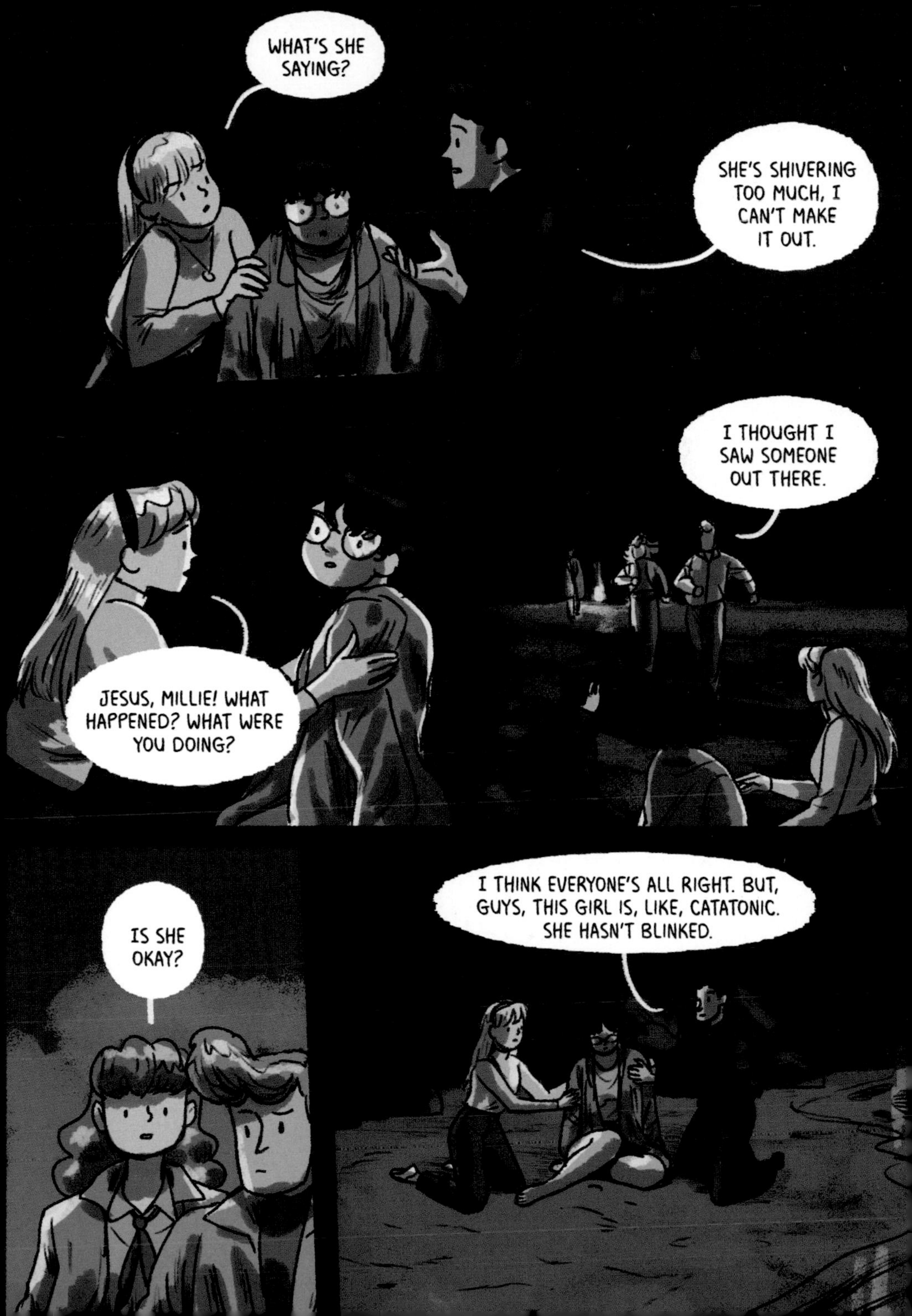
WHAT'S SHE SAYING?
SHE'S SHIVERING TOO MUCH, I CAN'T MAKE IT OUT.
I THOUGHT I SAW SOMEONE OUT THERE.
JESUS, MILLIE! WHAT HAPPENED? WHAT WERE YOU DOING?
IS SHE OKAY?
I THINK EVERYONE'S ALL RIGHT. BUT, GUYS, THIS GIRL IS, LIKE, CATATONIC. SHE HASN'T BLINKED.

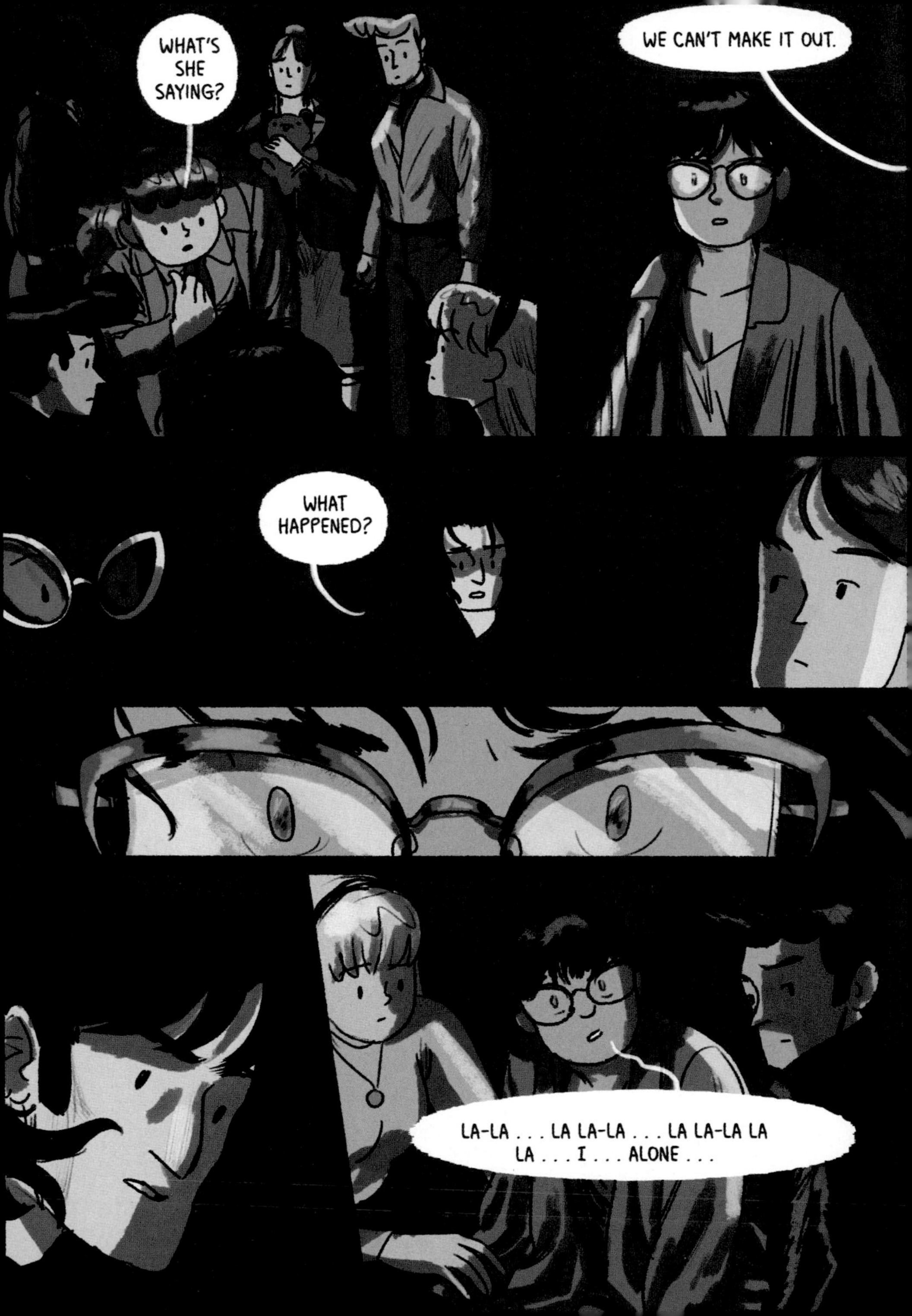
WHAT'S SHE SAYING?
WE CAN'T MAKE IT OUT.
WHAT HAPPENED?
LA-LA . . . LA LA-LA . . . LA LA-LA LA LA . . . I . . . ALONE . . .

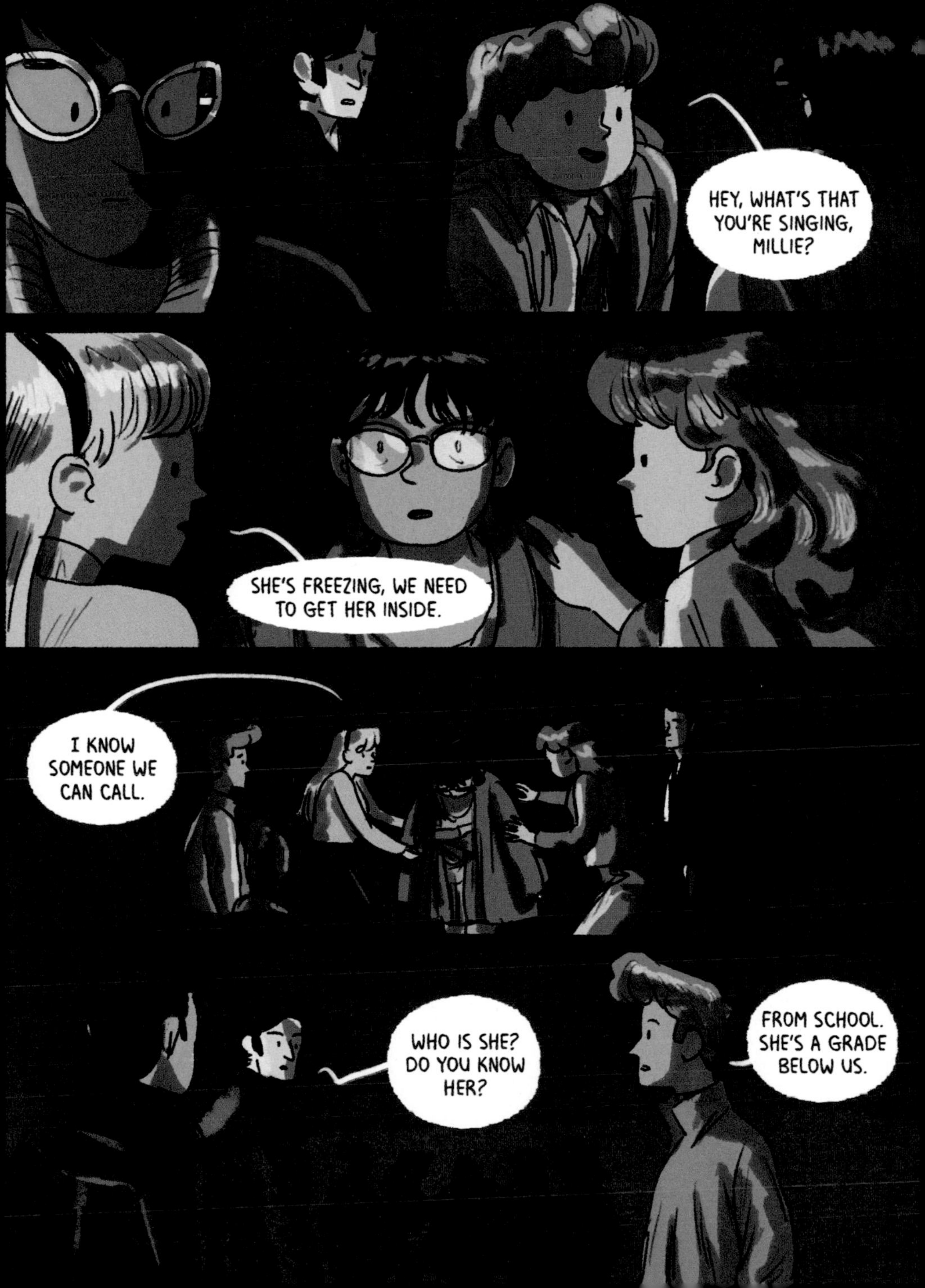
HEY, WHAT'S THAT YOU'RE SINGING, MILLIE?
SHE'S FREEZING, WE NEED TO GET HER INSIDE.
I KNOW SOMEONE WE CAN CALL.
WHO IS SHE? DO YOU KNOW HER?
FROM SCHOOL. SHE'S A GRADE BELOW US.

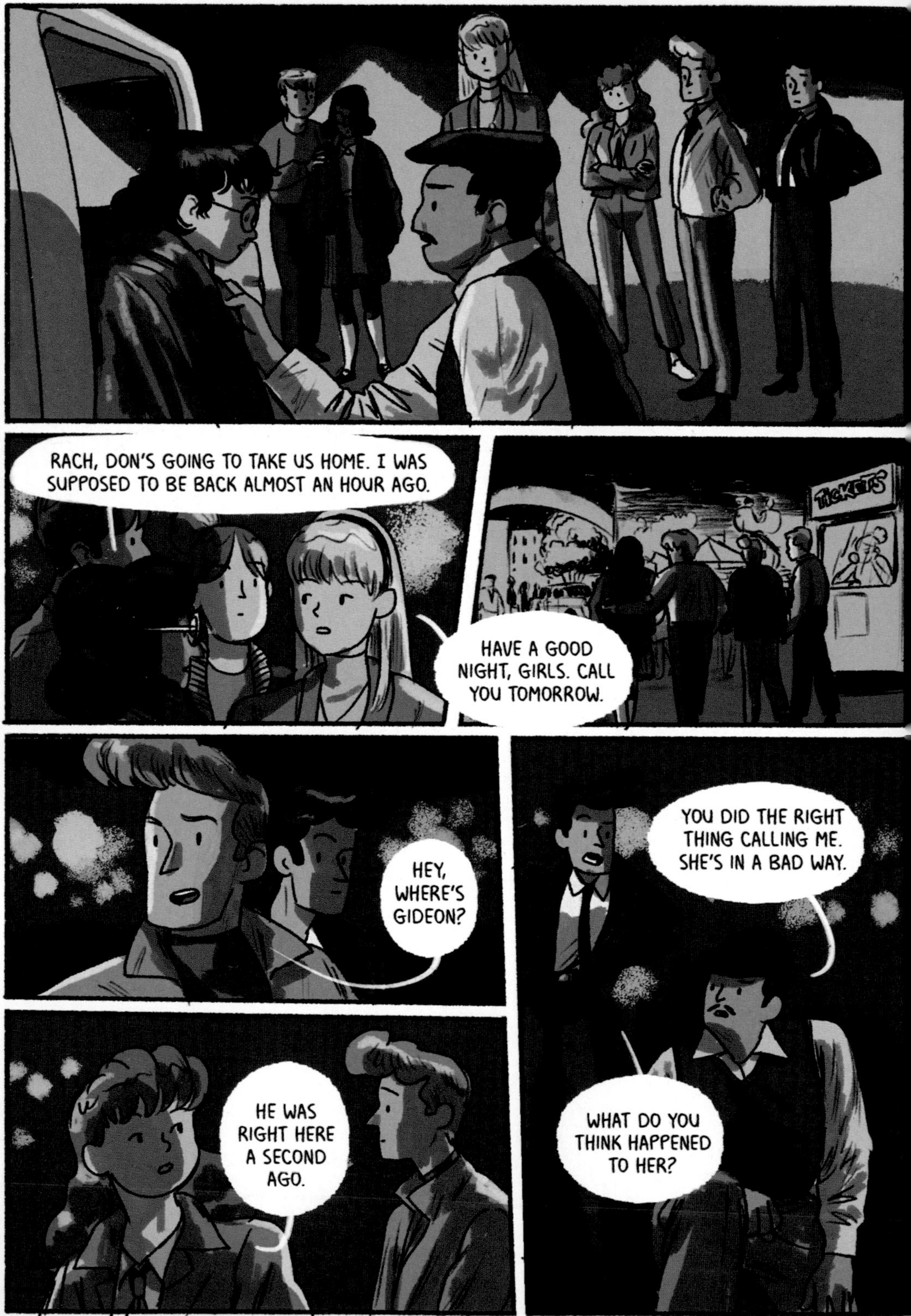
RACH, DON'S GOING TO TAKE US HOME. I WAS SUPPOSED TO BE BACK ALMOST AN HOUR AGO.
HAVE A GOOD NIGHT, GIRLS. CALL YOU TOMORROW.
TICKETS
HEY, WHERE'S GIDEON?
HE WAS RIGHT HERE A SECOND AGO.
YOU DID THE RIGHT THING CALLING ME. SHE'S IN A BAD WAY.
WHAT DO YOU THINK HAPPENED TO HER?

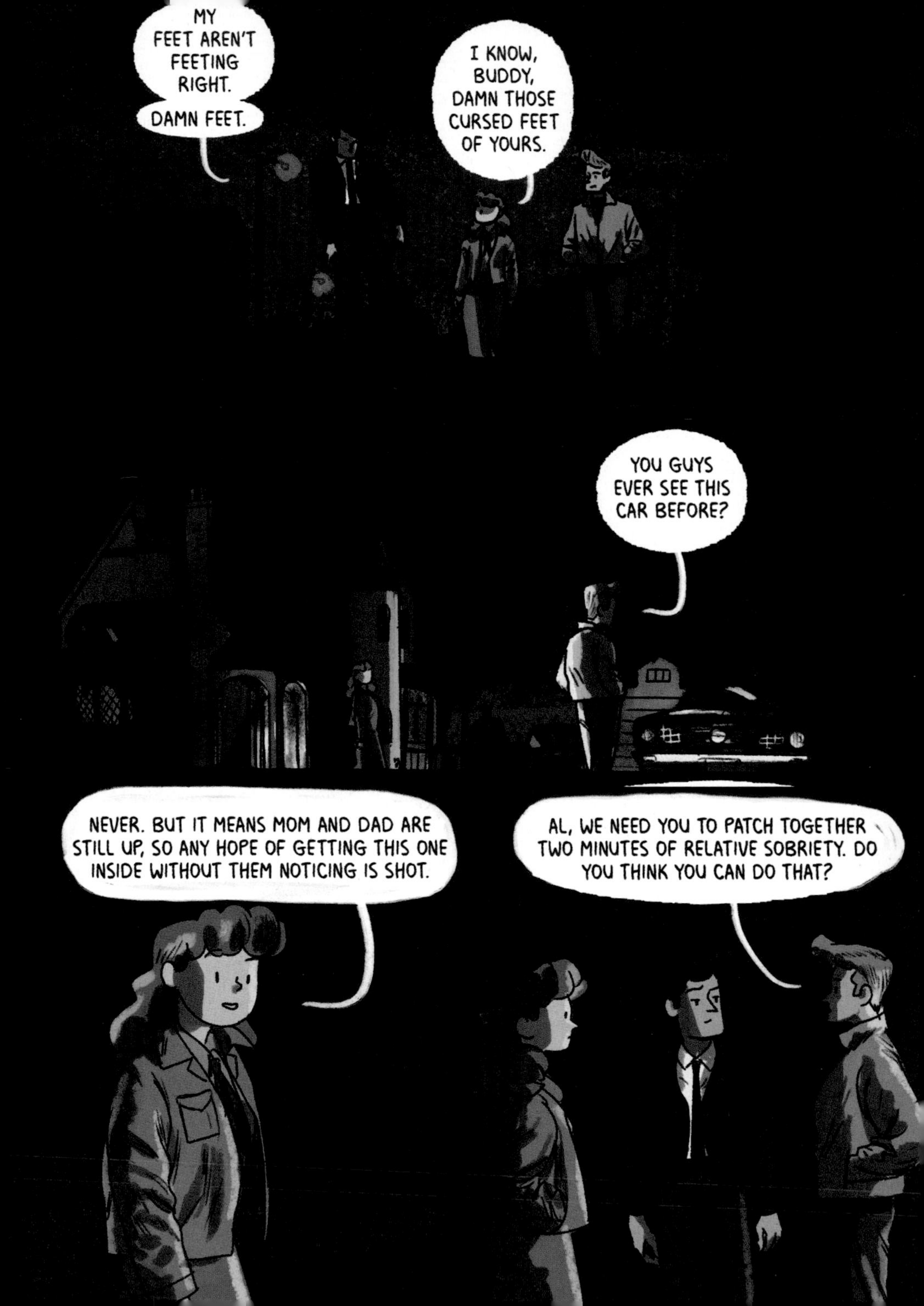
MY FEET AREN'T FEETING RIGHT.
DAMN FEET.
I KNOW, BUDDY, DAMN THOSE CURSED FEET OF YOURS.
YOU GUYS EVER SEE THIS CAR BEFORE?
NEVER. BUT IT MEANS MOM AND DAD ARE STILL UP, SO ANY HOPE OF GETTING THIS ONE INSIDE WITHOUT THEM NOTICING IS SHOT.
AL, WE NEED YOU TO PATCH TOGETHER TWO MINUTES OF RELATIVE SOBRIETY. DO YOU THINK YOU CAN DO THAT?

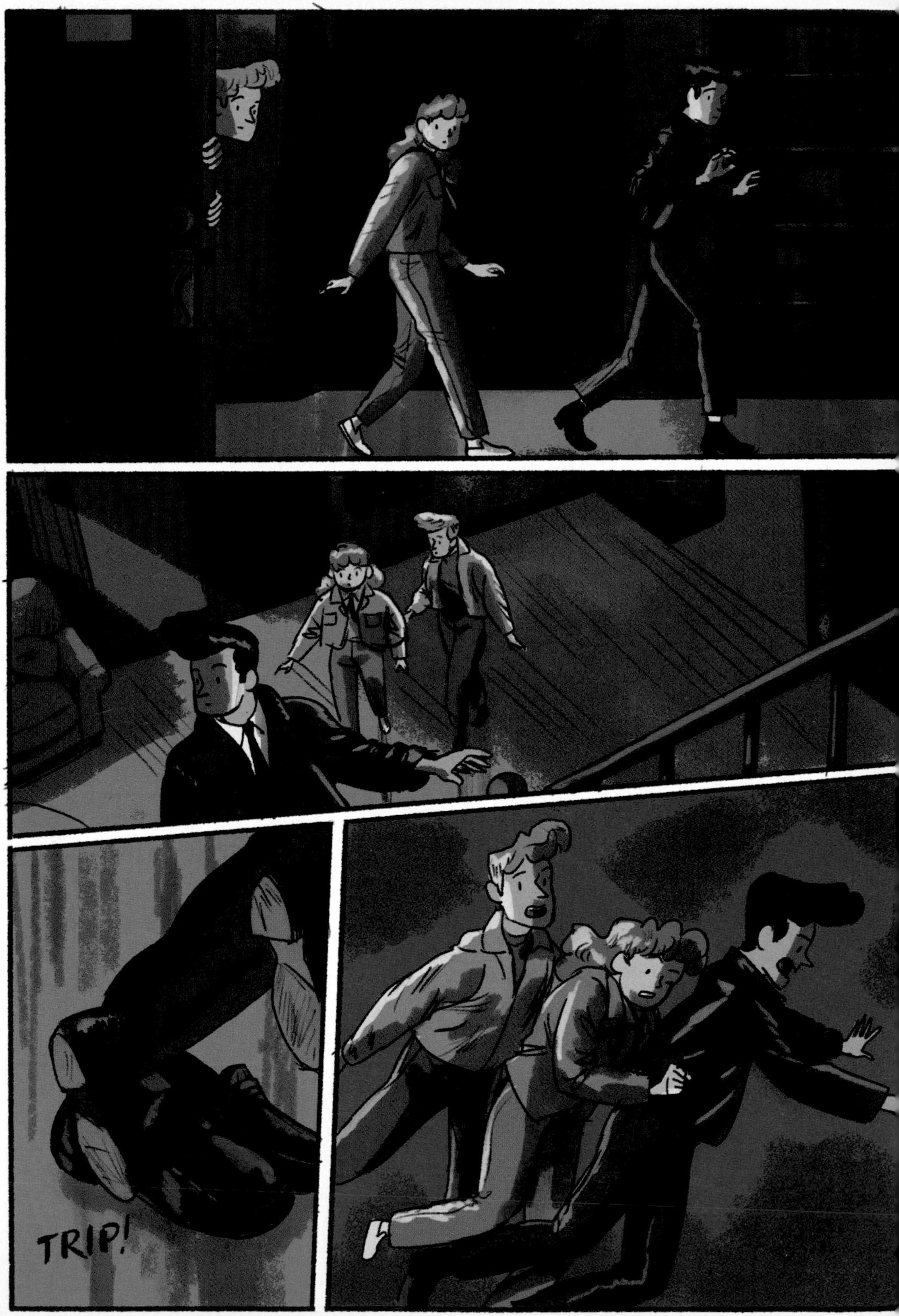
TRIP!

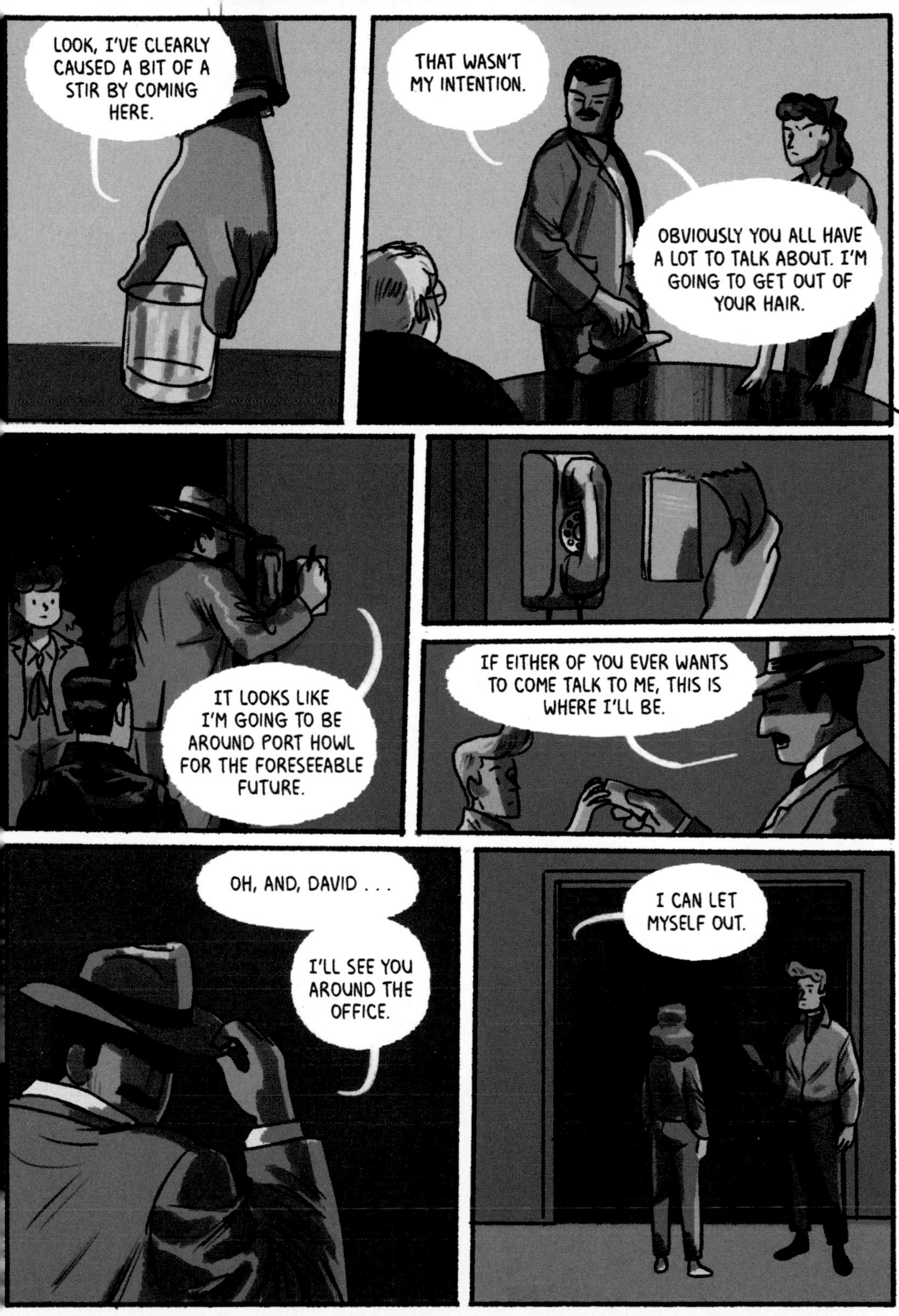
LOOK, I'VE CLEARLY CAUSED A BIT OF A STIR BY COMING HERE.
THAT WASN'T MY INTENTION.
OBVIOUSLY YOU ALL HAVE A LOT TO TALK ABOUT. I'M GOING TO GET OUT OF YOUR HAIR.
IT LOOKS LIKE I'M GOING TO BE AROUND PORT HOWL FOR THE FORESEEABLE FUTURE.
IF EITHER OF YOU EVER WANTS TO COME TALK TO ME, THIS IS WHERE I'LL BE.
OH, AND, DAVID . . .
I'LL SEE YOU AROUND THE OFFICE.
I CAN LET MYSELF OUT.

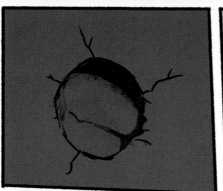

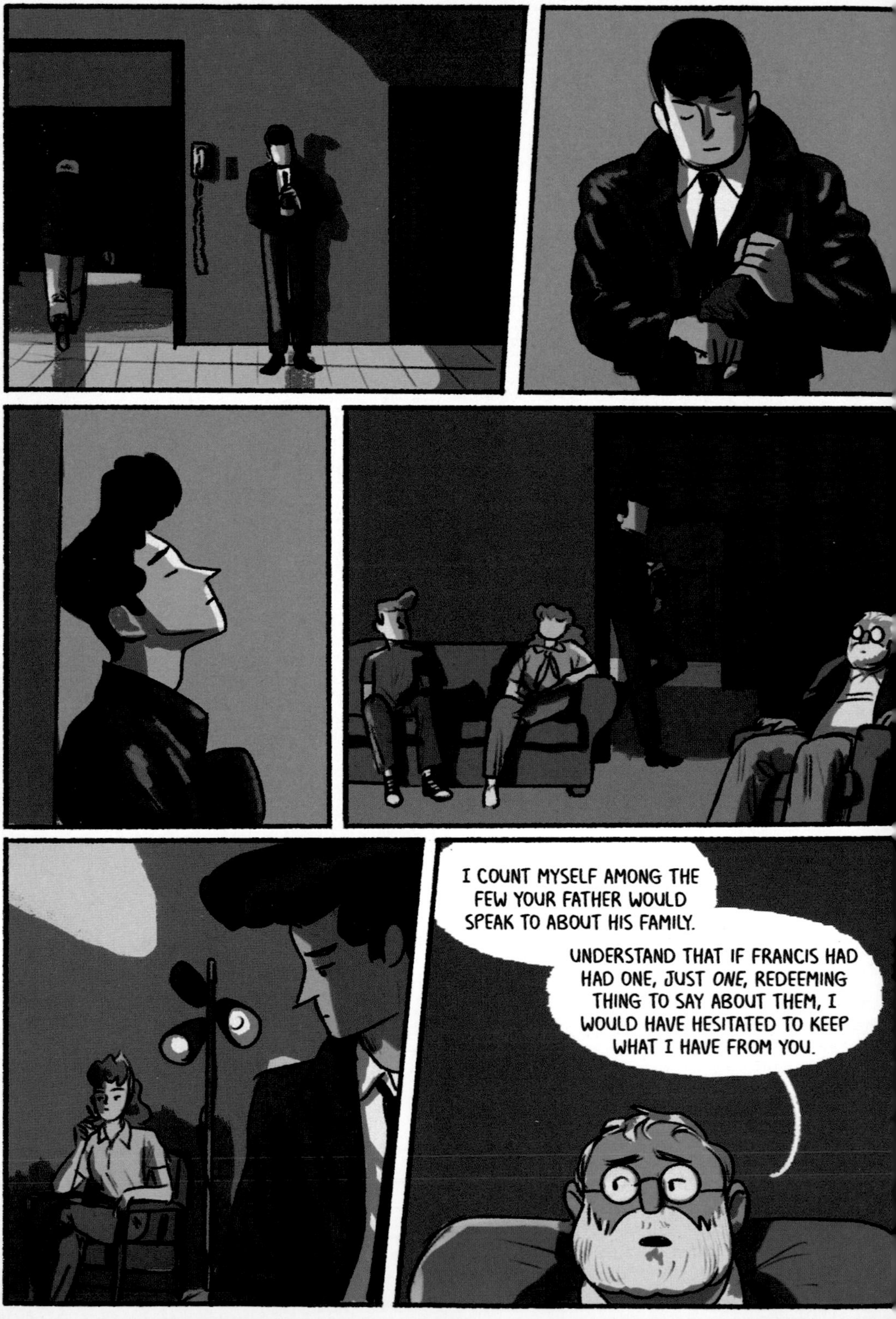
I COUNT MYSELF AMONG THE FEW YOUR FATHER WOULD SPEAK TO ABOUT HIS FAMILY.
UNDERSTAND THAT IF FRANCIS HAD HAD ONE, JUST *ONE*, REDEEMING THING TO SAY ABOUT THEM, I WOULD HAVE HESITATED TO KEEP WHAT I HAVE FROM YOU.

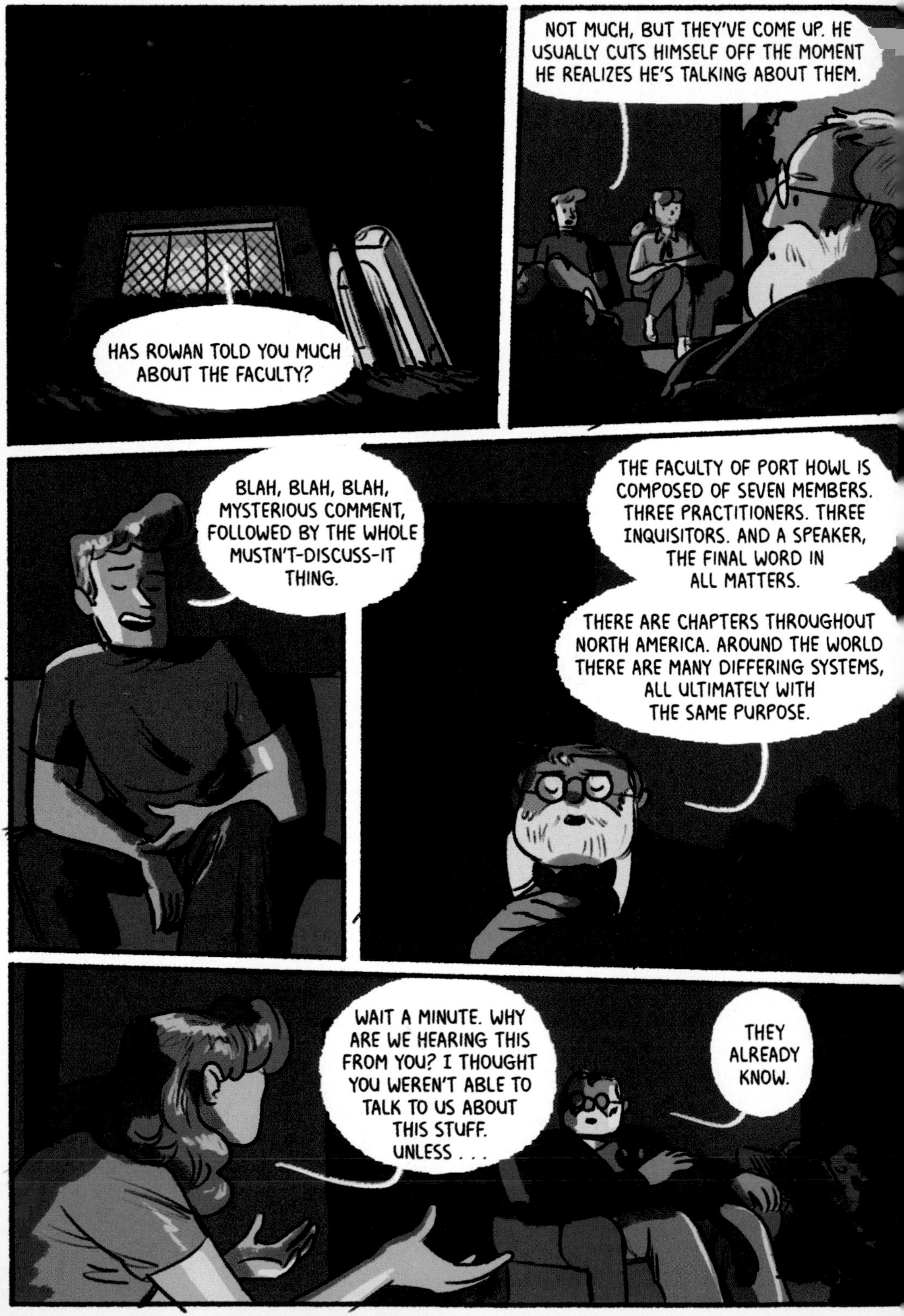
HAS ROWAN TOLD YOU MUCH ABOUT THE FACULTY?
NOT MUCH, BUT THEY'VE COME UP. HE USUALLY CUTS HIMSELF OFF THE MOMENT HE REALIZES HE'S TALKING ABOUT THEM.
BLAH, BLAH, BLAH, MYSTERIOUS COMMENT, FOLLOWED BY THE WHOLE MUSTN'T-DISCUSS-IT THING.
THE FACULTY OF PORT HOWL IS COMPOSED OF SEVEN MEMBERS. THREE PRACTITIONERS. THREE INQUISITORS. AND A SPEAKER, THE FINAL WORD IN ALL MATTERS.
THERE ARE CHAPTERS THROUGHOUT NORTH AMERICA. AROUND THE WORLD THERE ARE MANY DIFFERING SYSTEMS, ALL ULTIMATELY WITH THE SAME PURPOSE.
WAIT A MINUTE. WHY ARE WE HEARING THIS FROM YOU? I THOUGHT YOU WEREN'T ABLE TO TALK TO US ABOUT THIS STUFF. UNLESS . . .
THEY ALREADY KNOW.

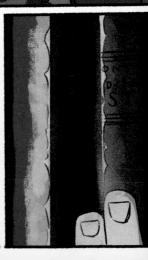

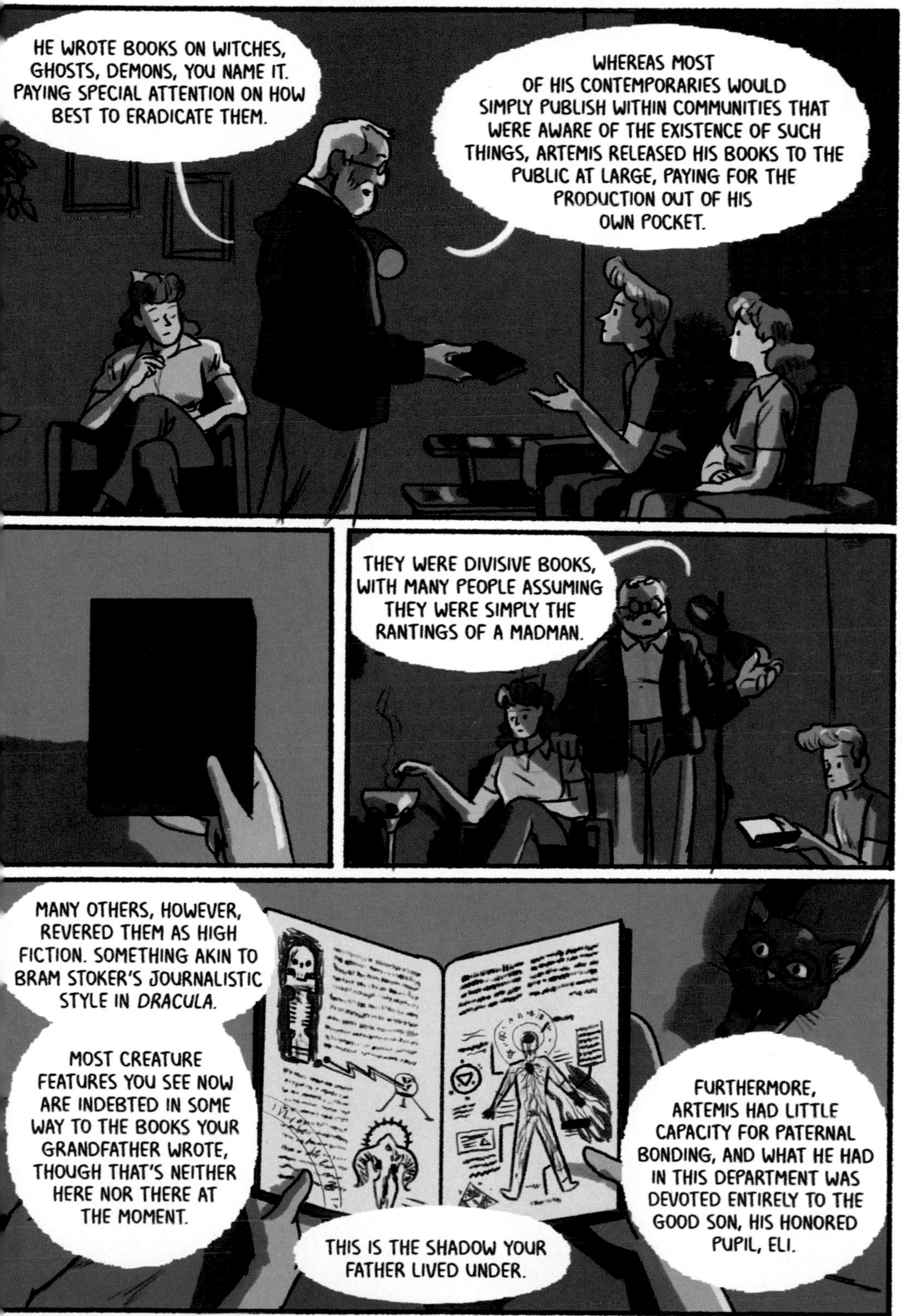
HE WROTE BOOKS ON WITCHES, GHOSTS, DEMONS, YOU NAME IT. PAYING SPECIAL ATTENTION ON HOW BEST TO ERADICATE THEM.
WHEREAS MOST OF HIS CONTEMPORARIES WOULD SIMPLY PUBLISH WITHIN COMMUNITIES THAT WERE AWARE OF THE EXISTENCE OF SUCH THINGS, ARTEMIS RELEASED HIS BOOKS TO THE PUBLIC AT LARGE, PAYING FOR THE PRODUCTION OUT OF HIS OWN POCKET.
THEY WERE DIVISIVE BOOKS, WITH MANY PEOPLE ASSUMING THEY WERE SIMPLY THE RANTINGS OF A MADMAN.
MANY OTHERS, HOWEVER, REVERED THEM AS HIGH FICTION. SOMETHING AKIN TO BRAM STOKER'S JOURNALISTIC STYLE IN *DRACULA*.
MOST CREATURE FEATURES YOU SEE NOW ARE INDEBTED IN SOME WAY TO THE BOOKS YOUR GRANDFATHER WROTE, THOUGH THAT'S NEITHER HERE NOR THERE AT THE MOMENT.
THIS IS THE SHADOW YOUR FATHER LIVED UNDER.
FURTHERMORE, ARTEMIS HAD LITTLE CAPACITY FOR PATERNAL BONDING, AND WHAT HE HAD IN THIS DEPARTMENT WAS DEVOTED ENTIRELY TO THE GOOD SON, HIS HONORED PUPIL, ELI.

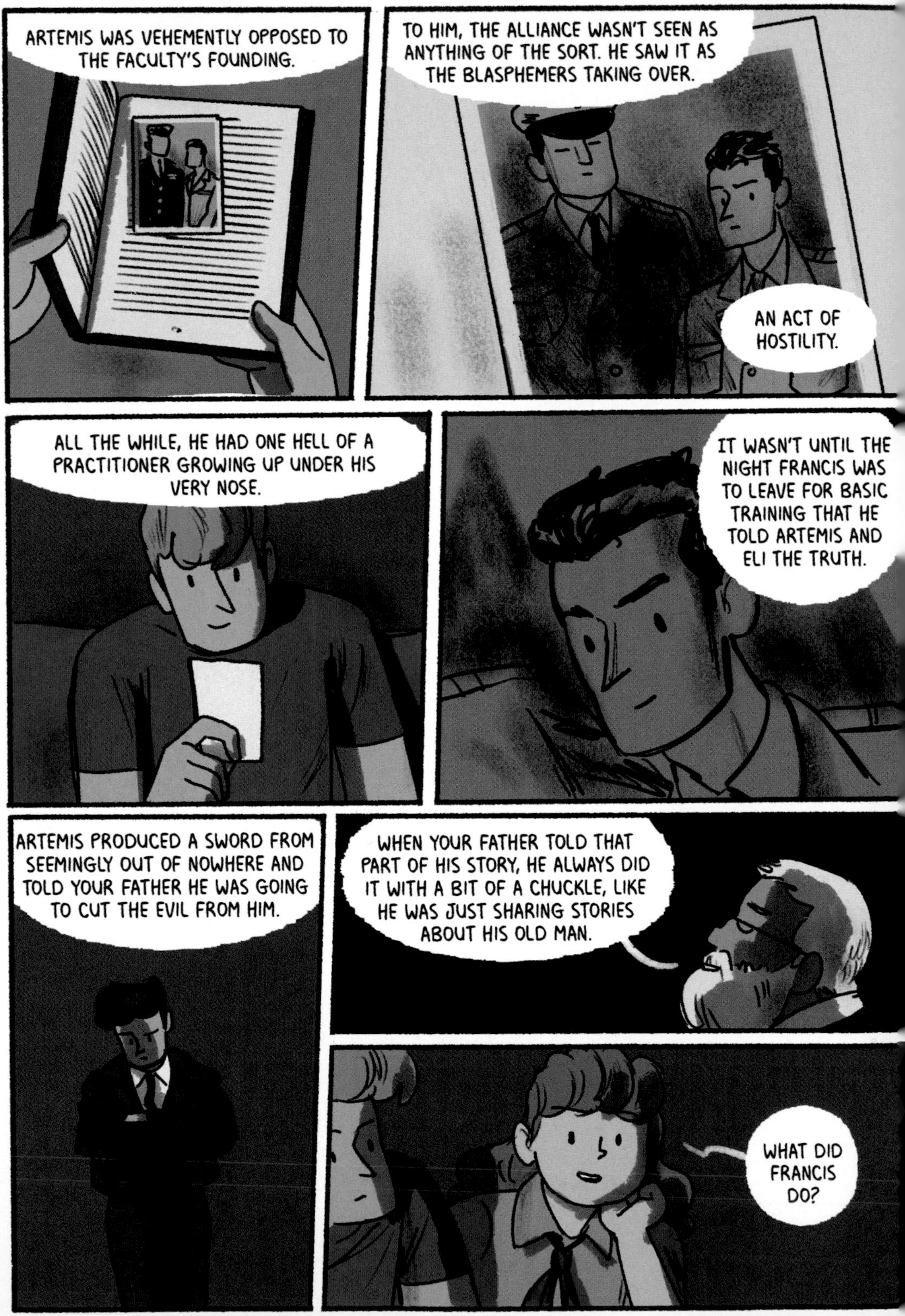
ARTEMIS WAS VEHEMENTLY OPPOSED TO THE FACULTY'S FOUNDING.
TO HIM, THE ALLIANCE WASN'T SEEN AS ANYTHING OF THE SORT. HE SAW IT AS THE BLASPHEMERS TAKING OVER.
AN ACT OF HOSTILITY.
ALL THE WHILE, HE HAD ONE HELL OF A PRACTITIONER GROWING UP UNDER HIS VERY NOSE.
IT WASN'T UNTIL THE NIGHT FRANCIS WAS TO LEAVE FOR BASIC TRAINING THAT HE TOLD ARTEMIS AND ELI THE TRUTH.
ARTEMIS PRODUCED A SWORD FROM SEEMINGLY OUT OF NOWHERE AND TOLD YOUR FATHER HE WAS GOING TO CUT THE EVIL FROM HIM.
WHEN YOUR FATHER TOLD THAT PART OF HIS STORY, HE ALWAYS DID IT WITH A BIT OF A CHUCKLE, LIKE HE WAS JUST SHARING STORIES ABOUT HIS OLD MAN.
WHAT DID FRANCIS DO?

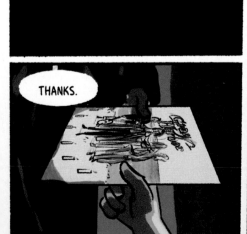

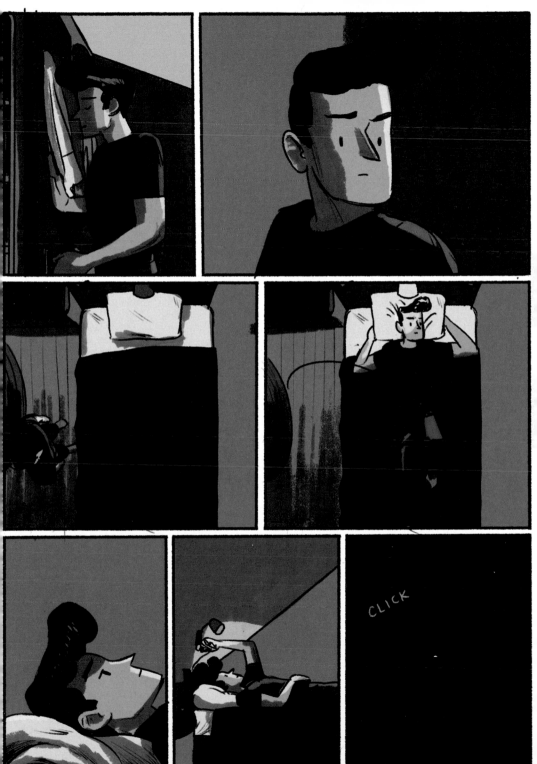

CLICK

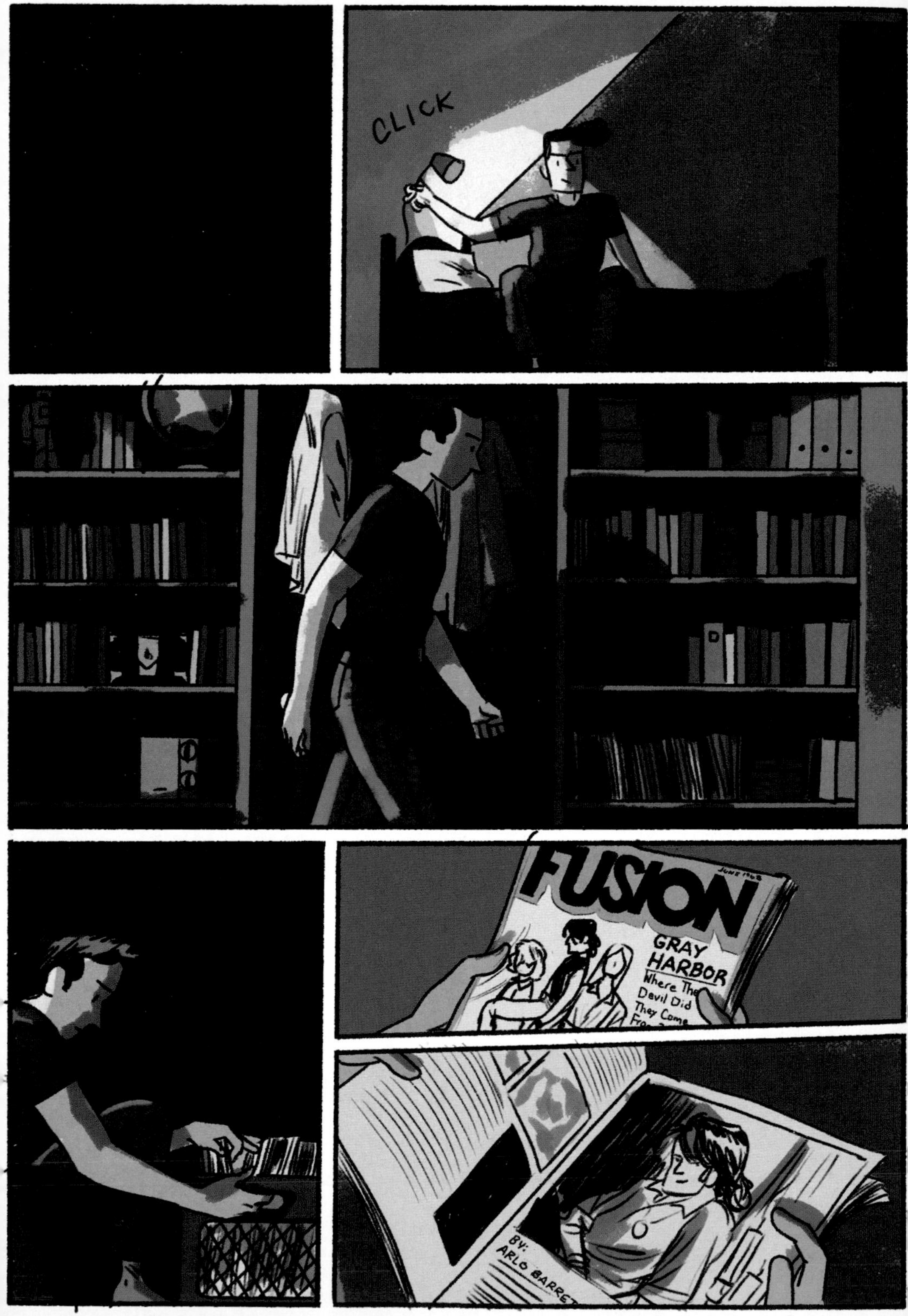
CLICK
FUSION
JUNE
GRAY HARBOR
Where The
Devil Did
They Come
BY: ARLO BARRET

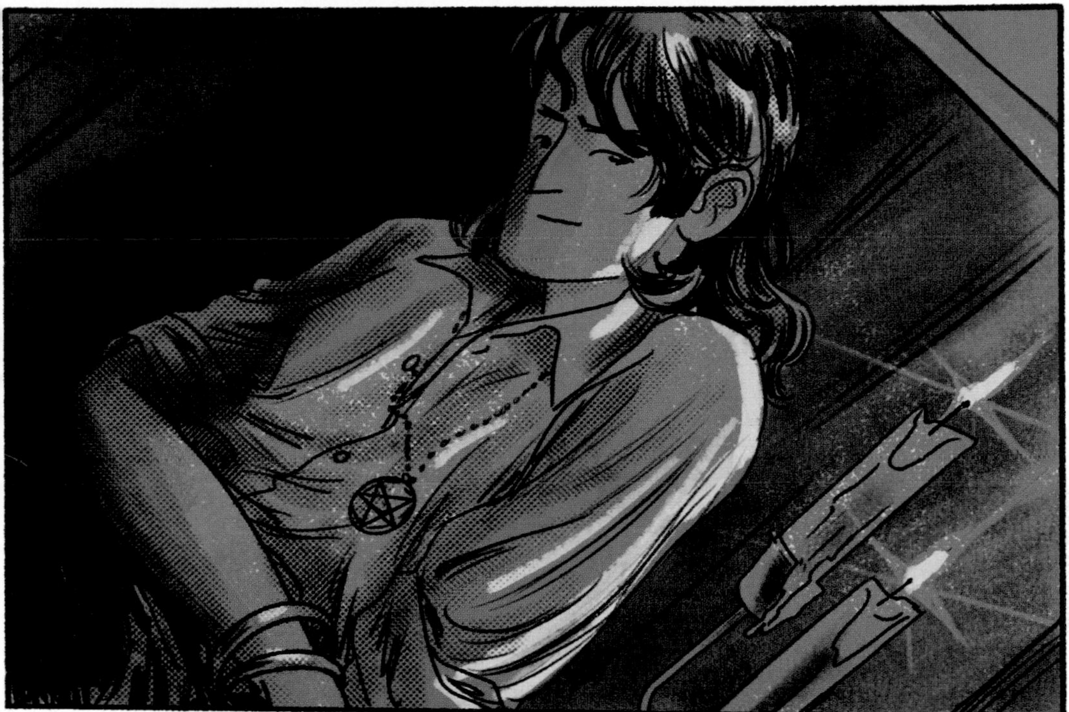

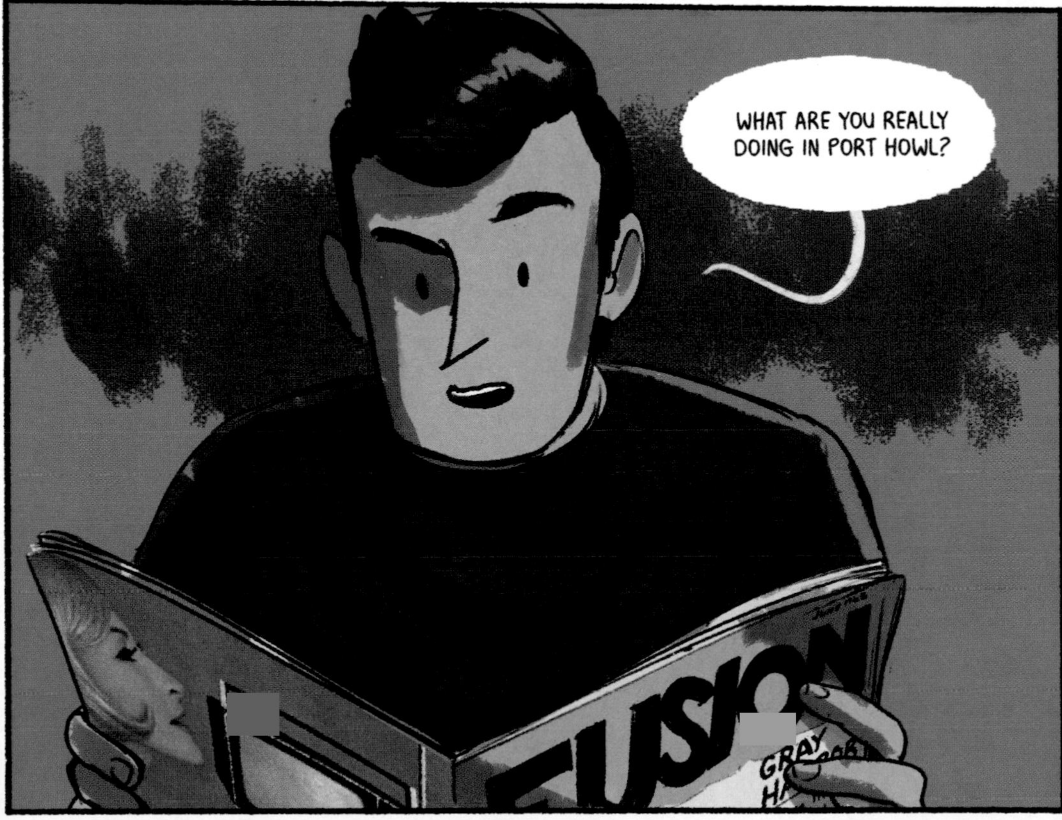
WHAT ARE YOU REALLY DOING IN PORT HOWL?

CHAPTER 3

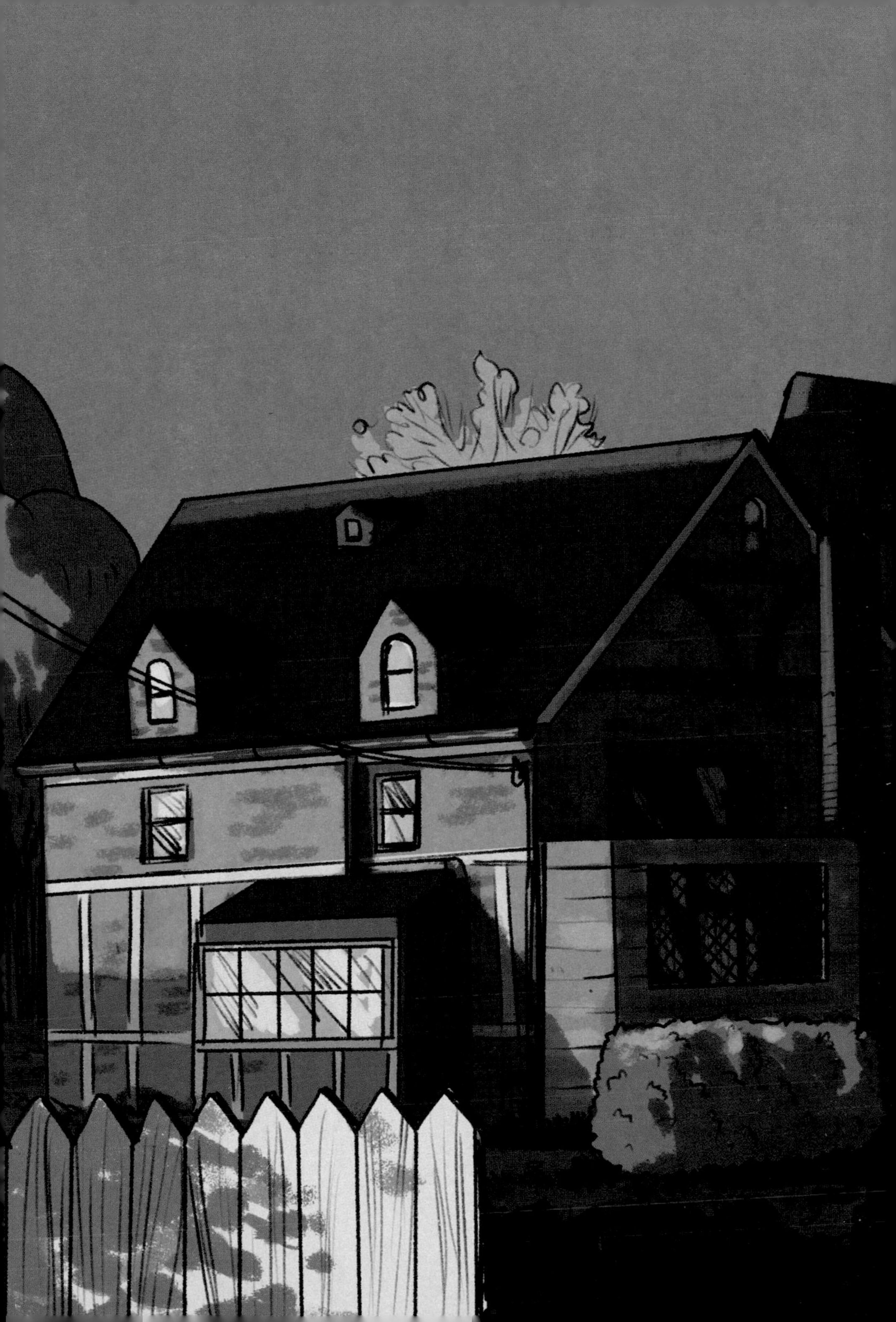

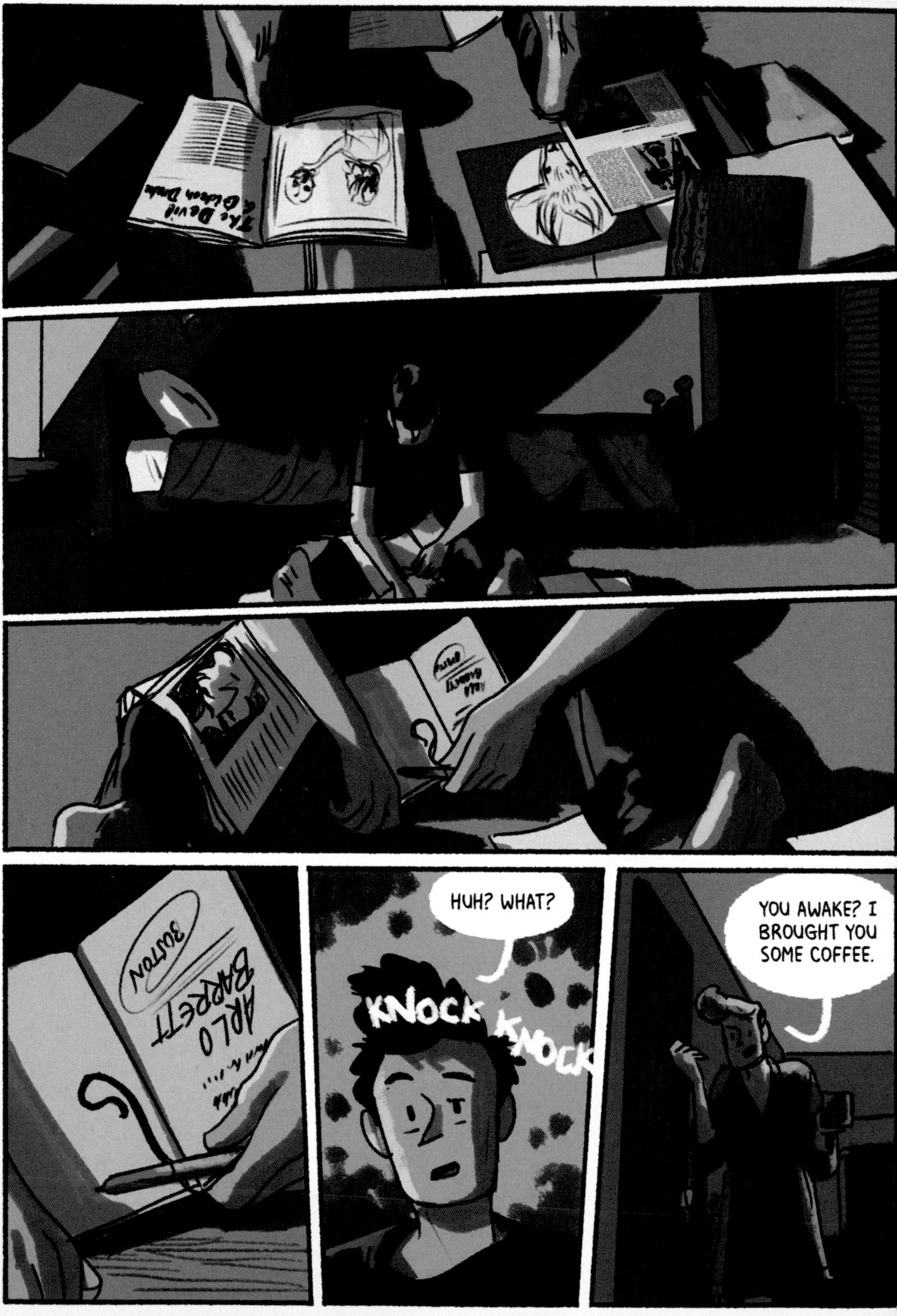
ARLO BARRETT
BUSTON
HUH? WHAT?
KNOCK KNOCK
YOU AWAKE? I BROUGHT YOU SOME COFFEE.

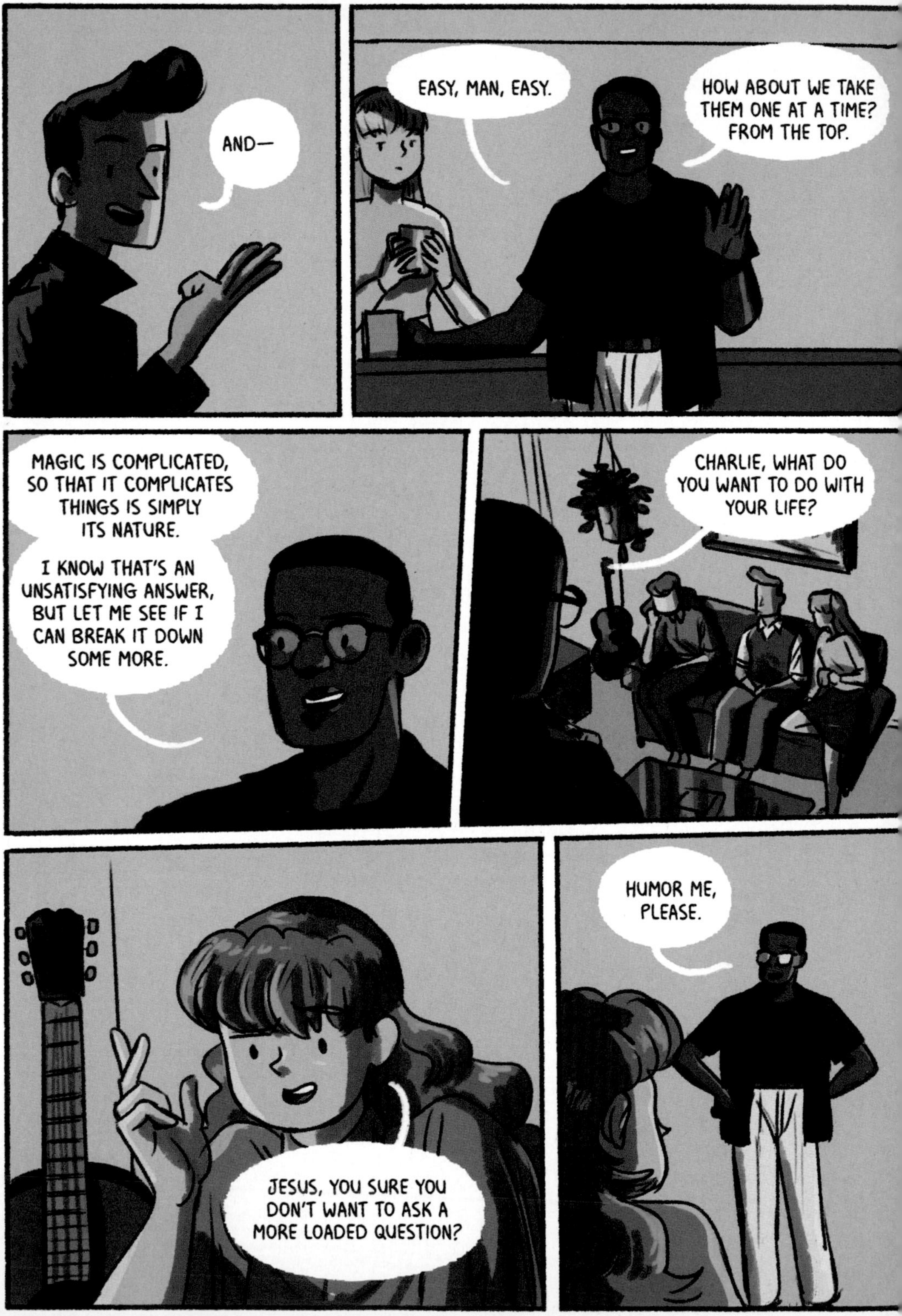
AND—
EASY, MAN, EASY.
HOW ABOUT WE TAKE THEM ONE AT A TIME? FROM THE TOP.
MAGIC IS COMPLICATED, SO THAT IT COMPLICATES THINGS IS SIMPLY ITS NATURE.
I KNOW THAT'S AN UNSATISFYING ANSWER, BUT LET ME SEE IF I CAN BREAK IT DOWN SOME MORE.
CHARLIE, WHAT DO YOU WANT TO DO WITH YOUR LIFE?
JESUS, YOU SURE YOU DON'T WANT TO ASK A MORE LOADED QUESTION?
HUMOR ME, PLEASE.

I'VE ALWAYS KINDA WANTED TO BE A JOURNALIST?

PERFECT! A JOURNALIST.

AND WHAT MAKES A GOOD JOURNALIST? I MEAN, BEYOND SOMEBODY WHO CAN WRITE WELL.

CLAP!

FAIRNESS, OBJECTIVITY, HONESTY . . . IN SHORT, SOMEONE WHO SEEKS TO FIND, AND COMMUNICATE, THE TRUTH.

NOW LET'S CONSIDER YOUR SPECIALTY. . . .

MY SPECIALTY?

WOULD YOU NOT SAY THAT ABILITY COULD AID YOU IN THE FIELD OF JOURNALISM?

SURE.

YOUR ABILITY TO READ OBJECTS. OR, TO USE THE MORE TECHNICAL TERM, PSYCHOMETRY.

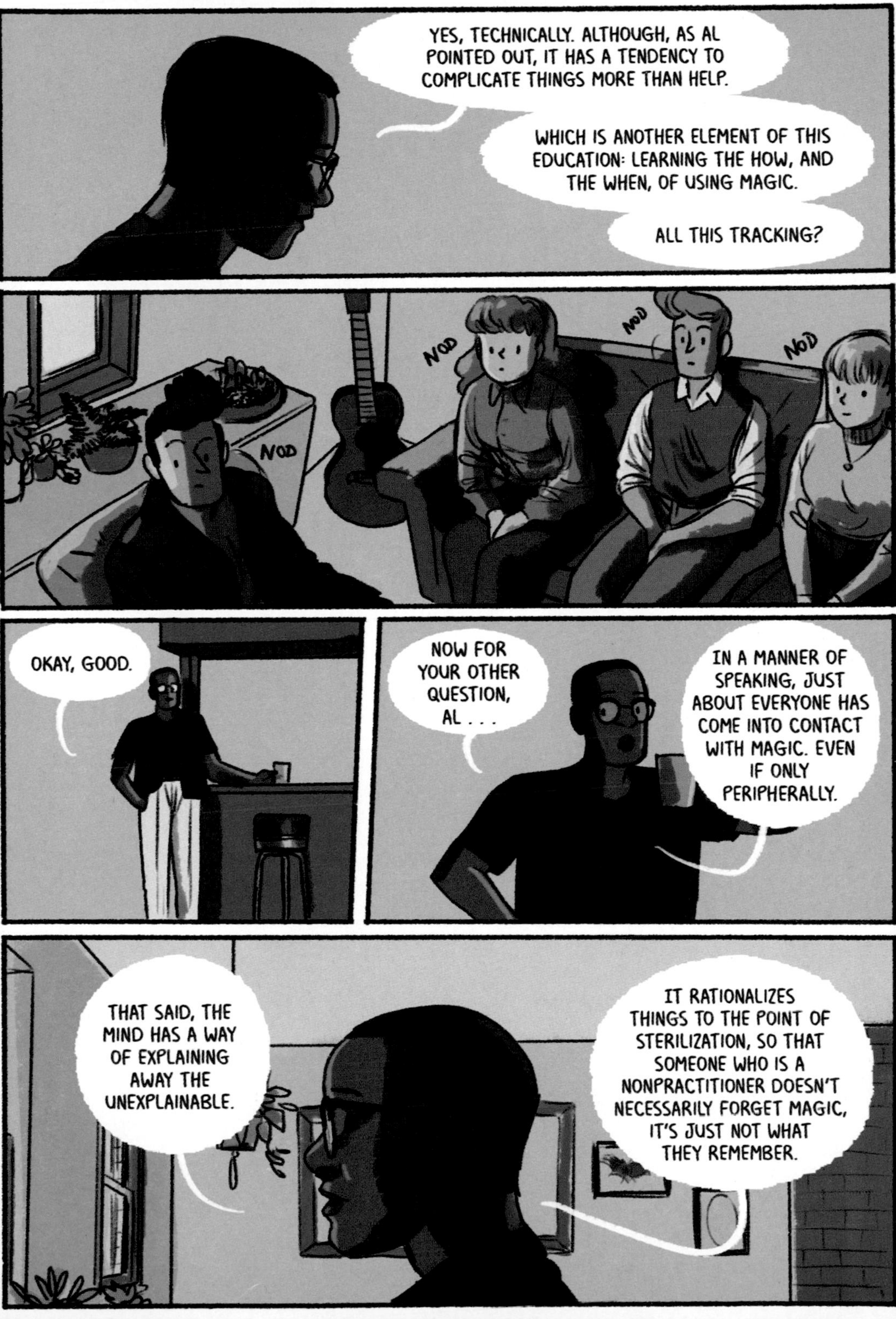
YES, TECHNICALLY. ALTHOUGH, AS AL POINTED OUT, IT HAS A TENDENCY TO COMPLICATE THINGS MORE THAN HELP.
WHICH IS ANOTHER ELEMENT OF THIS EDUCATION: LEARNING THE HOW, AND THE WHEN, OF USING MAGIC.
ALL THIS TRACKING?
NOD
NOD
NOD
NOD
OKAY, GOOD.
NOW FOR YOUR OTHER QUESTION, AL . . .
IN A MANNER OF SPEAKING, JUST ABOUT EVERYONE HAS COME INTO CONTACT WITH MAGIC. EVEN IF ONLY PERIPHERALLY.
THAT SAID, THE MIND HAS A WAY OF EXPLAINING AWAY THE UNEXPLAINABLE.
IT RATIONALIZES THINGS TO THE POINT OF STERILIZATION, SO THAT SOMEONE WHO IS A NONPRACTITIONER DOESN'T NECESSARILY FORGET MAGIC, IT'S JUST NOT WHAT THEY REMEMBER.

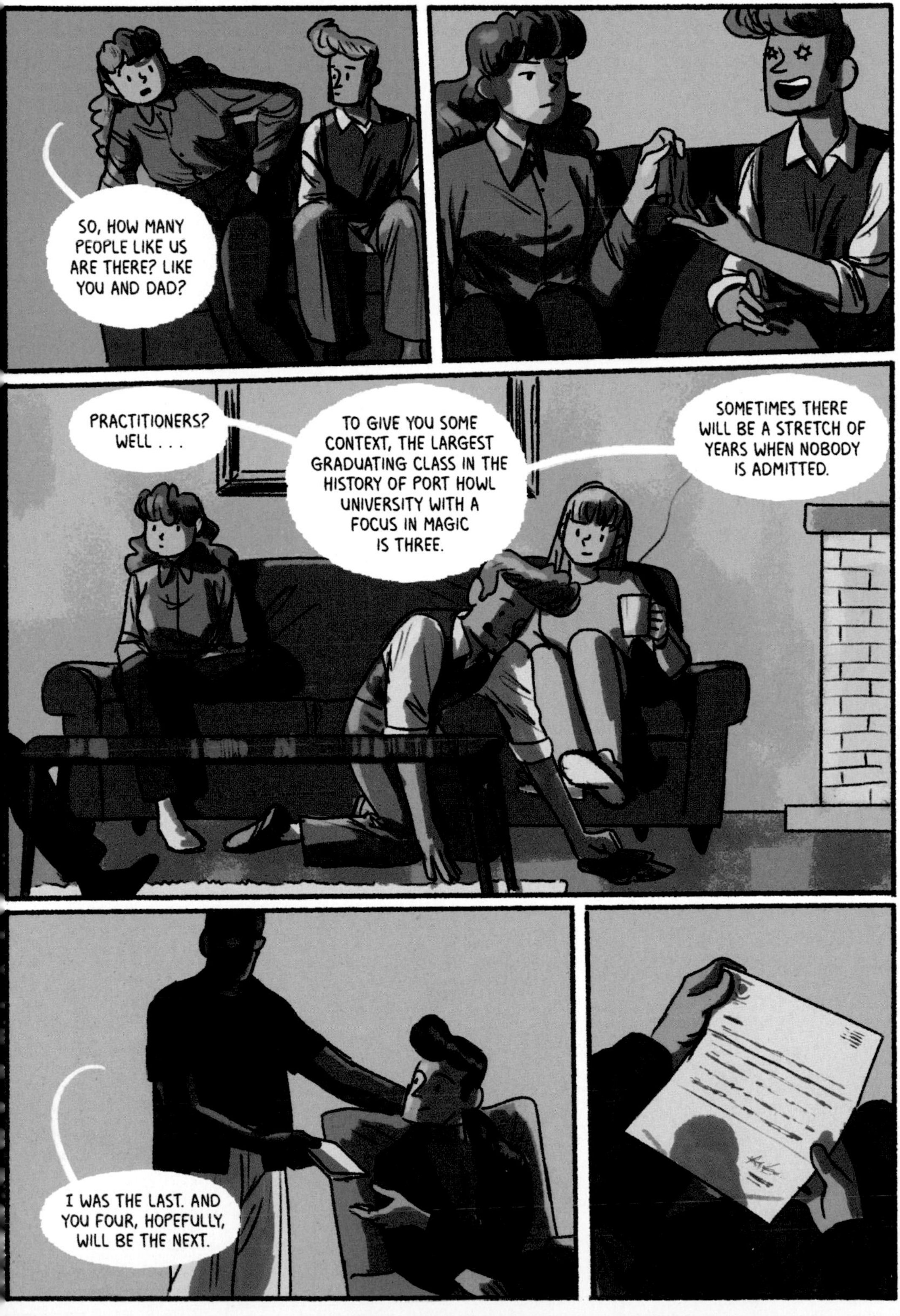
SO, HOW MANY PEOPLE LIKE US ARE THERE? LIKE YOU AND DAD?
PRACTITIONERS? WELL . . .
TO GIVE YOU SOME CONTEXT, THE LARGEST GRADUATING CLASS IN THE HISTORY OF PORT HOWL UNIVERSITY WITH A FOCUS IN MAGIC IS THREE.
SOMETIMES THERE WILL BE A STRETCH OF YEARS WHEN NOBODY IS ADMITTED.
I WAS THE LAST. AND YOU FOUR, HOPEFULLY, WILL BE THE NEXT.

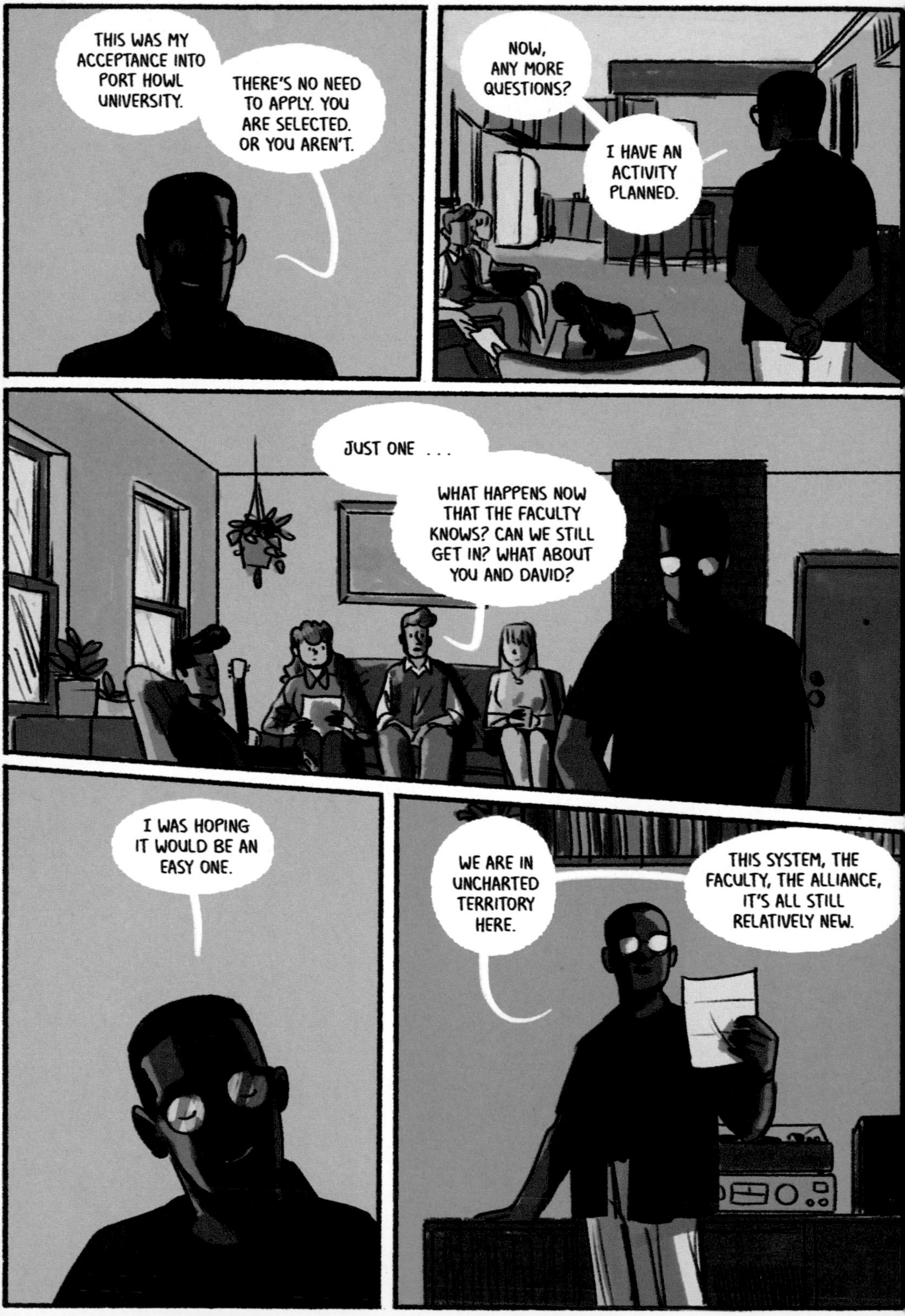
THIS WAS MY ACCEPTANCE INTO PORT HOWL UNIVERSITY.
THERE'S NO NEED TO APPLY. YOU ARE SELECTED. OR YOU AREN'T.
NOW, ANY MORE QUESTIONS?
I HAVE AN ACTIVITY PLANNED.
JUST ONE . . .
WHAT HAPPENS NOW THAT THE FACULTY KNOWS? CAN WE STILL GET IN? WHAT ABOUT YOU AND DAVID?
I WAS HOPING IT WOULD BE AN EASY ONE.
WE ARE IN UNCHARTED TERRITORY HERE.
THIS SYSTEM, THE FACULTY, THE ALLIANCE, IT'S ALL STILL RELATIVELY NEW.

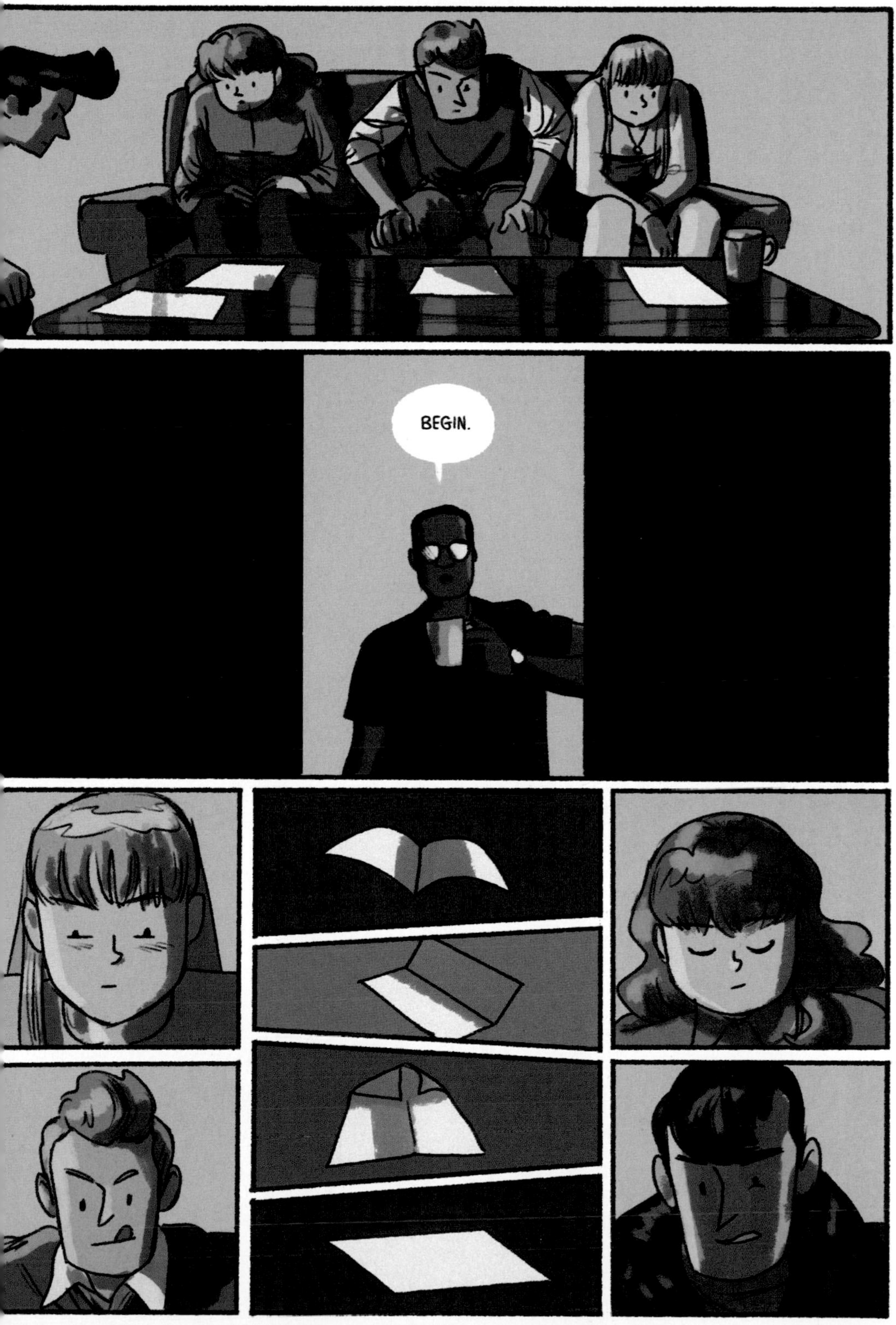
BEGIN.

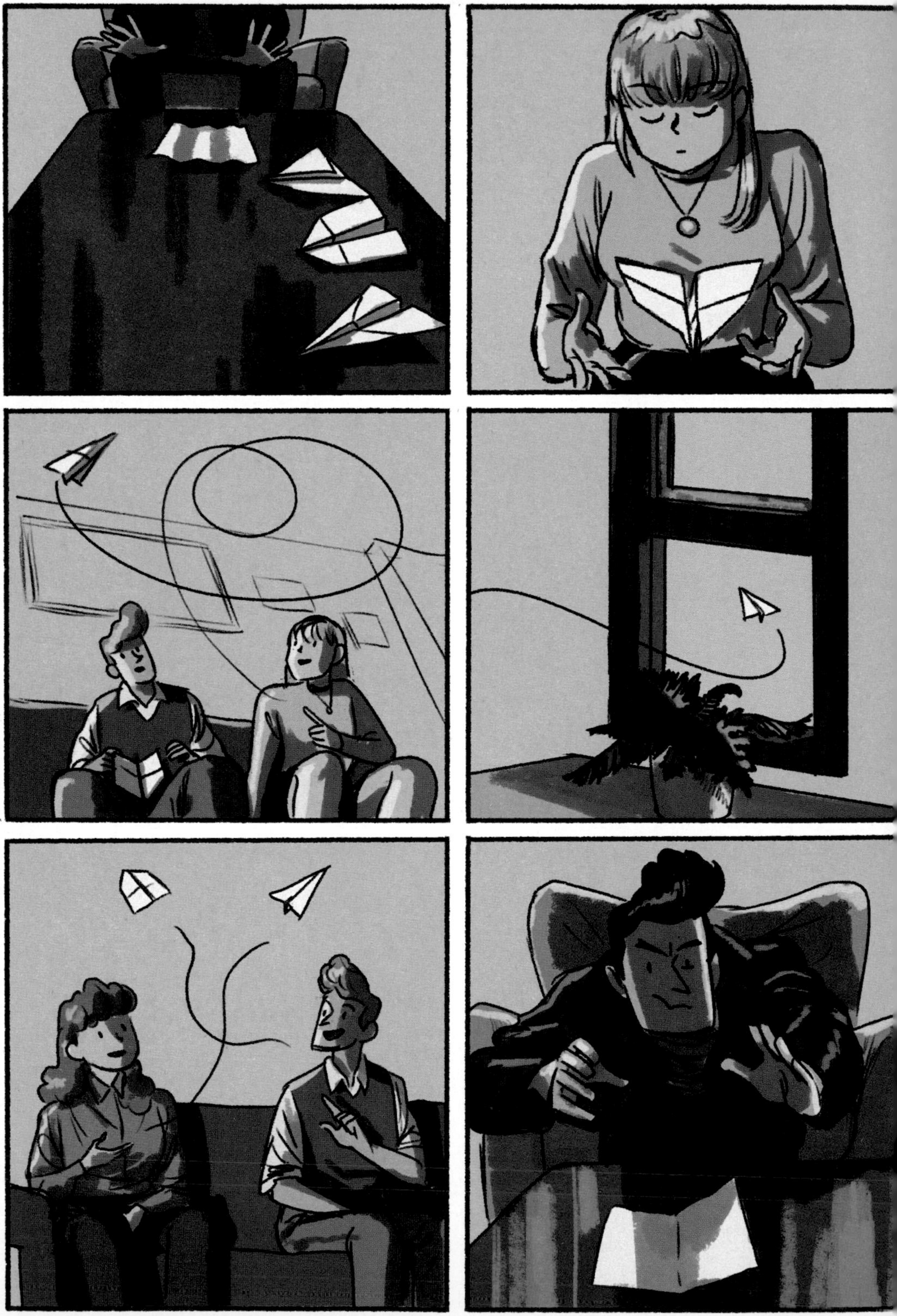

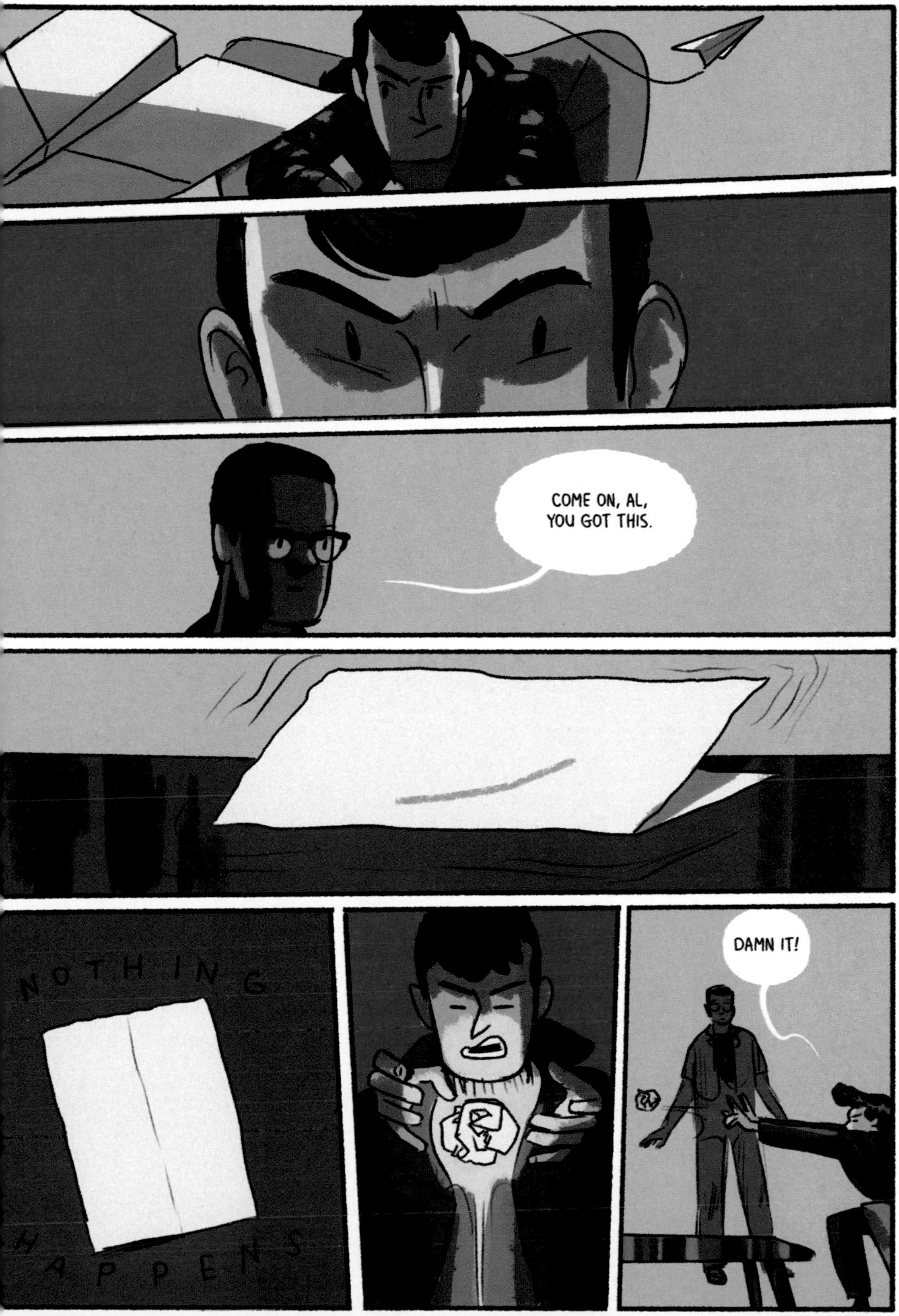
COME ON, AL,
YOU GOT THIS.
NOTHING
HAPPENS
DAMN IT!

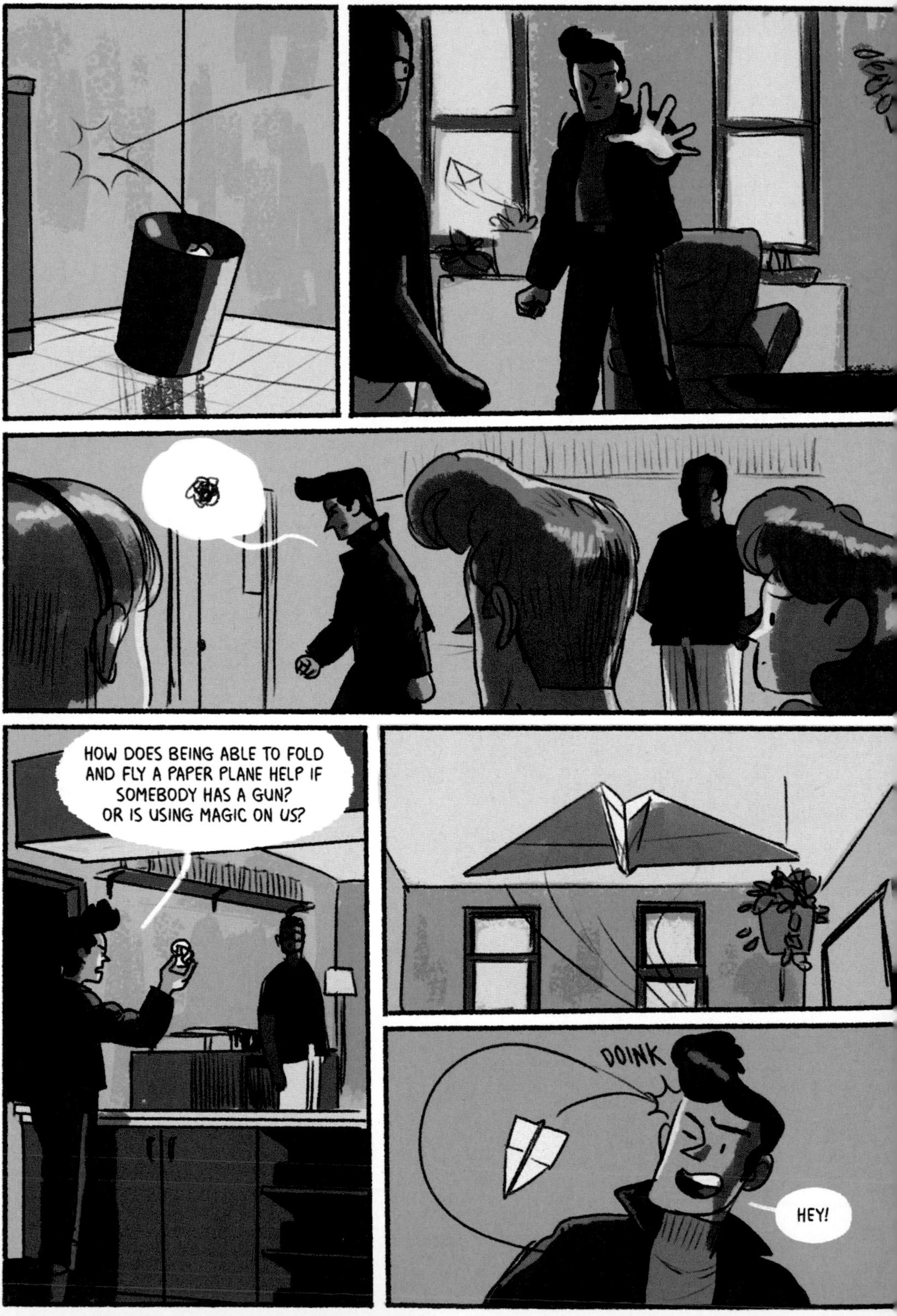
HOW DOES BEING ABLE TO FOLD AND FLY A PAPER PLANE HELP IF SOMEBODY HAS A GUN? OR IS USING MAGIC ON US?
DOINK
HEY!

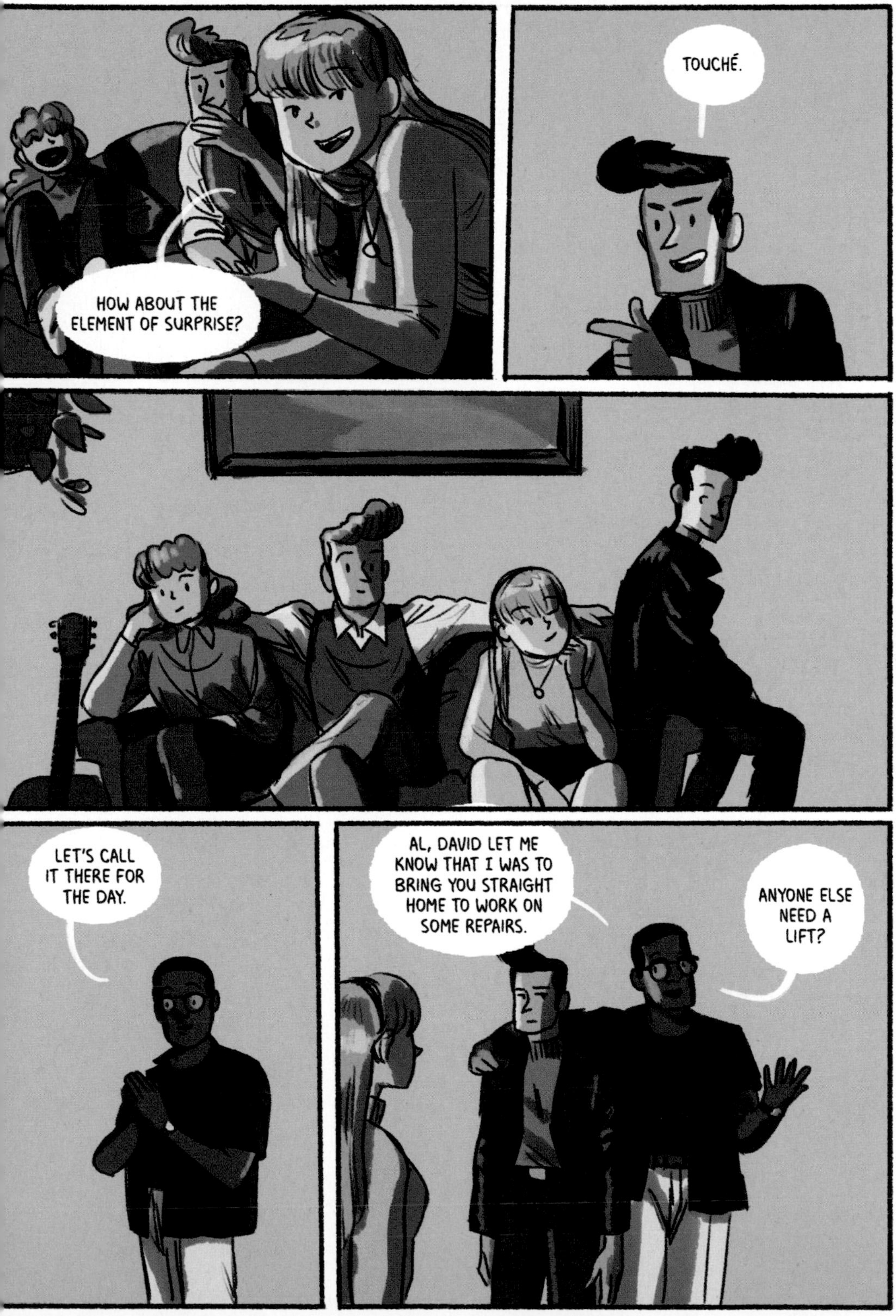
HOW ABOUT THE ELEMENT OF SURPRISE?
TOUCHÉ.
LET'S CALL IT THERE FOR THE DAY.
AL, DAVID LET ME KNOW THAT I WAS TO BRING YOU STRAIGHT HOME TO WORK ON SOME REPAIRS.
ANYONE ELSE NEED A LIFT?

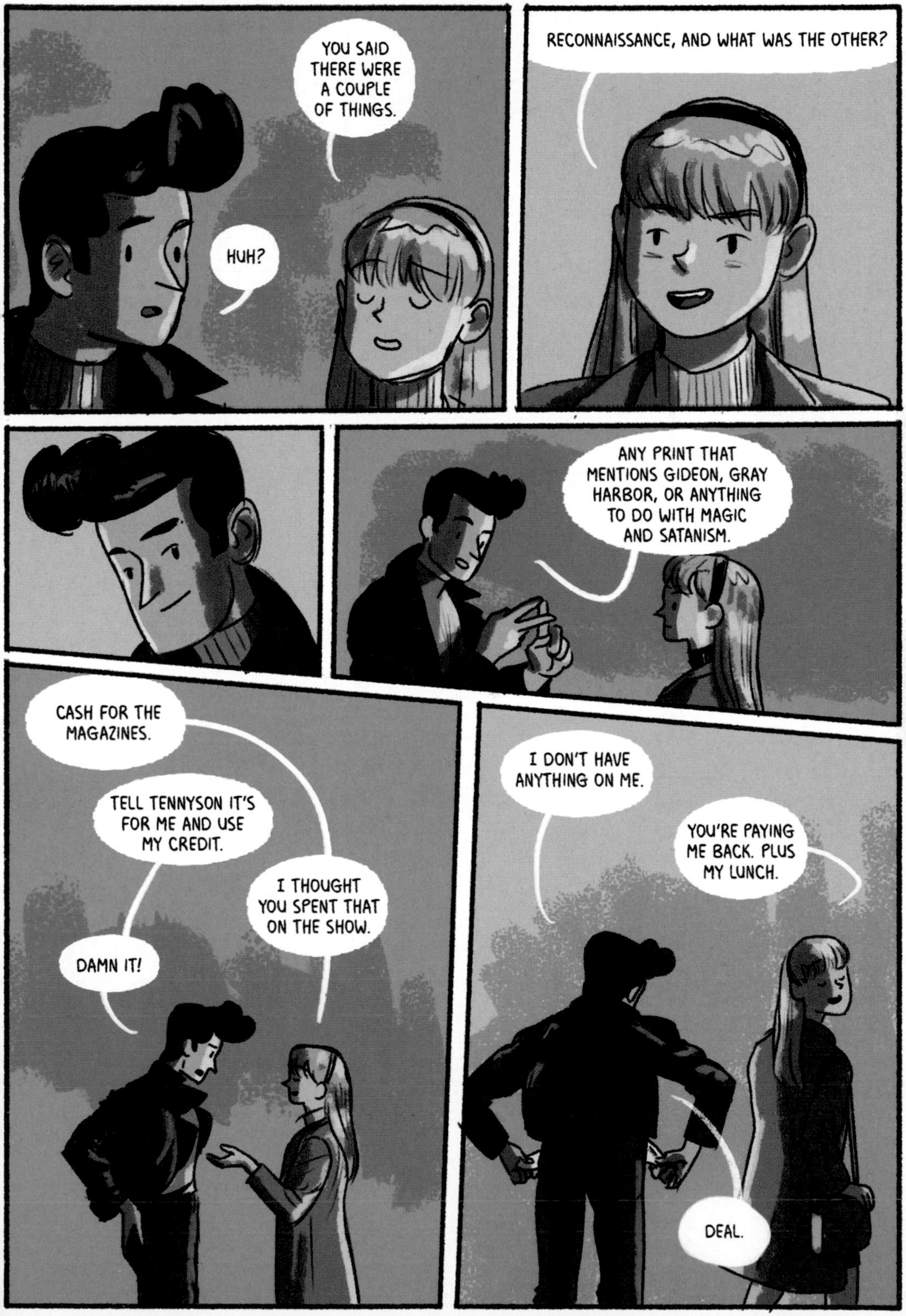
YOU SAID THERE WERE A COUPLE OF THINGS.
HUH?
RECONNAISSANCE, AND WHAT WAS THE OTHER?
ANY PRINT THAT MENTIONS GIDEON, GRAY HARBOR, OR ANYTHING TO DO WITH MAGIC AND SATANISM.
CASH FOR THE MAGAZINES.
TELL TENNYSON IT'S FOR ME AND USE MY CREDIT.
I THOUGHT YOU SPENT THAT ON THE SHOW.
DAMN IT!
I DON'T HAVE ANYTHING ON ME.
YOU'RE PAYING ME BACK. PLUS MY LUNCH.
DEAL.

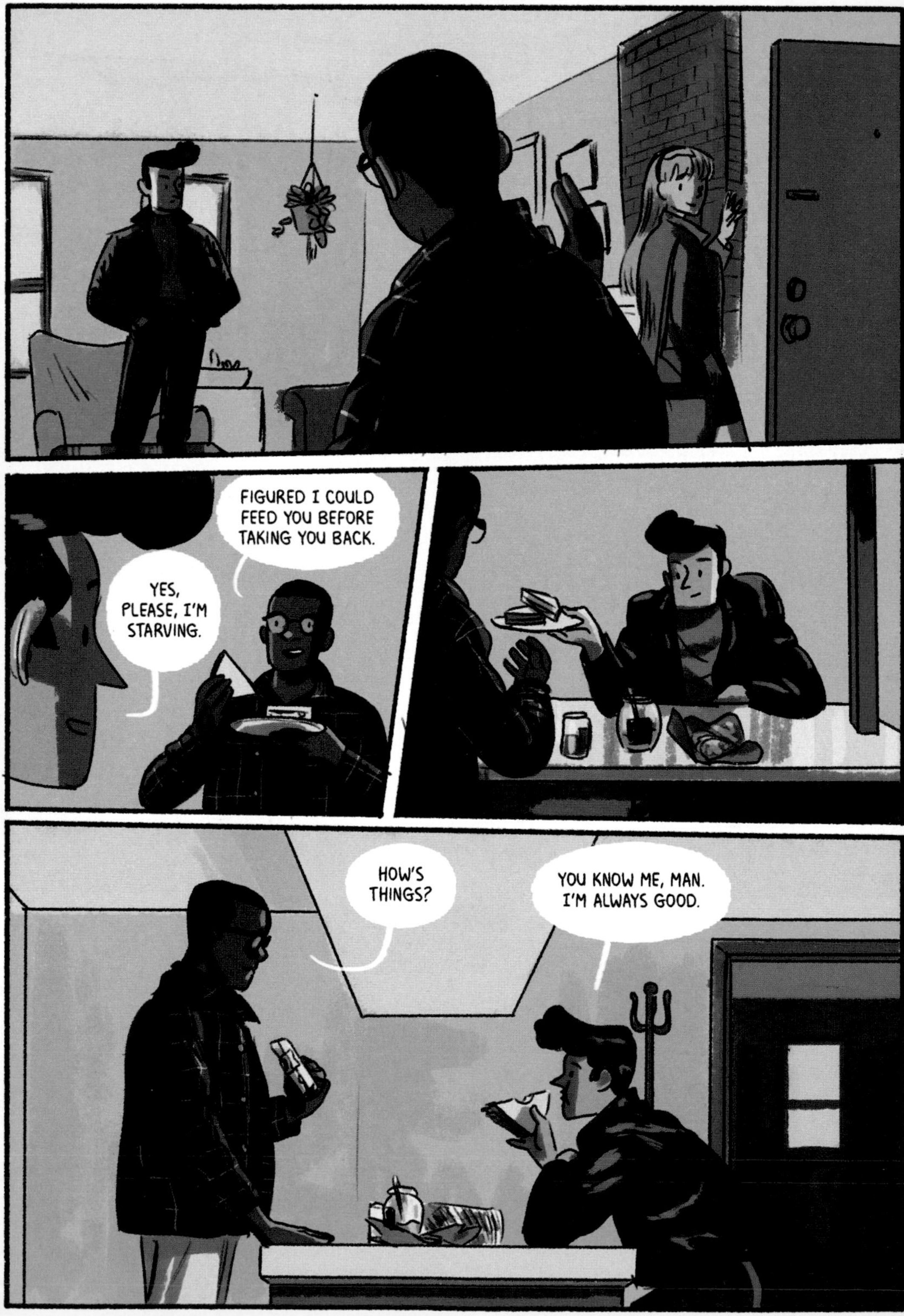
FIGURED I COULD FEED YOU BEFORE TAKING YOU BACK.
YES, PLEASE, I'M STARVING.
HOW'S THINGS?
YOU KNOW ME, MAN. I'M ALWAYS GOOD.

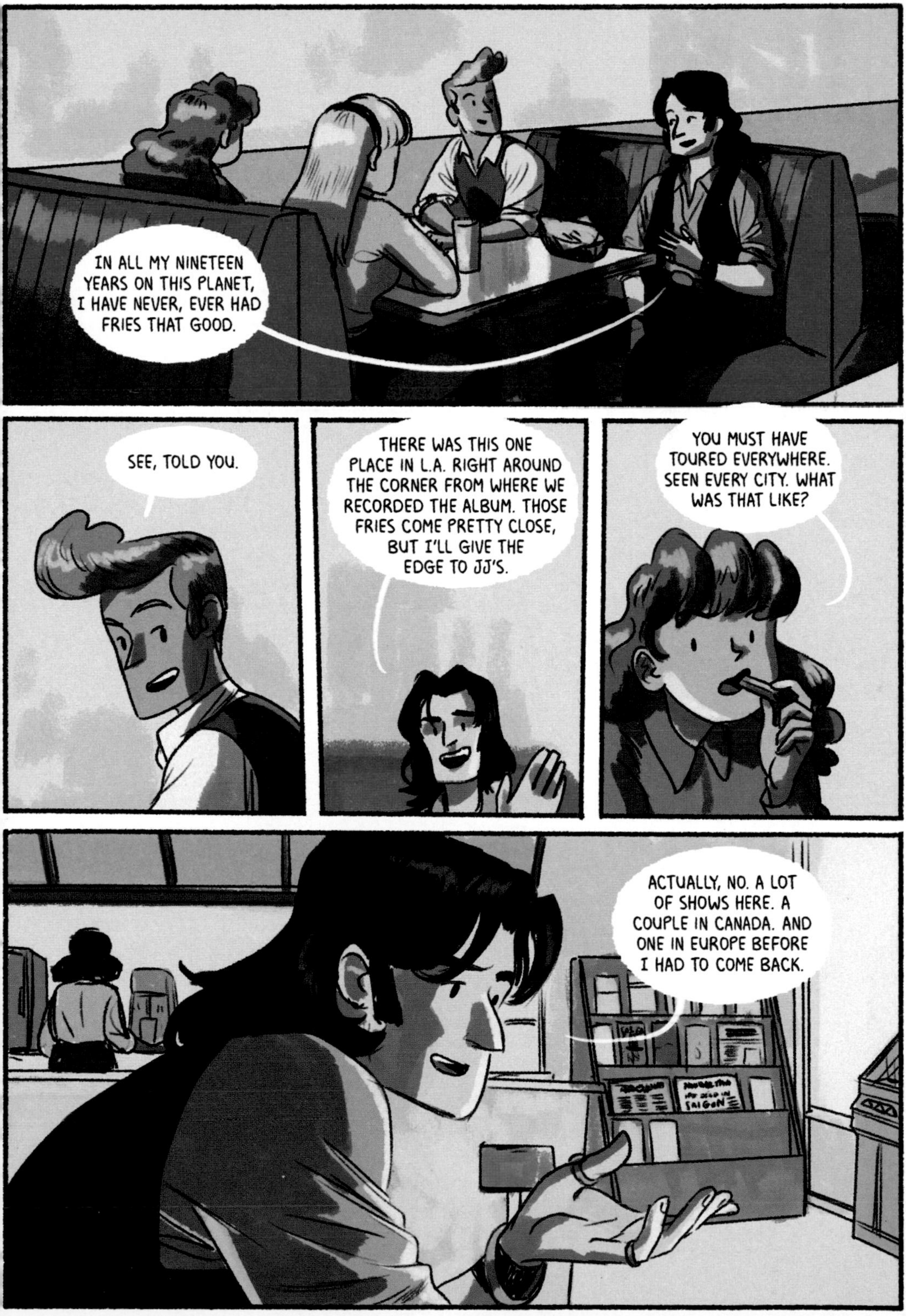
IN ALL MY NINETEEN YEARS ON THIS PLANET, I HAVE NEVER, EVER HAD FRIES THAT GOOD.
SEE, TOLD YOU.
THERE WAS THIS ONE PLACE IN L.A. RIGHT AROUND THE CORNER FROM WHERE WE RECORDED THE ALBUM. THOSE FRIES COME PRETTY CLOSE, BUT I'LL GIVE THE EDGE TO JJ'S.
YOU MUST HAVE TOURED EVERYWHERE. SEEN EVERY CITY. WHAT WAS THAT LIKE?
ACTUALLY, NO. A LOT OF SHOWS HERE. A COUPLE IN CANADA. AND ONE IN EUROPE BEFORE I HAD TO COME BACK.

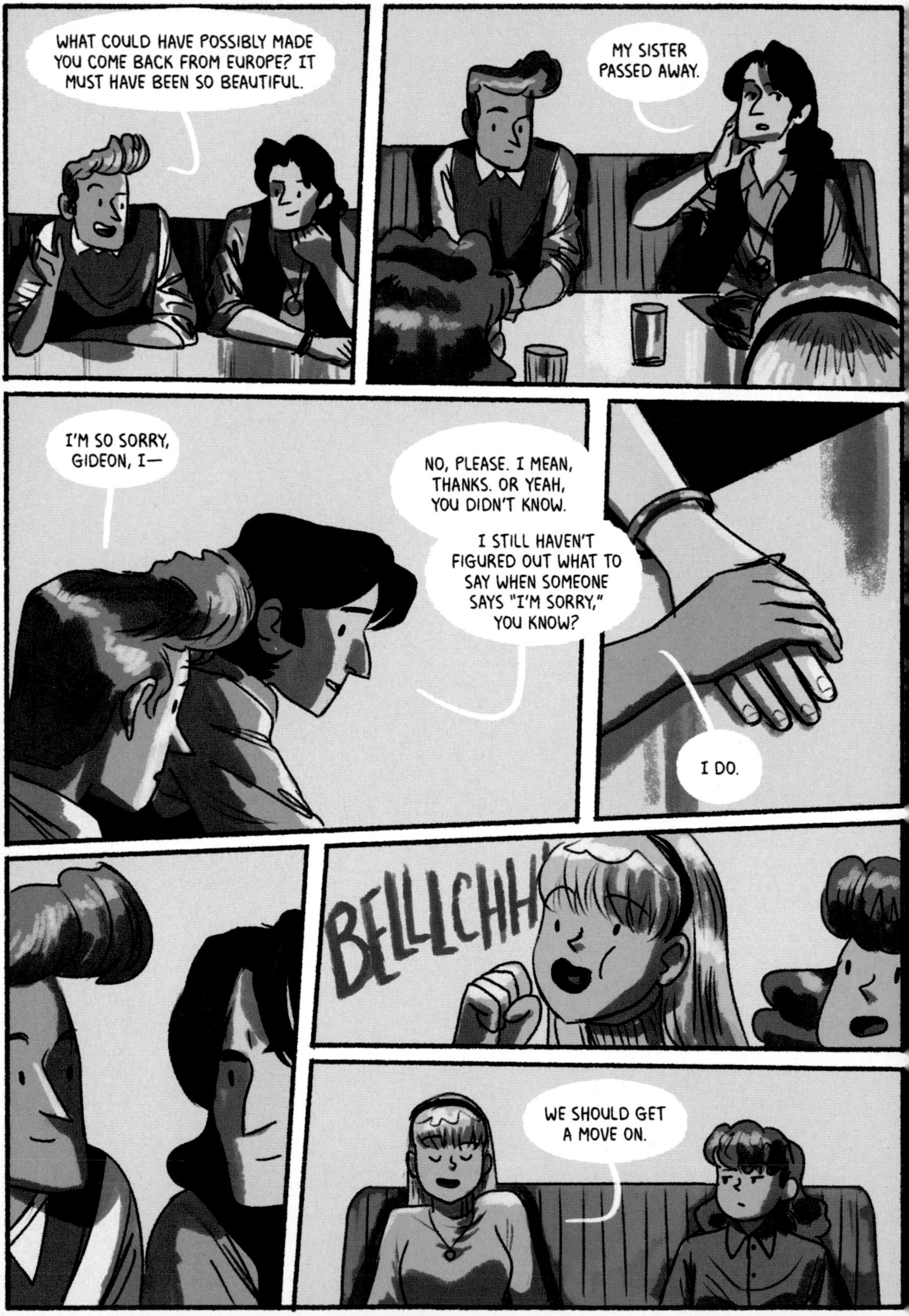
WHAT COULD HAVE POSSIBLY MADE YOU COME BACK FROM EUROPE? IT MUST HAVE BEEN SO BEAUTIFUL.
MY SISTER PASSED AWAY.
I'M SO SORRY, GIDEON, I—
NO, PLEASE. I MEAN, THANKS. OR YEAH, YOU DIDN'T KNOW.
I STILL HAVEN'T FIGURED OUT WHAT TO SAY WHEN SOMEONE SAYS "I'M SORRY," YOU KNOW?
I DO.
BELLLCHH
WE SHOULD GET A MOVE ON.

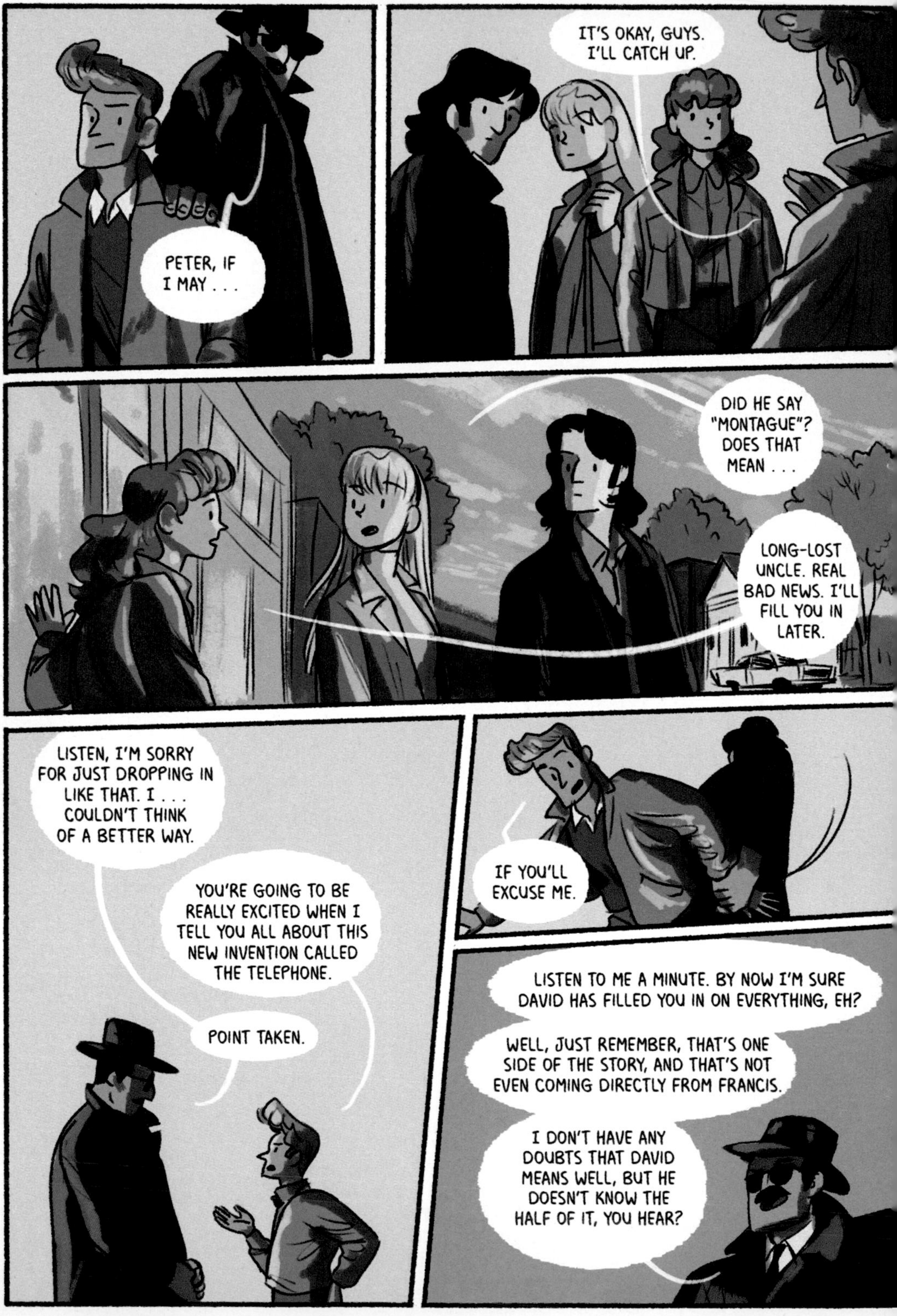
PETER, IF I MAY . . .
IT'S OKAY, GUYS. I'LL CATCH UP.
DID HE SAY "MONTAGUE"? DOES THAT MEAN . . .
LONG-LOST UNCLE. REAL BAD NEWS. I'LL FILL YOU IN LATER.
LISTEN, I'M SORRY FOR JUST DROPPING IN LIKE THAT. I . . . COULDN'T THINK OF A BETTER WAY.
YOU'RE GOING TO BE REALLY EXCITED WHEN I TELL YOU ALL ABOUT THIS NEW INVENTION CALLED THE TELEPHONE.
POINT TAKEN.
IF YOU'LL EXCUSE ME.
LISTEN TO ME A MINUTE. BY NOW I'M SURE DAVID HAS FILLED YOU IN ON EVERYTHING, EH?
WELL, JUST REMEMBER, THAT'S ONE SIDE OF THE STORY, AND THAT'S NOT EVEN COMING DIRECTLY FROM FRANCIS.
I DON'T HAVE ANY DOUBTS THAT DAVID MEANS WELL, BUT HE DOESN'T KNOW THE HALF OF IT, YOU HEAR?

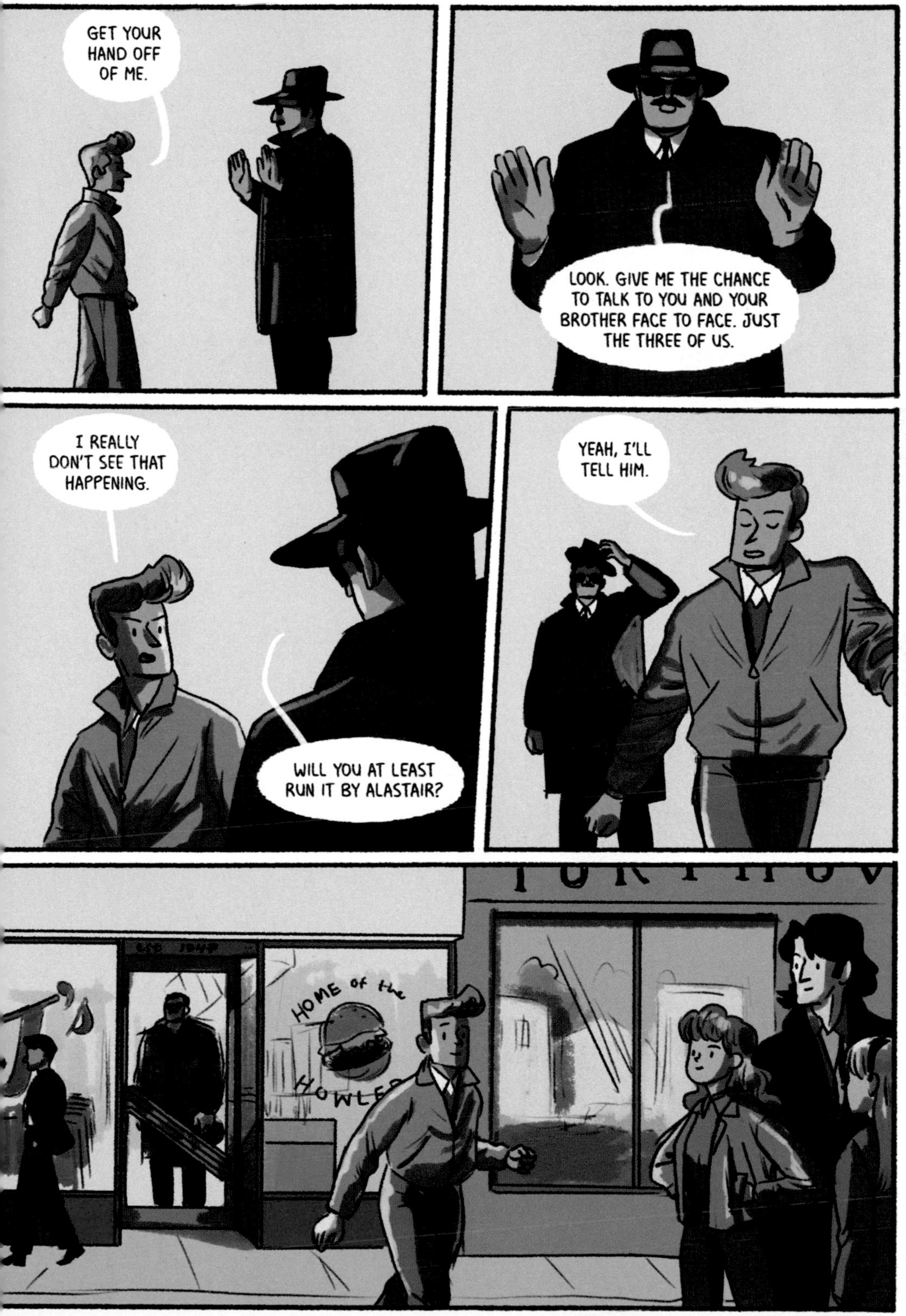
GET YOUR HAND OFF OF ME.
LOOK. GIVE ME THE CHANCE TO TALK TO YOU AND YOUR BROTHER FACE TO FACE. JUST THE THREE OF US.
I REALLY DON'T SEE THAT HAPPENING.
WILL YOU AT LEAST RUN IT BY ALASTAIR?
YEAH, I'LL TELL HIM.
HOME of the

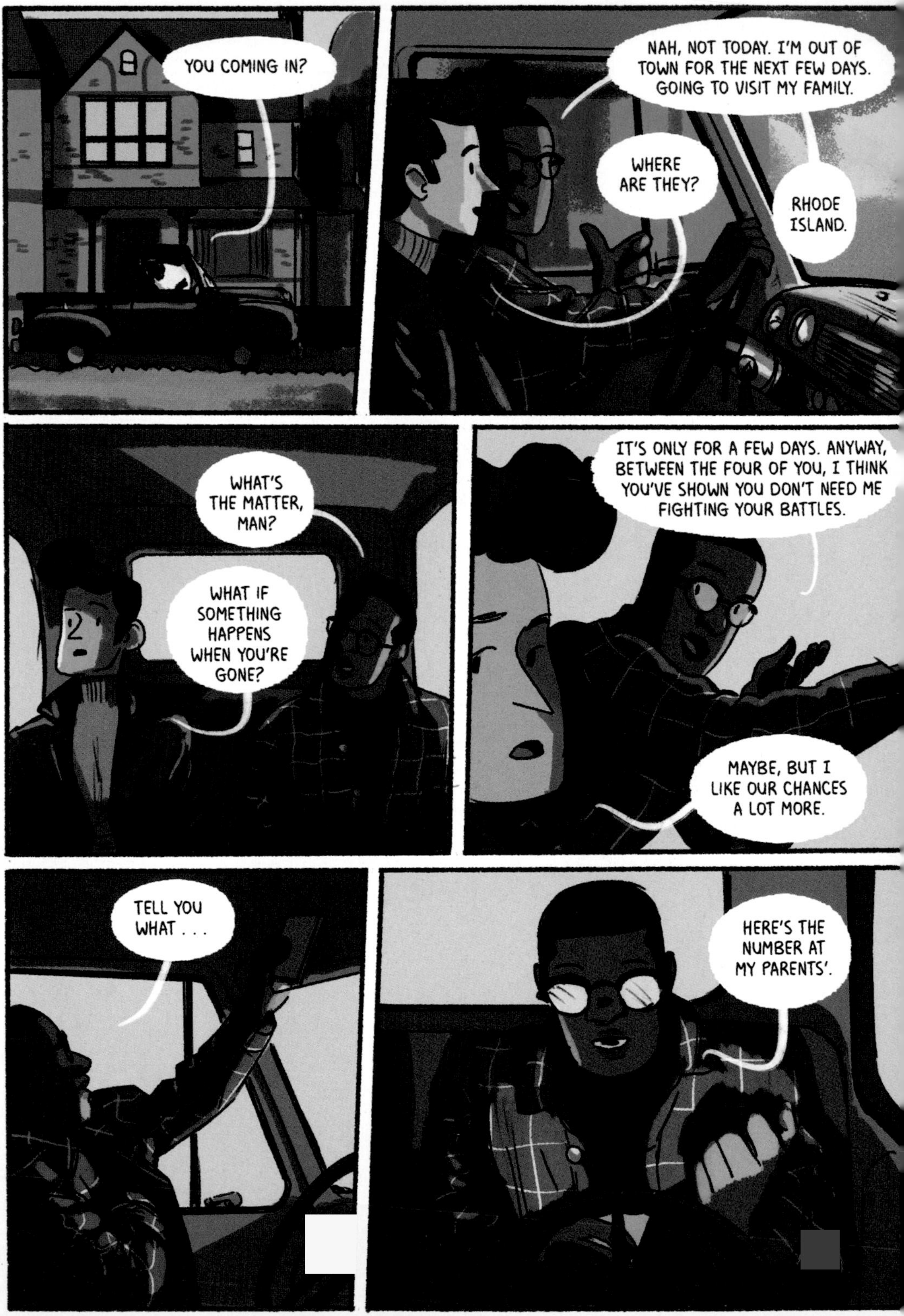
YOU COMING IN?
NAH, NOT TODAY. I'M OUT OF TOWN FOR THE NEXT FEW DAYS. GOING TO VISIT MY FAMILY.
WHERE ARE THEY?
RHODE ISLAND.
WHAT'S THE MATTER, MAN?
WHAT IF SOMETHING HAPPENS WHEN YOU'RE GONE?
IT'S ONLY FOR A FEW DAYS. ANYWAY, BETWEEN THE FOUR OF YOU, I THINK YOU'VE SHOWN YOU DON'T NEED ME FIGHTING YOUR BATTLES.
MAYBE, BUT I LIKE OUR CHANCES A LOT MORE.
TELL YOU WHAT . . .
HERE'S THE NUMBER AT MY PARENTS'.

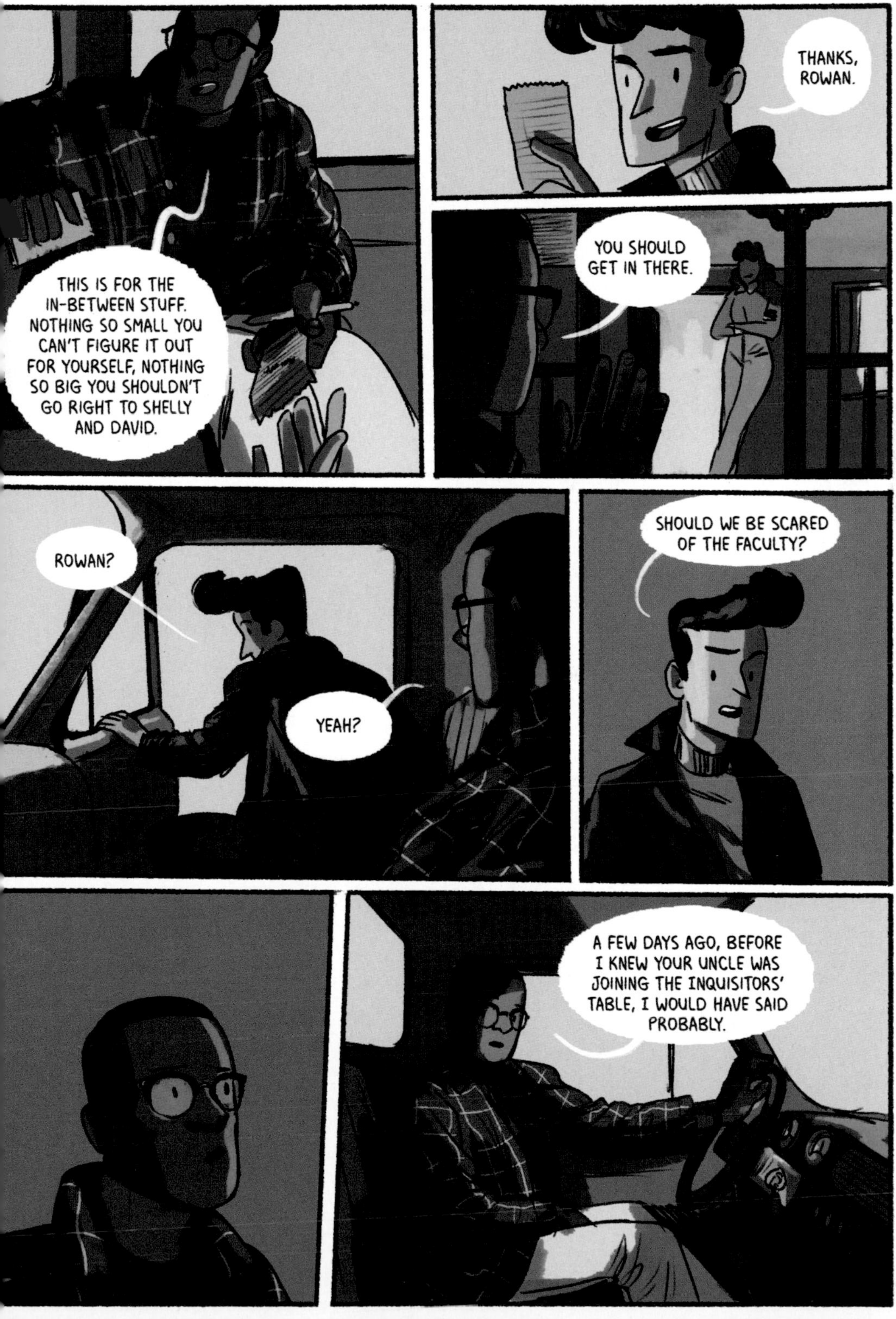
THIS IS FOR THE IN-BETWEEN STUFF. NOTHING SO SMALL YOU CAN'T FIGURE IT OUT FOR YOURSELF, NOTHING SO BIG YOU SHOULDN'T GO RIGHT TO SHELLY AND DAVID.
THANKS, ROWAN.
YOU SHOULD GET IN THERE.
ROWAN?
YEAH?
SHOULD WE BE SCARED OF THE FACULTY?
A FEW DAYS AGO, BEFORE I KNEW YOUR UNCLE WAS JOINING THE INQUISITORS' TABLE, I WOULD HAVE SAID PROBABLY.

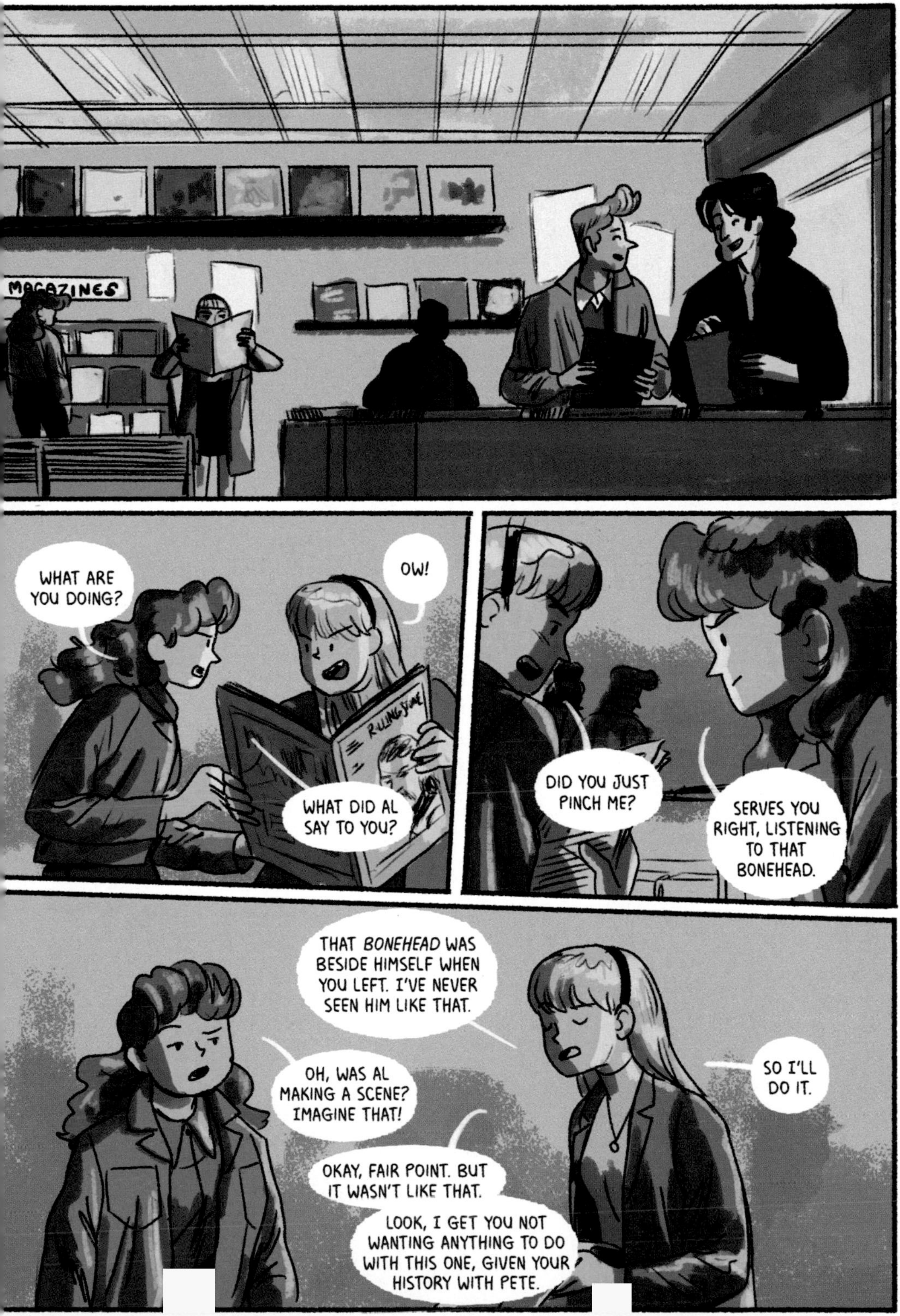
MAGAZINES
WHAT ARE YOU DOING?
OW!
WHAT DID AL SAY TO YOU?
DID YOU JUST PINCH ME?
SERVES YOU RIGHT, LISTENING TO THAT BONEHEAD.
THAT *BONEHEAD* WAS BESIDE HIMSELF WHEN YOU LEFT. I'VE NEVER SEEN HIM LIKE THAT.
OH, WAS AL MAKING A SCENE? IMAGINE THAT!
OKAY, FAIR POINT. BUT IT WASN'T LIKE THAT.
LOOK, I GET YOU NOT WANTING ANYTHING TO DO WITH THIS ONE, GIVEN YOUR HISTORY WITH PETE.
SO I'LL DO IT.

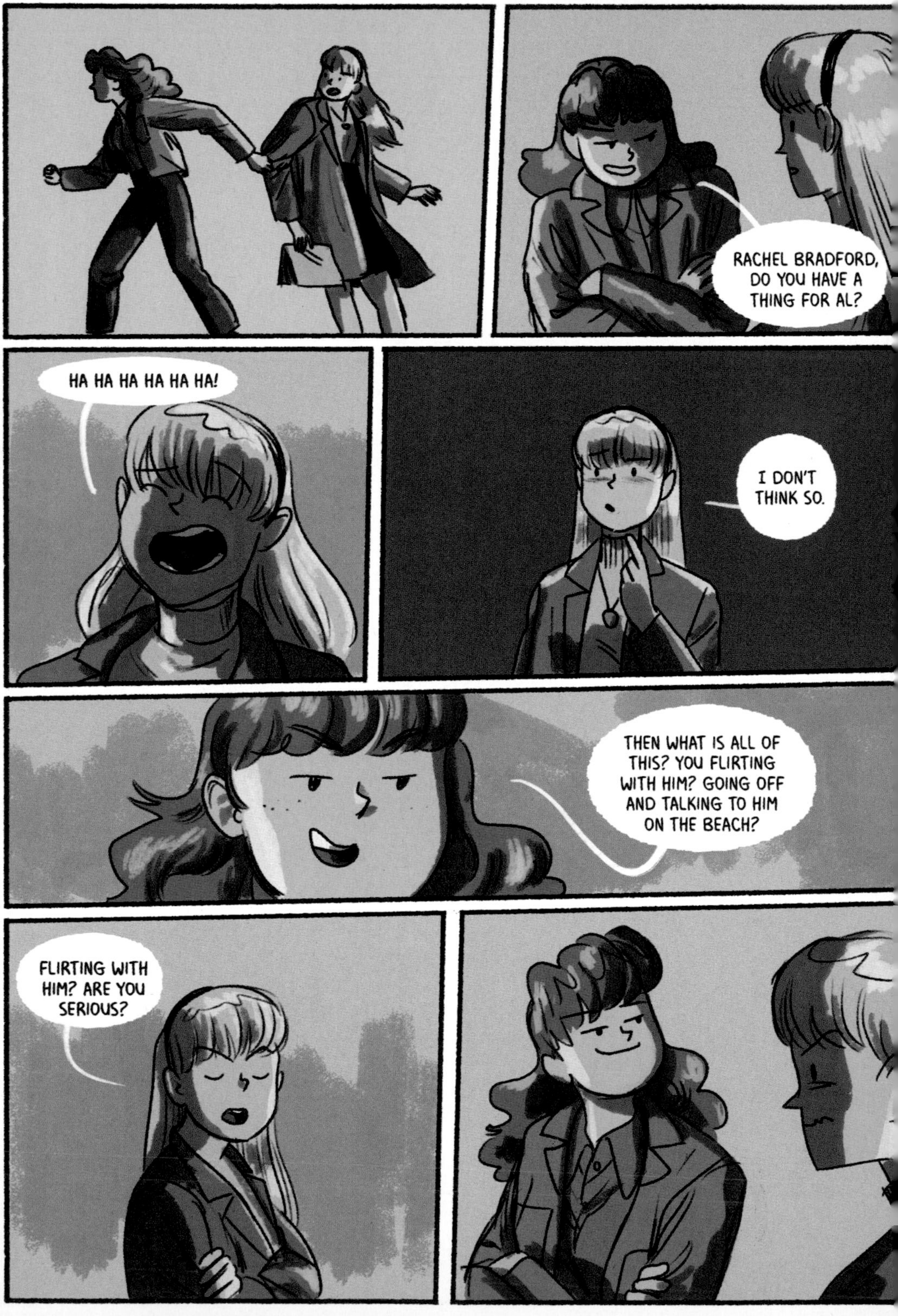
RACHEL BRADFORD, DO YOU HAVE A THING FOR AL?
HA HA HA HA HA HA!
I DON'T THINK SO.
THEN WHAT IS ALL OF THIS? YOU FLIRTING WITH HIM? GOING OFF AND TALKING TO HIM ON THE BEACH?
FLIRTING WITH HIM? ARE YOU SERIOUS?

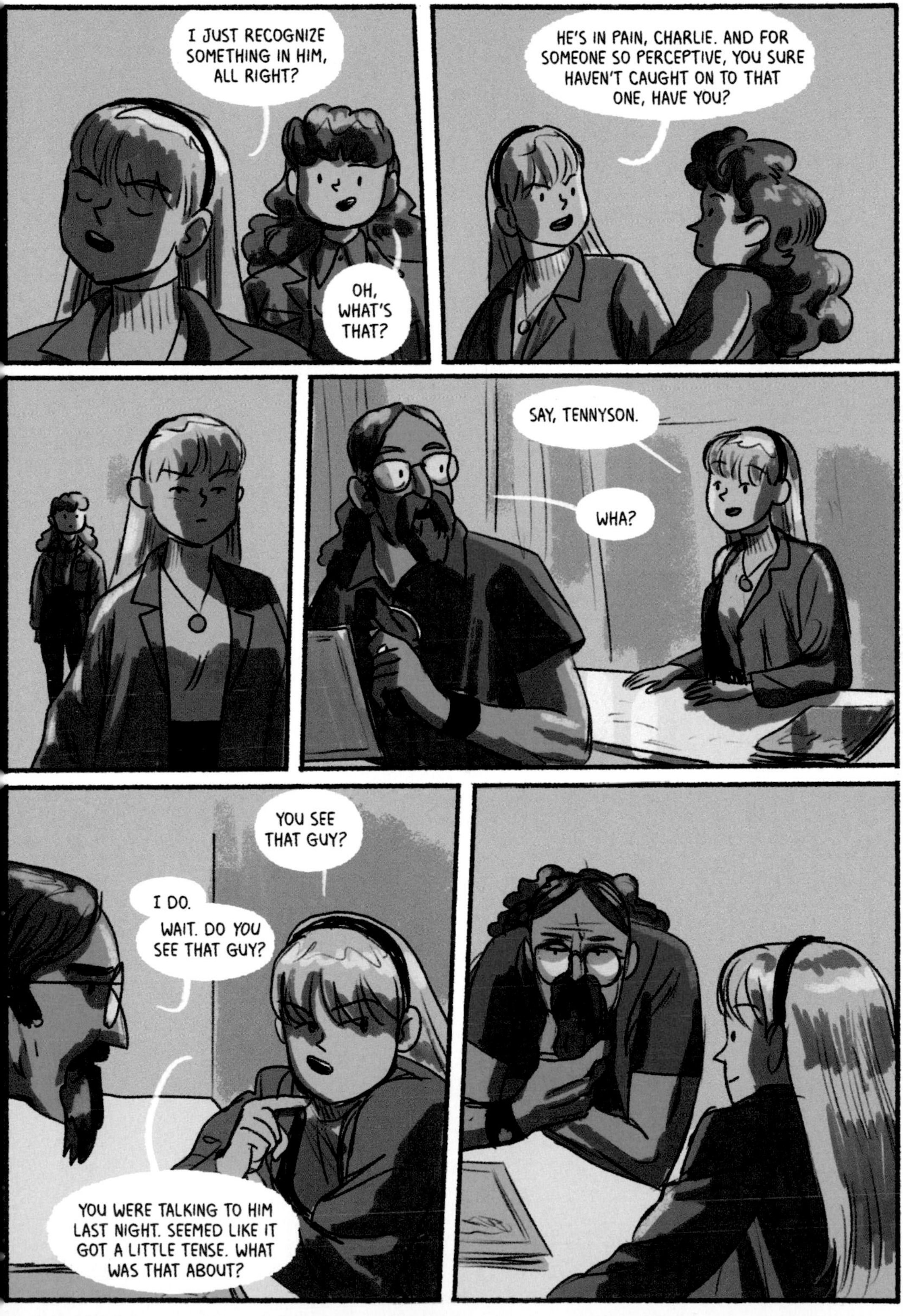
I JUST RECOGNIZE SOMETHING IN HIM, ALL RIGHT?
OH, WHAT'S THAT?
HE'S IN PAIN, CHARLIE. AND FOR SOMEONE SO PERCEPTIVE, YOU SURE HAVEN'T CAUGHT ON TO THAT ONE, HAVE YOU?
SAY, TENNYSON.
WHA?
YOU SEE THAT GUY?
I DO.
WAIT. DO *YOU* SEE THAT GUY?
YOU WERE TALKING TO HIM LAST NIGHT. SEEMED LIKE IT GOT A LITTLE TENSE. WHAT WAS THAT ABOUT?

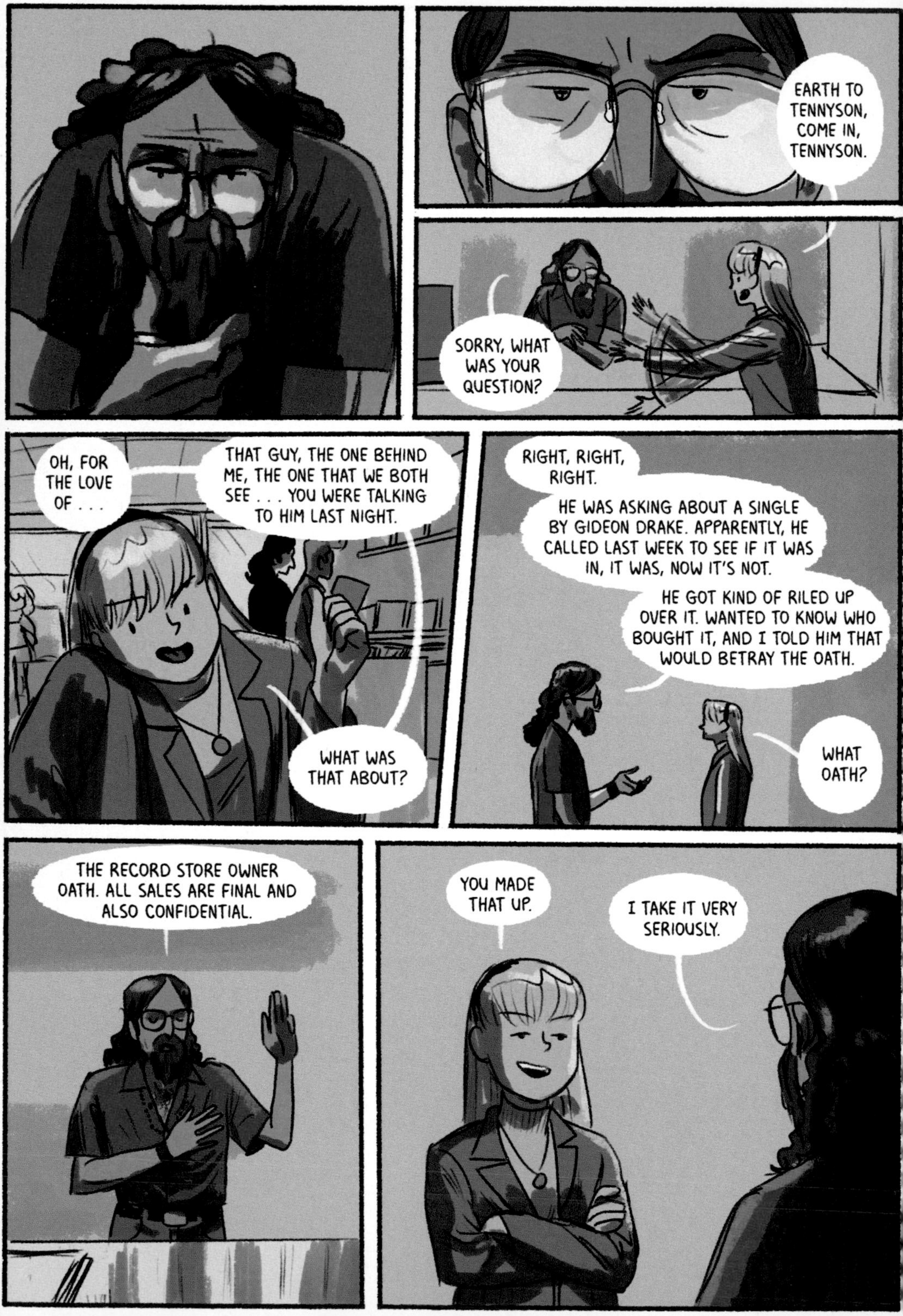
EARTH TO TENNYSON, COME IN, TENNYSON.
SORRY, WHAT WAS YOUR QUESTION?
OH, FOR THE LOVE OF . . .
THAT GUY, THE ONE BEHIND ME, THE ONE THAT WE BOTH SEE . . . YOU WERE TALKING TO HIM LAST NIGHT.
WHAT WAS THAT ABOUT?
RIGHT, RIGHT, RIGHT.
HE WAS ASKING ABOUT A SINGLE BY GIDEON DRAKE. APPARENTLY, HE CALLED LAST WEEK TO SEE IF IT WAS IN, IT WAS, NOW IT'S NOT.
HE GOT KIND OF RILED UP OVER IT. WANTED TO KNOW WHO BOUGHT IT, AND I TOLD HIM THAT WOULD BETRAY THE OATH.
WHAT OATH?
THE RECORD STORE OWNER OATH. ALL SALES ARE FINAL AND ALSO CONFIDENTIAL.
YOU MADE THAT UP.
I TAKE IT VERY SERIOUSLY.

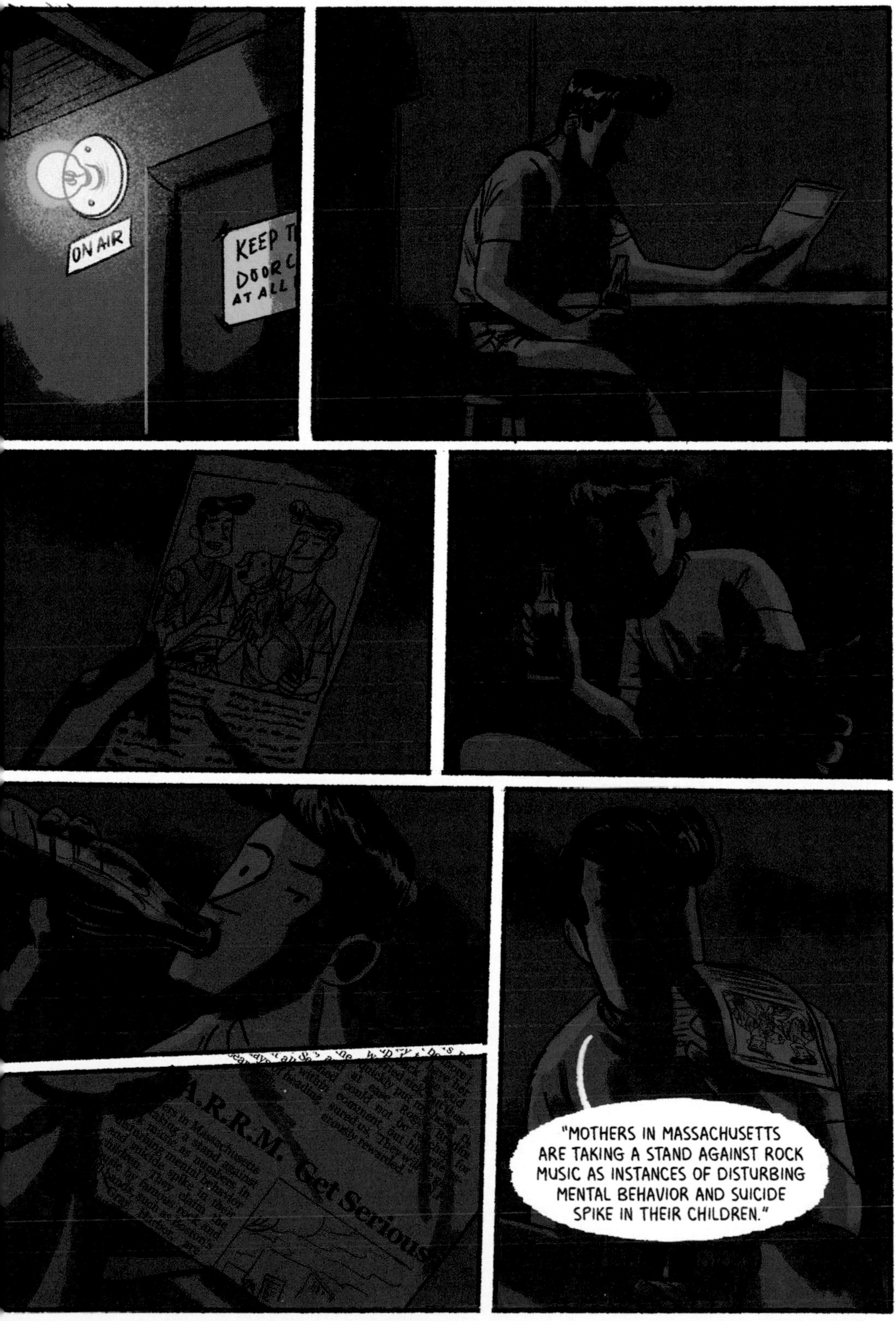
ON AIR
KEEP T
DOOR C
AT ALL
A.R.R.M. Get Serious
"MOTHERS IN MASSACHUSETTS ARE TAKING A STAND AGAINST ROCK MUSIC AS INSTANCES OF DISTURBING MENTAL BEHAVIOR AND SUICIDE SPIKE IN THEIR CHILDREN."

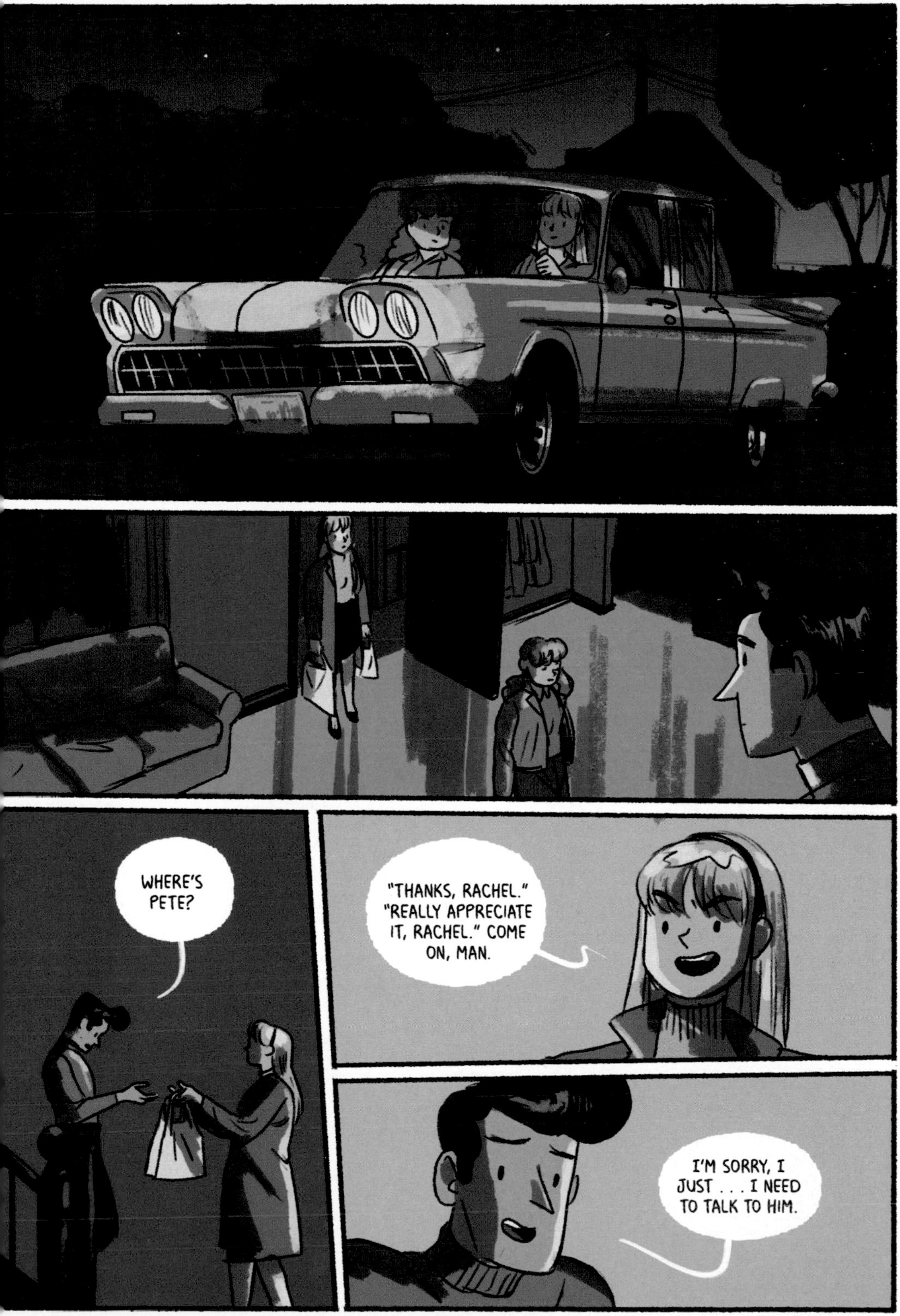
WHERE'S PETE?
"THANKS, RACHEL." "REALLY APPRECIATE IT, RACHEL." COME ON, MAN.
I'M SORRY, I JUST . . . I NEED TO TALK TO HIM.

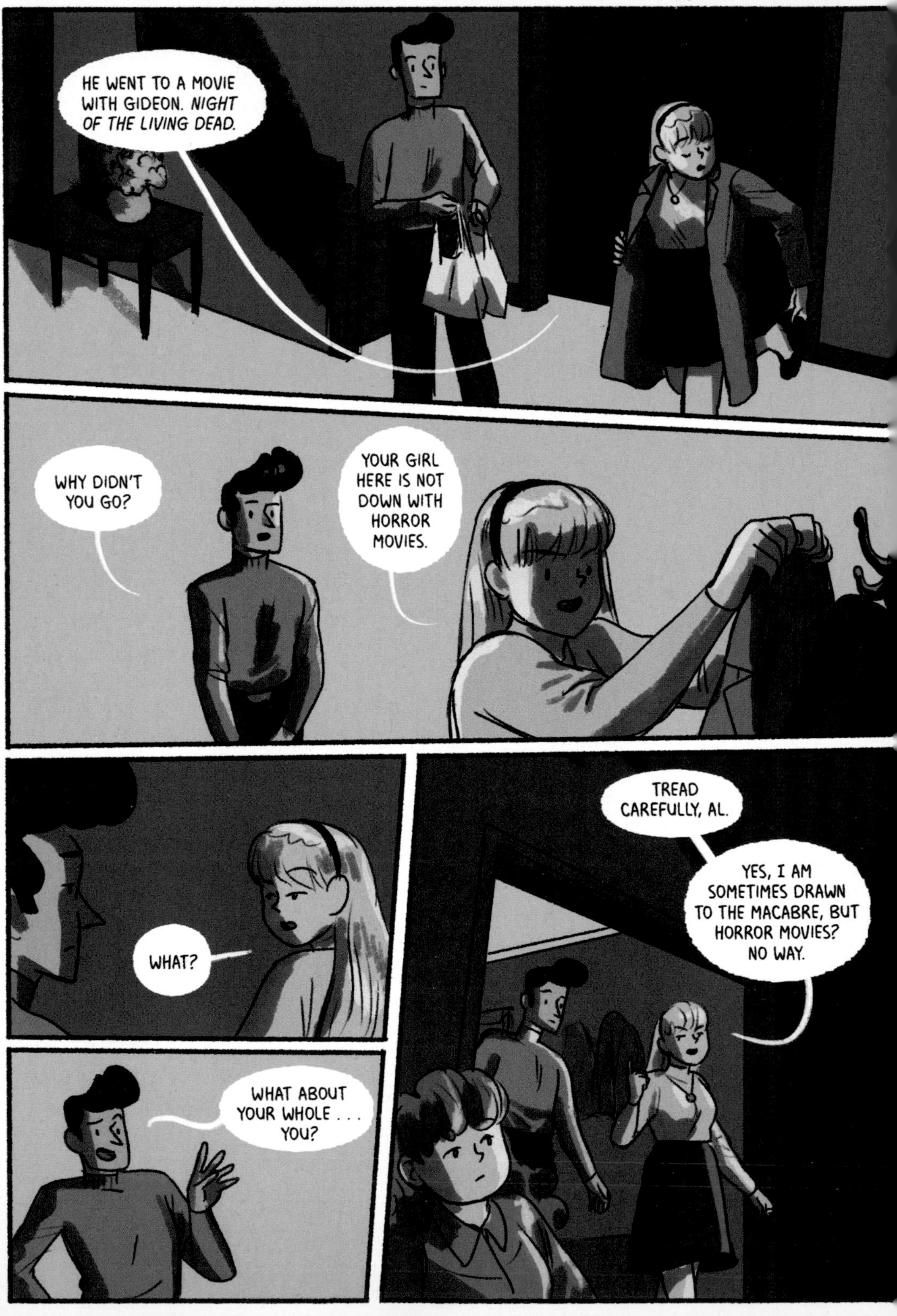
HE WENT TO A MOVIE WITH GIDEON. *NIGHT OF THE LIVING DEAD.*
WHY DIDN'T YOU GO?
YOUR GIRL HERE IS NOT DOWN WITH HORROR MOVIES.
WHAT?
WHAT ABOUT YOUR WHOLE . . . YOU?
TREAD CAREFULLY, AL.
YES, I AM SOMETIMES DRAWN TO THE MACABRE, BUT HORROR MOVIES? NO WAY.

AND WHY DIDN'T YOU GO?

SEEN IT.

LOOK AT THIS.

THIS IS A NEW LEVEL OF VANITY, AL. GREETING YOUR GUESTS WITH NEWSPAPER ARTICLES YOU'RE FEATURED IN?

'Hot Dog' Teen Sleuths Find Missing Dog

M.A.R.R.M. Get Serious in Boston

NO, LOOK AT THIS.

"A SOUTH BOSTON MOTHER BELIEVES THAT ONE HARD-TO-FIND RECORD IN PARTICULAR IS TO BLAME FOR THE DEATH OF HER SON. THAT IS THE FIRST SOLO PRESSING BY GRAY HARBOR SINGER GIDEON DRAKE.

DRAKE'S SINGLE HAS GAINED A CERTAIN AMOUNT OF NOTORIETY FOR BEING AN ELUSIVE COLLECTOR'S EDITION. THIS RECORD, SHE SAYS, WAS THE LAST SONG HER SON PLAYED RIGHT BEFORE TAKING HIS OWN LIFE UPON RETURNING HOME FROM DRAKE'S ONE AND ONLY SOLO SHOW THAT NIGHT."

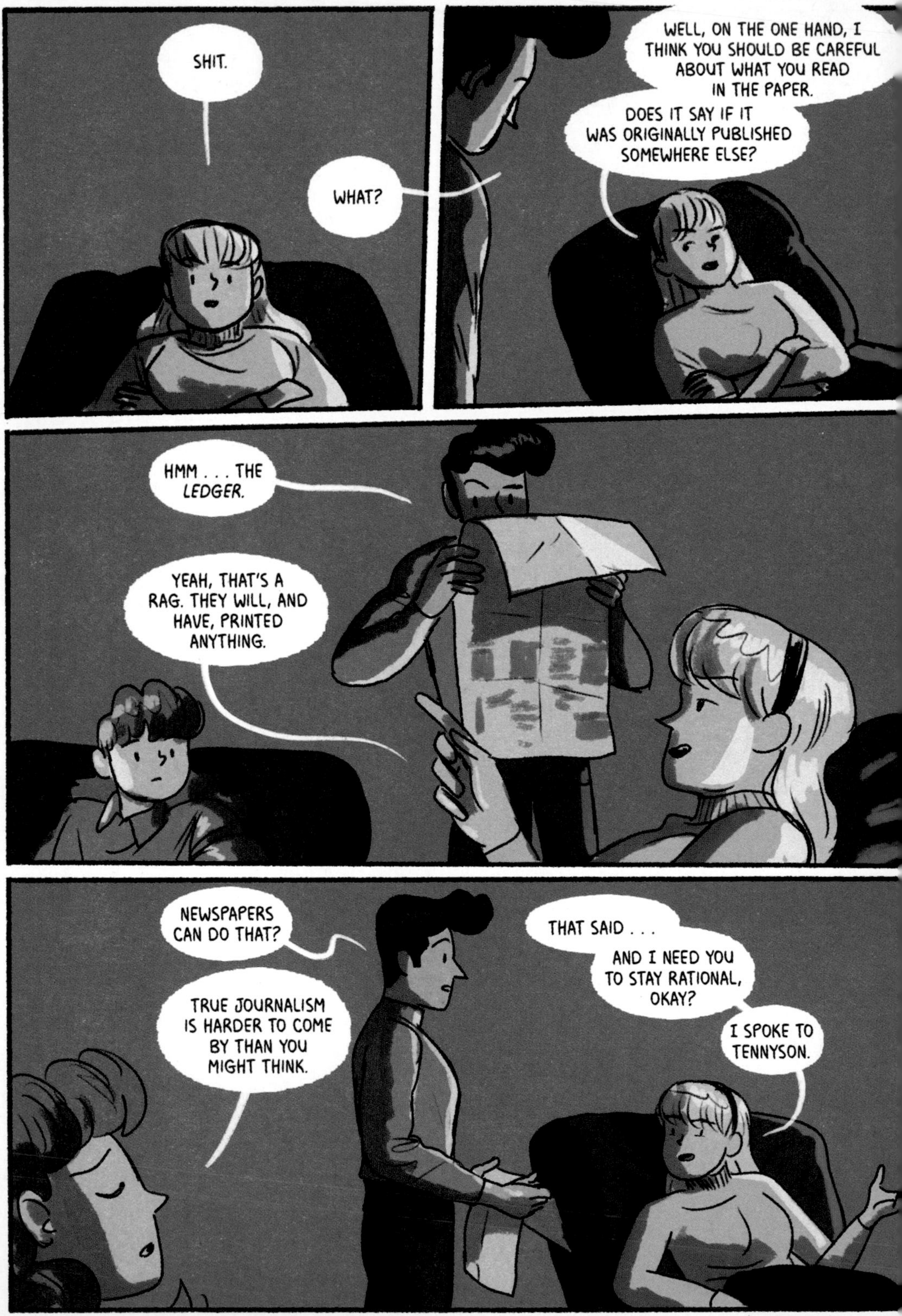
SHIT.
WHAT?
WELL, ON THE ONE HAND, I THINK YOU SHOULD BE CAREFUL ABOUT WHAT YOU READ IN THE PAPER.
DOES IT SAY IF IT WAS ORIGINALLY PUBLISHED SOMEWHERE ELSE?
HMM . . . THE *LEDGER.*
YEAH, THAT'S A RAG. THEY WILL, AND HAVE, PRINTED ANYTHING.
NEWSPAPERS CAN DO THAT?
TRUE JOURNALISM IS HARDER TO COME BY THAN YOU MIGHT THINK.
THAT SAID . . .
AND I NEED YOU TO STAY RATIONAL, OKAY?
I SPOKE TO TENNYSON.

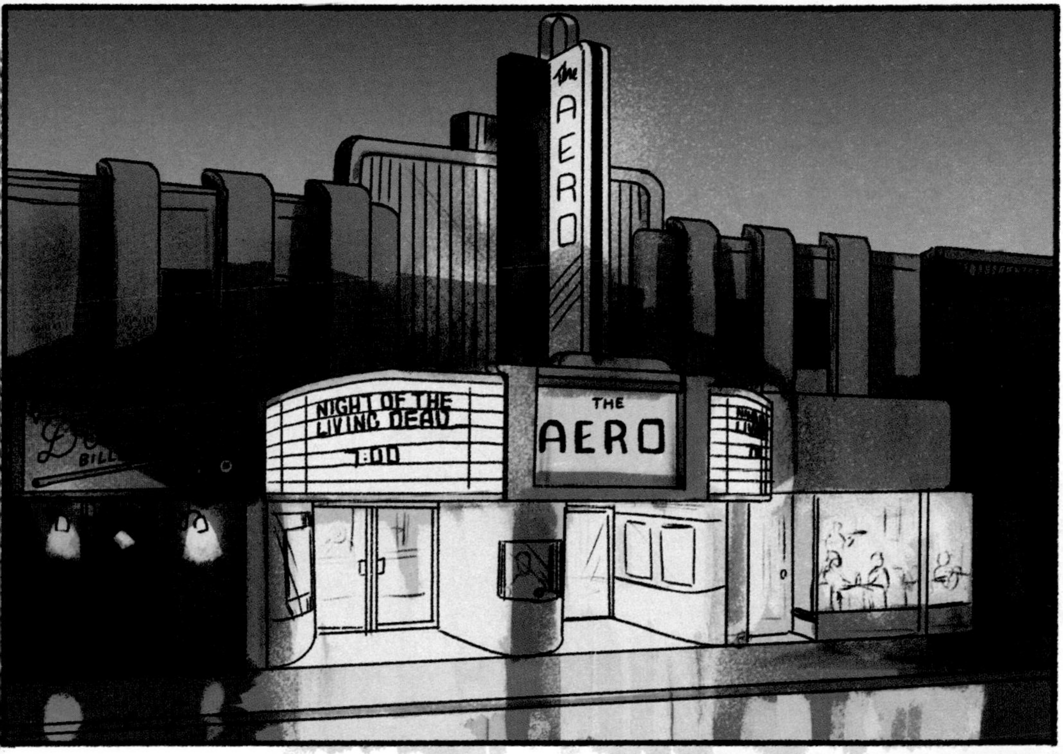
the AERO
NIGHT OF THE LIVING DEAD
7:00
THE AERO

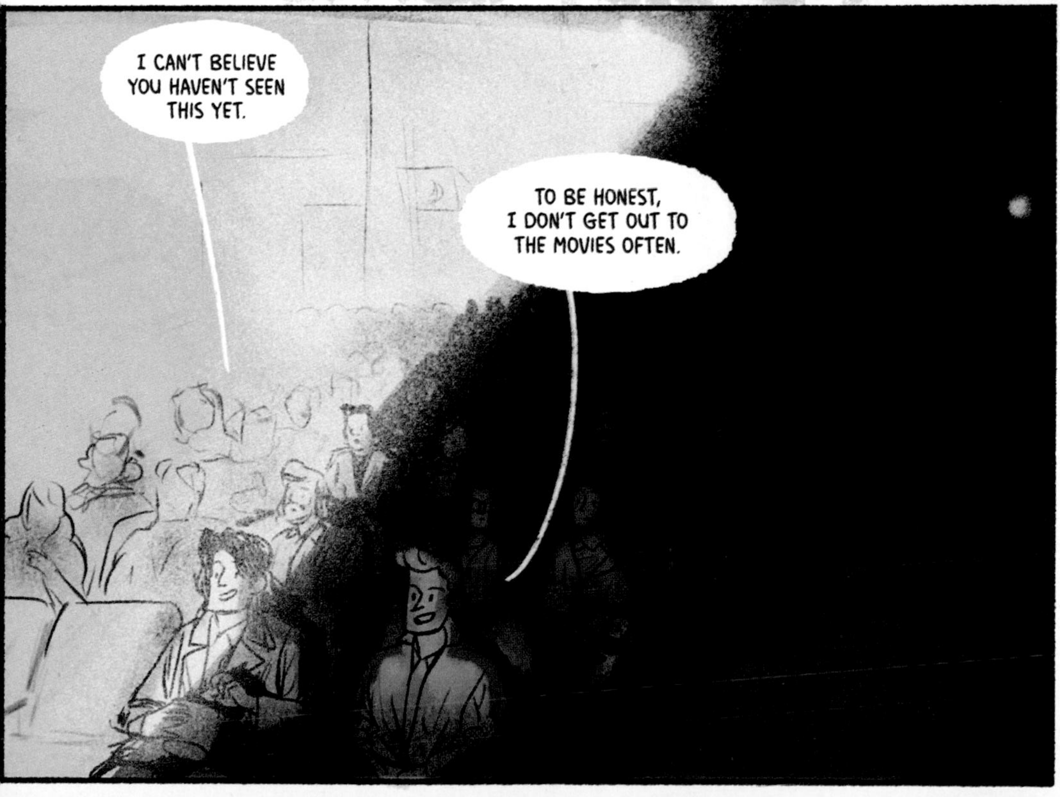
I CAN'T BELIEVE YOU HAVEN'T SEEN THIS YET.
TO BE HONEST, I DON'T GET OUT TO THE MOVIES OFTEN.

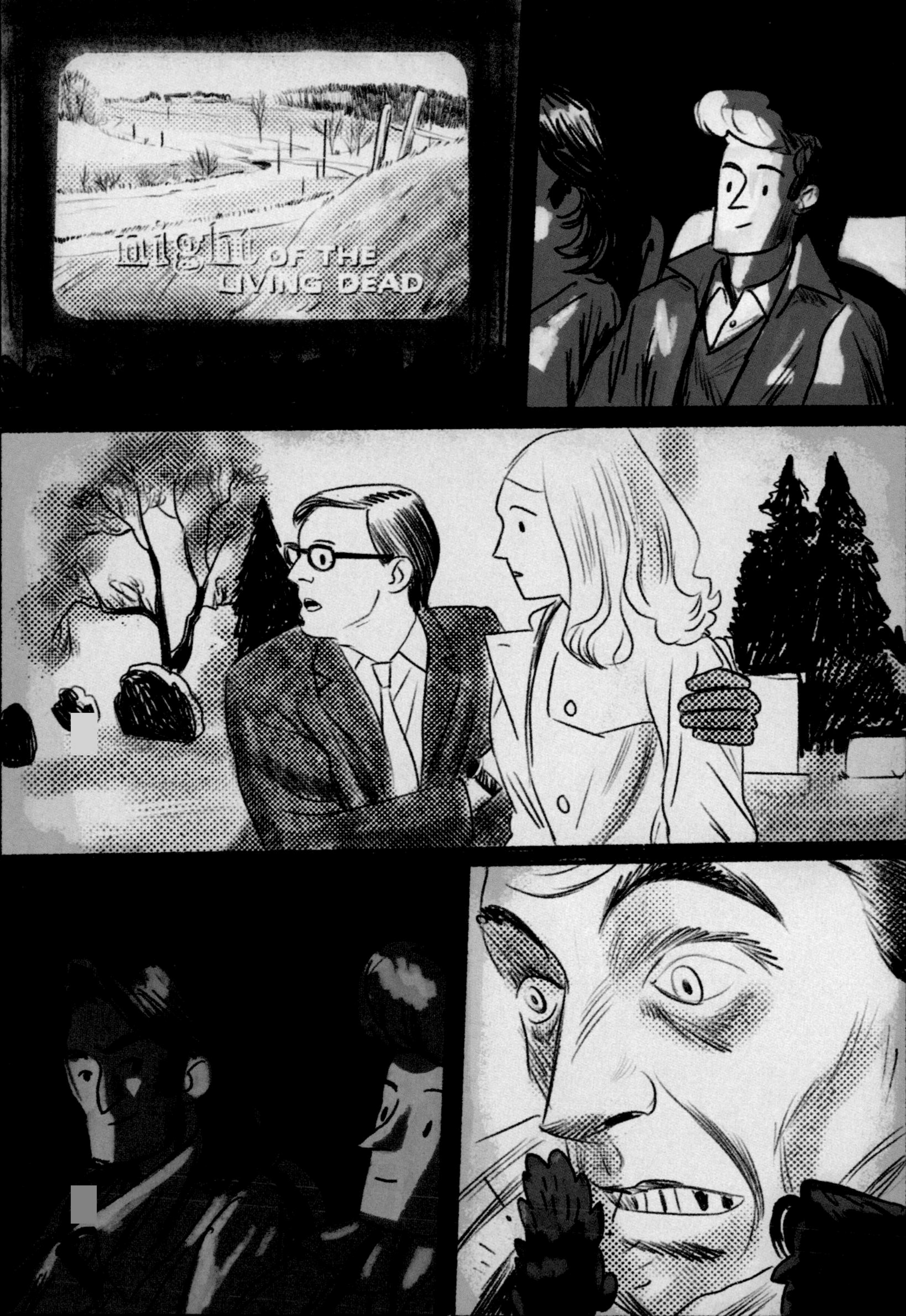
night OF THE
LIVING DEAD

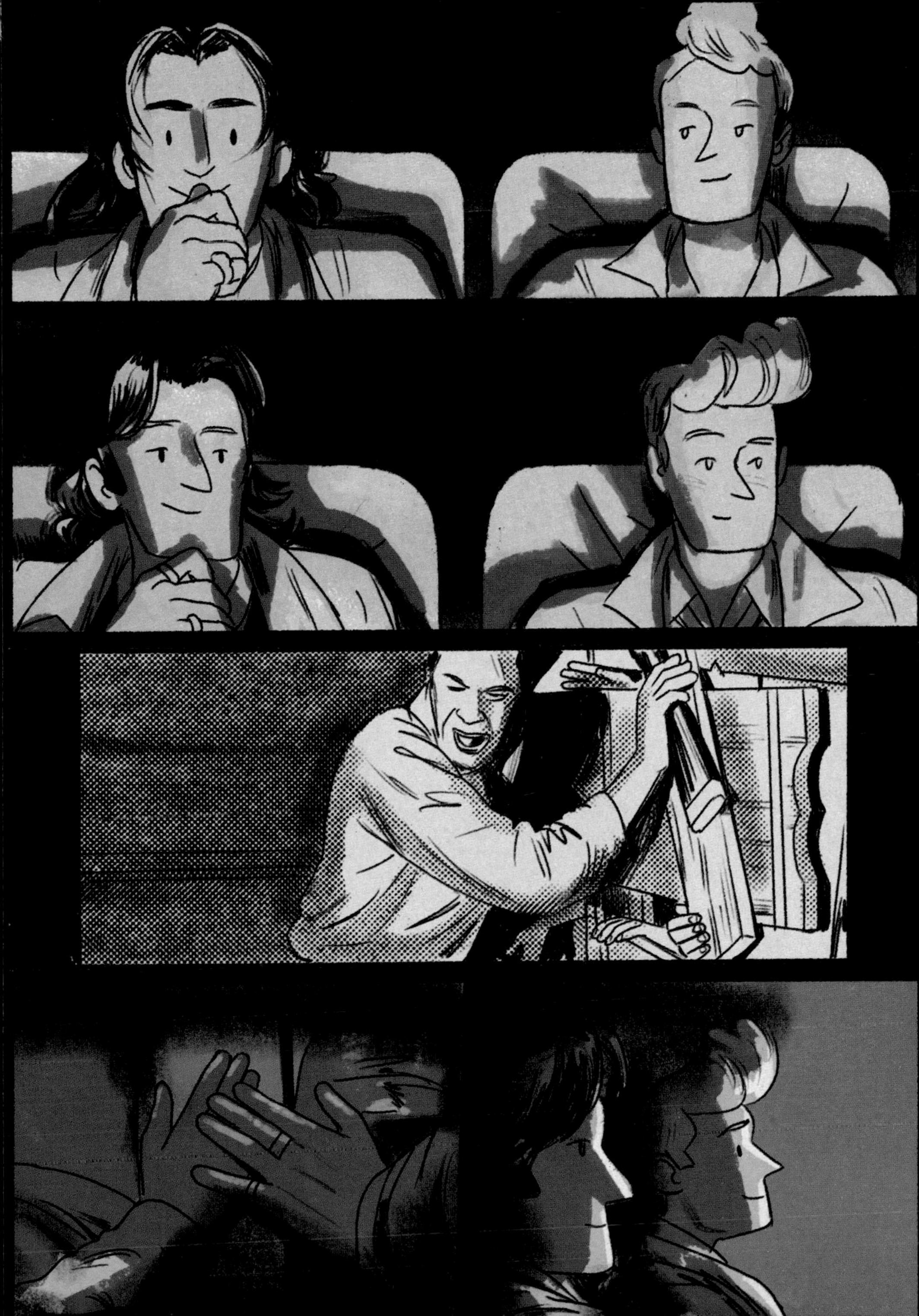

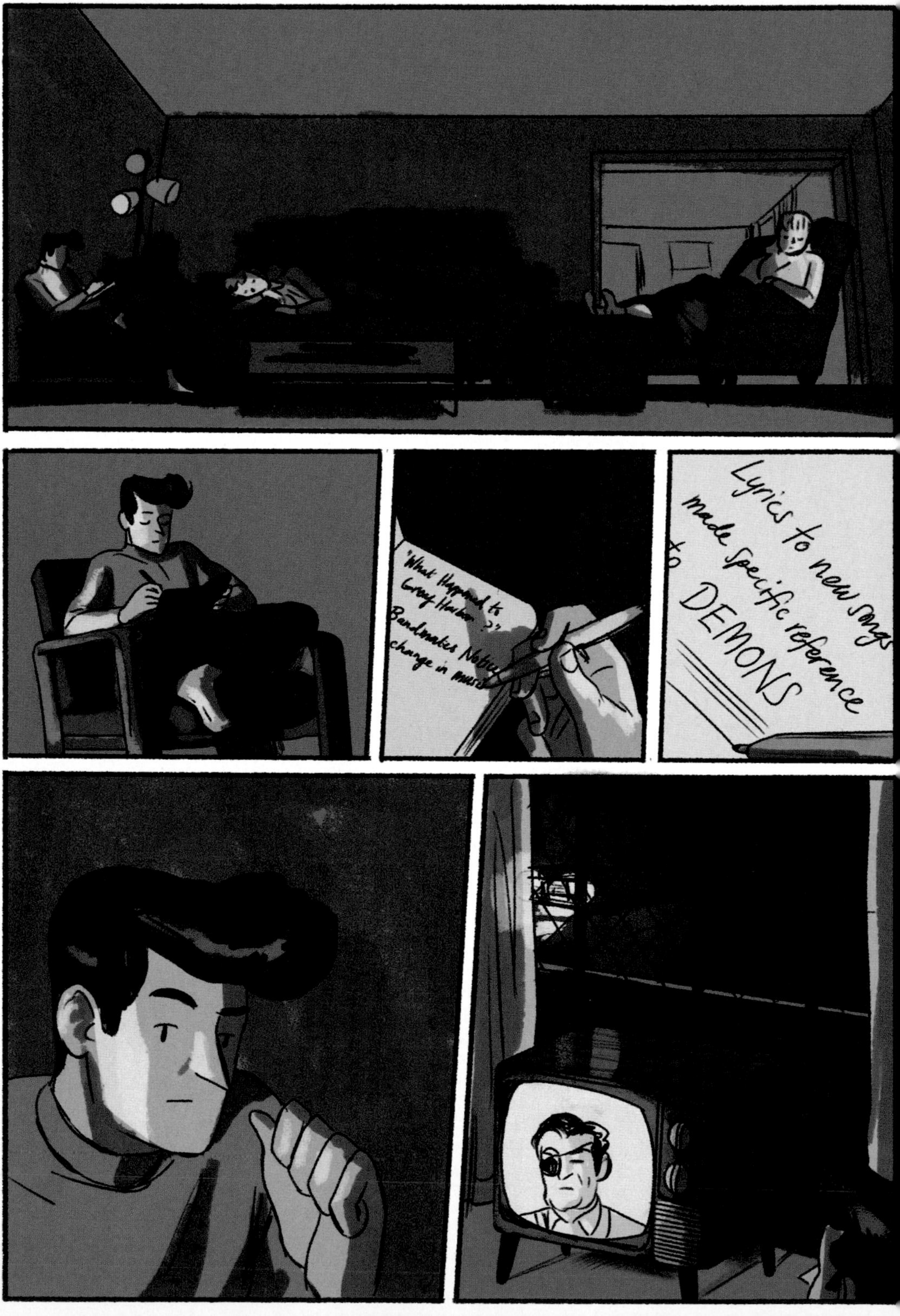
"What Happened to
Grey Harbor?"
Bandmakes Notic
change in musi
Lyrics to new songs
made specific reference
to DEMONS

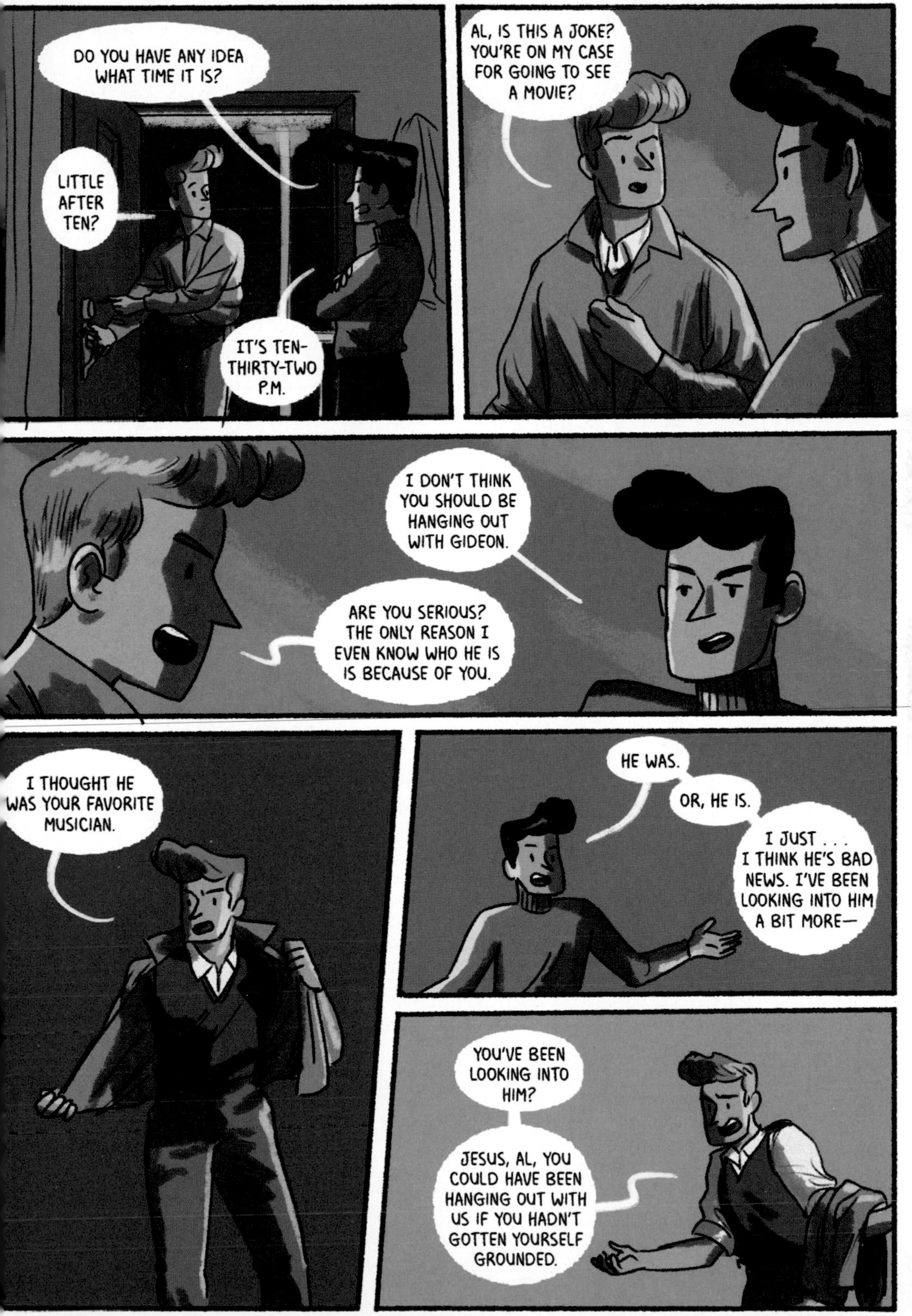
DO YOU HAVE ANY IDEA WHAT TIME IT IS?
LITTLE AFTER TEN?
IT'S TEN-THIRTY-TWO P.M.
AL, IS THIS A JOKE? YOU'RE ON MY CASE FOR GOING TO SEE A MOVIE?
I DON'T THINK YOU SHOULD BE HANGING OUT WITH GIDEON.
ARE YOU SERIOUS? THE ONLY REASON I EVEN KNOW WHO HE IS IS BECAUSE OF YOU.
I THOUGHT HE WAS YOUR FAVORITE MUSICIAN.
HE WAS.
OR, HE IS.
I JUST . . . I THINK HE'S BAD NEWS. I'VE BEEN LOOKING INTO HIM A BIT MORE—
YOU'VE BEEN LOOKING INTO HIM?
JESUS, AL, YOU COULD HAVE BEEN HANGING OUT WITH US IF YOU HADN'T GOTTEN YOURSELF GROUNDED.

CHAPTER 4

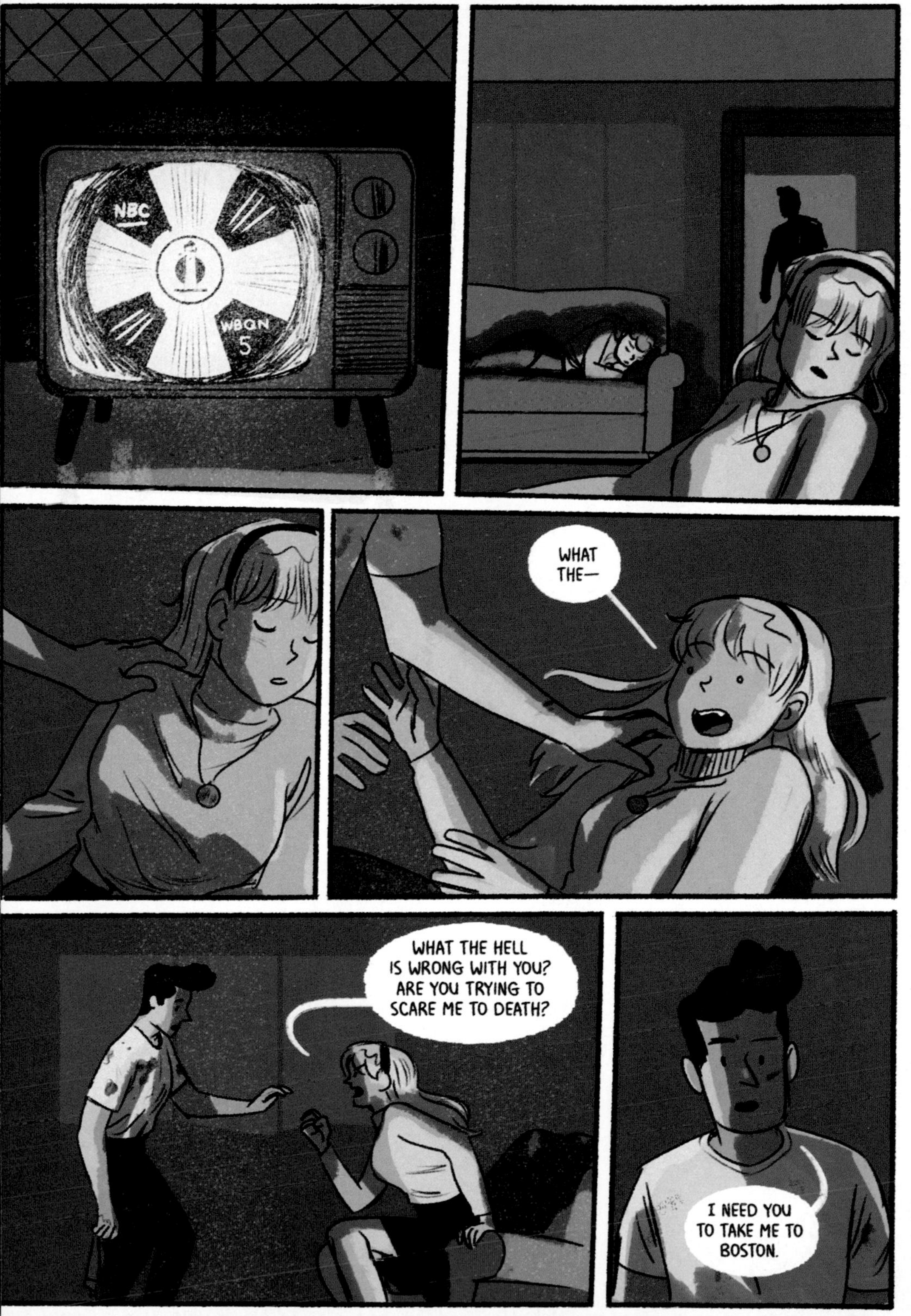
NBC
WBQN
5
WHAT THE—
WHAT THE HELL IS WRONG WITH YOU? ARE YOU TRYING TO SCARE ME TO DEATH?
I NEED YOU TO TAKE ME TO BOSTON.

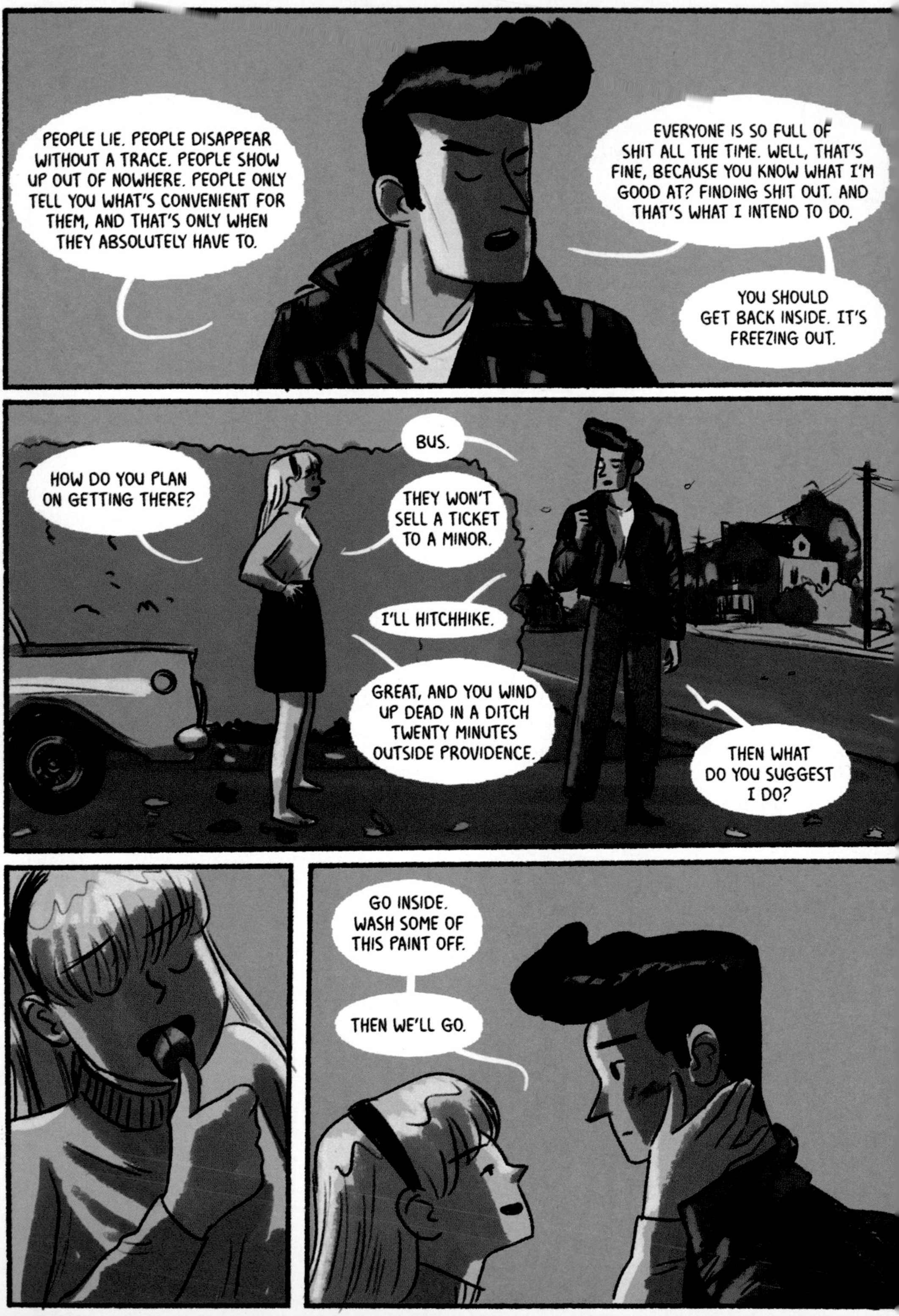
PEOPLE LIE. PEOPLE DISAPPEAR WITHOUT A TRACE. PEOPLE SHOW UP OUT OF NOWHERE. PEOPLE ONLY TELL YOU WHAT'S CONVENIENT FOR THEM, AND THAT'S ONLY WHEN THEY ABSOLUTELY HAVE TO.
EVERYONE IS SO FULL OF SHIT ALL THE TIME. WELL, THAT'S FINE, BECAUSE YOU KNOW WHAT I'M GOOD AT? FINDING SHIT OUT. AND THAT'S WHAT I INTEND TO DO.
YOU SHOULD GET BACK INSIDE. IT'S FREEZING OUT.
HOW DO YOU PLAN ON GETTING THERE?
BUS.
THEY WON'T SELL A TICKET TO A MINOR.
I'LL HITCHHIKE.
GREAT, AND YOU WIND UP DEAD IN A DITCH TWENTY MINUTES OUTSIDE PROVIDENCE.
THEN WHAT DO YOU SUGGEST I DO?
GO INSIDE. WASH SOME OF THIS PAINT OFF.
THEN WE'LL GO.

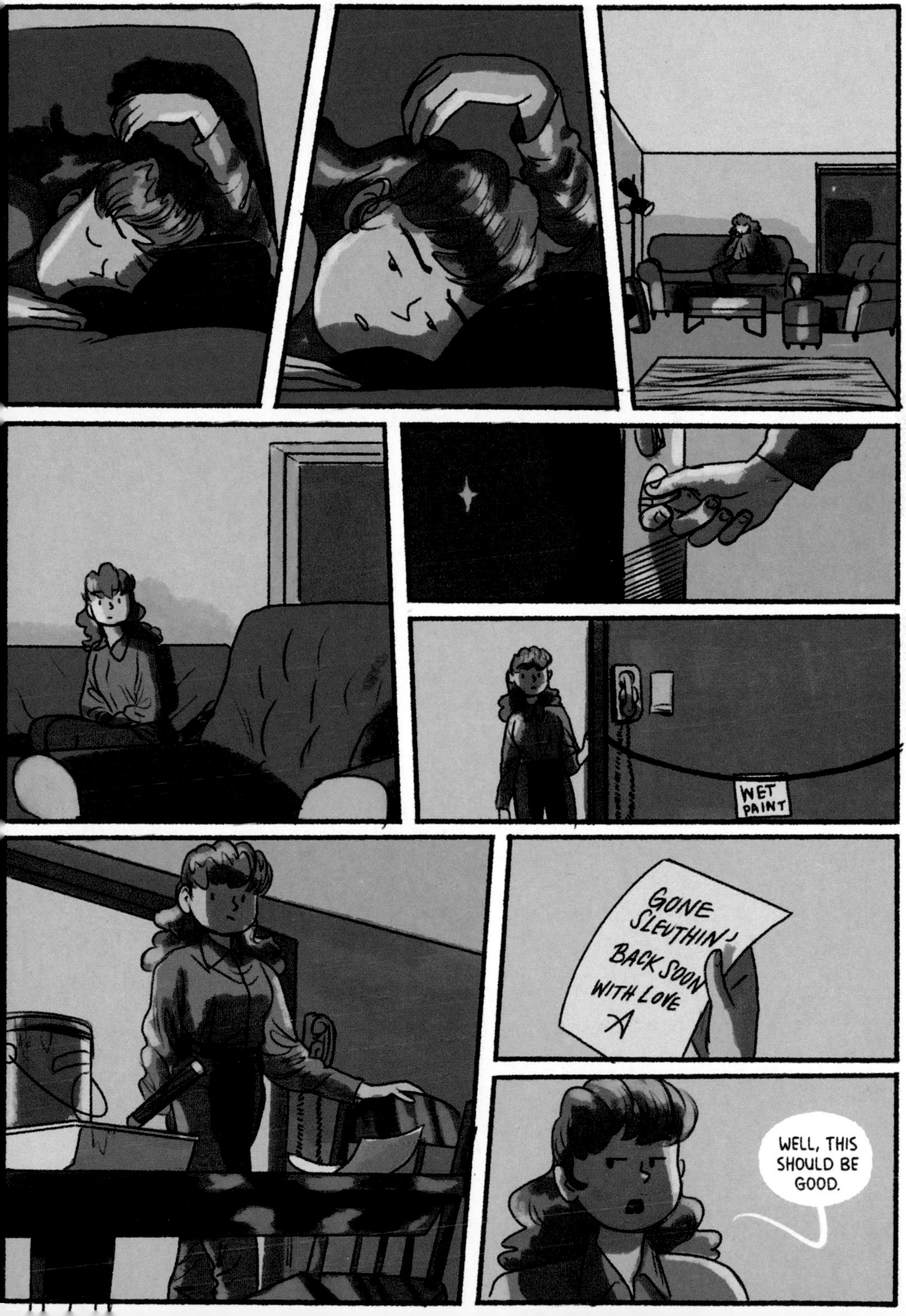
WET PAINT
GONE SLEUTHIN' BACK SOON WITH LOVE A
WELL, THIS SHOULD BE GOOD.

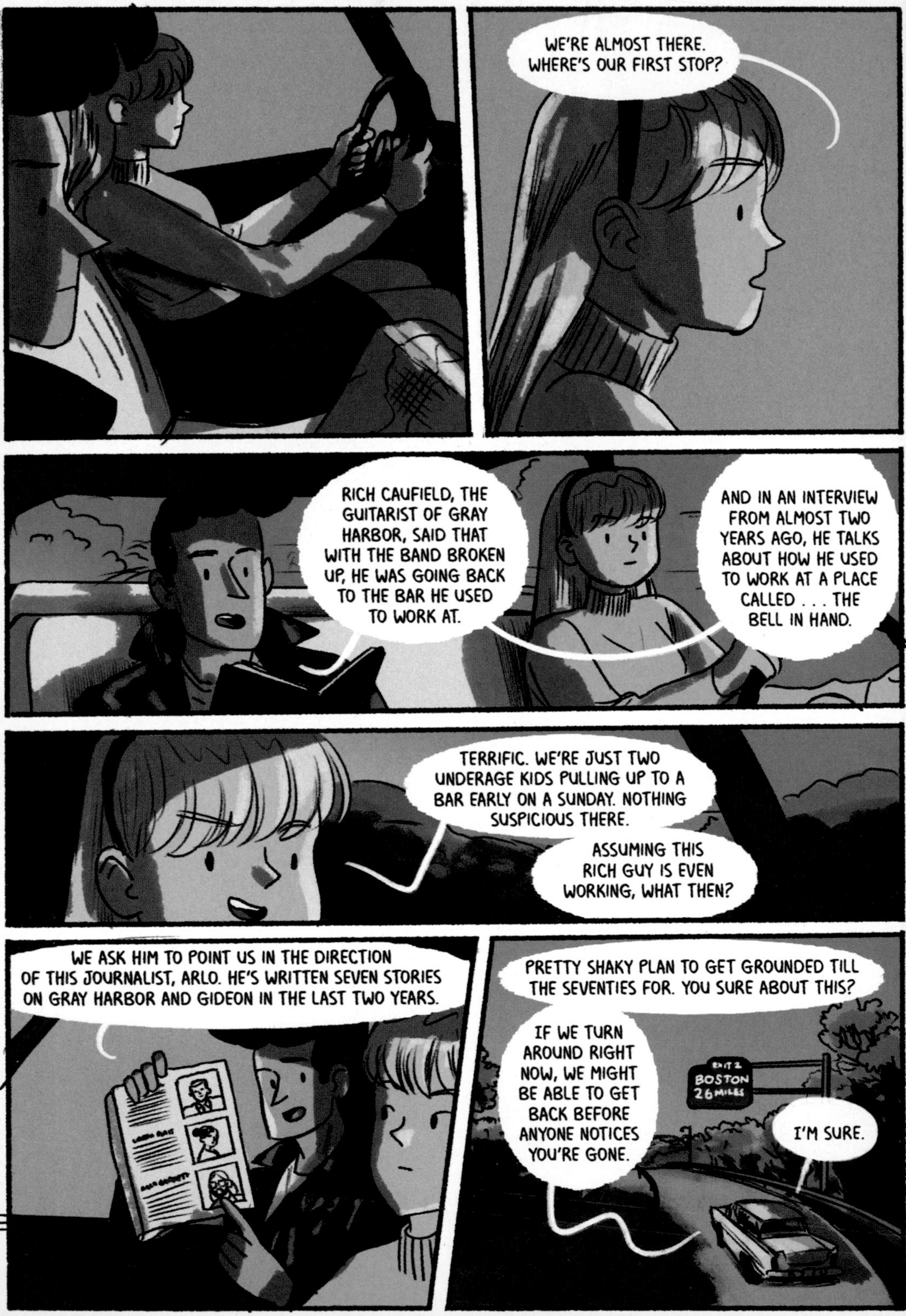
WE'RE ALMOST THERE. WHERE'S OUR FIRST STOP?
RICH CAUFIELD, THE GUITARIST OF GRAY HARBOR, SAID THAT WITH THE BAND BROKEN UP, HE WAS GOING BACK TO THE BAR HE USED TO WORK AT.
AND IN AN INTERVIEW FROM ALMOST TWO YEARS AGO, HE TALKS ABOUT HOW HE USED TO WORK AT A PLACE CALLED . . . THE BELL IN HAND.
TERRIFIC. WE'RE JUST TWO UNDERAGE KIDS PULLING UP TO A BAR EARLY ON A SUNDAY. NOTHING SUSPICIOUS THERE.
ASSUMING THIS RICH GUY IS EVEN WORKING, WHAT THEN?
WE ASK HIM TO POINT US IN THE DIRECTION OF THIS JOURNALIST, ARLO. HE'S WRITTEN SEVEN STORIES ON GRAY HARBOR AND GIDEON IN THE LAST TWO YEARS.
PRETTY SHAKY PLAN TO GET GROUNDED TILL THE SEVENTIES FOR. YOU SURE ABOUT THIS?
IF WE TURN AROUND RIGHT NOW, WE MIGHT BE ABLE TO GET BACK BEFORE ANYONE NOTICES YOU'RE GONE.
BOSTON
26 MILES
I'M SURE.

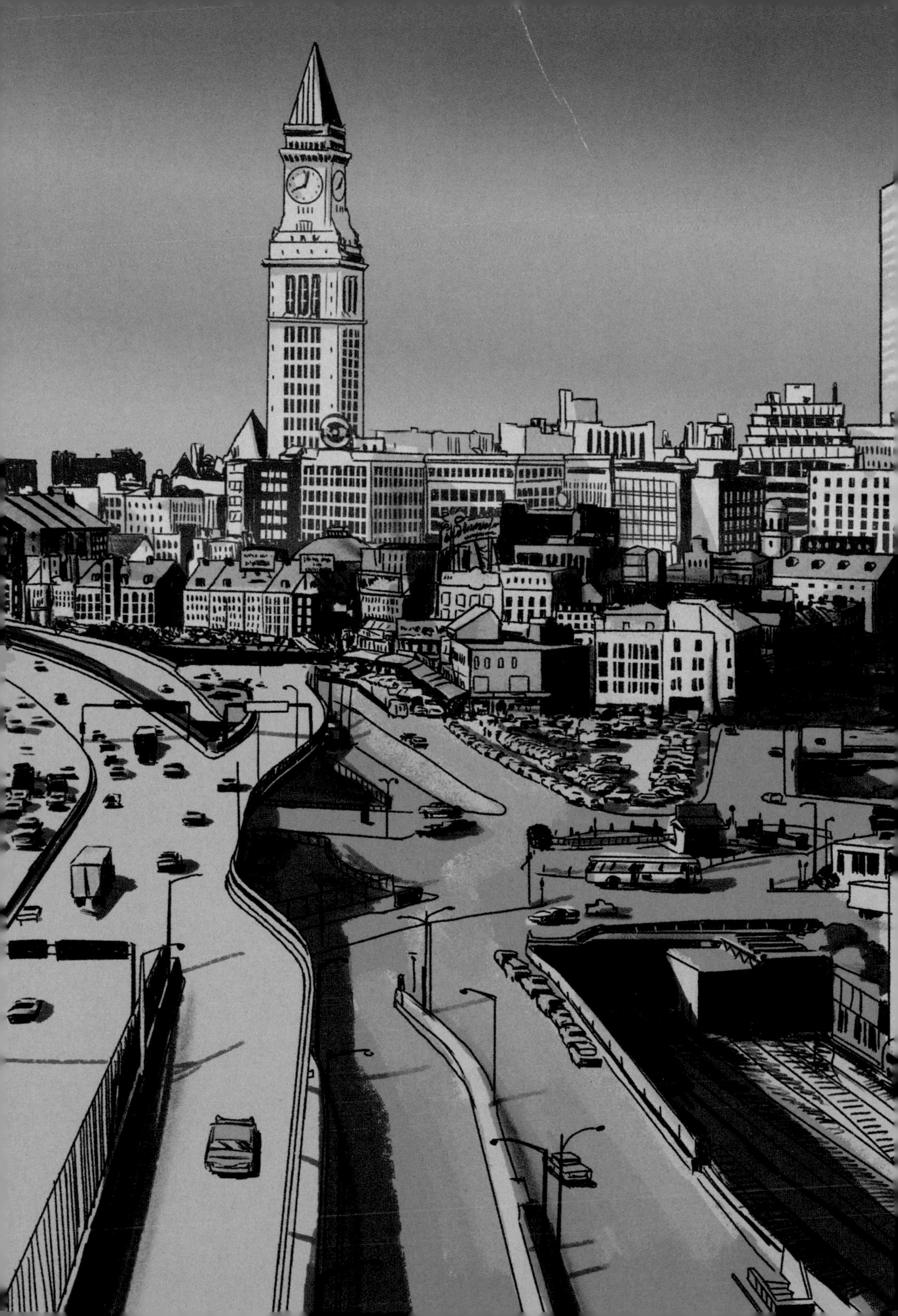

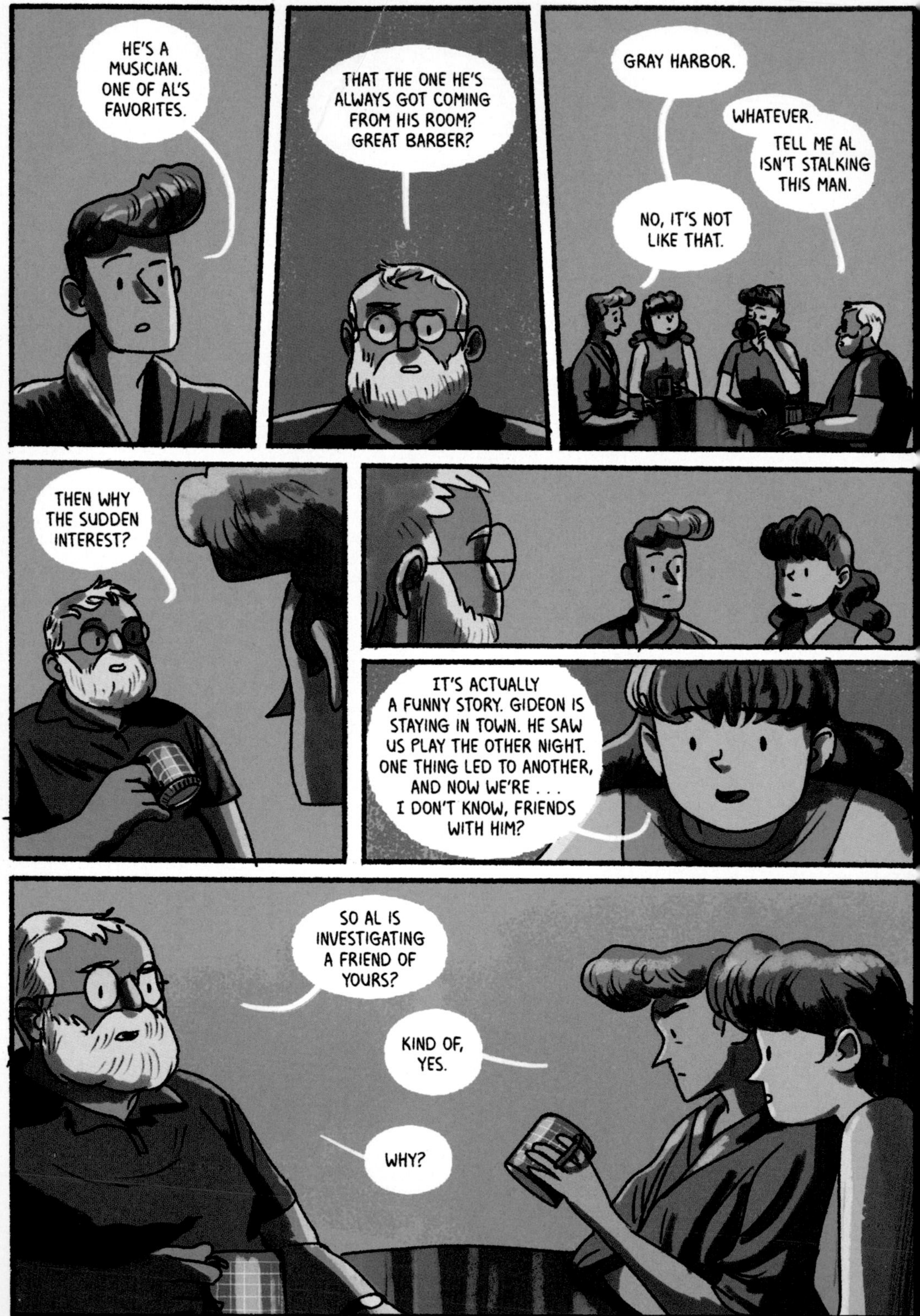
HE'S A MUSICIAN. ONE OF AL'S FAVORITES.
THAT THE ONE HE'S ALWAYS GOT COMING FROM HIS ROOM? GREAT BARBER?
GRAY HARBOR.
WHATEVER.
TELL ME AL ISN'T STALKING THIS MAN.
NO, IT'S NOT LIKE THAT.
THEN WHY THE SUDDEN INTEREST?
IT'S ACTUALLY A FUNNY STORY. GIDEON IS STAYING IN TOWN. HE SAW US PLAY THE OTHER NIGHT. ONE THING LED TO ANOTHER, AND NOW WE'RE . . . I DON'T KNOW, FRIENDS WITH HIM?
SO AL IS INVESTIGATING A FRIEND OF YOURS?
KIND OF, YES.
WHY?

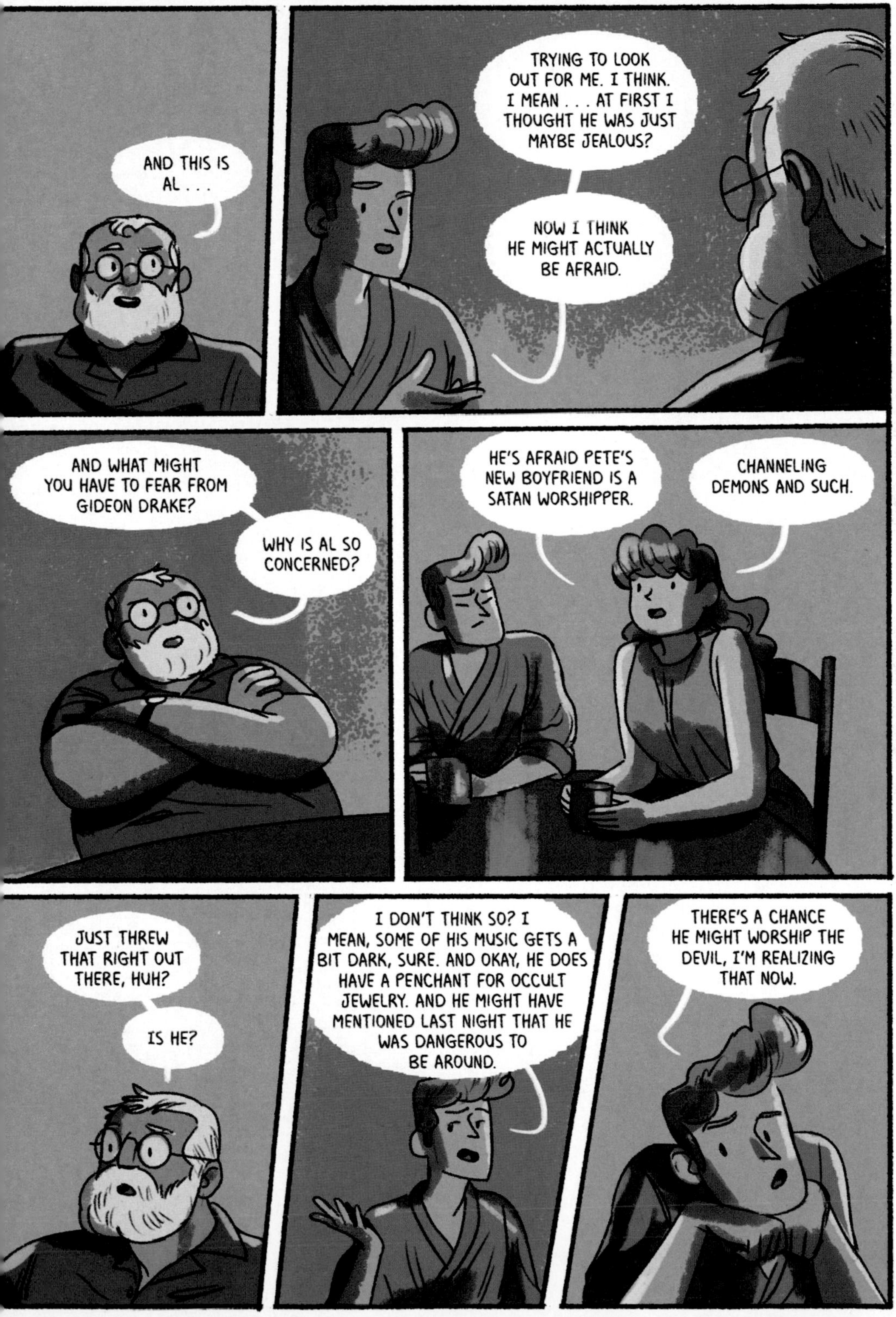
AND THIS IS AL . . .
TRYING TO LOOK OUT FOR ME. I THINK. I MEAN . . . AT FIRST I THOUGHT HE WAS JUST MAYBE JEALOUS?
NOW I THINK HE MIGHT ACTUALLY BE AFRAID.
AND WHAT MIGHT YOU HAVE TO FEAR FROM GIDEON DRAKE?
WHY IS AL SO CONCERNED?
HE'S AFRAID PETE'S NEW BOYFRIEND IS A SATAN WORSHIPPER.
CHANNELING DEMONS AND SUCH.
JUST THREW THAT RIGHT OUT THERE, HUH?
IS HE?
I DON'T THINK SO? I MEAN, SOME OF HIS MUSIC GETS A BIT DARK, SURE. AND OKAY, HE DOES HAVE A PENCHANT FOR OCCULT JEWELRY. AND HE MIGHT HAVE MENTIONED LAST NIGHT THAT HE WAS DANGEROUS TO BE AROUND.
THERE'S A CHANCE HE MIGHT WORSHIP THE DEVIL, I'M REALIZING THAT NOW.

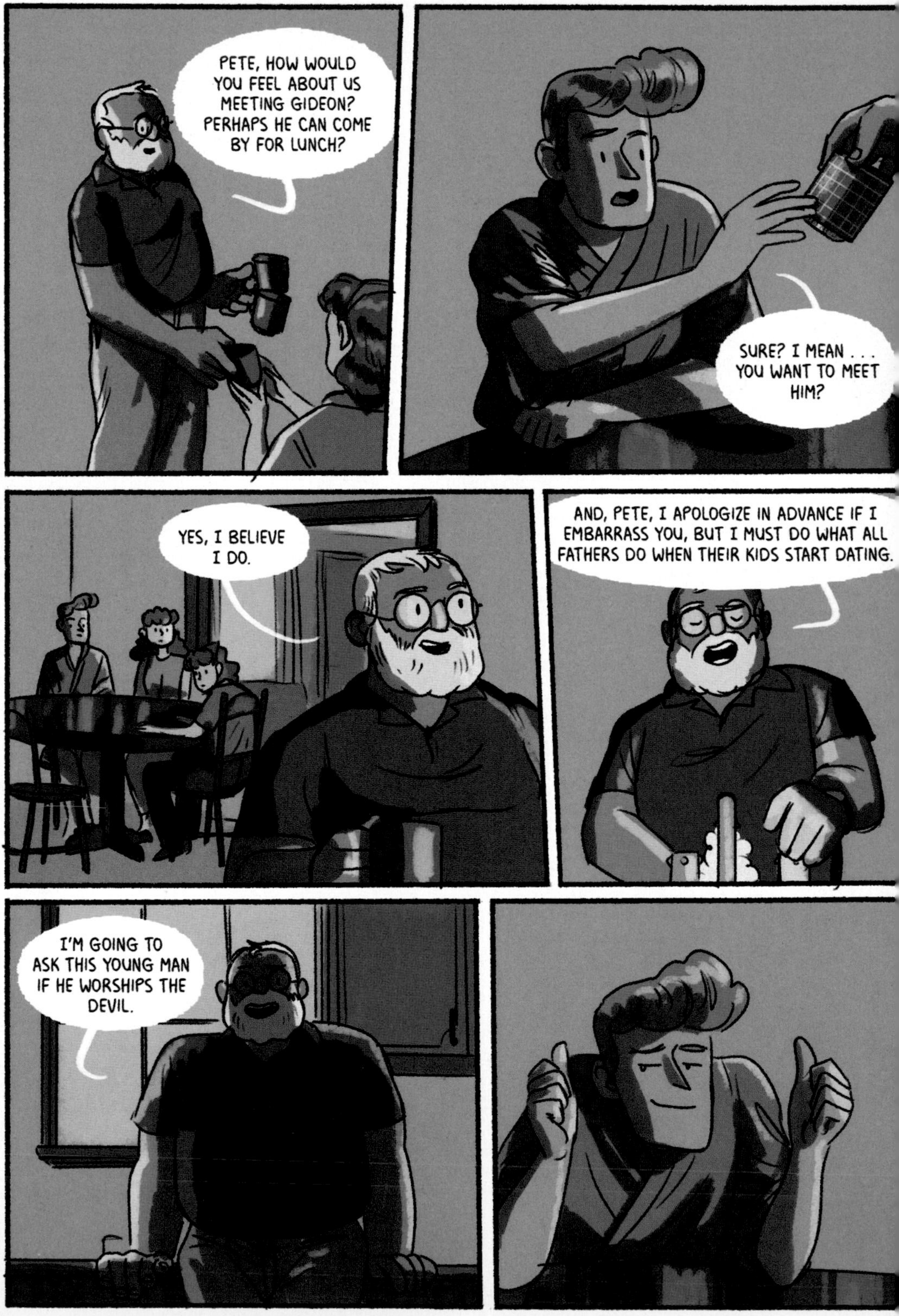
PETE, HOW WOULD YOU FEEL ABOUT US MEETING GIDEON? PERHAPS HE CAN COME BY FOR LUNCH?
SURE? I MEAN . . . YOU WANT TO MEET HIM?
YES, I BELIEVE I DO.
AND, PETE, I APOLOGIZE IN ADVANCE IF I EMBARRASS YOU, BUT I MUST DO WHAT ALL FATHERS DO WHEN THEIR KIDS START DATING.
I'M GOING TO ASK THIS YOUNG MAN IF HE WORSHIPS THE DEVIL.

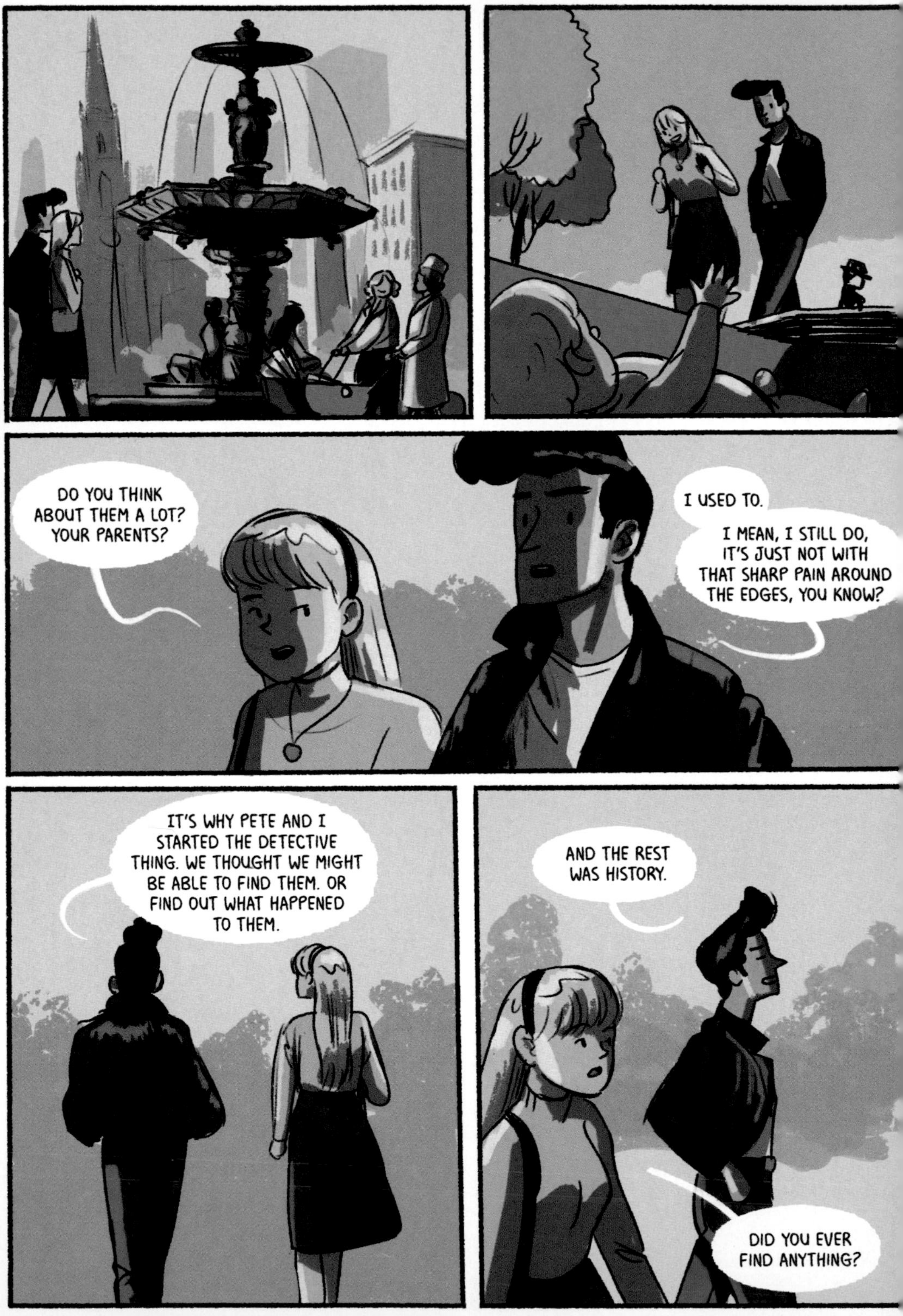
DO YOU THINK ABOUT THEM A LOT? YOUR PARENTS?
I USED TO.
I MEAN, I STILL DO, IT'S JUST NOT WITH THAT SHARP PAIN AROUND THE EDGES, YOU KNOW?
IT'S WHY PETE AND I STARTED THE DETECTIVE THING. WE THOUGHT WE MIGHT BE ABLE TO FIND THEM. OR FIND OUT WHAT HAPPENED TO THEM.
AND THE REST WAS HISTORY.
DID YOU EVER FIND ANYTHING?

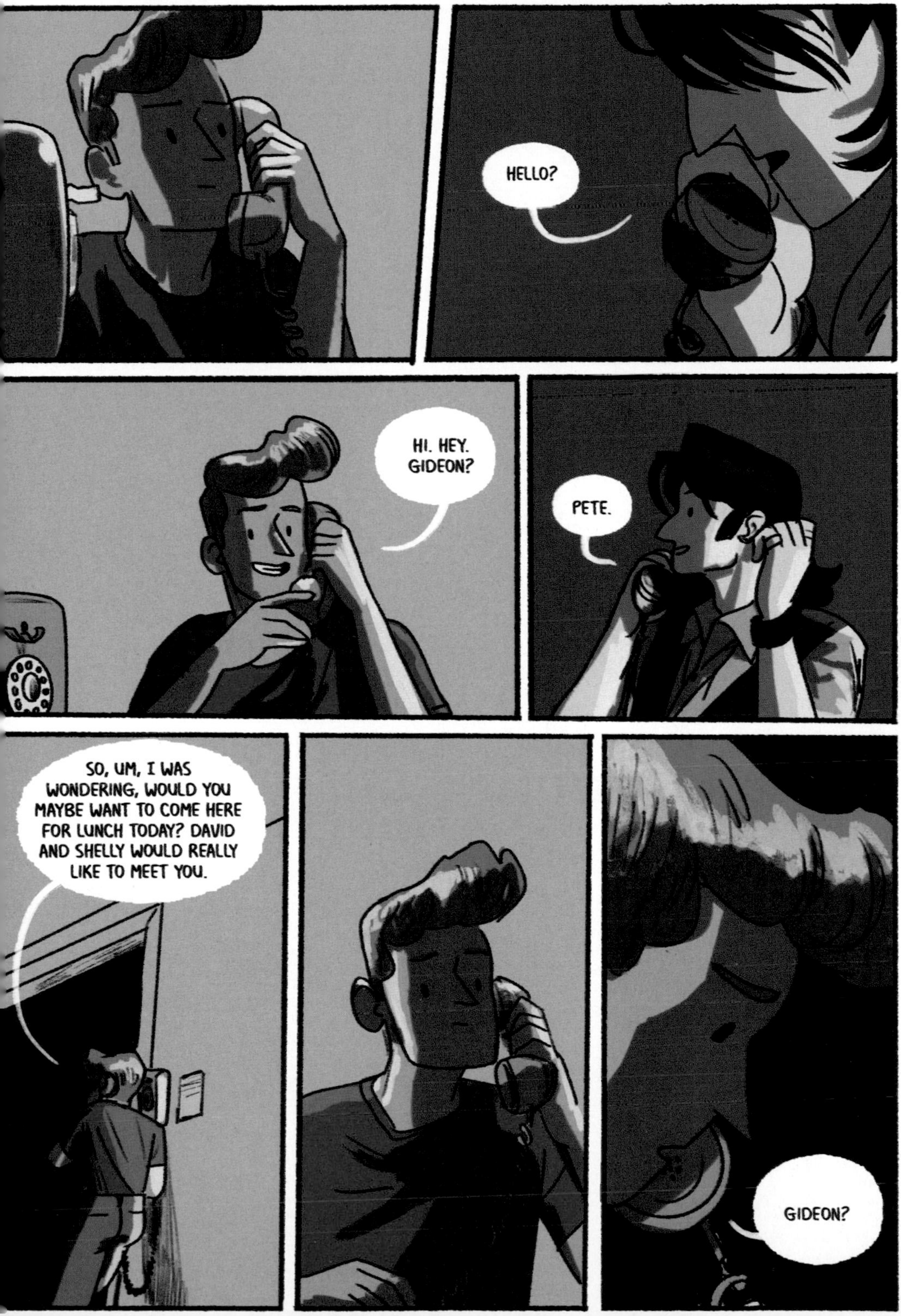
HELLO?
HI. HEY. GIDEON?
PETE.
SO, UM, I WAS WONDERING, WOULD YOU MAYBE WANT TO COME HERE FOR LUNCH TODAY? DAVID AND SHELLY WOULD REALLY LIKE TO MEET YOU.
GIDEON?

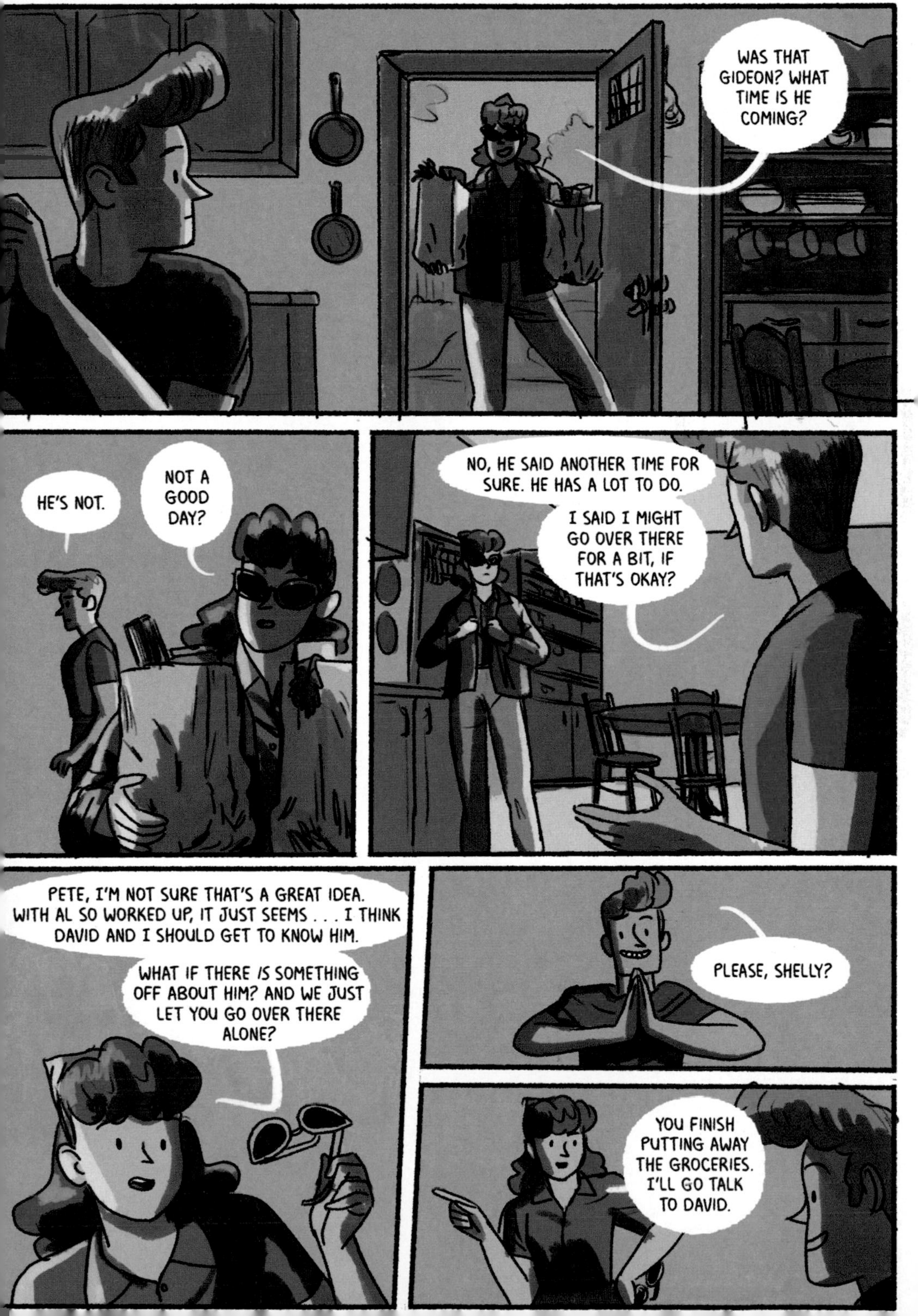
WAS THAT GIDEON? WHAT TIME IS HE COMING?
HE'S NOT.
NOT A GOOD DAY?
NO, HE SAID ANOTHER TIME FOR SURE. HE HAS A LOT TO DO.
I SAID I MIGHT GO OVER THERE FOR A BIT, IF THAT'S OKAY?
PETE, I'M NOT SURE THAT'S A GREAT IDEA. WITH AL SO WORKED UP, IT JUST SEEMS . . . I THINK DAVID AND I SHOULD GET TO KNOW HIM.
WHAT IF THERE *IS* SOMETHING OFF ABOUT HIM? AND WE JUST LET YOU GO OVER THERE ALONE?
PLEASE, SHELLY?
YOU FINISH PUTTING AWAY THE GROCERIES. I'LL GO TALK TO DAVID.

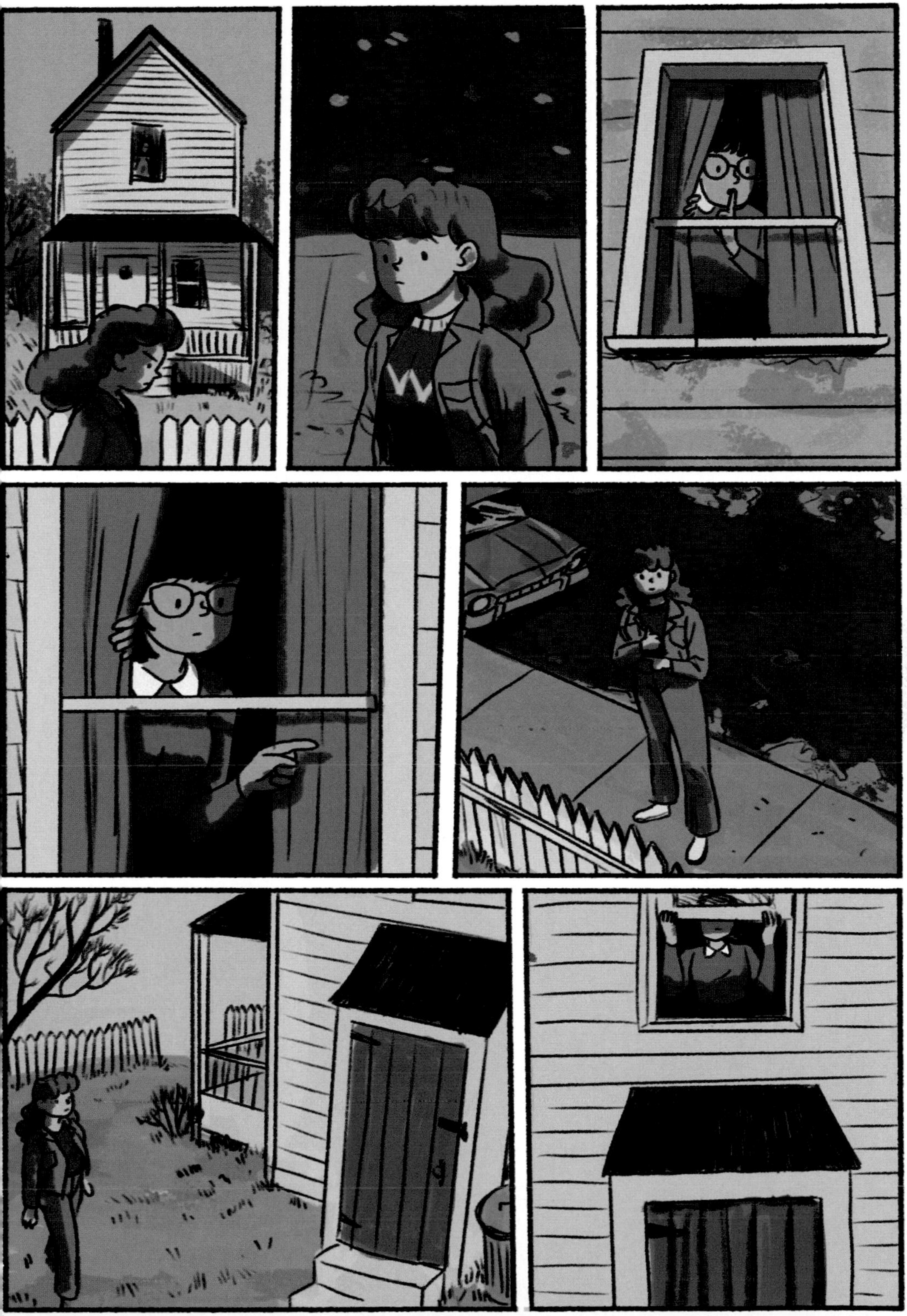

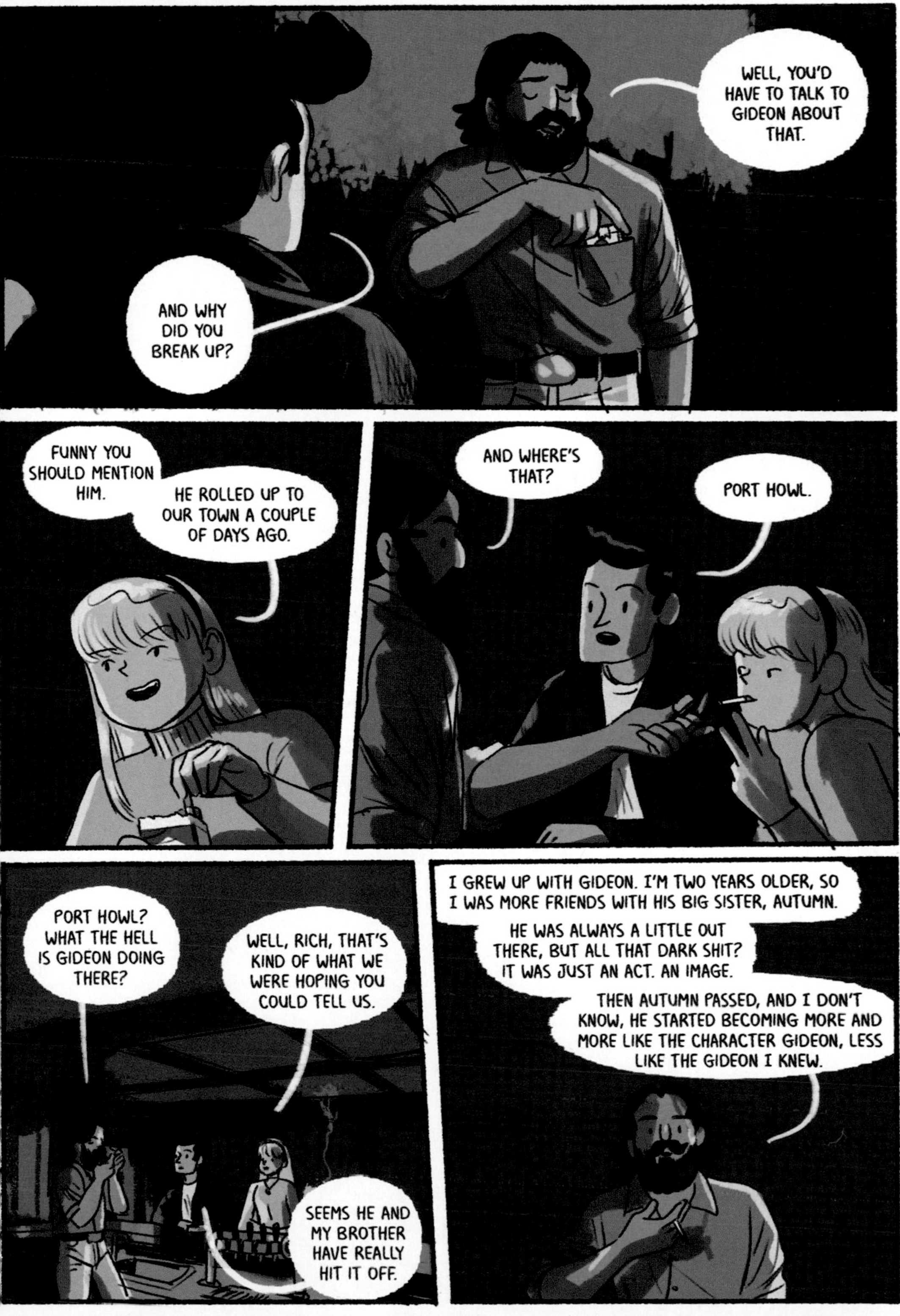
WELL, YOU'D HAVE TO TALK TO GIDEON ABOUT THAT.
AND WHY DID YOU BREAK UP?
FUNNY YOU SHOULD MENTION HIM.
HE ROLLED UP TO OUR TOWN A COUPLE OF DAYS AGO.
AND WHERE'S THAT?
PORT HOWL.
PORT HOWL? WHAT THE HELL IS GIDEON DOING THERE?
WELL, RICH, THAT'S KIND OF WHAT WE WERE HOPING YOU COULD TELL US.
SEEMS HE AND MY BROTHER HAVE REALLY HIT IT OFF.
I GREW UP WITH GIDEON. I'M TWO YEARS OLDER, SO I WAS MORE FRIENDS WITH HIS BIG SISTER, AUTUMN.
HE WAS ALWAYS A LITTLE OUT THERE, BUT ALL THAT DARK SHIT? IT WAS JUST AN ACT. AN IMAGE.
THEN AUTUMN PASSED, AND I DON'T KNOW, HE STARTED BECOMING MORE AND MORE LIKE THE CHARACTER GIDEON, LESS LIKE THE GIDEON I KNEW.

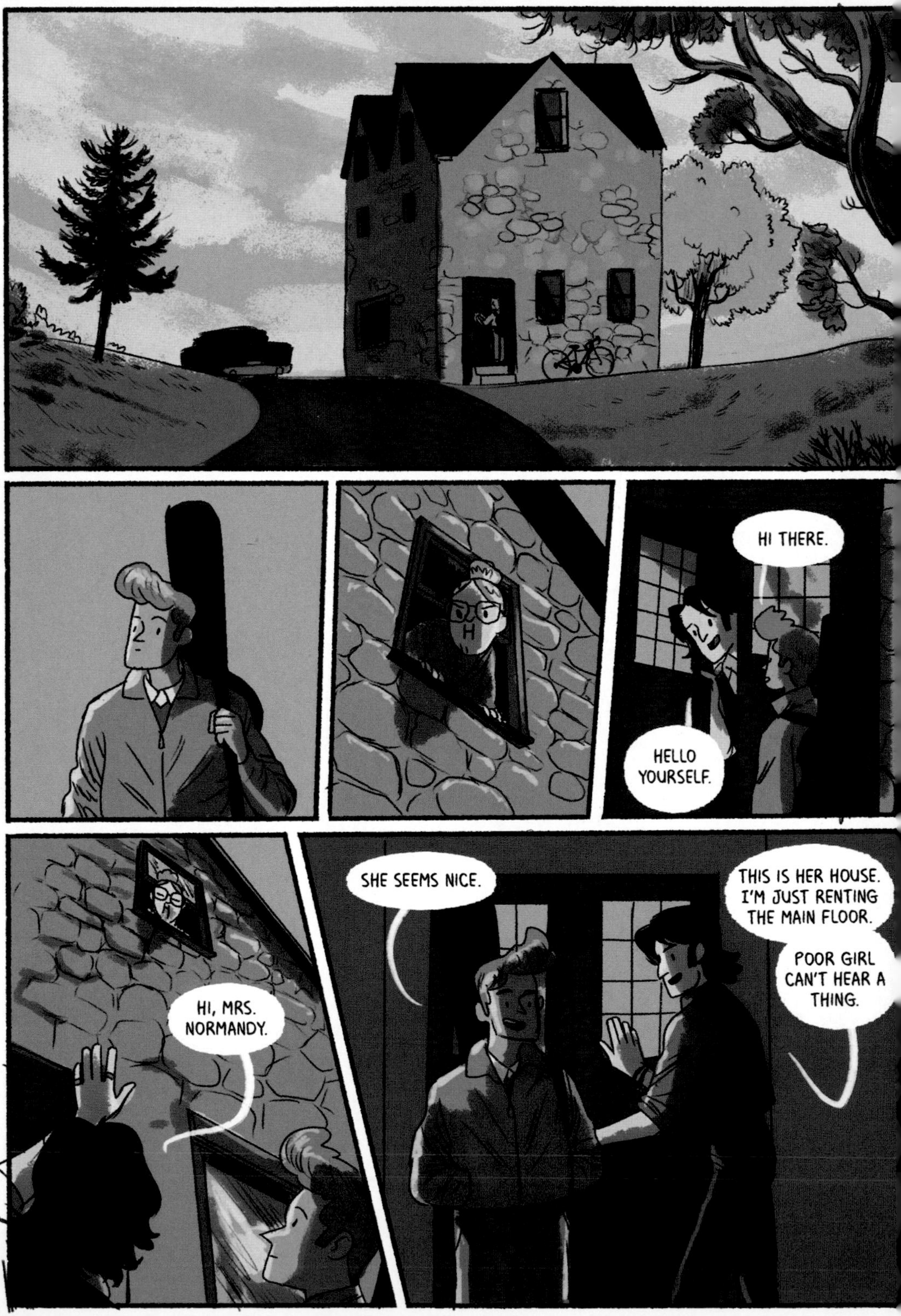
HI THERE.
HELLO YOURSELF.
HI, MRS. NORMANDY.
SHE SEEMS NICE.
THIS IS HER HOUSE. I'M JUST RENTING THE MAIN FLOOR.
POOR GIRL CAN'T HEAR A THING.

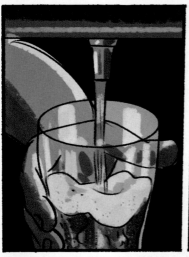

LOOK, GUYS, THE BAR IS STARTING TO FILL UP. IS THERE ANYTHING ELSE I CAN HELP YOU WITH?

DO YOU KNOW HOW WE CAN GET A HOLD OF THIS MAN?

Journalist
ARLO BARRETT

ARLO?

I DON'T MAKE A HABIT OUT OF MEMORIZING MUSIC JOURNALISTS' HOME ADDRESSES.

BUT I GOT HIS PHONE NUMBER. YOU CAN CALL THE OPERATOR FOR THE ADDRESS.

THAT WILL DO JUST FINE, THANKS. THEN WE'LL GET OUT OF YOUR HAIR.

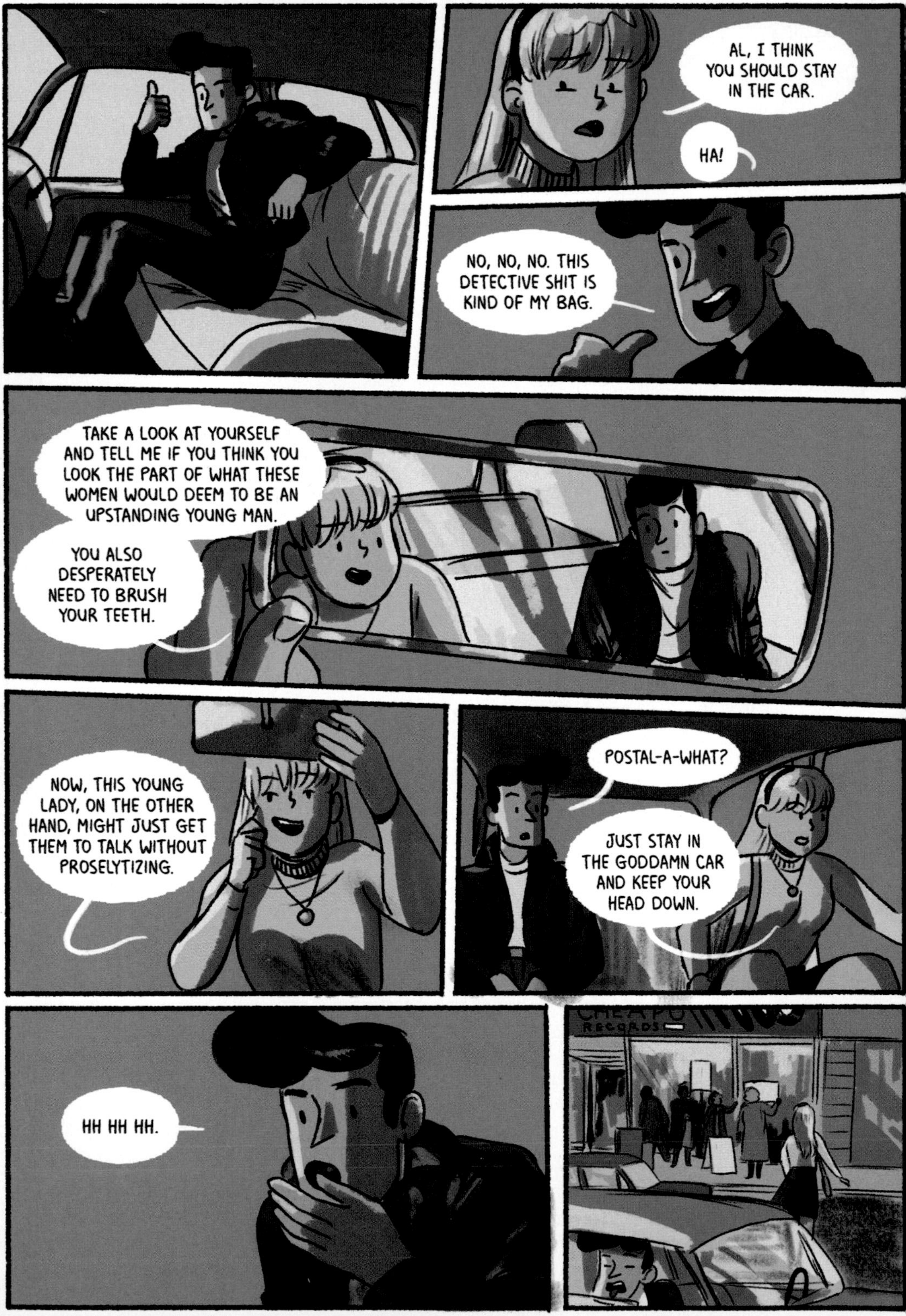
AL, I THINK YOU SHOULD STAY IN THE CAR.
HA!
NO, NO, NO. THIS DETECTIVE SHIT IS KIND OF MY BAG.
TAKE A LOOK AT YOURSELF AND TELL ME IF YOU THINK YOU LOOK THE PART OF WHAT THESE WOMEN WOULD DEEM TO BE AN UPSTANDING YOUNG MAN.
YOU ALSO DESPERATELY NEED TO BRUSH YOUR TEETH.
NOW, THIS YOUNG LADY, ON THE OTHER HAND, MIGHT JUST GET THEM TO TALK WITHOUT PROSELYTIZING.
POSTAL-A-WHAT?
JUST STAY IN THE GODDAMN CAR AND KEEP YOUR HEAD DOWN.
HH HH HH.
RECORDS

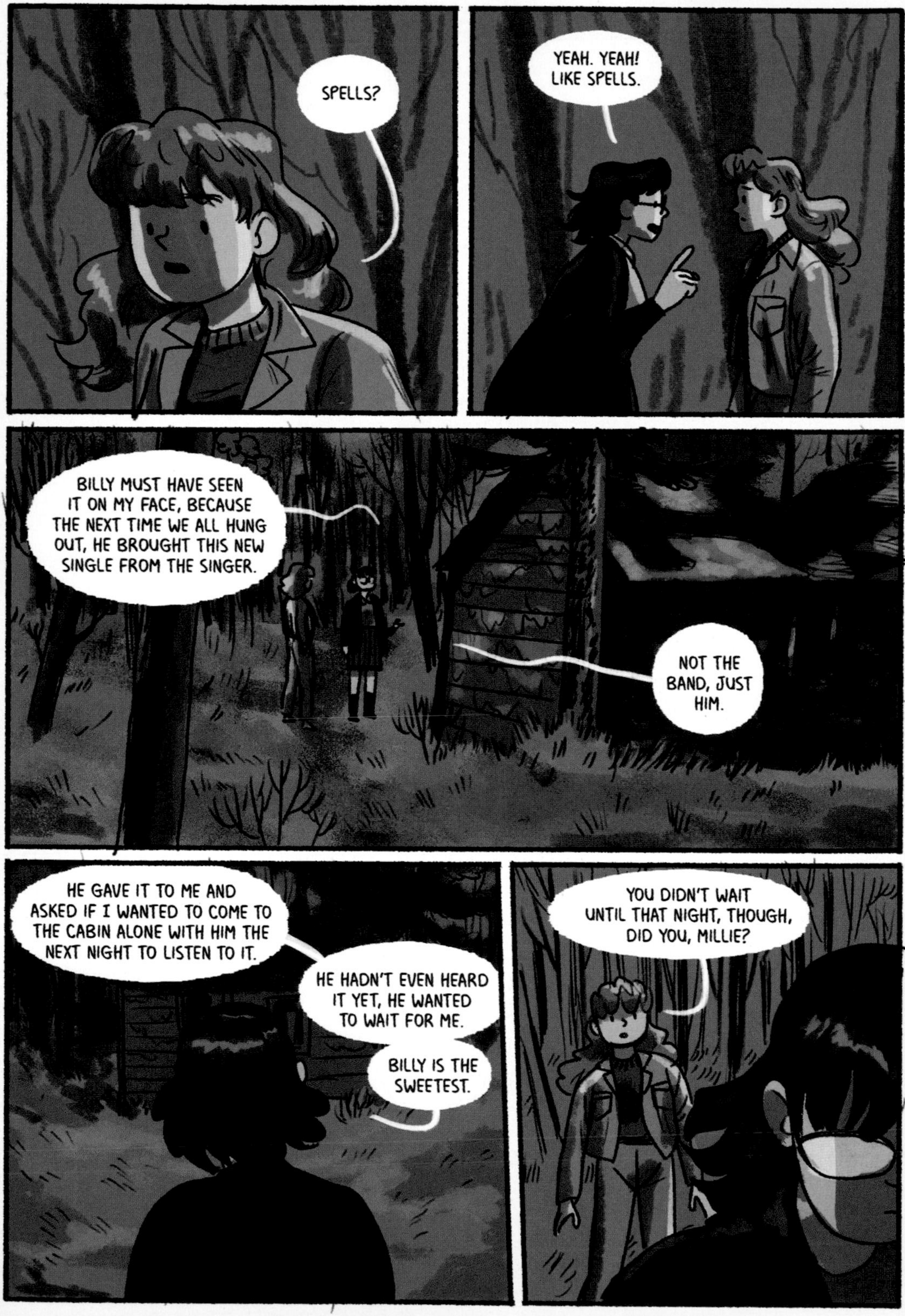
SPELLS?
YEAH. YEAH! LIKE SPELLS.
BILLY MUST HAVE SEEN IT ON MY FACE, BECAUSE THE NEXT TIME WE ALL HUNG OUT, HE BROUGHT THIS NEW SINGLE FROM THE SINGER.
NOT THE BAND, JUST HIM.
HE GAVE IT TO ME AND ASKED IF I WANTED TO COME TO THE CABIN ALONE WITH HIM THE NEXT NIGHT TO LISTEN TO IT.
HE HADN'T EVEN HEARD IT YET, HE WANTED TO WAIT FOR ME.
BILLY IS THE SWEETEST.
YOU DIDN'T WAIT UNTIL THAT NIGHT, THOUGH, DID YOU, MILLIE?

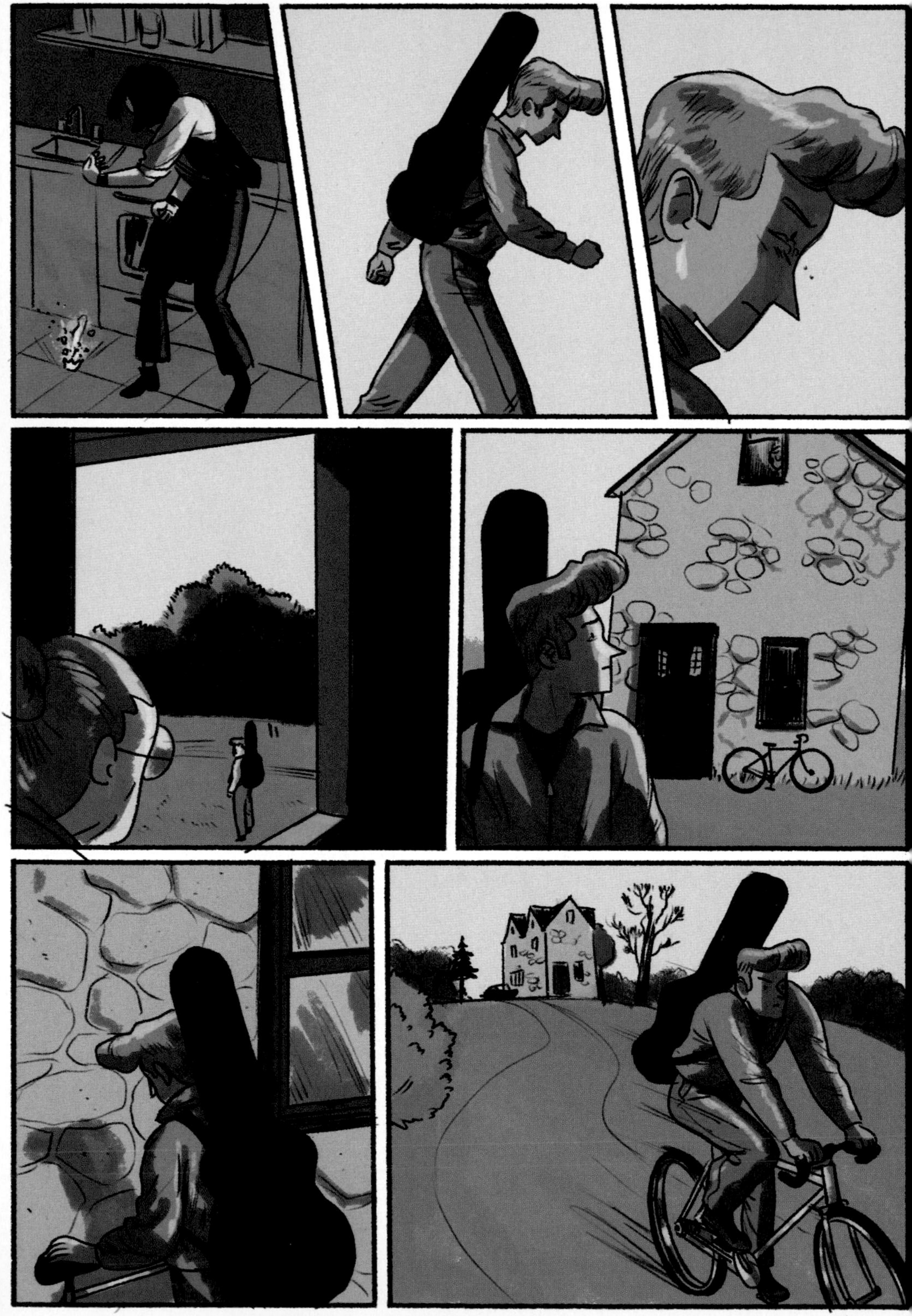

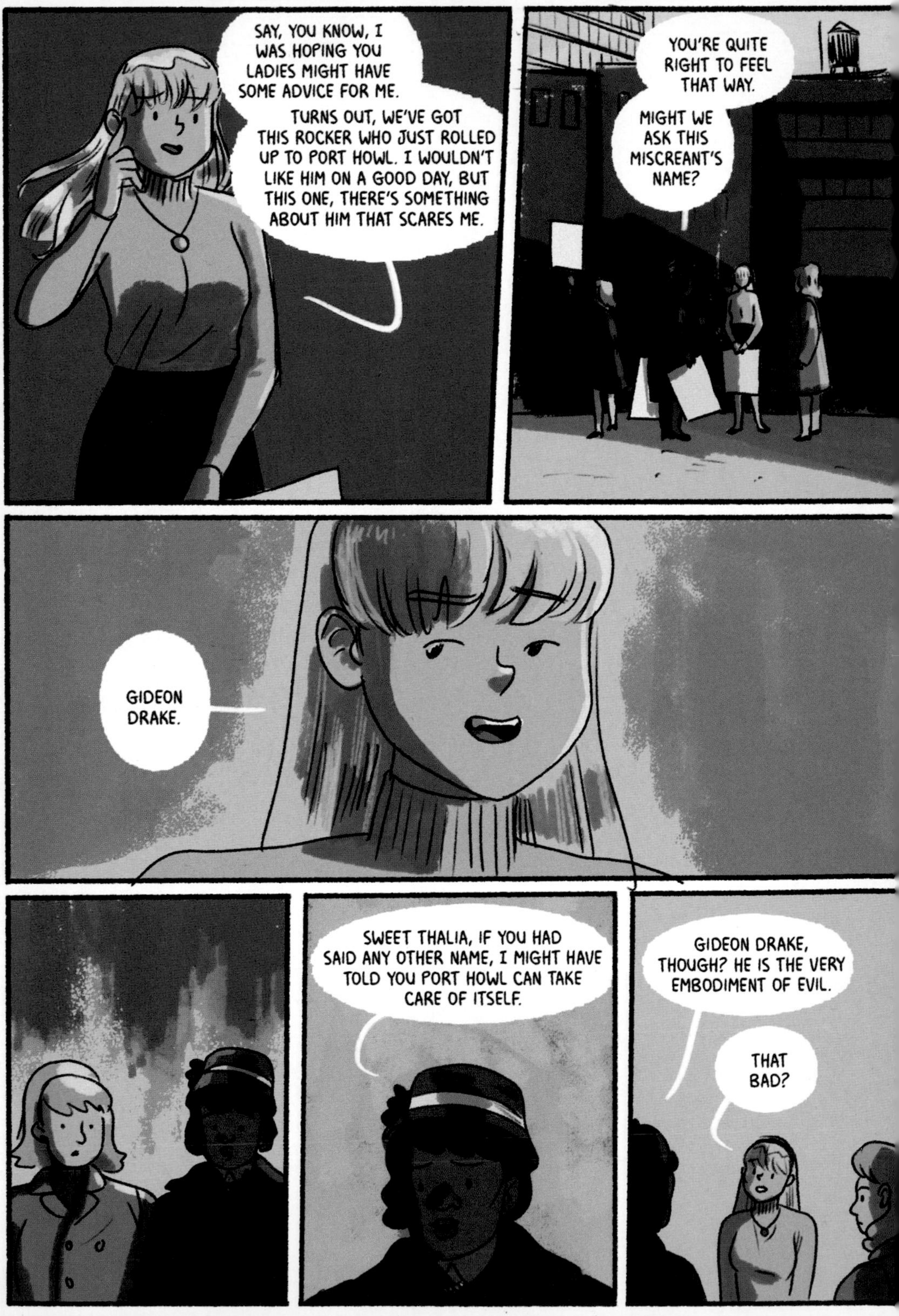
SAY, YOU KNOW, I WAS HOPING YOU LADIES MIGHT HAVE SOME ADVICE FOR ME.
TURNS OUT, WE'VE GOT THIS ROCKER WHO JUST ROLLED UP TO PORT HOWL. I WOULDN'T LIKE HIM ON A GOOD DAY, BUT THIS ONE, THERE'S SOMETHING ABOUT HIM THAT SCARES ME.
YOU'RE QUITE RIGHT TO FEEL THAT WAY.
MIGHT WE ASK THIS MISCREANT'S NAME?
GIDEON DRAKE.
SWEET THALIA, IF YOU HAD SAID ANY OTHER NAME, I MIGHT HAVE TOLD YOU PORT HOWL CAN TAKE CARE OF ITSELF.
GIDEON DRAKE, THOUGH? HE IS THE VERY EMBODIMENT OF EVIL.
THAT BAD?

I'LL EXPLAIN ON THE WAY TO ARLO'S.

YOU'LL BURN IN HELLFIRE!

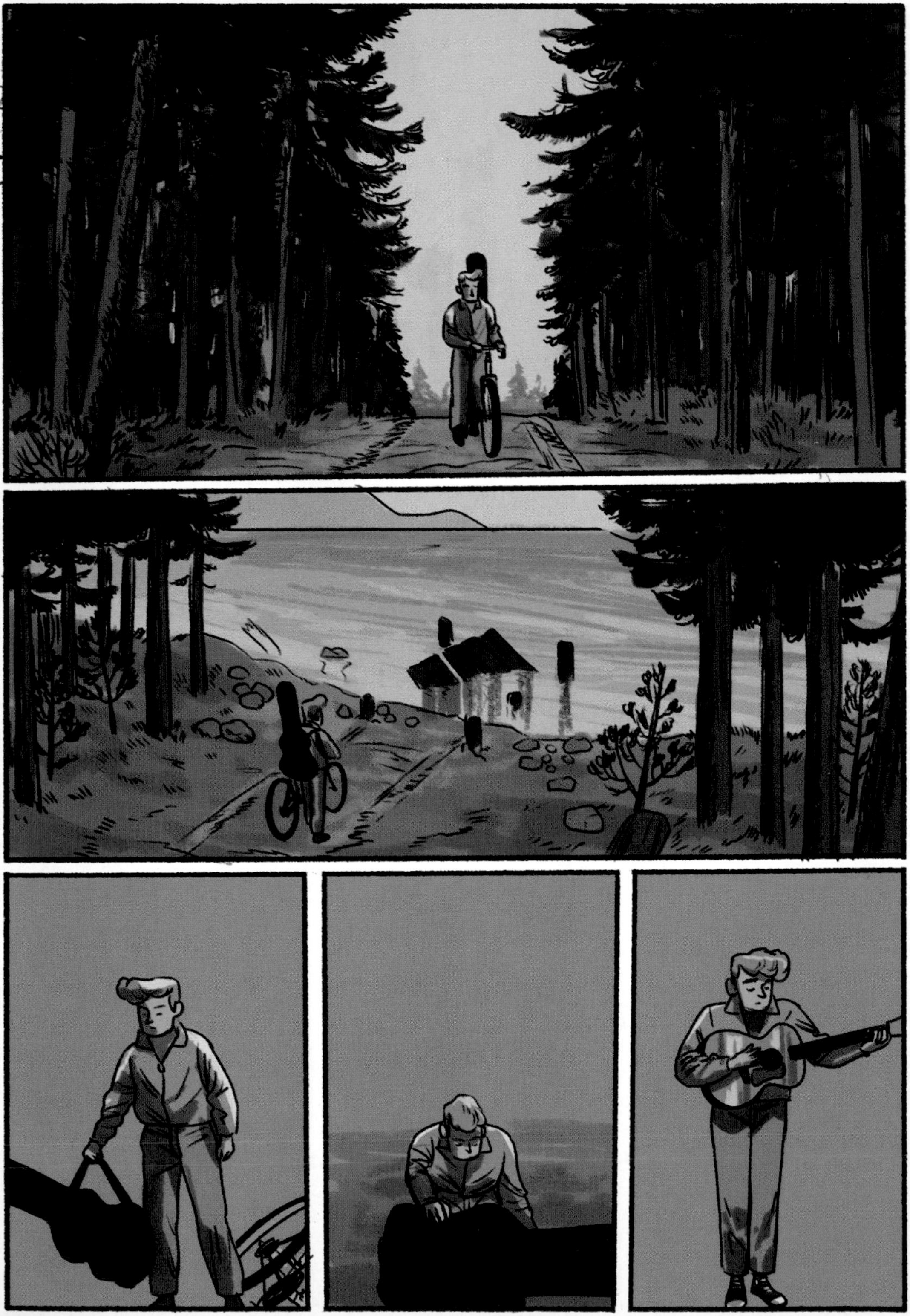

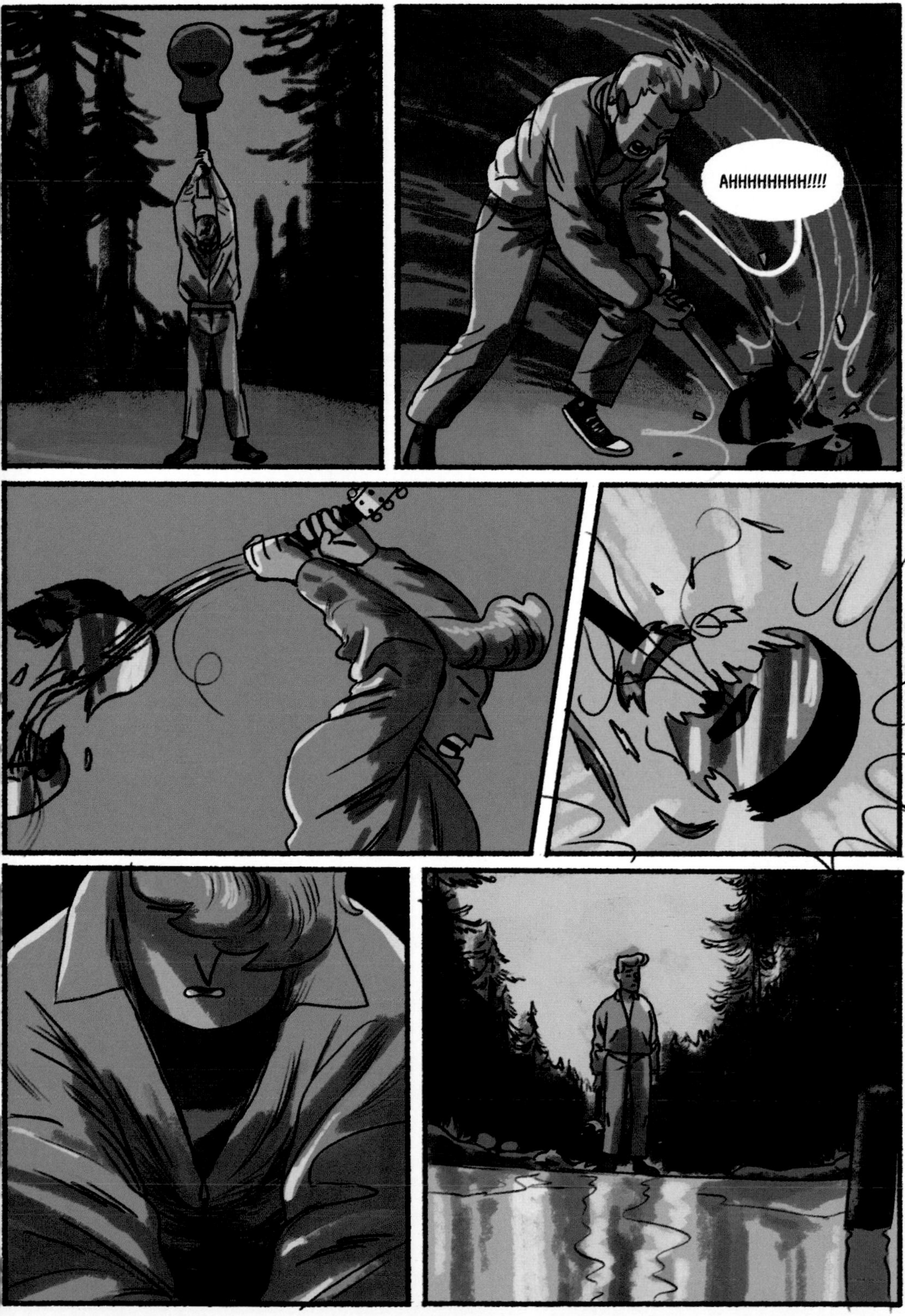
AHHHHHHHH!!!!

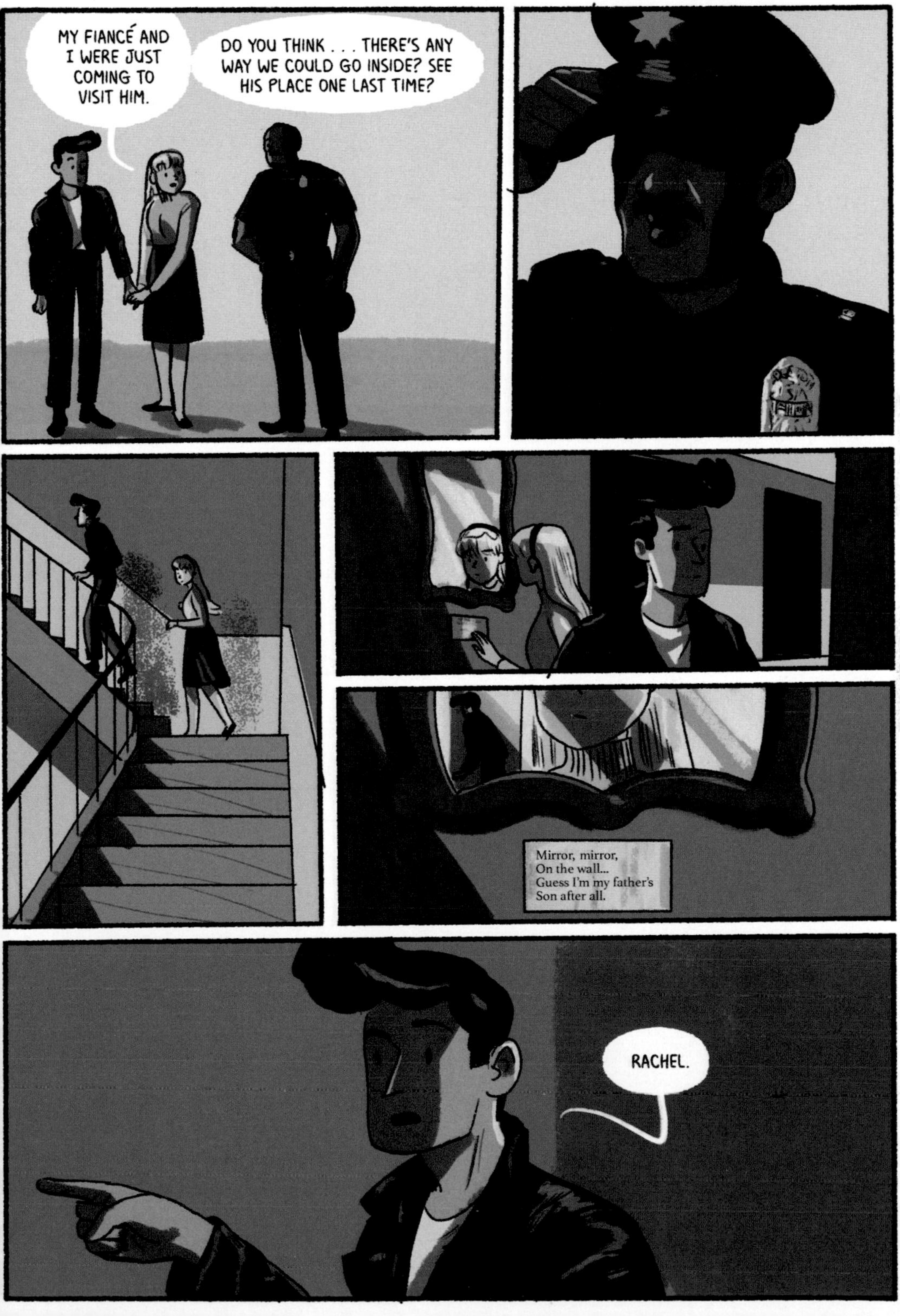
MY FIANCÉ AND I WERE JUST COMING TO VISIT HIM.
DO YOU THINK . . . THERE'S ANY WAY WE COULD GO INSIDE? SEE HIS PLACE ONE LAST TIME?
Mirror, mirror,
On the wall...
Guess I'm my father's
Son after all.
RACHEL.

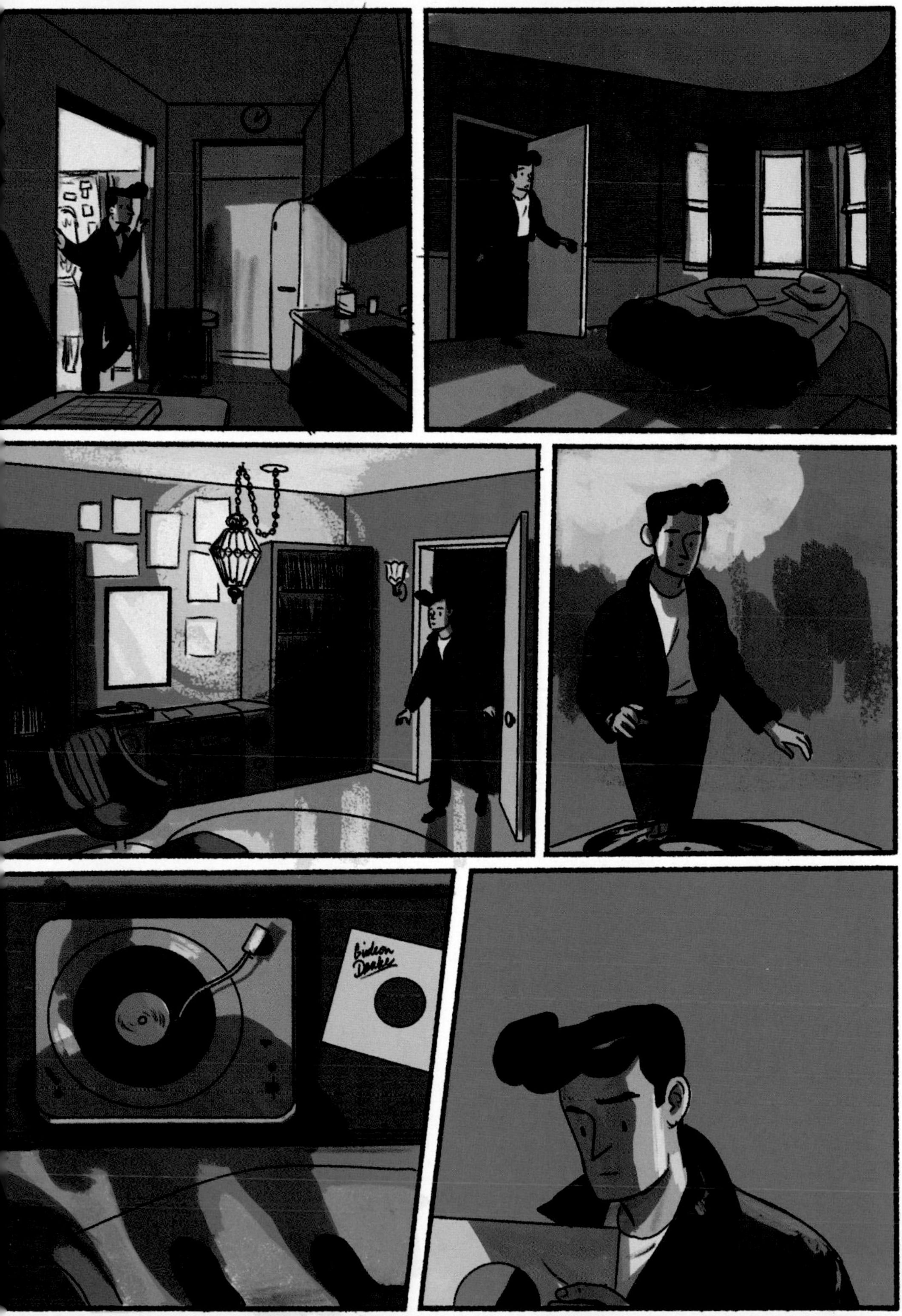

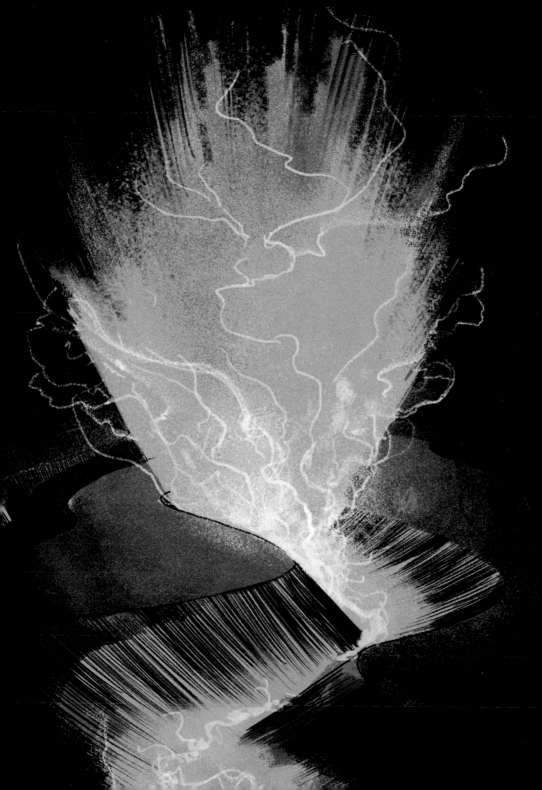

CHAPTER 5

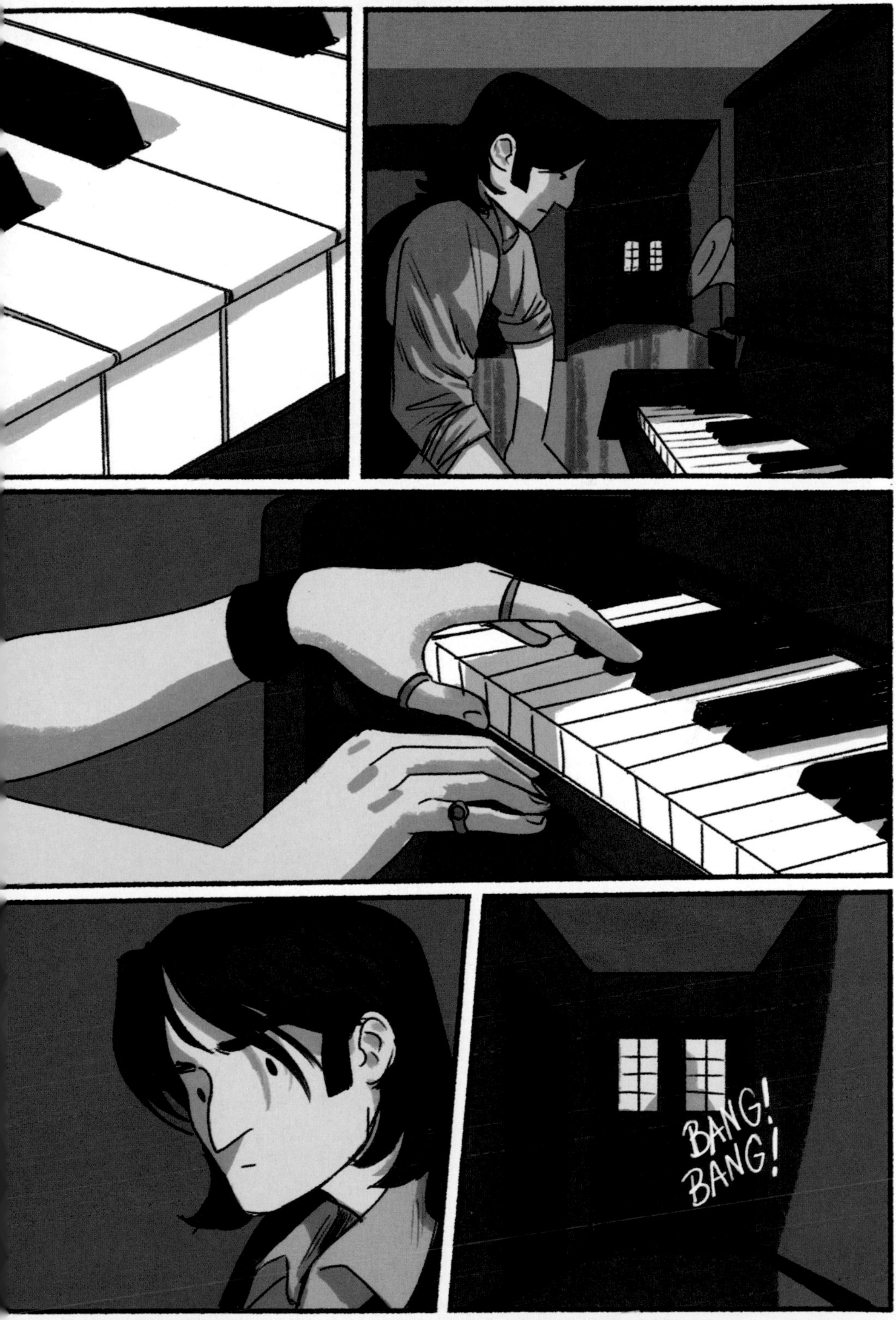
BANG!
BANG!

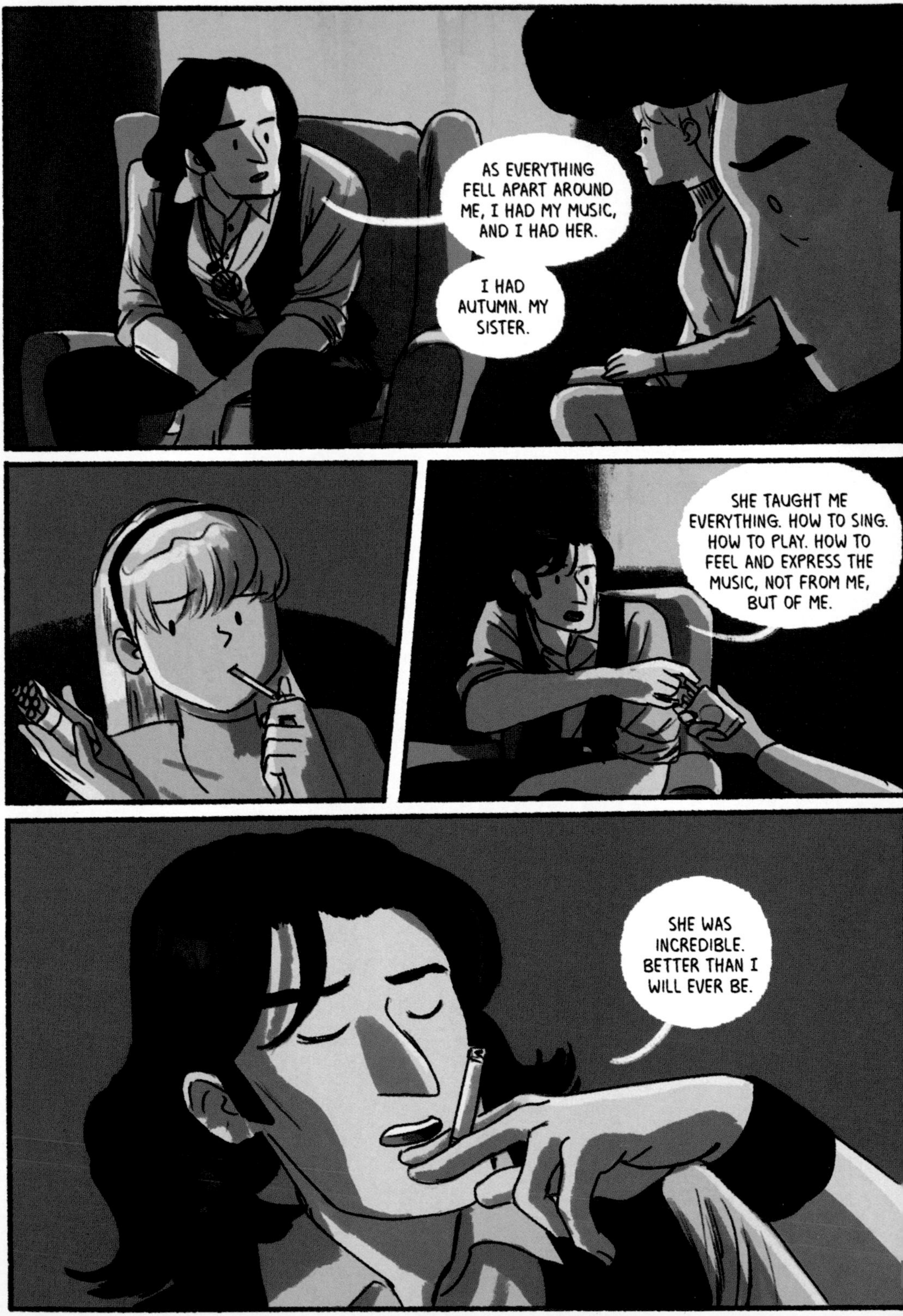
AS EVERYTHING FELL APART AROUND ME, I HAD MY MUSIC, AND I HAD HER.
I HAD AUTUMN. MY SISTER.
SHE TAUGHT ME EVERYTHING. HOW TO SING. HOW TO PLAY. HOW TO FEEL AND EXPRESS THE MUSIC, NOT FROM ME, BUT OF ME.
SHE WAS INCREDIBLE. BETTER THAN I WILL EVER BE.

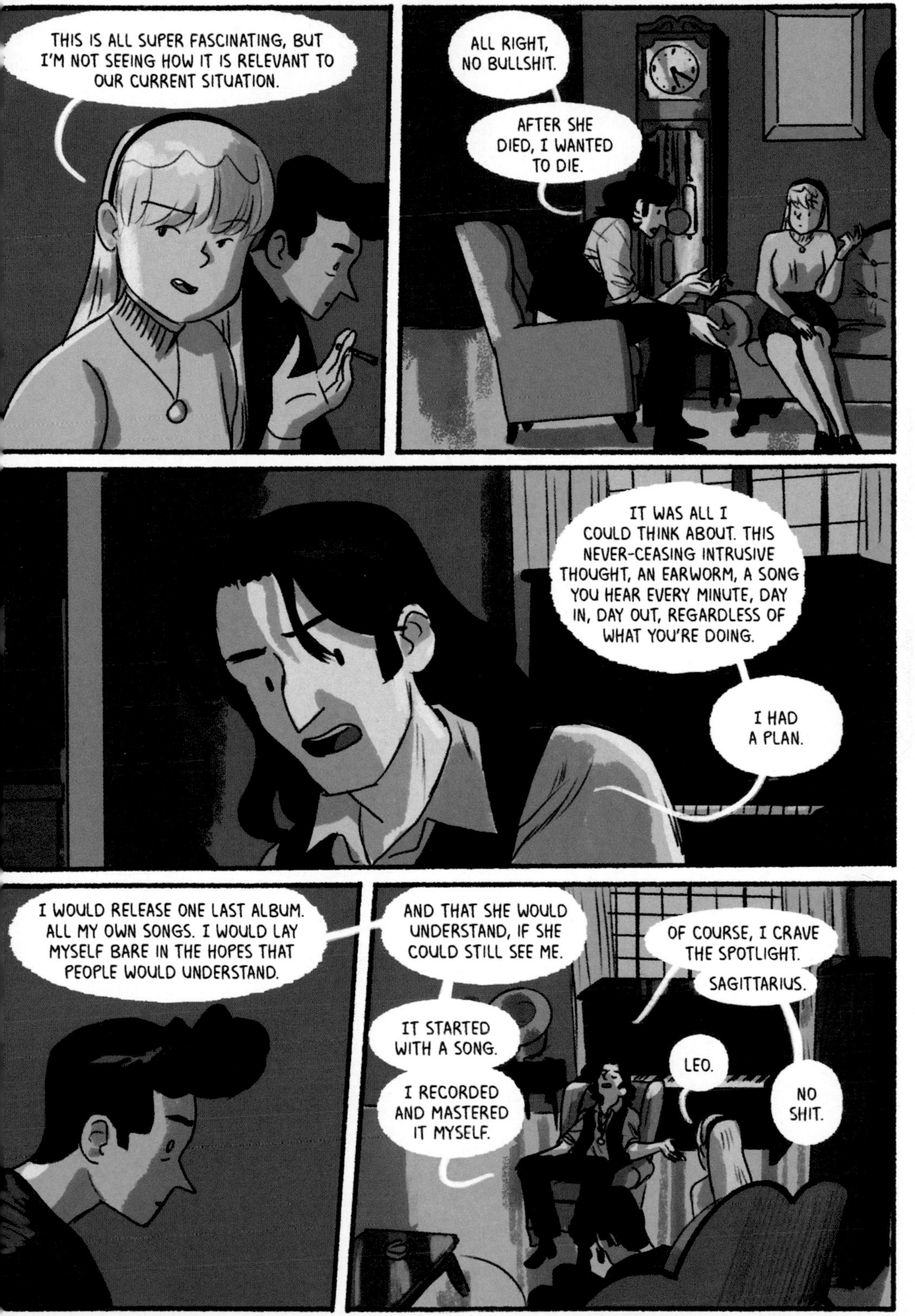
THIS IS ALL SUPER FASCINATING, BUT I'M NOT SEEING HOW IT IS RELEVANT TO OUR CURRENT SITUATION.
ALL RIGHT, NO BULLSHIT.
AFTER SHE DIED, I WANTED TO DIE.
IT WAS ALL I COULD THINK ABOUT. THIS NEVER-CEASING INTRUSIVE THOUGHT, AN EARWORM, A SONG YOU HEAR EVERY MINUTE, DAY IN, DAY OUT, REGARDLESS OF WHAT YOU'RE DOING.
I HAD A PLAN.
I WOULD RELEASE ONE LAST ALBUM. ALL MY OWN SONGS. I WOULD LAY MYSELF BARE IN THE HOPES THAT PEOPLE WOULD UNDERSTAND.
AND THAT SHE WOULD UNDERSTAND, IF SHE COULD STILL SEE ME.
IT STARTED WITH A SONG.
I RECORDED AND MASTERED IT MYSELF.
OF COURSE, I CRAVE THE SPOTLIGHT.
LEO.
SAGITTARIUS.
NO SHIT.

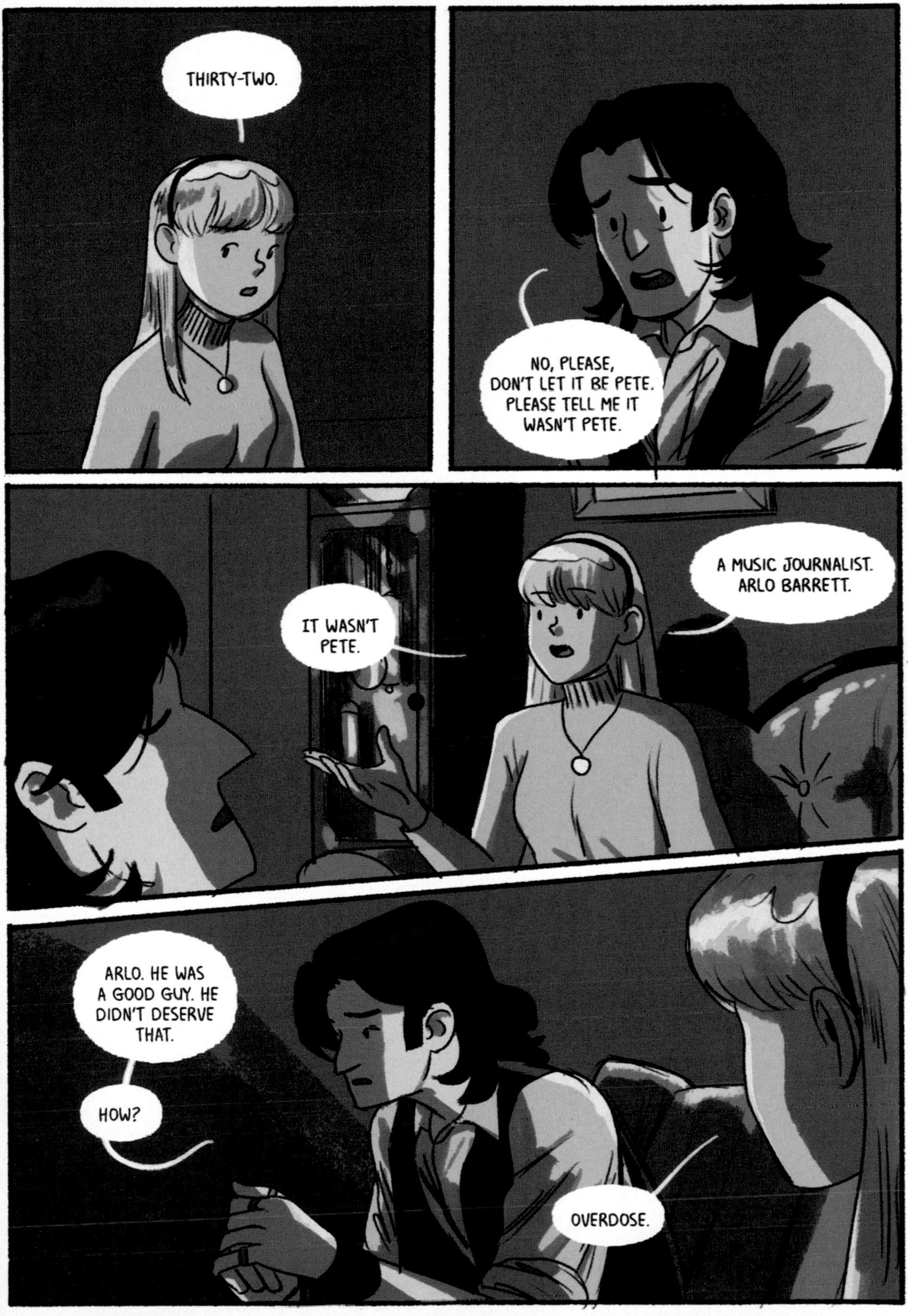
THIRTY-TWO.
NO, PLEASE, DON'T LET IT BE PETE. PLEASE TELL ME IT WASN'T PETE.
A MUSIC JOURNALIST. ARLO BARRETT.
IT WASN'T PETE.
ARLO. HE WAS A GOOD GUY. HE DIDN'T DESERVE THAT.
HOW?
OVERDOSE.

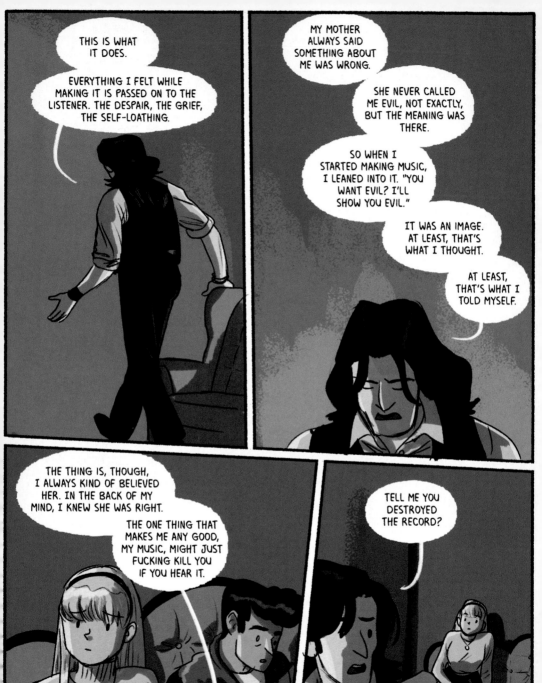

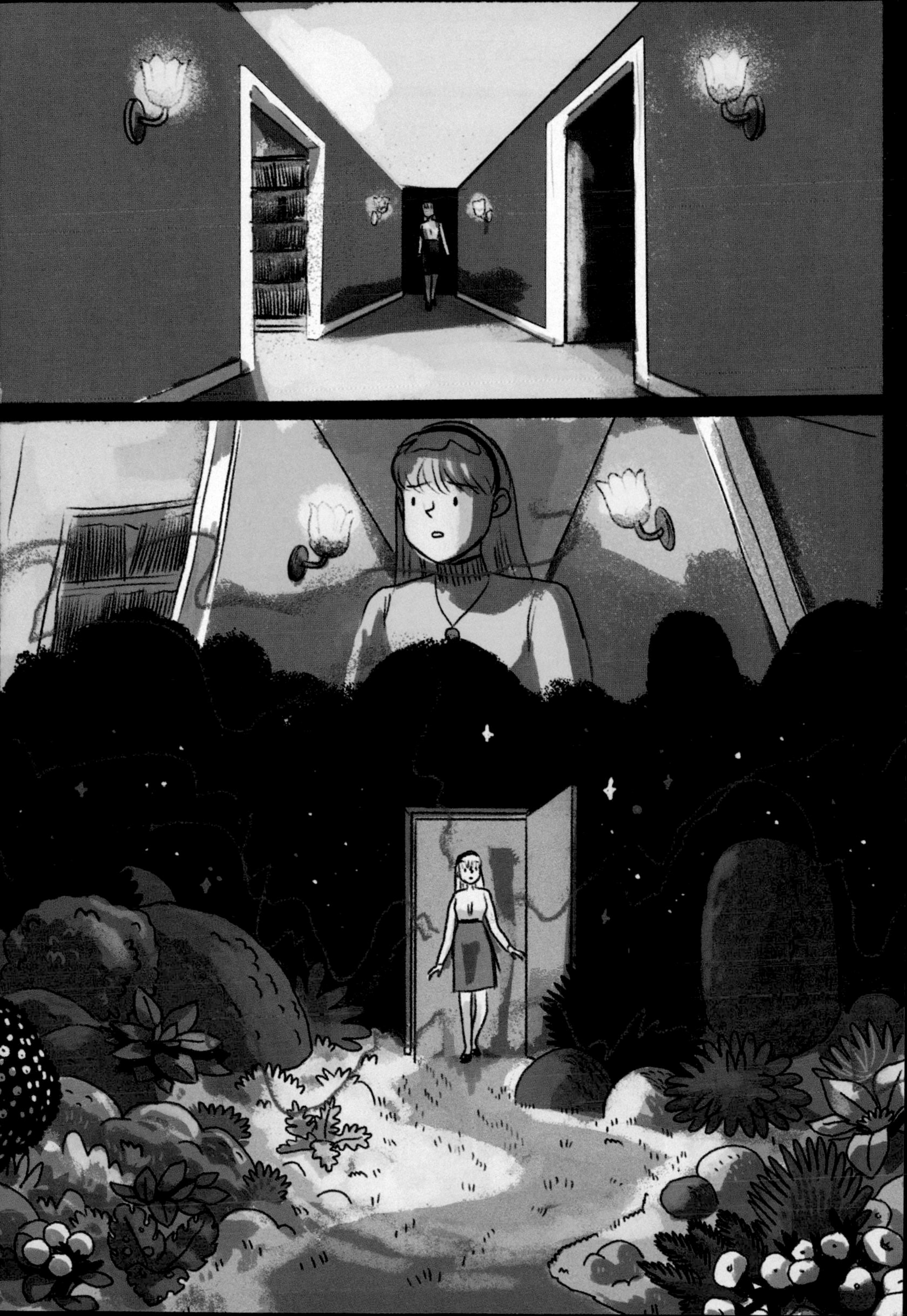

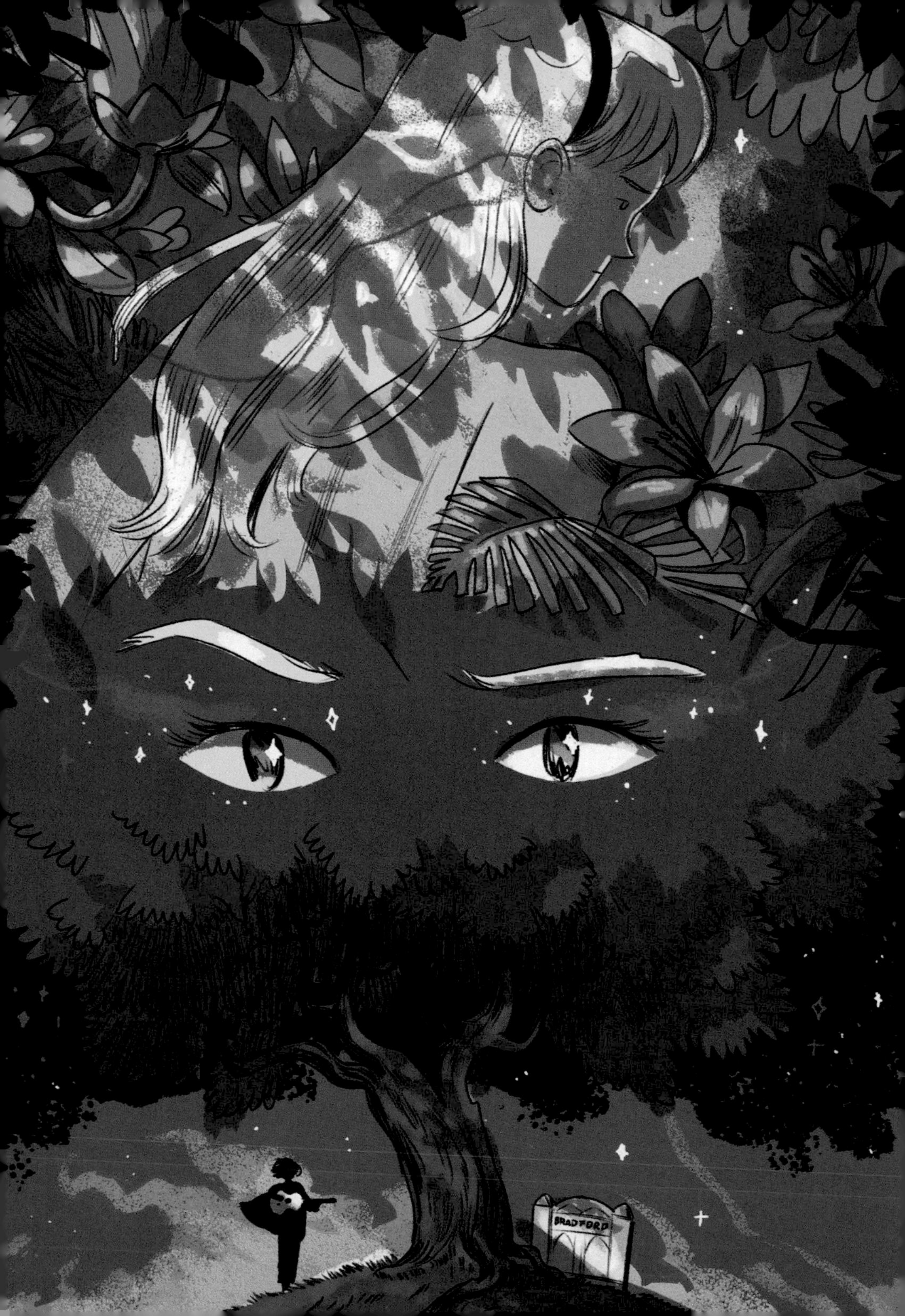
BRADFORD

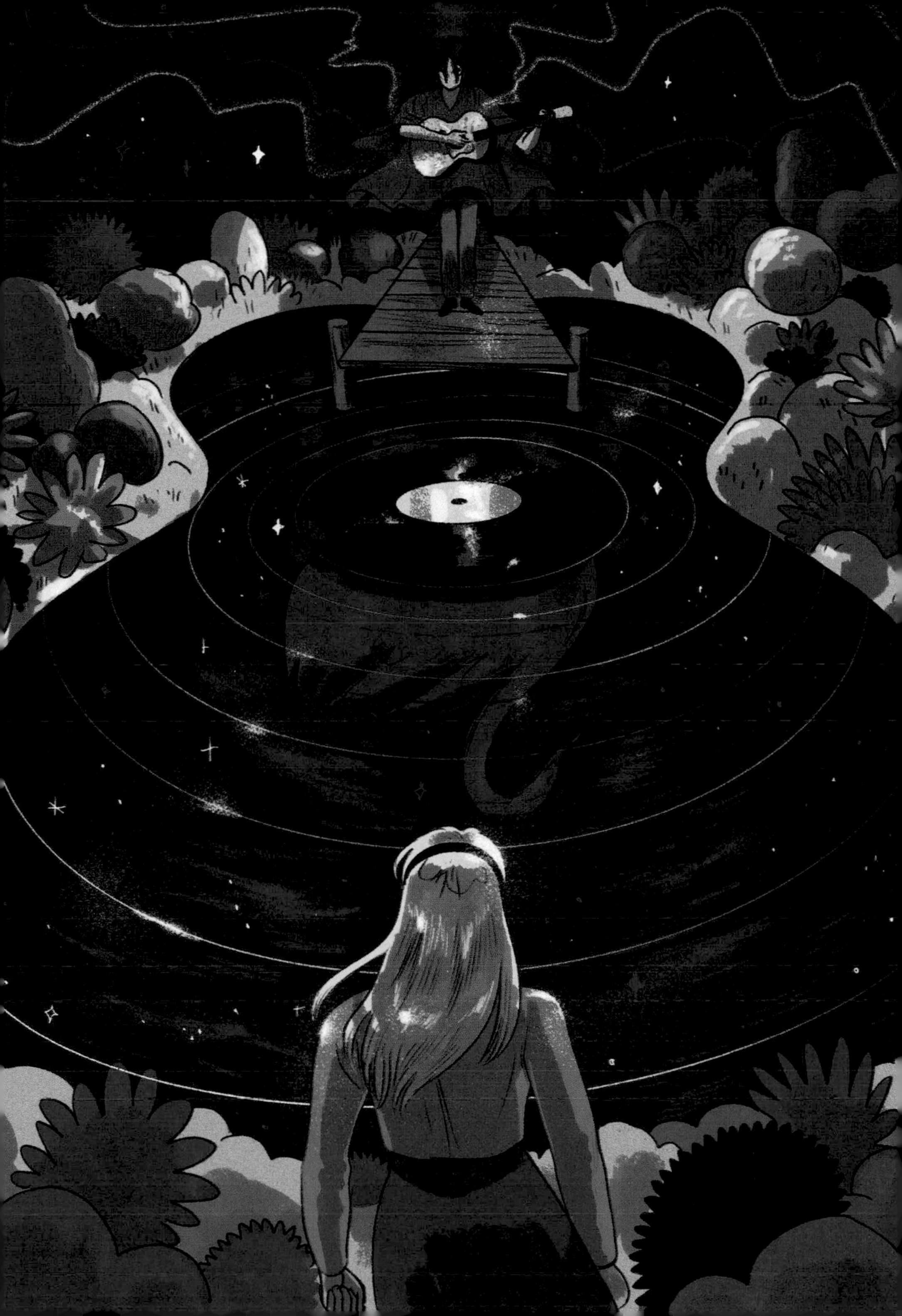

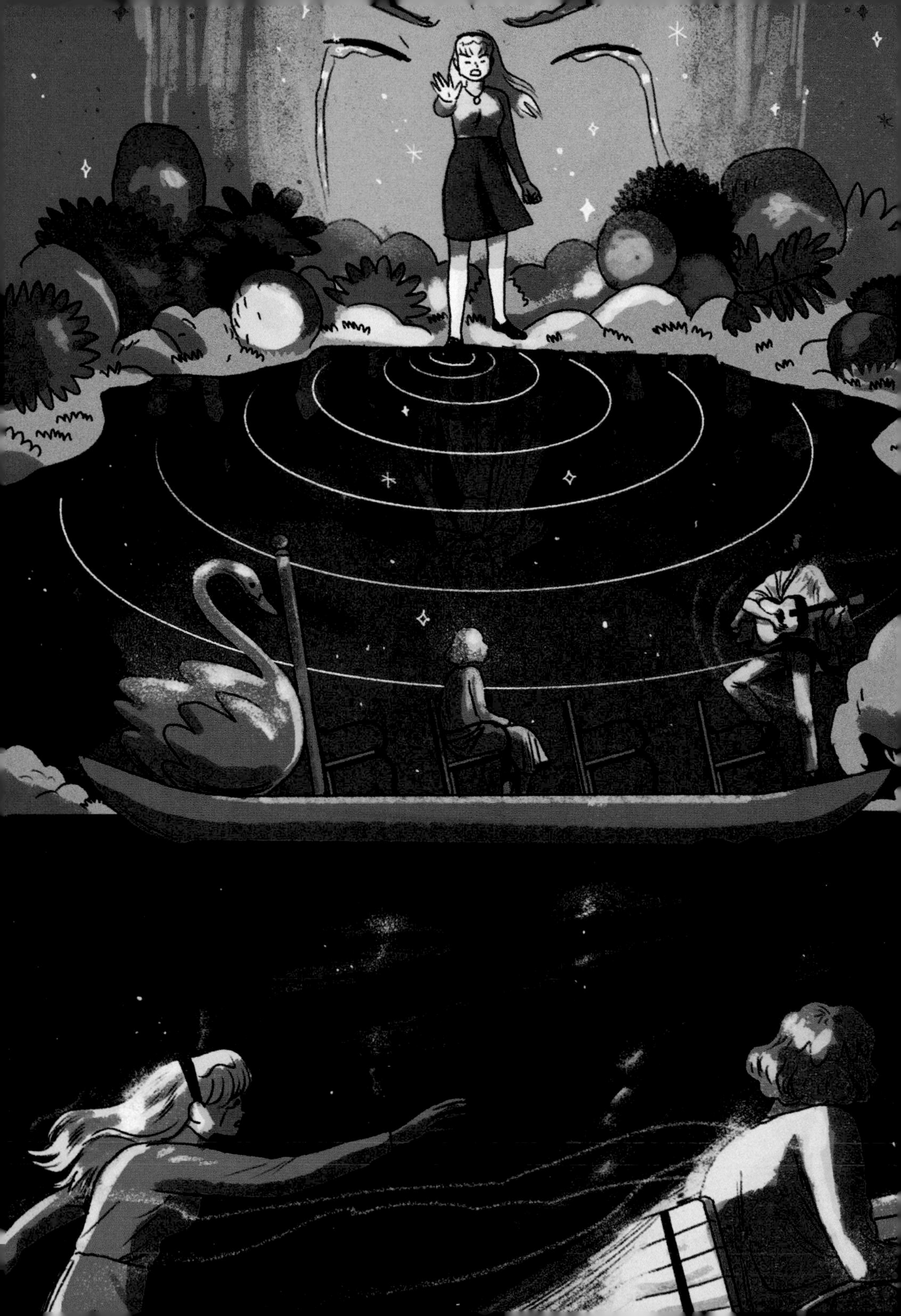

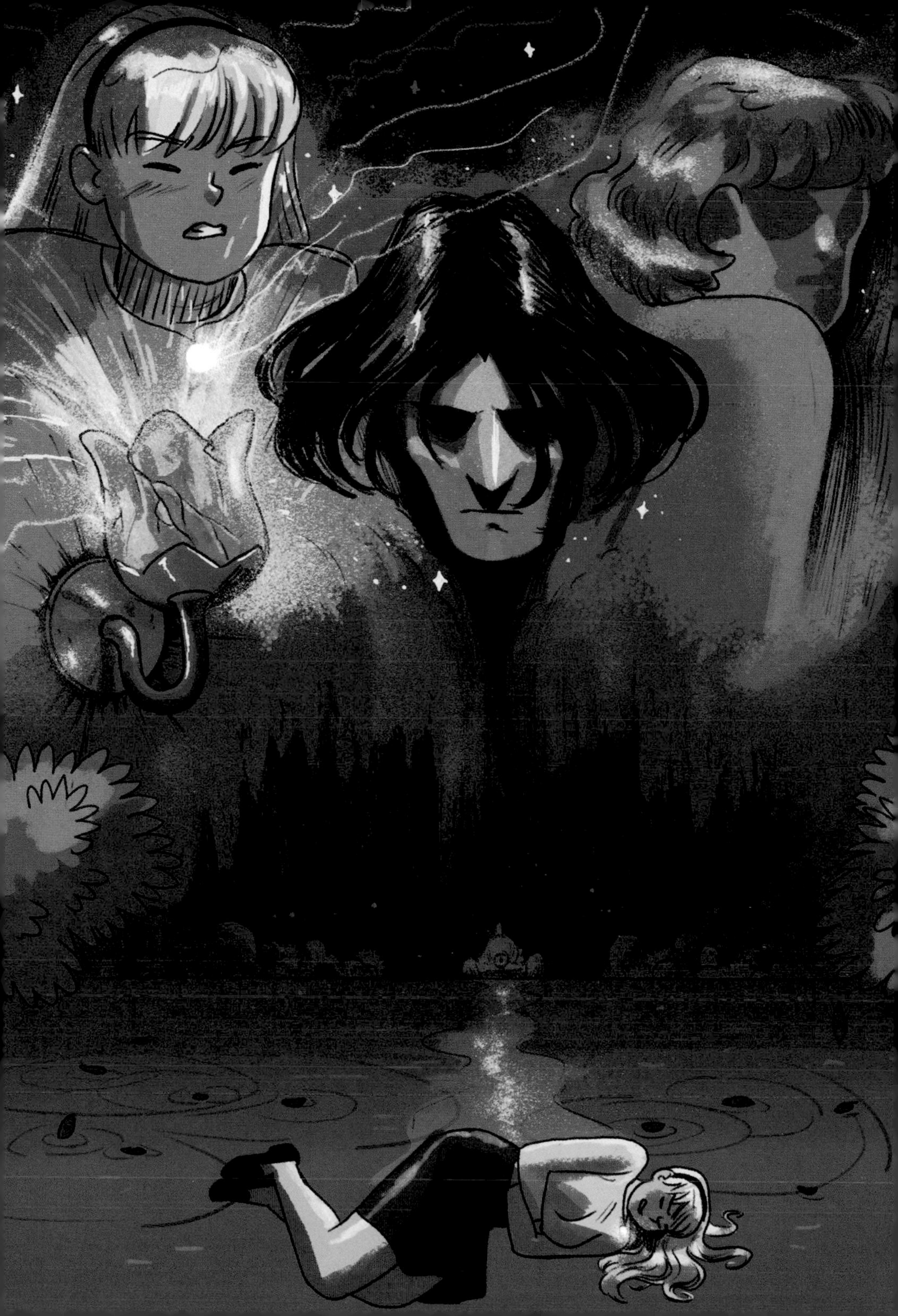

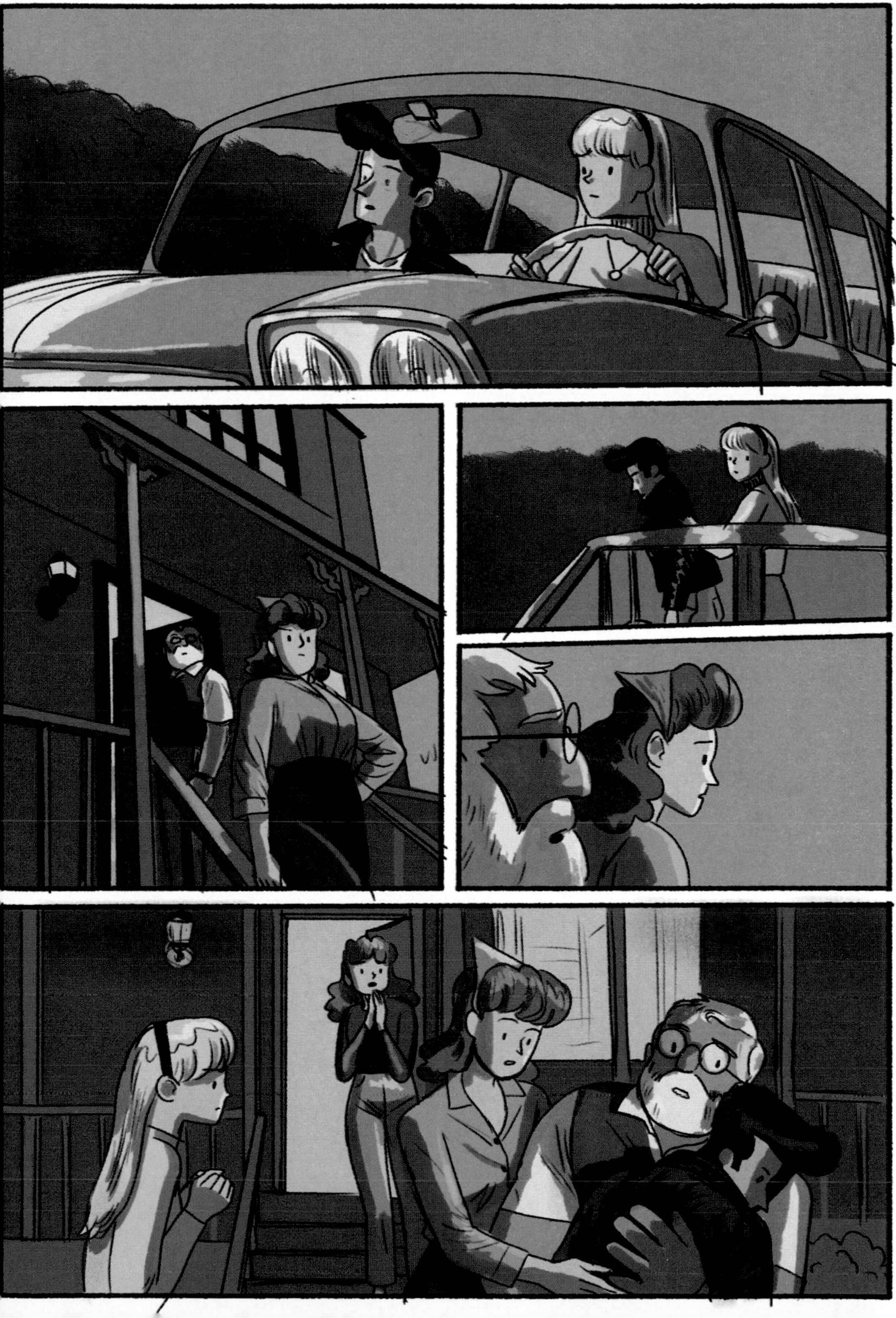

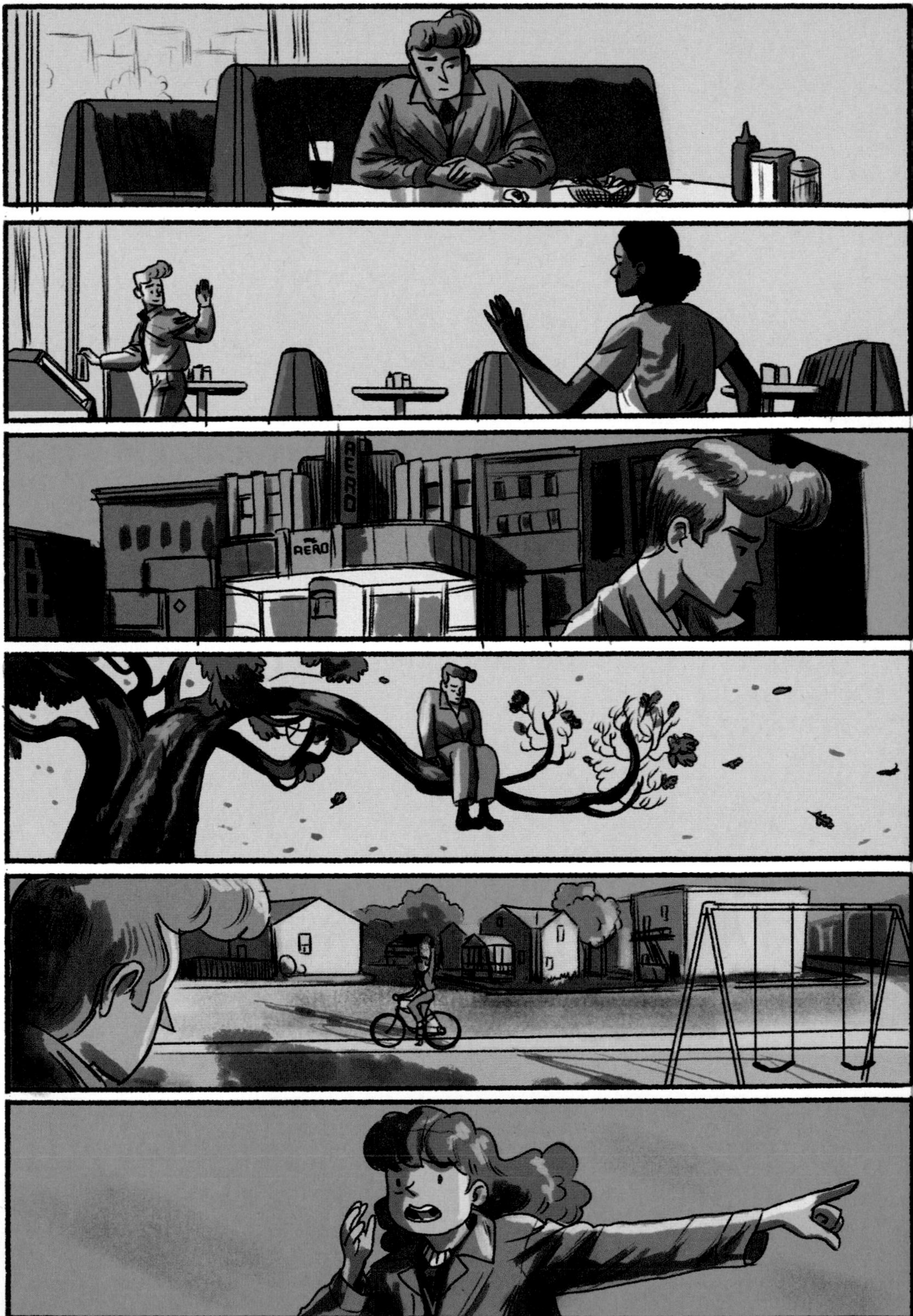
AERO
AERO

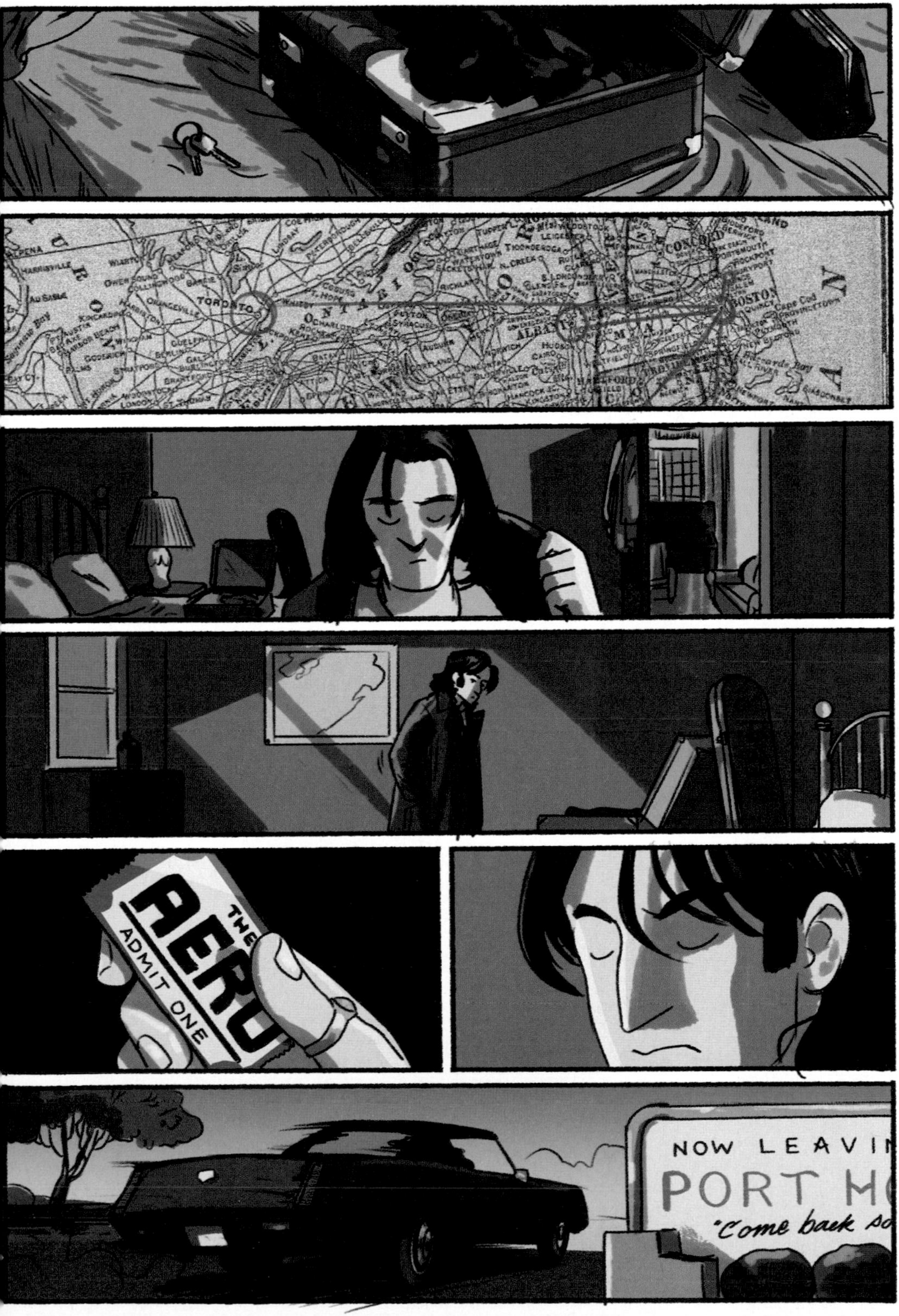
TORONTO
ALBANY
CONCORD
BOSTON
THE
AERO
ADMIT ONE
NOW LEAVIN
PORT H
"Come back so

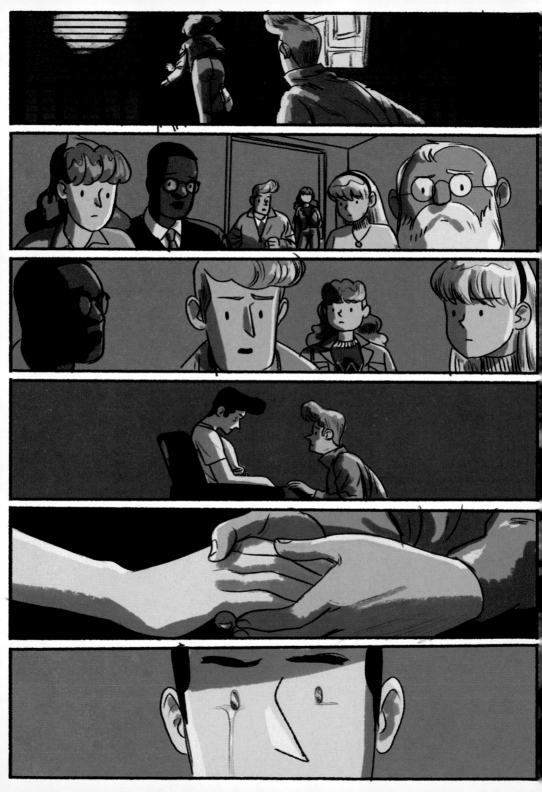

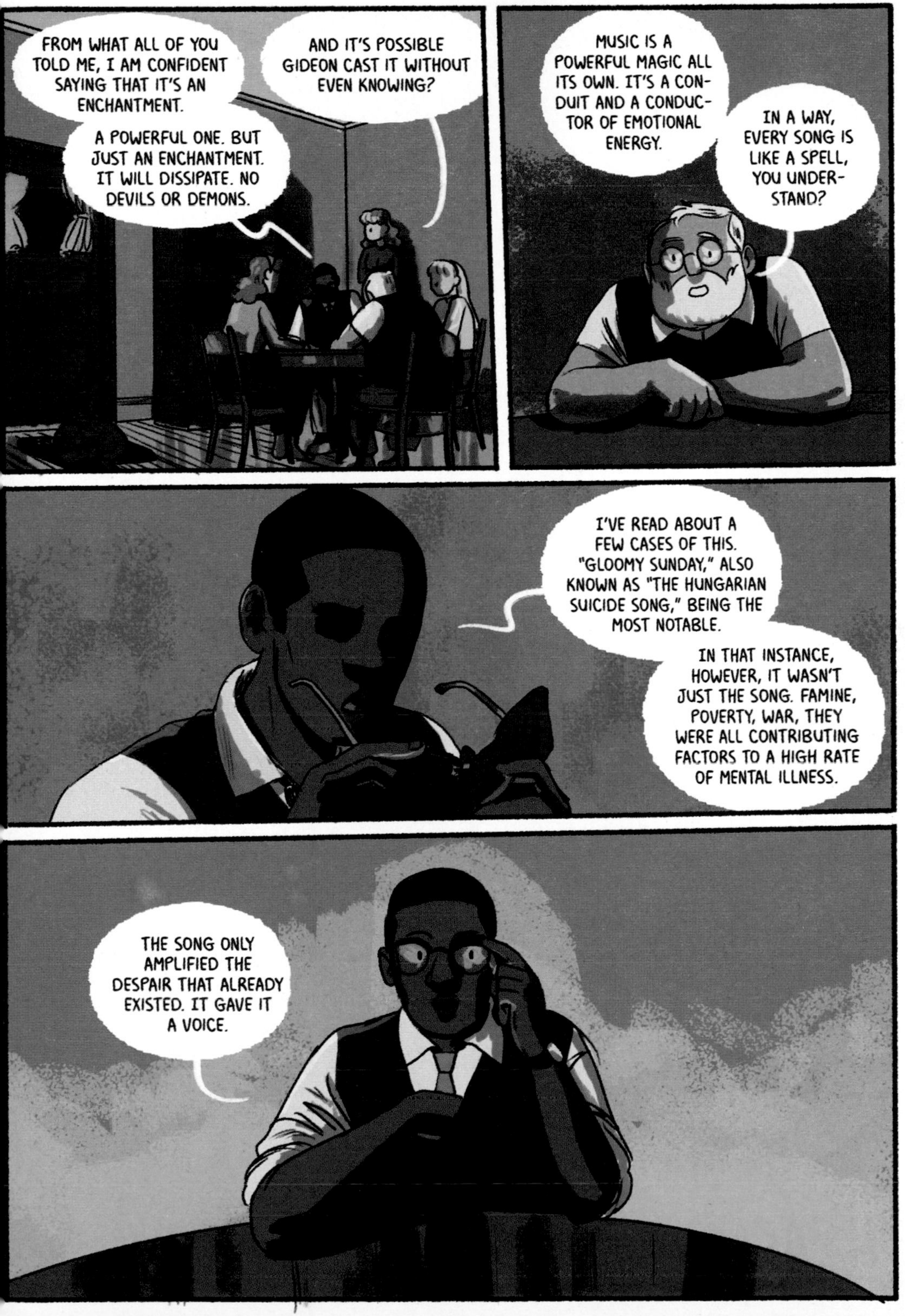
FROM WHAT ALL OF YOU TOLD ME, I AM CONFIDENT SAYING THAT IT'S AN ENCHANTMENT.
A POWERFUL ONE. BUT JUST AN ENCHANTMENT. IT WILL DISSIPATE. NO DEVILS OR DEMONS.
AND IT'S POSSIBLE GIDEON CAST IT WITHOUT EVEN KNOWING?
MUSIC IS A POWERFUL MAGIC ALL ITS OWN. IT'S A CONDUIT AND A CONDUCTOR OF EMOTIONAL ENERGY.
IN A WAY, EVERY SONG IS LIKE A SPELL, YOU UNDERSTAND?
I'VE READ ABOUT A FEW CASES OF THIS. "GLOOMY SUNDAY," ALSO KNOWN AS "THE HUNGARIAN SUICIDE SONG," BEING THE MOST NOTABLE.
IN THAT INSTANCE, HOWEVER, IT WASN'T JUST THE SONG. FAMINE, POVERTY, WAR, THEY WERE ALL CONTRIBUTING FACTORS TO A HIGH RATE OF MENTAL ILLNESS.
THE SONG ONLY AMPLIFIED THE DESPAIR THAT ALREADY EXISTED. IT GAVE IT A VOICE.

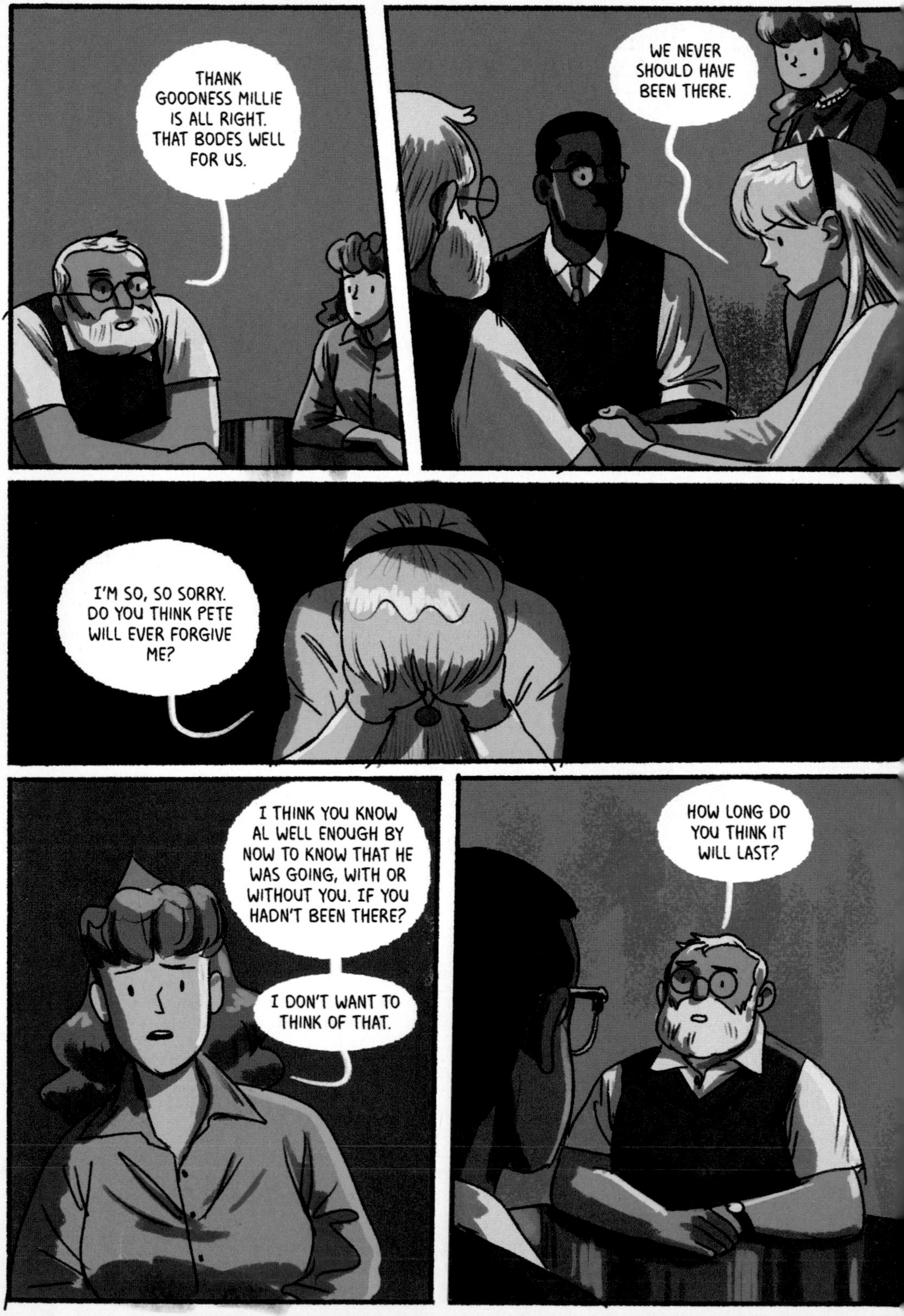
THANK GOODNESS MILLIE IS ALL RIGHT. THAT BODES WELL FOR US.
WE NEVER SHOULD HAVE BEEN THERE.
I'M SO, SO SORRY. DO YOU THINK PETE WILL EVER FORGIVE ME?
I THINK YOU KNOW AL WELL ENOUGH BY NOW TO KNOW THAT HE WAS GOING, WITH OR WITHOUT YOU. IF YOU HADN'T BEEN THERE?
I DON'T WANT TO THINK OF THAT.
HOW LONG DO YOU THINK IT WILL LAST?

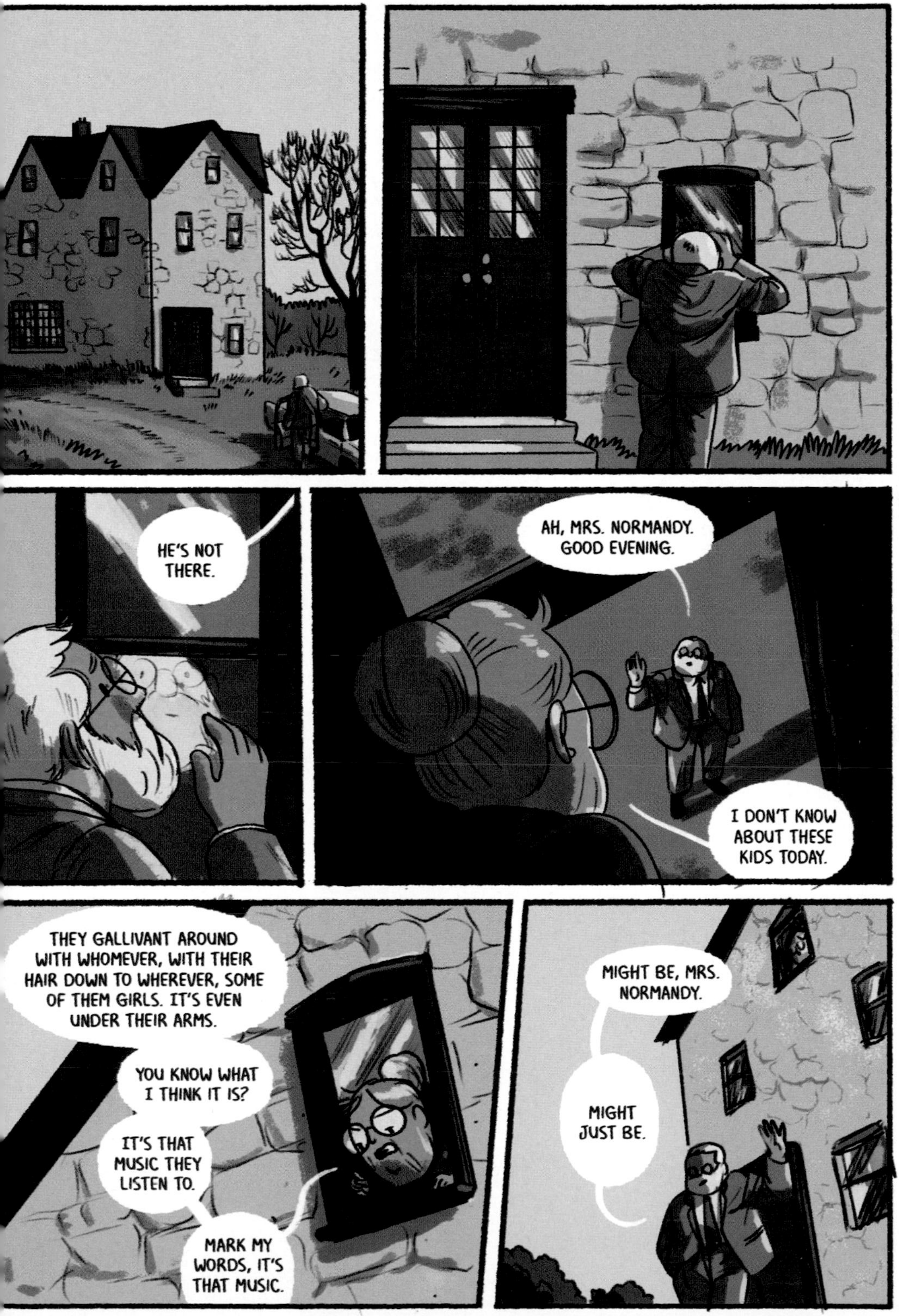
HE'S NOT THERE.
AH, MRS. NORMANDY. GOOD EVENING.
I DON'T KNOW ABOUT THESE KIDS TODAY.
THEY GALLIVANT AROUND WITH WHOMEVER, WITH THEIR HAIR DOWN TO WHEREVER, SOME OF THEM GIRLS. IT'S EVEN UNDER THEIR ARMS.
YOU KNOW WHAT I THINK IT IS?
IT'S THAT MUSIC THEY LISTEN TO.
MARK MY WORDS, IT'S THAT MUSIC.
MIGHT BE, MRS. NORMANDY.
MIGHT JUST BE.

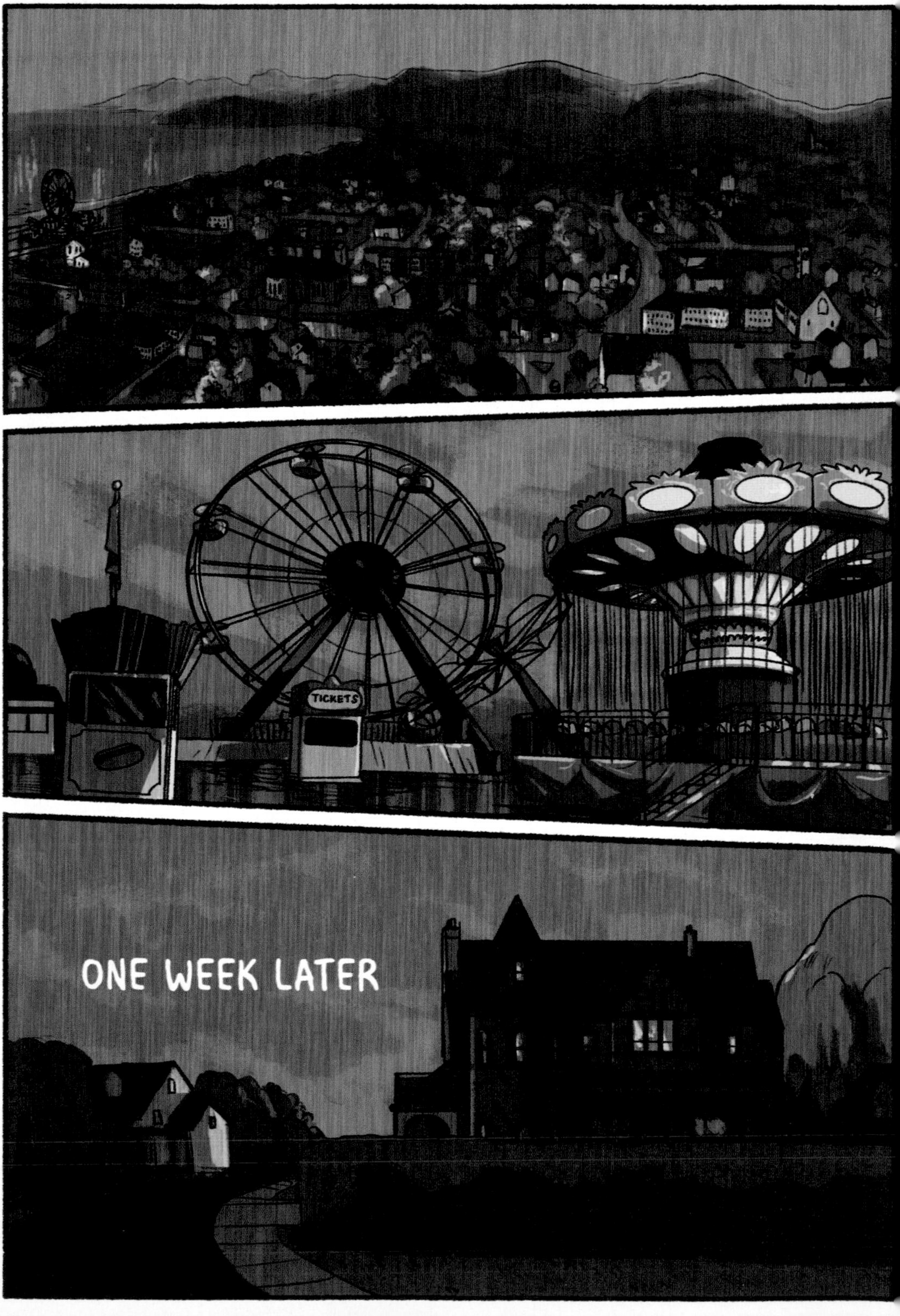
TICKETS
ONE WEEK LATER

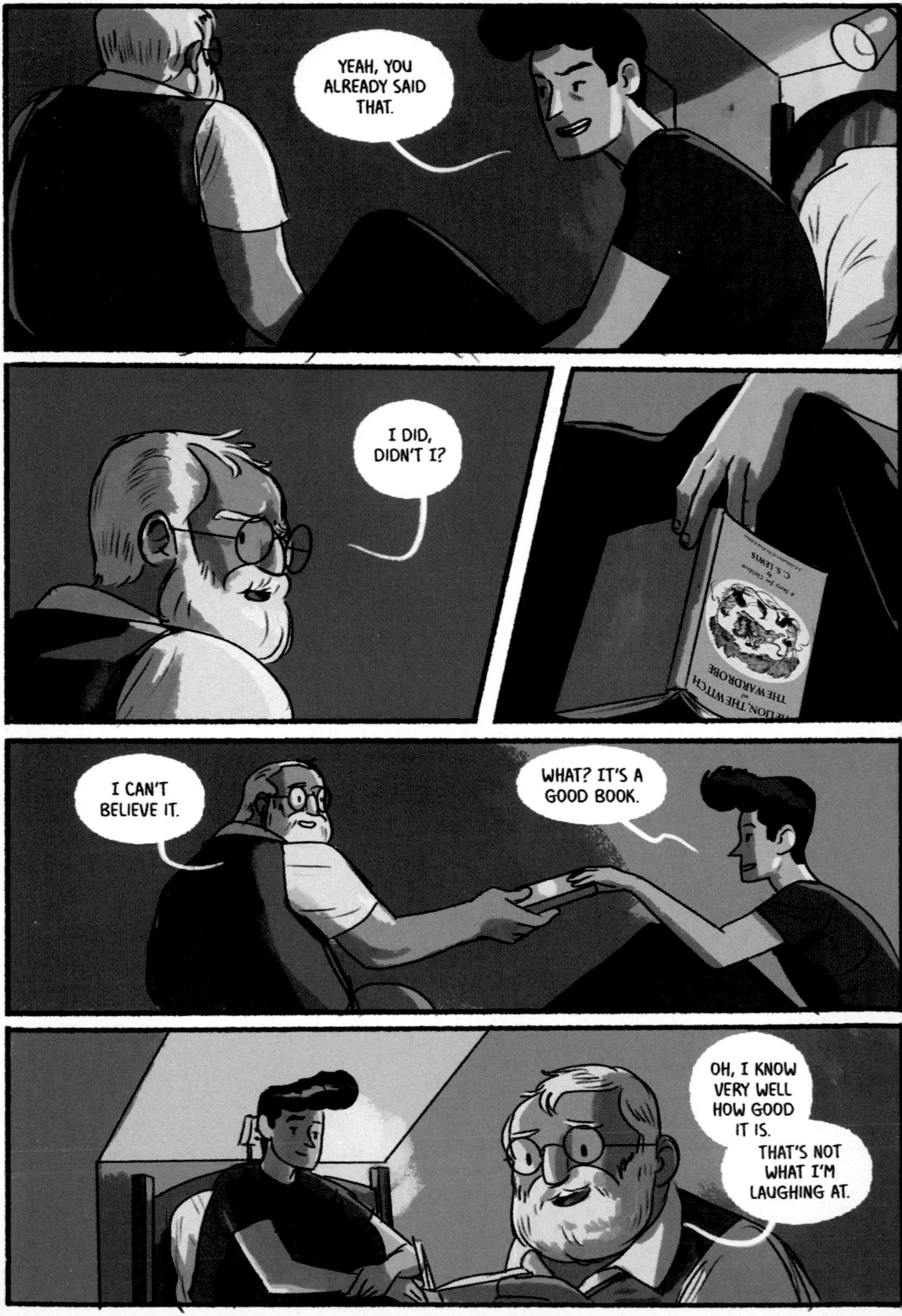
YEAH, YOU ALREADY SAID THAT.
I DID, DIDN'T I?
THE WARDROBE
C. S. LEWIS
I CAN'T BELIEVE IT.
WHAT? IT'S A GOOD BOOK.
OH, I KNOW VERY WELL HOW GOOD IT IS.
THAT'S NOT WHAT I'M LAUGHING AT.

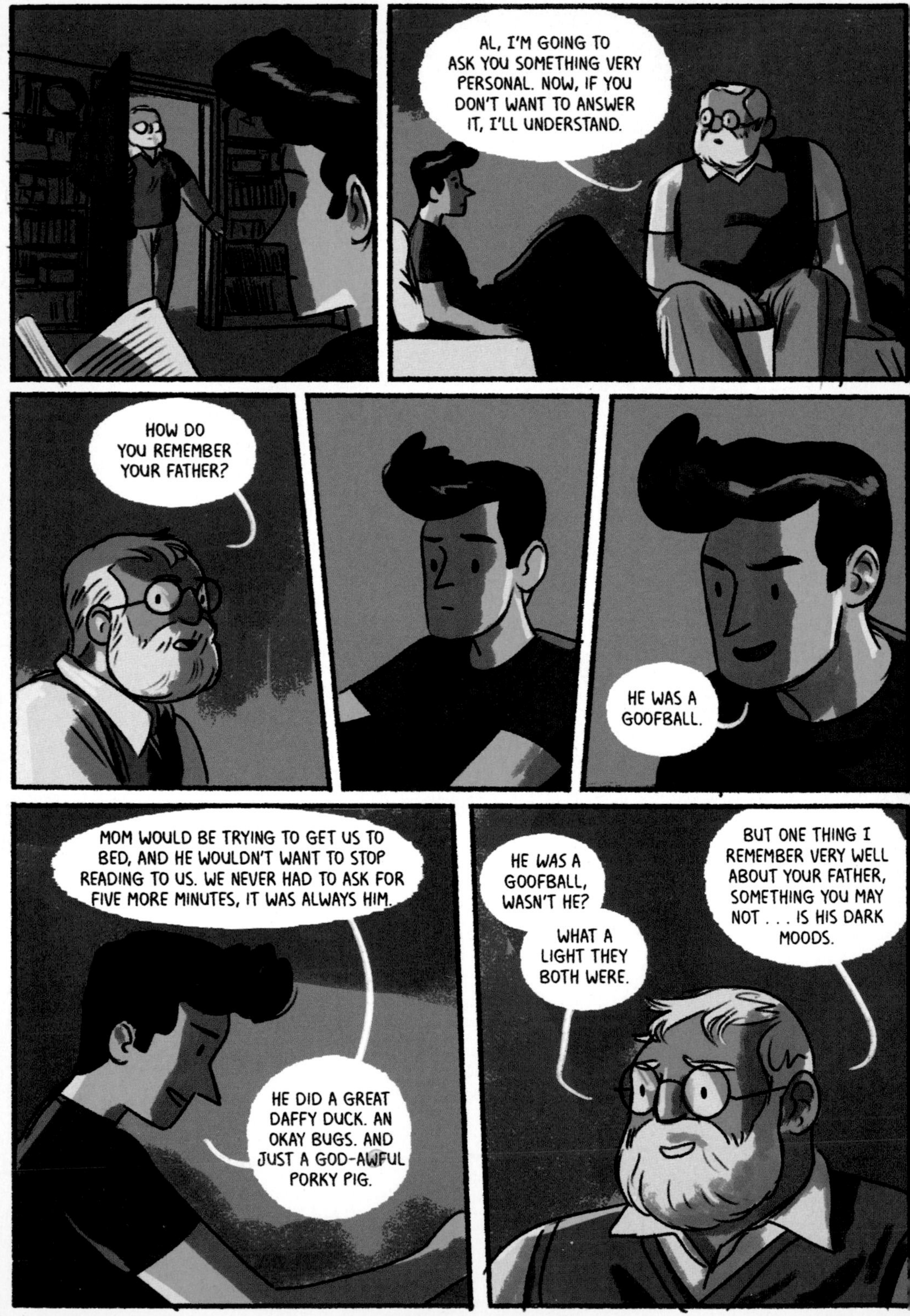
AL, I'M GOING TO ASK YOU SOMETHING VERY PERSONAL. NOW, IF YOU DON'T WANT TO ANSWER IT, I'LL UNDERSTAND.
HOW DO YOU REMEMBER YOUR FATHER?
HE WAS A GOOFBALL.
MOM WOULD BE TRYING TO GET US TO BED, AND HE WOULDN'T WANT TO STOP READING TO US. WE NEVER HAD TO ASK FOR FIVE MORE MINUTES, IT WAS ALWAYS HIM.
HE DID A GREAT DAFFY DUCK. AN OKAY BUGS. AND JUST A GOD-AWFUL PORKY PIG.
HE WAS A GOOFBALL, WASN'T HE?
WHAT A LIGHT THEY BOTH WERE.
BUT ONE THING I REMEMBER VERY WELL ABOUT YOUR FATHER, SOMETHING YOU MAY NOT . . . IS HIS DARK MOODS.

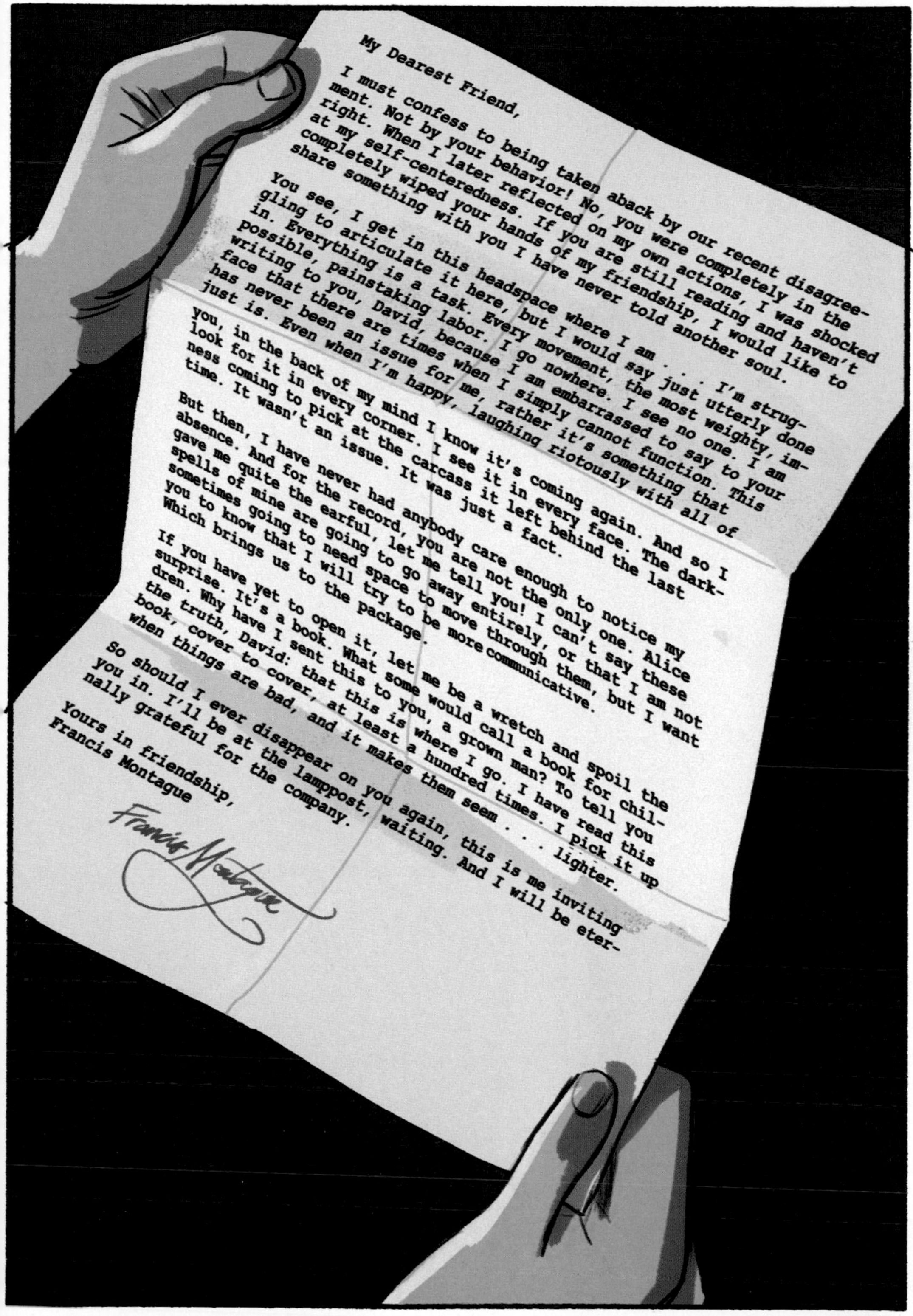

My Dearest Friend,

I must confess to being taken aback by our recent disagreement. Not by your behavior! No, you were completely in the right. When I later reflected on my own actions, I was shocked at my self-centeredness. If you are still reading and haven't completely wiped your hands of my friendship, I would like to share something with you I have never told another soul.

You see, I get in this headspace where I am . . . I'm struggling to articulate it here, but I would say just utterly done in. Everything is a task. Every movement, the most weighty, impossible, painstaking labor. I go nowhere. I see no one. I am writing to you, David, because I simply cannot function. This face that there are times when I am embarrassed to say to your has never been an issue for me, rather it's something that just is. Even when I'm happy, laughing riotously with all of

you, in the back of my mind I know it's coming again. And so I look for it in every corner. I see it in every face. The darkness coming to pick at the carcass it left behind the last time. It wasn't an issue. It was just a fact.

But then, I have never had anybody care enough to notice my absence. And for the record, you are not the only one. Alice gave me quite the earful, let me tell you! I can't say these spells of mine are going to need space to move through them, but I want sometimes going to you to know that I will try to be more communicative.

Which brings us to the package.

If you have yet to open it, let me be a wretch and spoil the surprise. It's a book. What some would call a book for children. Why have I sent this to you, a grown man? To tell you the truth, David: that this is where I go. I have read this book, cover to cover, at least a hundred times. I pick it up when things are bad, and it makes them seem . . . lighter.

So should I ever disappear on you again, this is me inviting you in. I'll be at the lamppost, waiting. And I will be eternally grateful for the company.

Yours in friendship,
Francis Montague

Francis Montague

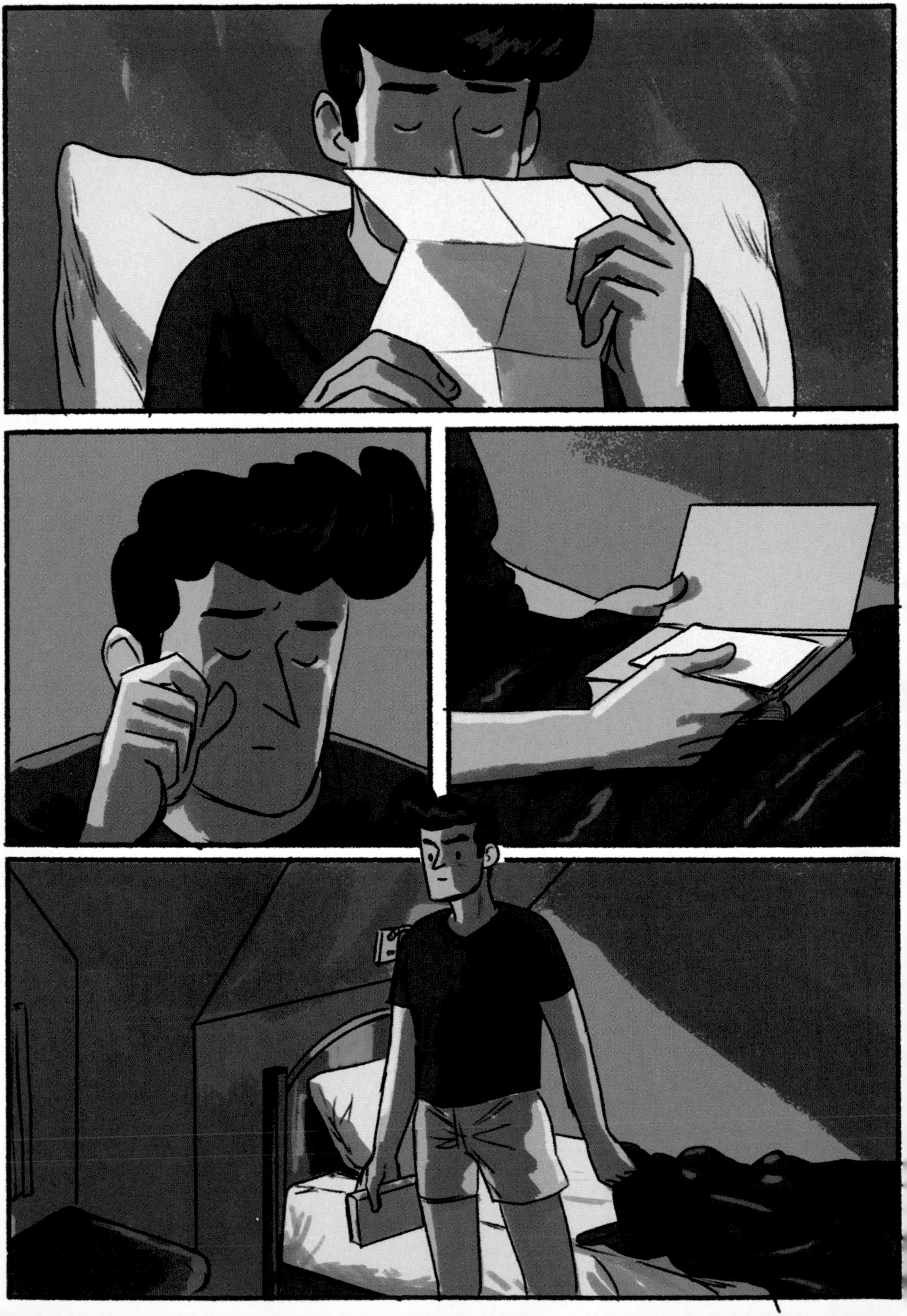

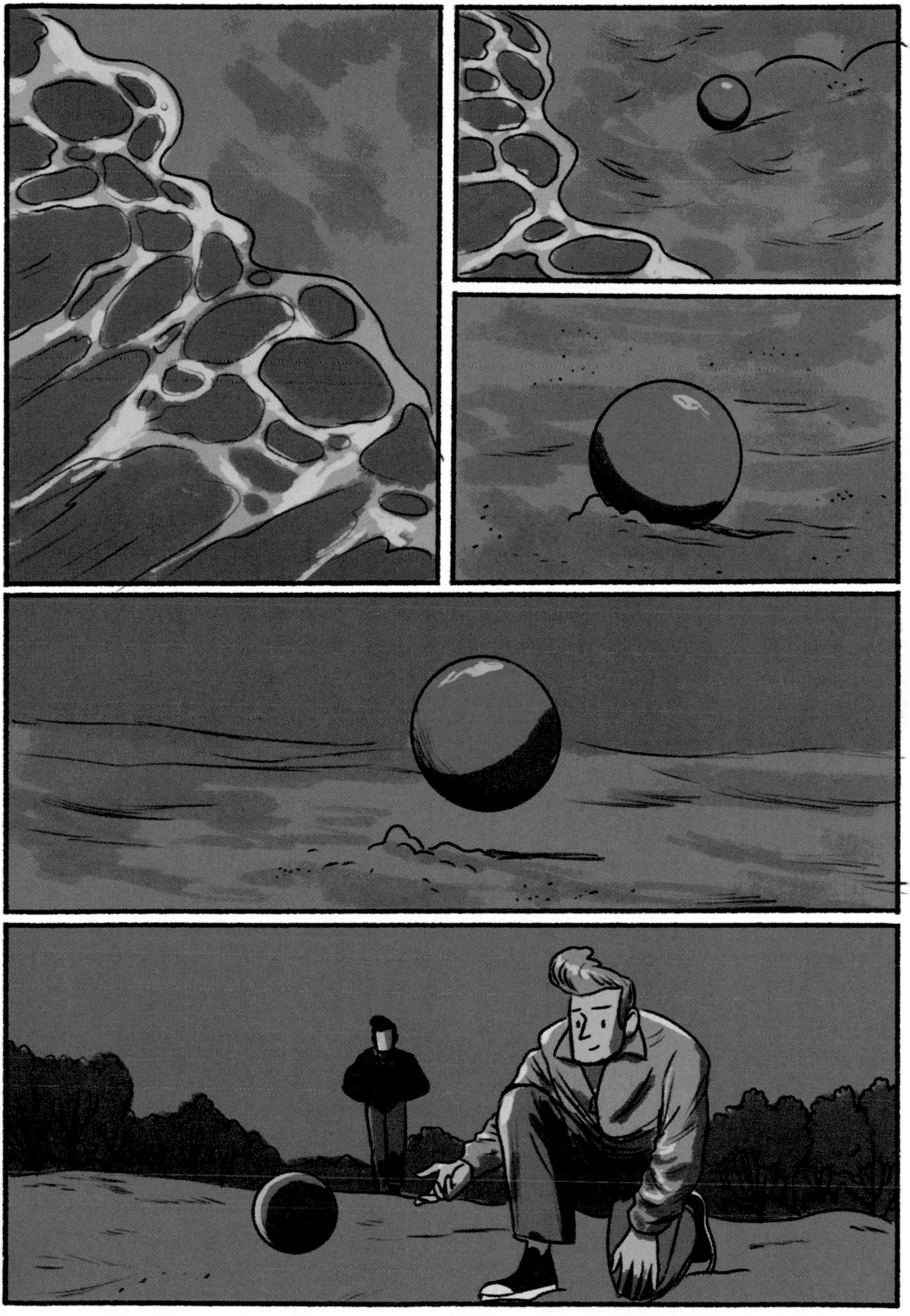

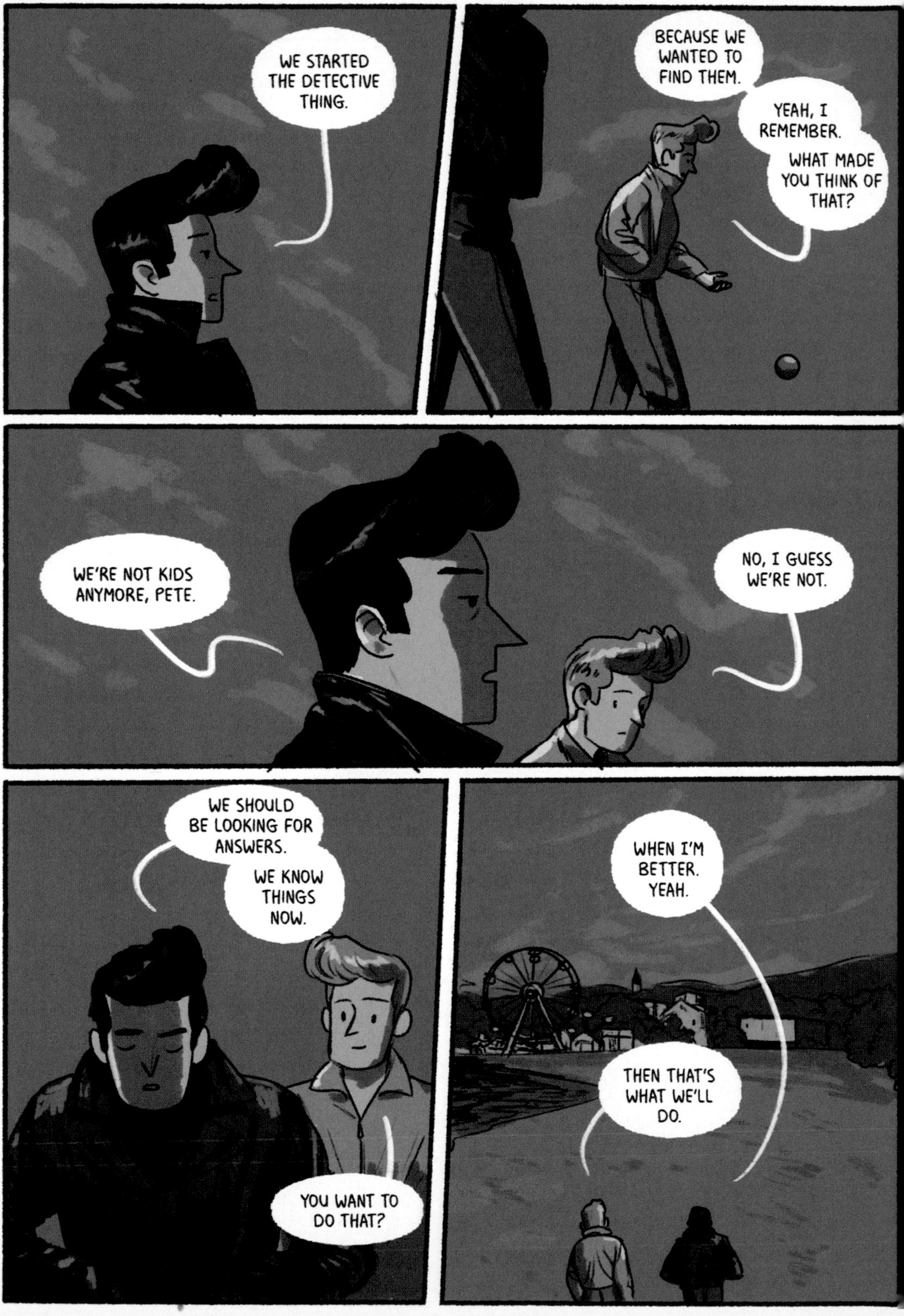
WE STARTED THE DETECTIVE THING.
BECAUSE WE WANTED TO FIND THEM.
YEAH, I REMEMBER.
WHAT MADE YOU THINK OF THAT?
WE'RE NOT KIDS ANYMORE, PETE.
NO, I GUESS WE'RE NOT.
WE SHOULD BE LOOKING FOR ANSWERS.
WE KNOW THINGS NOW.
YOU WANT TO DO THAT?
WHEN I'M BETTER. YEAH.
THEN THAT'S WHAT WE'LL DO.

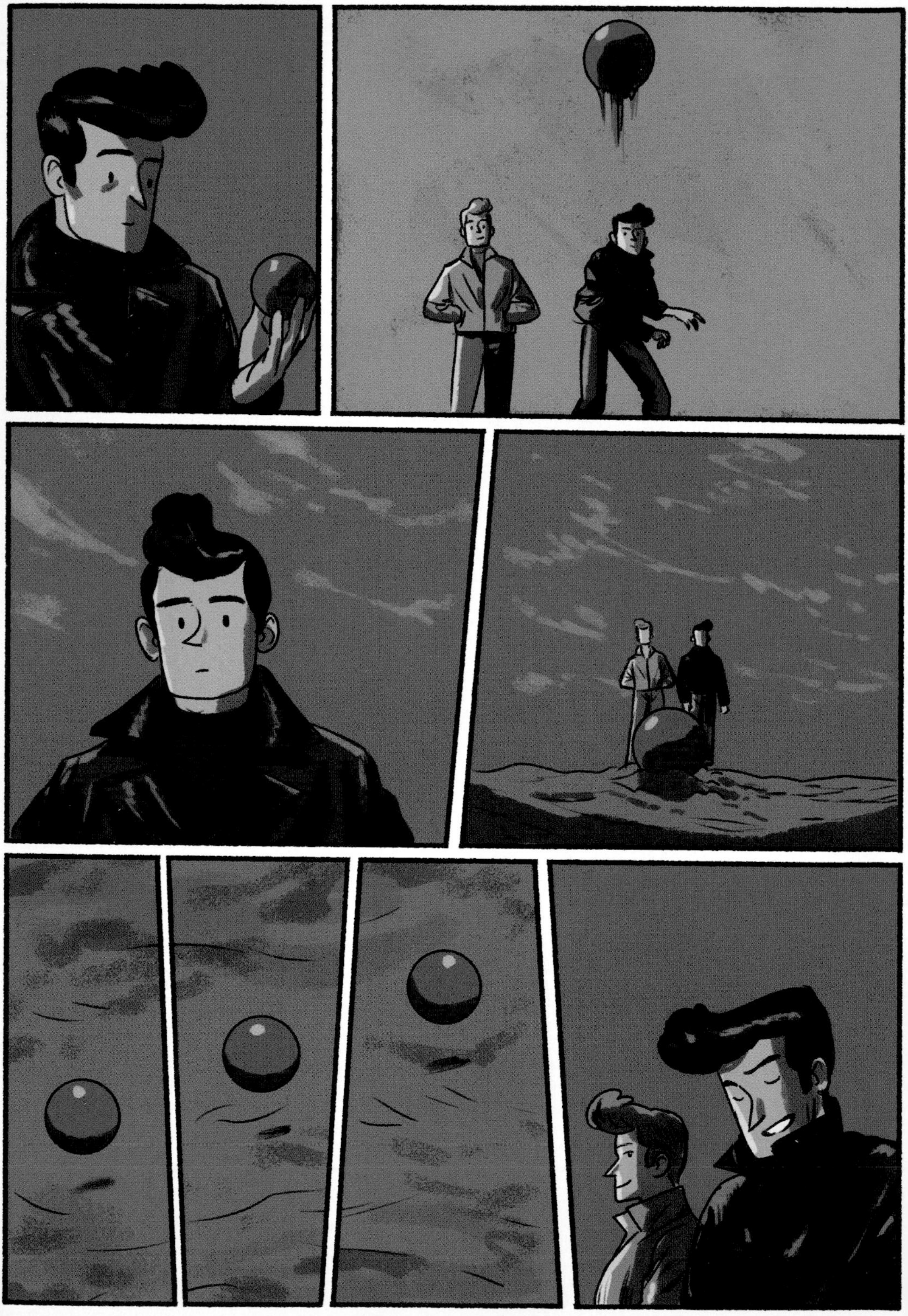

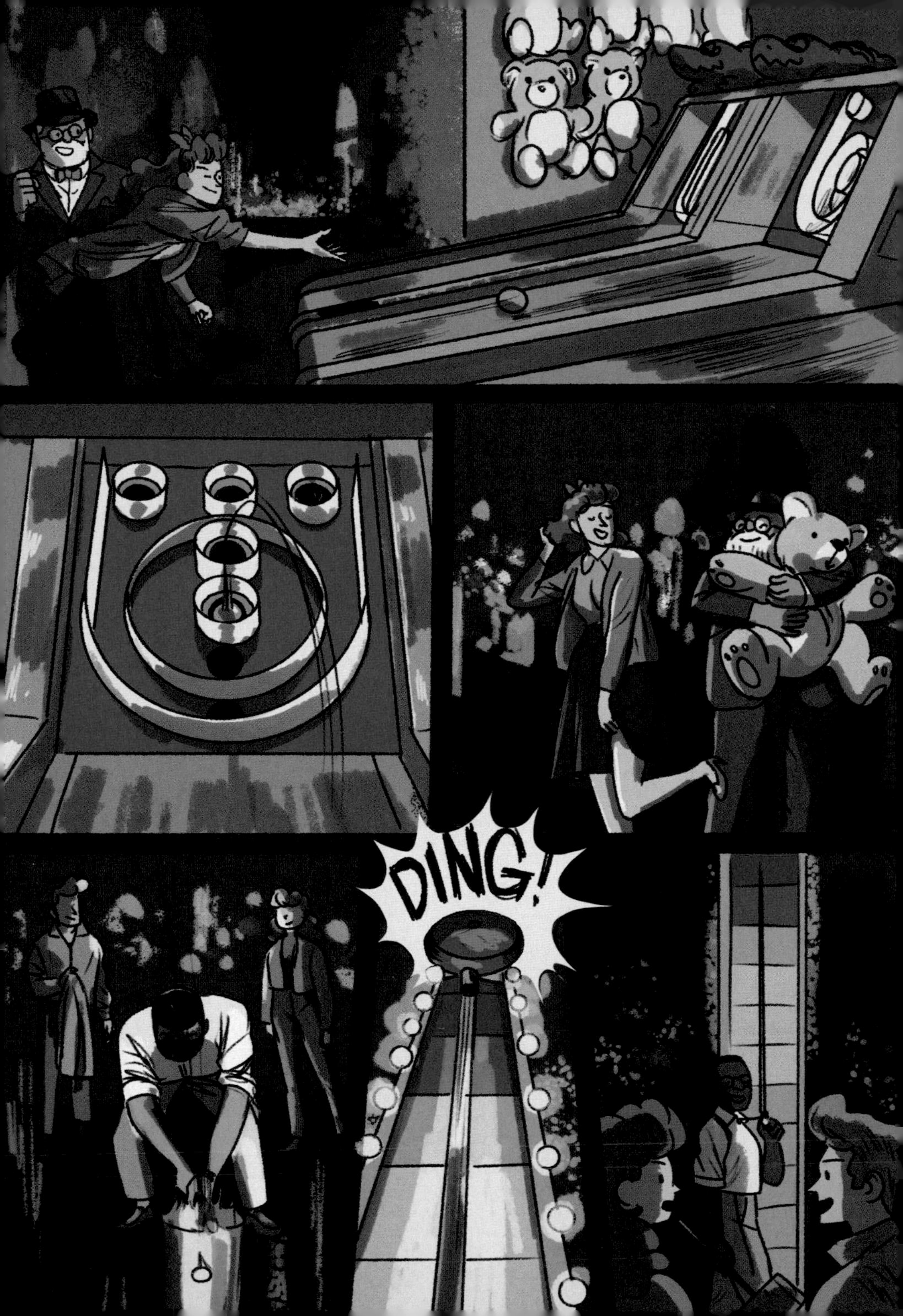
DING!

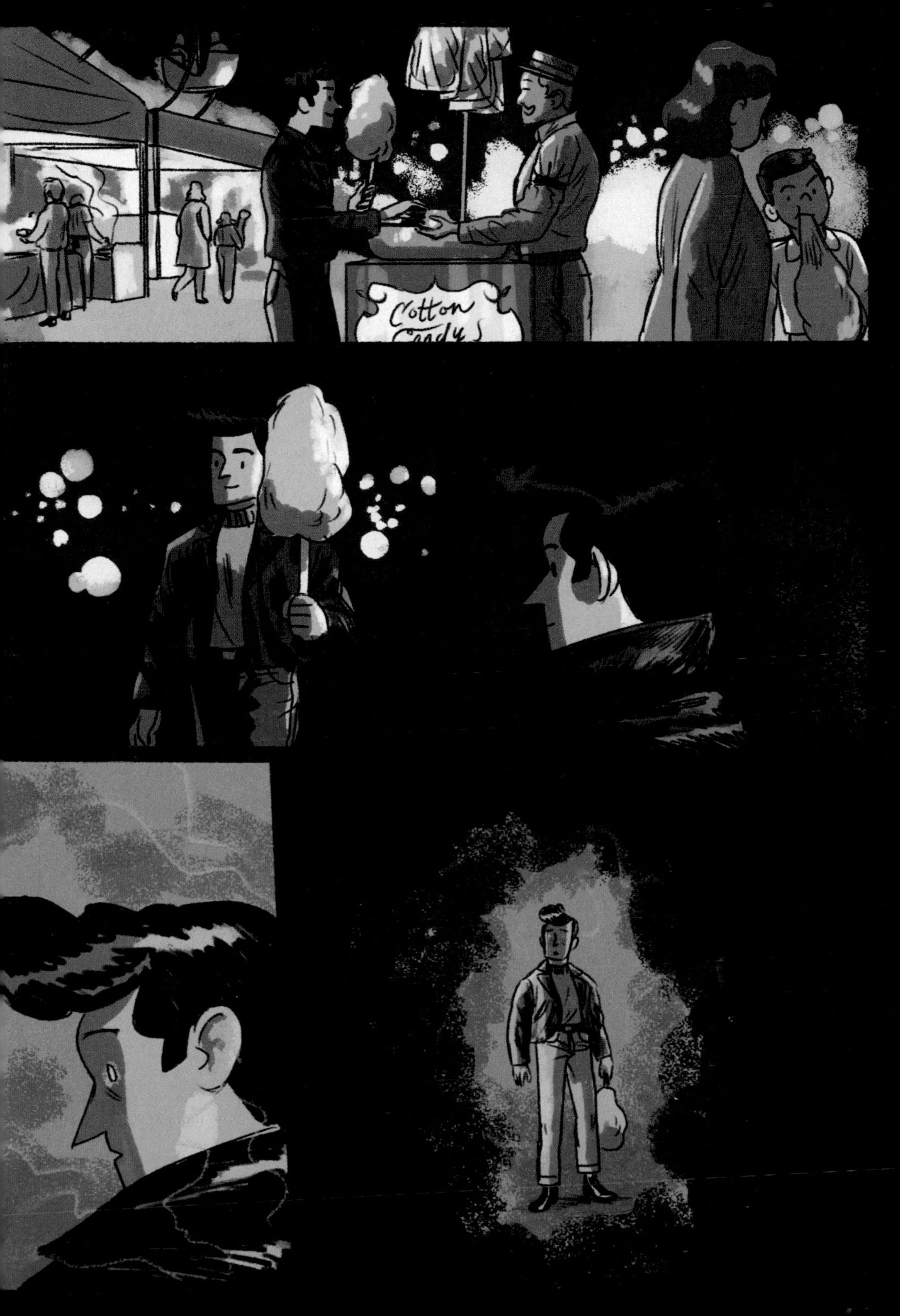
Cotton

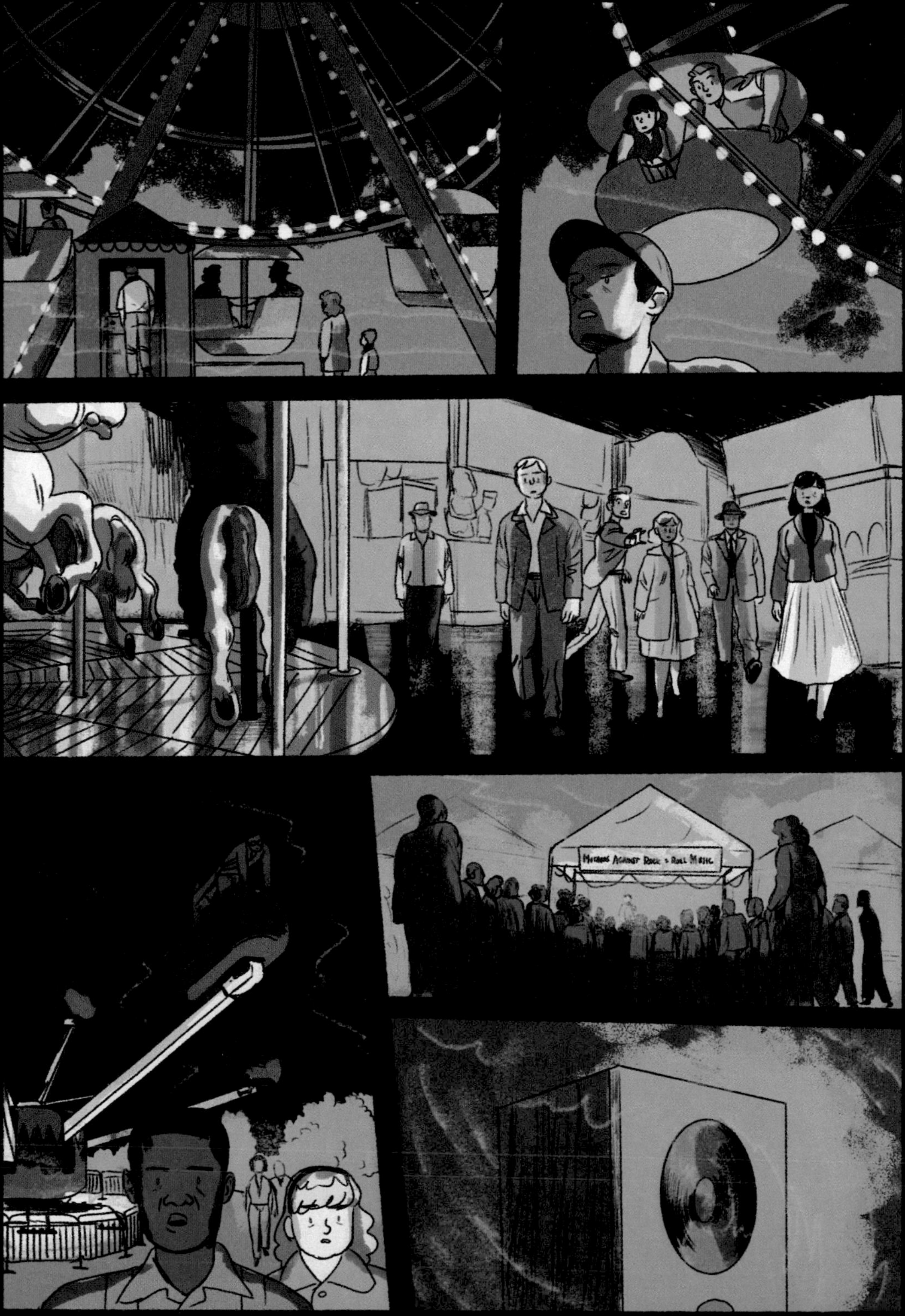
MOTHERS AGAINST ROCK & ROLL MUSIC

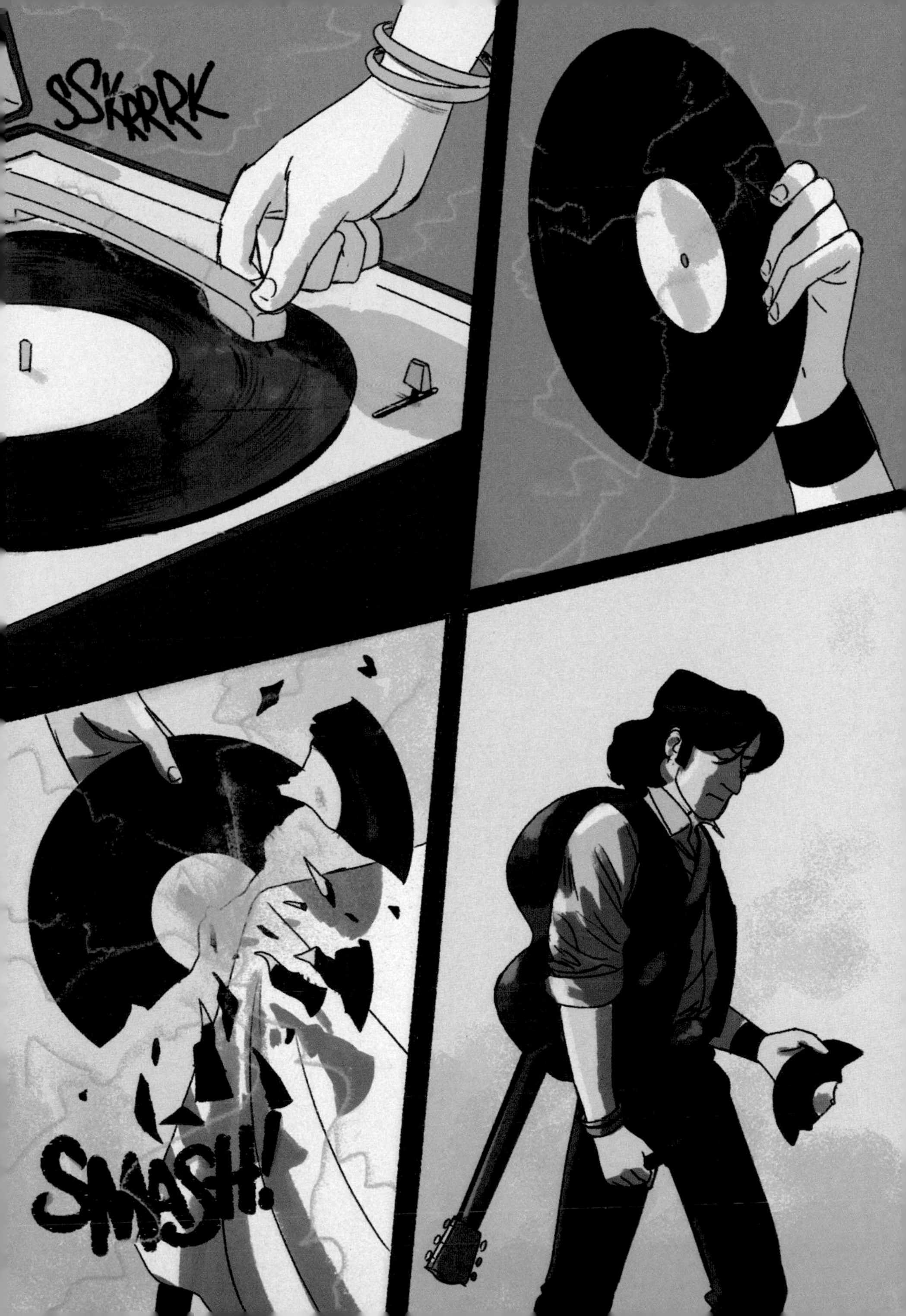
SSKRRRK
SMASH!

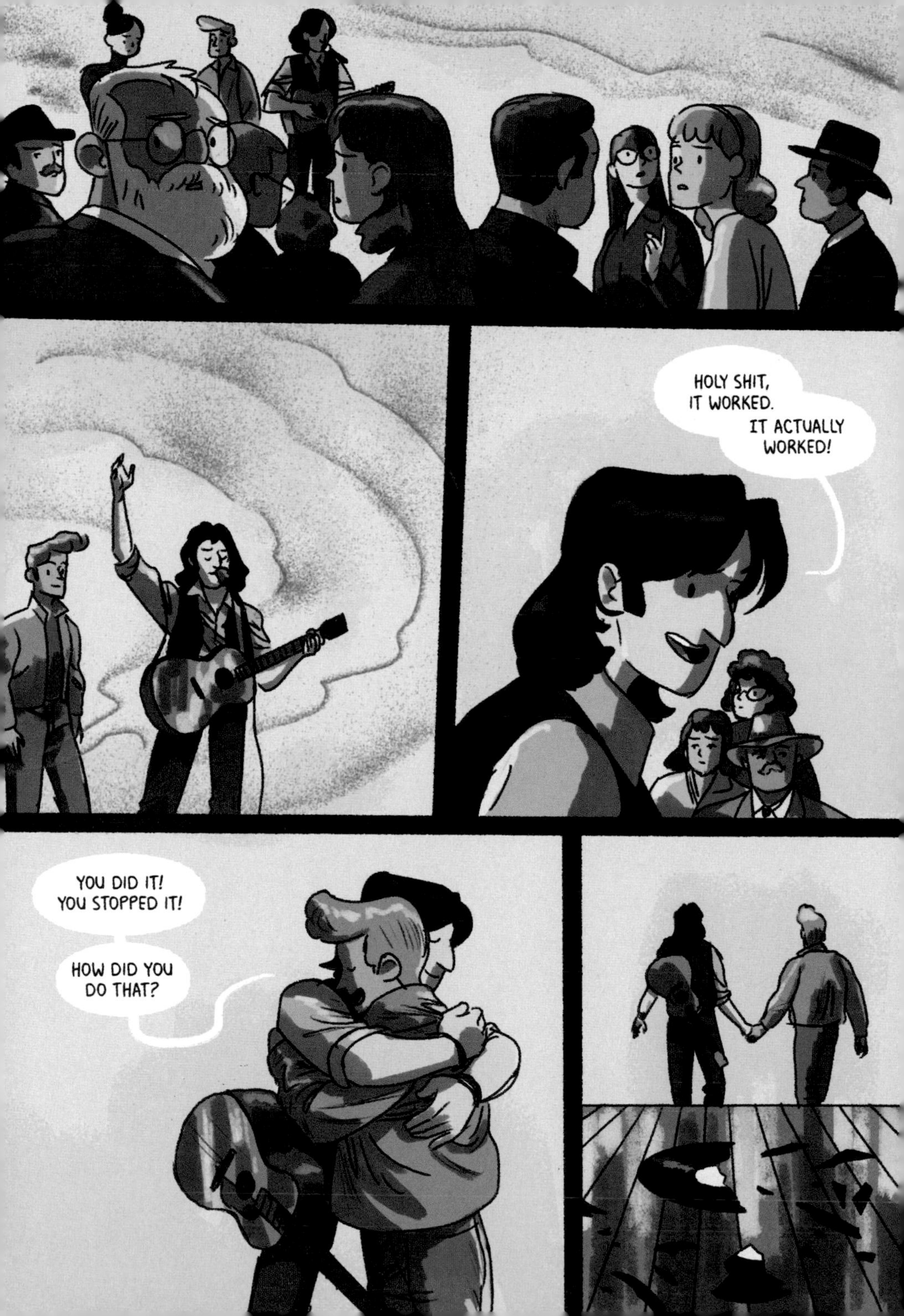
HOLY SHIT, IT WORKED.
IT ACTUALLY WORKED!
YOU DID IT! YOU STOPPED IT!
HOW DID YOU DO THAT?

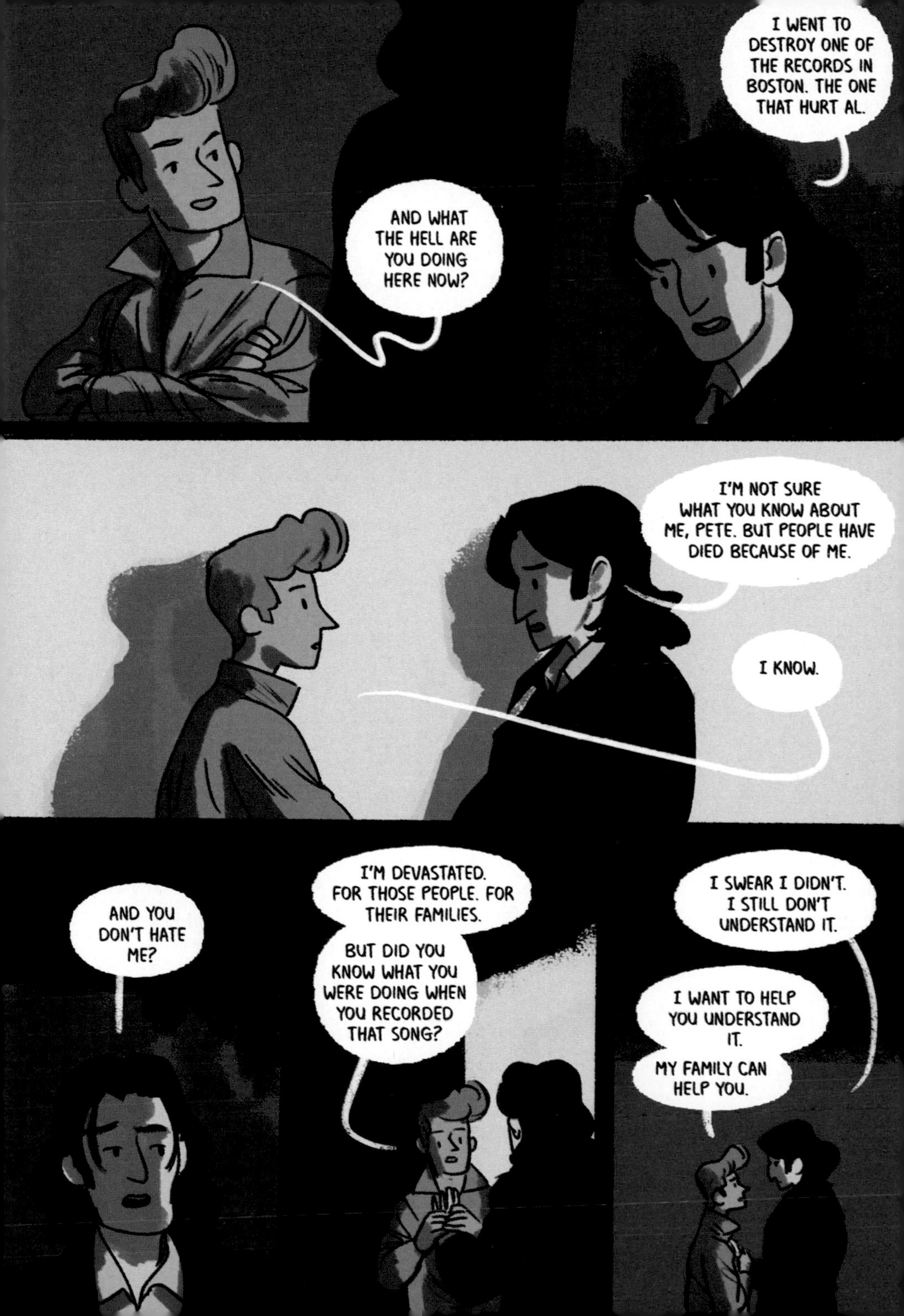
AND WHAT THE HELL ARE YOU DOING HERE NOW?
I WENT TO DESTROY ONE OF THE RECORDS IN BOSTON. THE ONE THAT HURT AL.
I'M NOT SURE WHAT YOU KNOW ABOUT ME, PETE. BUT PEOPLE HAVE DIED BECAUSE OF ME.
I KNOW.
AND YOU DON'T HATE ME?
I'M DEVASTATED. FOR THOSE PEOPLE. FOR THEIR FAMILIES.
BUT DID YOU KNOW WHAT YOU WERE DOING WHEN YOU RECORDED THAT SONG?
I SWEAR I DIDN'T. I STILL DON'T UNDERSTAND IT.
I WANT TO HELP YOU UNDERSTAND IT.
MY FAMILY CAN HELP YOU.

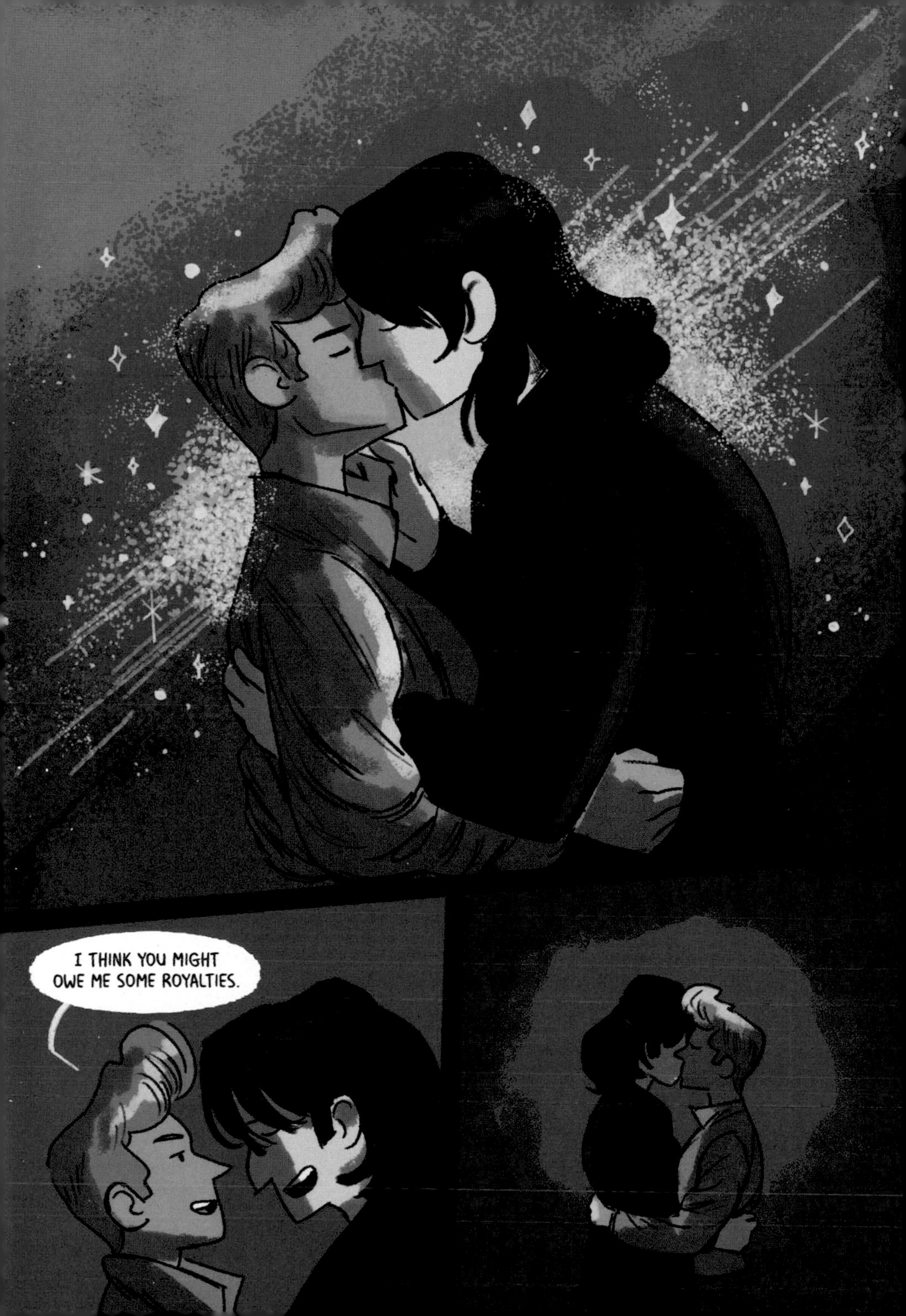
I THINK YOU MIGHT OWE ME SOME ROYALTIES.

CHAPTER 6

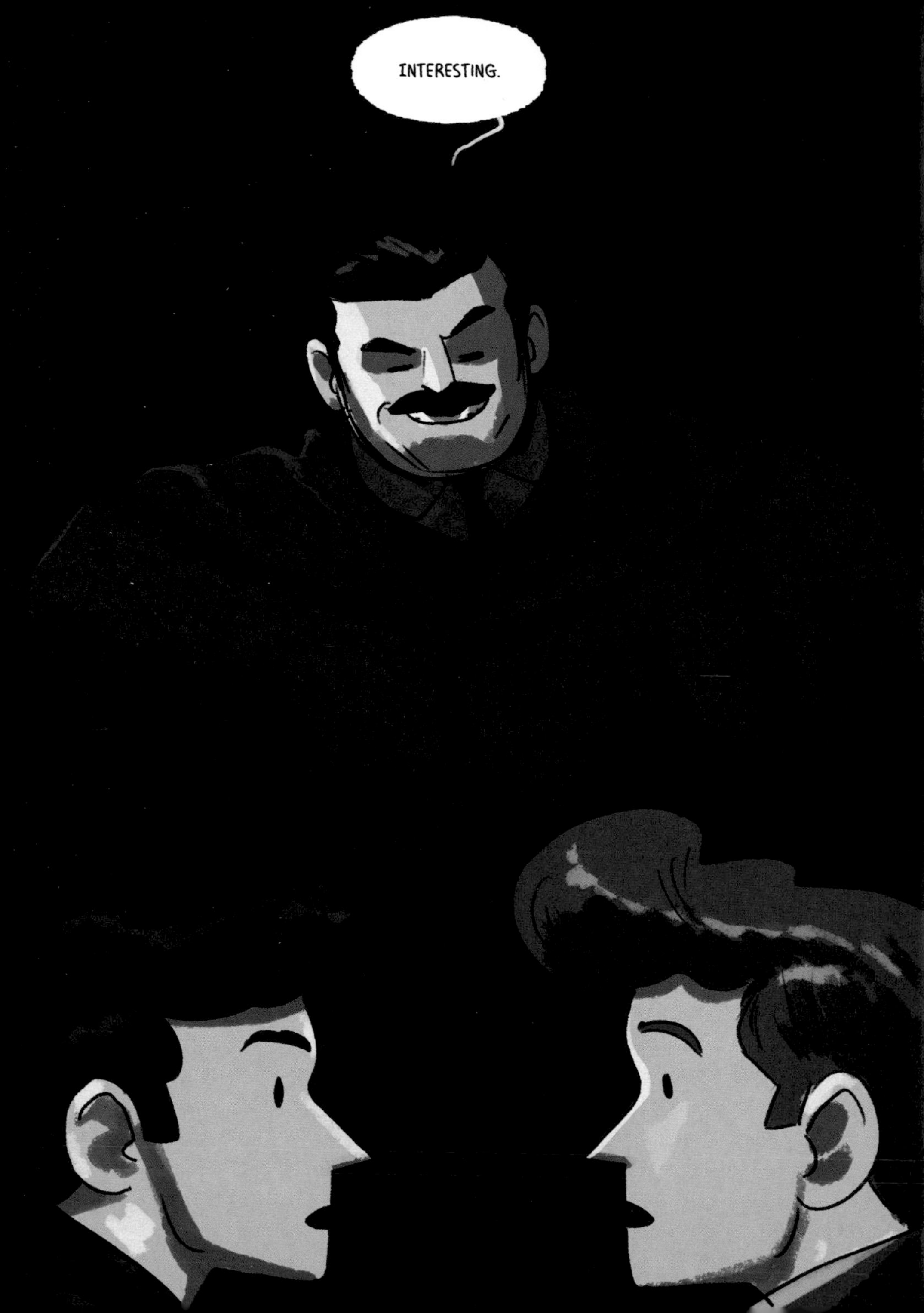
INTERESTING.

Mental Health Resources

RESOURCES IN THE U.S.

The Jed Foundation is a national nonprofit that exists to protect the emotional health of—and to prevent suicide among—our nation's teens and young adults. You can find more information at jedfoundation.org.

The National Suicide Prevention Lifeline provides 24/7 free and confidential support for people in distress, prevention and crisis resources for you or your loved ones, and best practices for professionals. You can find out more at suicidepreventionlifeline.org. If you need help now, text "START" to 741-741 to immediately connect with help at the Jed Foundation or call 1-800-273-TALK (8255) for free, confidential services with the Jed Foundation and the National Suicide Prevention Lifeline.

The Trevor Project is the leading national organization providing crisis intervention and suicide prevention services to lesbian, gay, bisexual, transgender, queer, and questioning young people under age twenty-five. The Trevor Project has a staff of trained counselors available for support 24/7. If you are in crisis, feeling suicidal, or in need of a safe and judgment-free place to talk, call the TrevorLifeline now at 1-800-488-7386 or text "START" to 678-678.

RESOURCES IN CANADA

To contact the Canada Suicide Prevention Service, call 1-833-456-4566 or text 45645 from 4 p.m. to midnight EST daily.

Crisis Services Canada (CSC) is a national network of existing distress, crisis, and suicide prevention line services. They are committed to supporting any person living in Canada who is affected by suicide, in the most caring and least intrusive manner possible. For more information, visit crisisservicescanada.ca.

To contact the Youthspace Text Line (across Canada), text 778-783-0177 from 6 p.m. to midnight PST daily.

Anyone in Canada under thirty years old is welcome to chat with a diverse community of trained volunteers.

They encourage and welcome all youth to contact them, no matter their background, religion, race, ability, sexual orientation, gender identity, lifestyle, or culture. Youthspace's goal is to create inclusive and safer spaces for all visitors to Youthspace.ca.

Acknowledgments

Every project has its heroes behind the scenes, and during such a wild year, we needed all the help we could get. Here's to our amazing team for your dedication and hard work. As always, we would be nowhere without our amazing agent, Maria Vicente, who possesses a magic far beyond that of even David. To our editor, Marisa: thank you for guiding us through the tangled garden of this story and for all your invaluable insights. Thanks so much to Joan Lee and Heather Mullan for your color-flatting mastery. To Maggie Stiefvater and Sam Maggs for saying such nice things; your encouragement means more than you could ever know. Thanks to the entire team at Knopf and Random House Graphic for the tireless job they do, not just for our books but for the medium at large. And, of course, to our support network of friends and family, without whom the Montague Twins could not exist. Thank you. We love you all.